NORA ROBERTS

Accidentally
in Love

Includes *Convincing Alex* & *The Perfect Neighbor*

Silhouette Books

 SILHOUETTE™

Accidentally in Love

ISBN-13: 978-1-335-14613-7

Copyright © 2025 by Harlequin Enterprises ULC

Convincing Alex
First published in 1994. This edition published in 2025.
Copyright © 1994 by Nora Roberts

The Perfect Neighbor
First published in 1999. This edition published in 2025.
Copyright © 1999 by Nora Roberts

Silhouette
22 Adelaide St. West, 41st Floor
Toronto, Ontario M5H 4E3, Canada
www.Harlequin.com

Printed in U.S.A.

CONTENTS

Chapter 1

The curvy blonde in hot-pink spandex tottered on stiletto heels as she worked her corner. Her eyes, heavily painted with a sunburst of colors, kept a sharp watch on her associates, those spangled shadows of the night. There was a great deal of laughter on the street. After all, it was springtime in New York. But beneath the laughter there was a flat sheen of boredom that no amount of glitter or sex could disguise.

For these ladies, business was business.

After popping in some fresh gum, she adjusted the large canvas bag on her bare shoulder. Thank God it was warm, she thought. It would be hell to strut around half-dressed if the weather was ugly.

A gorgeous black woman in red leather that barely covered the essentials languidly lit a cigarette and cocked her hip. "Come on, baby," she said to no one in par-

ticular, in a voice husky from the smoke she exhaled.
"Wanna have some fun?"

Some did, Bess noted, her eyes skimming the block.
Some didn't. All in all, she thought, business was pretty
brisk on this spring night. She'd observed several trans-
actions, and the varied ways they were contracted. It
was too bad boredom was the byword here. Boredom,
and a defiant kind of hopelessness.

"You talking to yourself, honey?"

"Huh?" Bess blinked up into the shrewd eyes of
the black goddess in red leather who had strolled over.
"Was I?"

"You're new?" Studying Bess, she blew out smoke.
"Who's your man?"

"My... I don't have one."

"Don't have one?" The woman arched her ruthlessly
plucked brows and sneered. "Girl, you can't work this
street without a man."

"That's what I'm doing." Since she didn't have a cigarette, Bess blew a bubble with her gum. Then snapped
it.

"Bobby or Big Ed find out, they're going to mess
you up." She shrugged. After all, it wasn't her problem.

"Free country."

"Girl, ain't nothing free." With a laugh, she ran a
hand down her slick, leather-covered hip. "Nothing at
all." She flicked her cigarette into the street, where it
bounced off the rear fender of a cab.

There were dozens of questions on Bess's lips. It was
in her nature to ask them, but she remembered that she
had to go slow. "So who's *your* man?"

"Bobby." With her lips pursed, the woman skimmed
her gaze up and down Bess. "He'd take you on. A little

skinny through the butt, but you'd do. You need protection when you work the streets." And she could use the extra money Bobby would pass her way if she brought him a new girl.

"Nobody protected the two girls who got murdered last month."

The black woman's eyes flickered. Bess considered herself an excellent judge of emotion, and she saw grief, regret and sorrow before the eyes hardened again. "You a cop?"

Bess's mouth fell open before she laughed. That was a good one, she thought. Sort of flattering. "No, I'm not a cop. I'm just trying to make a living. Did you know either of them? The women who were killed?"

"We don't like questions around here." The woman tilted her head. "If you're trying to make a living, let's see you do it."

Bess felt a quick ripple of unease. Not only was the woman gorgeous, she was big. Big and suspicious. Both qualities were going to make it difficult for Bess to hang back on the fringes and observe. But she considered herself an agile thinker and a quick study. After all, she reminded herself, she'd come here tonight to do business.

"Sure." Turning, she strutted slowly along the sidewalk. Her hips—and she didn't for a minute believe that her butt was skinny—swayed seductively.

Maybe her throat was a little dry. Maybe her heart was pounding a bit too quickly. But Bess McNee took a great deal of pride in her work.

She spotted the two men half a block away and licked her lips. The one on the left, the dark one, looked very promising.

* * *

"Look, rookie, the idea's to take one, maybe two." Alex scanned the sidewalk ahead. Hookers, drunks, junkies and those unfortunate enough to have to pass through them to get home. "My snitch says that the tall black one—Rosalie—knew both the victims."

"So why don't we just pick her up and take her in for questioning?" Judd Malloy was anxious for action. His detective's shield was only forty-eight hours old. And he was working with Alexi Stanislaski, a cop who had a reputation for moving quickly and getting the job done. "Better yet, why don't we go roust her pimp?"

Rookies, Alex thought. Why were they always teaming him up with rookies? "Because we want her cooperation. We're going to pick her up, book her for solicitation. Then we're going to talk to her, real nice, before Bobby can come along and tell her to clam up."

"If my wife finds out I spent the night picking up hookers—"

"A smart cop doesn't tell his family anything they'd don't need to know. And they don't need to know much." Alex's dark brown eyes were cool, very cool, as they flicked over his new partner's face. "Stanislaski's rule number one."

He spotted the blonde. She was staring at him. Alex stared back. Odd face, he thought. Sharp, sexy, despite the makeup she'd troweled on. Beneath all the gunk, her eyes were a vivid green. The face itself was all angles, some of them wrong. Her nose was slightly crooked, as if it had been broken. Some john or pimp, he figured, then skimmed his eyes down to her mouth.

Full, overfull, and a glossy red. It didn't please him at all that he felt a reaction to it. Not knowing what she was, what she did. Her chin came to a slight point, and with her prominent cheekbones it gave her face a triangular, foxlike look.

The clinging tube top and spandex capri pants showed every inch of her curvy, athletic little body. He'd always been a sucker for the athletic type—but he reminded himself just where this particular number got her exercise.

In any case, she wasn't the one he was looking for.

Now or never, Bess told herself, feeling her new acquaintance's eyes on her.

"Hey, baby…" Though she hadn't smoked since she'd been fifteen, her voice was husky. Saying a prayer to whatever gods were listening, she veered in on Alex. "Want to party?"

"Maybe." He hooked a finger in the top of her tube, and was surprised when she flinched. "You're not quite what I had it mind, sweetie."

"Oh?" What next? Combining instinct with her observations, she tossed her head and leaned into him. She had the quick impression of pressing against steel— hard, unyielding and very cool. "Just what *did* you have in mind?"

Then, for a moment, she had nothing at all on hers. Not with the way those dark eyes cut into her, through her. His knuckles were brushing her skin, just above the breasts. She felt the heat from them, from him. As she continued to stare, she was struck by a vivid image of the two of them, rolling on a narrow bed in some dark room.

And it had nothing to do with business.

It was the first time Alex had ever seen a hooker blush. It threw him off, made him want to apologize for the fantasy that had just whipped through his brain. Then he remembered himself.

"Just a different type, babe."

In her heels, they were eye-to-eye. It made him want to rub off the powders and paints to see what was beneath.

"I can be a different type," Bess said, delighted with her inspired response.

"Hey, girlfriend." Rosalie strutted over and slipped a friendly arm around Bess's shoulders. "You're not going to be greedy and take both of these boys, are you?"

"I—"

Pay dirt, Alex thought, and shifted his attention to Rosalie. "You two a team?"

"We are tonight." She glanced from Alex to his partner. "How 'bout you two?"

Judd searched for his voice. He'd rather have been facing a gunman in an alley. And he simply couldn't put his hands on this big, beautiful woman, when a picture of his wife's trusting face was flashing in his head like a neon light.

"Sure." He let out a long breath and tried to emulate some of Alex's cocky confidence.

Rosalie threw back her head and laughed before she stepped forward, bumping bodies with Judd. He gave way instinctively as a dark red flush crept up his neck. "I believe you're new at this, honey. Why don't you let Rosalie show you the ropes?"

Because his partner seemed to have developed laryngitis, Alex took over. "How much?"

"Well..." Rosalie didn't bother to look over at Bess, who had gone dead pale. "Special rate tonight. You get both of us for a hundred. That's the first hour." She leaned down and whispered something in Judd's ear that had him babbling. "After that," she continued, "we can negotiate."

"I don't—" Bess began, then felt Rosalie's fingers dig into her bare shoulder like sharp little knives.

"I think that'll do it," Alex said, and pulled out his badge. "Ladies, you're busted."

Cops, Bess realized on a wave of sweet relief. While Rosalie expressed her opinion with a single vicious word, Bess struggled not to burst into wild laughter.

Perfect, Bess thought as she was bumped along into the squad room. She'd been arrested for solicitation, and life couldn't be better. Trying to take everything in at once, she grinned as she scanned the station house. She'd been in one before, of course. As she always said, she took her work seriously. But not in this precinct. Not downtown.

It was dirty—grimy, really, she decided, making mental notes and muttering to herself. Floors, walls, the barred windows. Everything had a nice, picturesque coat of crud.

It smelled, too. She took a deep breath so that she wouldn't forget the ripe stench of human sweat, bitter coffee and strong disinfectant.

And it was noisy. With every nerve on sensory alert, she separated the din into ringing phones, angry curses, weeping, and the clickety-clack of keyboards at work.

Man, oh, man, she thought. Her luck was really in.

"You're not a tourist, sweetheart," Alex reminded her, adding a firm nudge.

"Sorry."

The vibrant excitement in her eyes was so out of

place that he stared. Then, with a shake of his head, he jabbed a finger toward a chair. He was letting the rookie get his feet wet getting the vitals from Rosalie. Once they had her booked, he'd take over himself, using charm or threats or whatever seemed most expedient to make her talk to him about her two murdered associates.

"Okay." He took his seat behind his battered and overcrowded desk. "You know the drill."

She'd been staring at a young man of about twenty with a face full of bruises and a torn denim jacket. "Excuse me?"

Alex just sighed as he rolled a form onto his typewriter. "Name?"

"Oh, I'm Bess." She held out her hand in a gesture so natural and friendly he nearly took it.

Instead, he swore softly. "Bess what?"

"McNee. And you're?"

"In charge. Date of birth."

"Why?"

His eyes flicked up, arrowed hers. "Why what?"

"Why do you want to know?"

Patience, never his strong suit, strained. He tapped a finger on the form. "Because I've got this space to fill."

"Okay. I'm twenty-eight. A Gemini. I was born on June the first."

Alex did the math and typed in the year. "Residence."

Natural curiosity had her poking through the folders and papers on his desk until he slapped her hand. "You're awfully tense," she commented. "Is it because you work undercover?"

Damn that smile, he thought. It was sassy, sexy, and far from stupid. That, and those sharp, intelligent green eyes, might have fooled him. But she looked like a hooker, and she smelled like a hooker. Therefore...

"Listen, doll, here's the way this works. I ask the questions, you answer them."

"Tough, cynical, street-smart."

One dark brow lifted. "Excuse me?"

"Just a quick personality check. You want my address, right?" she rattled off an address that made both of Alex's brows raise.

"Let's get serious."

"Okay." Willing to oblige, Bess folded her hands on the edge of his desk.

"Your address," he repeated.

"I just gave it to you."

"I know what real estate goes for in that area. Maybe you're good." Thoughtful, he scanned her attributes one more time. "Maybe you're better than you look. But you don't make enough working the streets to pop for that kind of rent."

Bess knew an insult when it hit her over the head. What made it worse was that she'd spent over an hour on her makeup. And she happened to know that her body was good. Lord knew, she sweated to keep it that way by working out three days a week. "That's where I live, cop." Her temper, which had a habit of flaring quickly, had her upending her enormous canvas tote onto his desk.

Alex watched, fascinated, as she pawed through the pile of contents. There were enough cosmetics to supply a small department store. And they weren't the cheap kind. Six lipsticks, two compacts, several mascara sticks and pots of eye shadow. A rainbow of eyeliner pencils. Scattered with them were two sets of keys, a snowfall of credit-card receipts, rubber bands, paper clips, twelve pens—he counted—a few broken pencils, a steno pad, two paperback books, matches, a leather address book embossed with the initials *ELM,* a stapler—he didn't even pause to wonder why she would carry one—tissues and crumpled papers, a tiny microcassette recorder. And a gun.

He whipped it out of the pile and stared at it. A water gun.

"Careful with that," she warned as she found her overburdened wallet. "It's full of ammonia."

"Ammonia?"

"I used to carry Mace, but this works fine. Here." Pleased with herself, she pushed the open wallet under his nose.

It might have been her in the picture. The hair was short and curly and chic, a deep chestnut rather than a brassy blonde. But that nose, that chin. And those eyes. He frowned over the driver's license. The address was right.

"You got a car?"

She shrugged and began to dump things back into her purse. "So?"

"Women in your position usually don't."

Because it made sense, Bess stalled. "I've got a license. Everybody who has a license doesn't have to have a car, do they?"

"No." He jerked the wallet out of her reach. "Take off the wig."

Pouting a little, she patted it. "How come?"

He reached across the desk and yanked it off himself. She scowled at him while she ran her fingers through short, springy red curls. "I want that back. It's borrowed."

"Sure." He tossed it onto his desk before he leaned back in his squeaky chair for a fresh evaluation. If this lady was a hooker, he was Clark Kent. "What the hell *are* you?"

It was time to come clean. She knew it. But something about him egged her on. "I'm just a woman trying to make a living, Officer." That was how Jade would handle it, Bess was sure. And since Jade was her creation, Bess was determined to do right by her.

He opened the wallet, skimmed through the bills. She was carrying around what would be for him more than two weeks' pay. "Right."

"Can you do that?" she demanded, more curious than annoyed. "Go through my personal property?"

"Honey, right now *you* are *my* personal property." There were pictures in the wallet, as well. Snapshots of people, some with her, some without her. And the lady was a card-carrying member of dozens of groups, including Greenpeace, the World Wildlife Federation, Amnesty International and the Writers' Guild. The last brought him back to the tape recorder. When he picked up the little toy, he noted that it was running. "Let's have it, Bess."

God, he was cute. The thought passed through her head as she smiled at him. "Have what?"

"What were you doing hanging around with Rosalie and the rest of the girls?"

"My job." When his eyes narrowed that way, Bess thought, he was downright irresistible. Impatient, a little mean, with a flash of recklessness just barely under control.

Fabulous.

"Really." All honesty and cheap perfume, she leaned

forward. "You see, it all has to do with Jade, and how she's having this problem with a dual personality. By day, she's a dedicated lawyer—a real straight arrow, *you* know—but by night she hits the streets. She's blocking what happened between her and Brock, and coupled with a childhood memory that's begun to resurface, the strain's been too much for her. She's on a path of self-destruction."

The frown in his eyes turned them nearly black. "Who the hell is Jade?"

"Jade Sullivan Carstairs. Don't you watch daytime TV?"

His head was beginning to buzz. "No."

"You don't know what you're missing. You'd probably really enjoy the Jade-Storm-Brock story line. Storm's a cop, you see, and he's falling in love with Jade. Her emotional problems, and the hold Brock has on her, complicate things. Then there was a miscarriage, and the kidnapping. Naturally, Storm has problems of his own."

"Naturally. What's your point?"

"Oh, sorry. I get offtrack. I write for 'Secret Sins' daytime drama."

"You're a soap-opera writer?"

"Yeah." Unlike many in the trade, she wasn't bothered by that particular label. "And I like to get the feel of the situations I put my characters into. Since Jade is a special pet of mine, I—"

"Are you out of your mind?" Alex barked the question as he leaned over into her face. "Do you have any idea what you were doing?"

She blinked, at once innocent and amused. "Research?"

He swore again, and Bess found she liked the way he raked impatient fingers through his thick black hair. "Lady, just how far were you intending to take your research?"

"How—? Oh." Her eyes brightened with laughter. "Well no, not quite that far."

"What the hell would you have done if I hadn't been a cop?"

"I'd have thought of something." She continued to smile. He had a fascinating face—golden skin, dark eyes, wonderful bones. And that mouth, so beautifully sculpted, even if it did tend to scowl. "It's my job to think of things. And when I spotted you, I thought you looked safe. What I mean is, you didn't strike me as the kind of man who'd be interested in…" What was a delicate way of putting it? she wondered. "Paying for pleasure."

He was so angry he wanted to yank her up and toss her over his lap. The idea of administering a few good whacks to that cute little butt was tremendously appealing. "And if you'd guessed wrong?"

"I didn't," she pointed out. "For a minute there, I was worried, but it all worked out. Better than I expected, really, because I had a chance to ride in a— Do you still call them paddy wagons?"

He'd been so sure he'd seen everything. Heard everything. With his temper straining at the bit, he spoke through clenched teeth. "Two hookers are dead. Two who worked that area."

"I know," she said quickly, as if that explained it all. "That was one of the reasons I chose it. You see, I plan to have Jade—"

"I'm talking about you," he interrupted in a voice

that had her wincing. "You. Some bubbleheaded hack writer who thinks she can strut around in spandex and a half a ton of makeup, then go home to her nice neighborhood and wash it all off."

"Hack?" It was the only thing she took offense to. "Look, cop—"

"*You* look. You stay out of my territory, and out of those slut clothes. Do your research out of a book."

Her chin shot out. "I can go where I want, wearing what I want."

"You think so?" There was a way to teach her a lesson. A perfect way. "Fine." He rose, tugged the tote out of her hands, then took a firm grip on her arm. "Let's go."

"Where?"

"To holding, babe. You're under arrest, remember?"

She stumbled in the three-inch heels and squawked, "But I just explained—"

"I hear better stories before breakfast every day."

"You're not going to put me in a cell." Bess was sure of it. Positive. Right up until the moment the bars closed in her face.

It took about ten minutes for the shock to wear off. When it did, Bess decided it wasn't such a bad turn. She could be furious with the cop—whoever he was—but she could appreciate and take advantage of the unique opportunity he'd given her. She was in a holding cell with several other women. There was atmosphere to be absorbed, and there were interviews to be conducted.

When one of her cellmates informed her that she was entitled to a phone call, she demanded one. Pleased with the progress she was making, she settled back on her hard cot to talk to her new acquaintances.

It was thirty minutes later when she looked up and spotted her friend and cowriter Lori Banes, standing beside a uniformed policeman.

"Bess, you look so natural here."

With a grin, Bess popped up as the guard unlocked the door. "It's been great."

"Hey!" one of her cellmates called out. "I'm telling you that Vicki's a witch, and Jeffrey should boot her out. Amelia's the right woman for him."

Bess sent back a wink. "I'll see what I can do. Bye, girls."

Lori didn't consider herself long-suffering. She didn't consider herself a prude or a stuffed shirt. And she said as much to Bess as they walked through the corridors, up the stairs and back into the lobby area outside the squad room. "But," she added, pressing fingers to her tired eyes. "There's something that puts me off about being woken up at 2:00 a.m. to come bail you out of jail."

"Sorry, but it's been great. Wait until I tell you."

"Do you know what you look like, dear?"

"Yep." Unconcerned, Bess craned her neck. The chair behind Alex's desk was empty. "I had no idea that so many of the working girls watched the show. But they do work nights, mostly. Uh, excuse me…" She caught the sleeve of one of New York's finest as he walked by. "The officer who uses that desk?"

The cop swallowed the best part of a bite of his pastrami sandwich. "Stanislaski?"

"Whew. That's a mouthful. Is he still around?"

"He's in Interrogation."

"Oh. Thanks."

"Come on, Bess, we've got to pick up your things."

Bess had signed for her purse and its contents, still keeping an eye out for Alex. "Stanislaski," she repeated to herself. "Is that Polish, do you think?"

"How the hell do I know?" Out of patience, Lori steered her toward the door. "Let's get out of here. The place is lousy with criminals."

"I know. It's fabulous." With a laugh, she tucked an arm around Lori's waist. "I got ideas for the next three years. If we decide to have Elana arrested for Reed's murder..."

"I don't know about having Reed murdered."

With a sigh, Bess looked around for a cab. "Lori, we both know Jim isn't going to sign another contract. He wants to try the big leagues. Having his character offed is the perfect way to beef up Elana's story line."

"Maybe."

Bess slyly pulled out her ace. "'Our Lives, Our Loves' picked up two points in the ratings last month."

Lori only grunted.

"Word is Dr. Amanda Jamison is going to have twins."

"Twins?" Lori shut her eyes. Soap diva Ariel Kirkwood, who played the long-suffering psychiatrist on the competing soap, was daytime's most popular star. "It had to be twins," Lori muttered. "Okay, Reed dies."

Bess allowed herself one quick victory smile, then hurried on.

"Anyway, while I was in there, I was picturing the elegant, cool Dr. Elana Warfield Stafford Carstairs in prison. Fabulous, Lori. It'd be fabulous. I wish you'd seen the cop."

They'd walked to the corner, and there wasn't a cab in sight. "What cop?"

"The one who arrested me. He was incredibly sexy."

Lori only had the energy to sigh. "Leave it to you to get busted by a sexy cop."

"Really. All this thick black hair. His eyes were nearly black, too. Very intense. He had all those hollows and planes in his face, and this beautiful mouth. Nice build, too. Sort of rough-and-ready. Like a boxer, maybe."

"Don't start, Bess."

"I'm not. I can find a man sexy and attractive without falling in love."

Lori shot her a look. "Since when?"

"Since the last time. I've sworn off, remember?" Her smile perked up when she spotted a cab heading their way. "I'm interested in this Stanislaski for strictly professional reasons."

"Right." Resigned, Lori climbed in when the cab swung to the curb.

"I swear." She lifted her right hand to add impact to the oath. "We want to get into Storm's head more, into his background and stuff. So I pick this cop's brain a little." She gave a cabbie both her address and Lori's. "After Jade gets attacked by the Millbrook Maniac, Storm isn't going to be able to hold back his feelings for her. More has to come out about who and what he is. If we do have Elana arrested for Reed's murder, that's going to complicate his life—you know, family loyalty versus professional ethics. And once he confronts Brock—"

"Hey." At a red light, the cabbie turned, peering at

them from under his fading Mets cap. "You talking about 'Secret Sins'?"

"Yeah." Bess brightened. "Do you watch it?"

"The wife tapes it every day. You don't look familiar."

"We're not on it," Bess explained. "We write it."

"Gotcha." Satisfied, he punched the accelerator when the light changed. "Let me tell you what I think about that two-timing Vicki."

As he proceeded to do just that, Bess leaned forward, debating with him. Lori closed her eyes and tried to catch up on lost sleep.

Chapter 2

"My wife went nuts." Judd Malloy munched on his cherry Danish while Alex swung in and out of downtown traffic. "She's a big fan of that soap, you know? Tapes it every day when she's in school."

"Terrific." Alex had been doing his best to forget his little encounter with the soap queen, but his partner wasn't cooperating.

"Holly figures it was just like meeting a celebrity."

"You don't find many celebrities turning tricks."

"Come on, Alex." Judd washed down the Danish with heavily sugared coffee. "She wasn't, really. You said so yourself, or the charges wouldn't have been dropped."

"She was stupid," Alex said between his teeth. "Carrying a damn water pistol in that suitcase of hers. I guess she figured if a john got rough, she'd blast him between the eyes and that would be that."

Judd started to comment on how it might feel to get a blast of ammonia in the eyes, but didn't think his partner wanted to hear it. "Well, Holly was impressed, and we got some fresh juice out of Rosalie, so we didn't waste our time."

"Malloy, you'd better get used to wasting time. Stanislaski's rule number four." Alex spotted the building he was looking for and double-parked. He was already out of the car and across the sidewalk before Judd found the NYPD sign and stuck it in the window. "We sure as hell could be wasting it here with this Domingo."

"Rosalie said—"

"Rosalie said what we wanted to hear so we'd spring her," Alex told him. His cop's eyes were already studying the building, noting windows, fire escapes, roof. "Maybe she gave us the straight shot on Domingo, and maybe she pulled it out of a hat. We'll see."

The place was in good repair. No graffiti, no broken glass or debris. Lower-middle-income, Alex surmised. Established families, mostly blue-collar. He pulled open the heavy entrance door, then scanned the names above the line of mailboxes.

"J. Domingo. 212." Alex pushed the buzzer for 110, waited, then hit 305. The answering buzz released the inner door. "People are so careless," he commented. He could feel Judd's nerves shimmering as they climbed the stairs, but he could tell he was holding it together. He'd damn well better hold it together, Alex thought as he gestured Judd into position, then knocked on the door of 212. He knocked a second time before he heard the cursing answer.

When the door opened a crack, Alex braced his body against it to keep it that way. "How's it going, Jesús?"

"What the hell do you want?"

He fit Rosalie's description, Alex noted. Right down to the natty Clark Gable moustache and the gold incisor. "Conversation, Jesús. Just a little conversation."

"I don't talk to nobody at this hour."

When he tried to shove the door to, Alex merely leaned on it and flipped open his badge. "You don't want to be rude, do you? Why don't you ask us in?"

Swearing in Spanish, Jesús Domingo cracked the door a little wider. "You got a warrant?"

"I can get one, if you want more than conversation. I can take you down for questioning, get the paperwork and do the job before your shyster lawyer can tap-dance you out. Want a team of badges in here, Jesús?"

"I haven't done nothing." He stepped back from the door, a small man with wiry muscles who was wearing nothing but a pair of gym shorts.

"Nobody said you did. Did I say he did, Malloy?"

Enjoying himself, Judd stepped in behind Alex. "Nope."

The building might be lower-middle-class, but Domingo's apartment was a small high-tech palace. State-of-the-art stereo equipment, Alex noted. A big-screen TV with some very classy video toys. The wall of tapes ran mostly to the X-rated.

"Nice place," Alex commented. "You sure know how to make your unemployment check stretch."

"I got a good head for figures." Domingo plucked up a pack of cigarettes from a table, lighted one. "So?"

"So, let's talk about Angie Horowitz."

Domingo blew out smoke and scratched at the hair on his chest. "Never heard of her."

"Funny, we got word you were one of her regulars, and her main supplier."

"You got the wrong word."

"Maybe you don't recognize the name." Alex reached into his inside jacket pocket, and his fingers brushed over his leather shoulder harness as he pulled out a manila envelope. "Why don't you take a look?" He stuck the police shot under Domingo's nose and watched his olive complexion go a sickly gray. "Look familiar?"

"Man." Domingo's fingers shook as he brought his cigarette to his lips.

"Problem?" Alex glanced down at the photo himself. There hadn't been much left of Angie for the camera. "Oh, hey, sorry about that, Jesús. Malloy, didn't I tell you not to put the dead shot in?"

Judd shrugged, feigning casualness. He was thinking he was glad he didn't have to look at it again himself. "Guess I made a mistake."

"Yeah." All the while he spoke, Alex held the photo where Domingo could see it. "Guy's a rookie," he explained. "Always screwing up. You know. Poor little Angie sure got sliced, didn't she? Coroner said the guy put about forty holes in her. You can see most of them. Poor Malloy here took one look and lost his breakfast. I keep telling him not to eat those damned greasy Danishes before we go check out a stiff, but like I said..." Alex grinned to himself as Domingo made a dash for the bathroom.

"That was cold, Stanislaski," Judd said, grinning.

"Yeah, I'm that kind of guy."

"And I didn't throw up my breakfast."

"You wanted to." The sounds coming from the bathroom were as unpleasant as they get. Alex tapped on the door. "Hey, Jesús, you okay, man? I'm really sorry about that." He passed the photo and envelope to Judd. "Tell you what, let me get you some nice cold water, okay?"

The answer was a muffled retch that Alex figured anyone could take for assent. He moved into the kitchen and opened the freezer. The two kilos were exactly where Rosalie had said he'd find them. He took one out just as Domingo rushed in.

"You got no warrant. You got no right."

"I was getting you some ice." Alex turned the frozen cocaine over in his hands. "This doesn't look like a TV dinner to me. What do you think, Malloy?"

By leaning a shoulder against the door jamb, Judd blocked the doorway. "Not the kind my mother used to make."

"You son of a bitch." Domingo wiped his mouth with a clenched fist. "You violated my civil rights. I'll be out before you can blink."

"Could be." Taking an evidence bag out of his pocket, Alex slipped both kilos inside. "Malloy, why don't you read our friend his rights while he's getting dressed? And, Jesús, try some mouthwash."

"Stanislaski," the desk sergeant called out when Alex came up from seeing Domingo into a cell. "You got company."

Alex glanced over toward his desk, seeing that several cops were huddled around it. There was quite a bit of laughter overriding the usual squad room noise. Curiosity had him moving forward even before he saw the legs. Legs he recognized. They were crossed at the knee and covered almost modestly in a canary-yellow skirt.

He recognized the rest of her, too, though the tough

little body was clad in a multihued striped blazer and a scoop-necked blouse the same color as the skirt. Half a dozen slim columns of gold danced at her ears as she laughed. She looked better, sexier, he was forced to admit, with her mouth unpainted, her freckles showing, and those big green eyes subtly smudged with color. Her hair was artfully tousled, a rich, deep red that made him think of a mahogany statue his brother had carved for him.

"So I told the mayor we'd try to work it in, and we'd love for him to come on the show and do a cameo." She shifted on the desk and spotted Alex. He was frowning at her, his thumbs tucked into the pockets of a leather bomber jacket. "Officer Stanislaski."

"McNee." He inclined his head, then swept his gaze over his fellow officers. "The boss comes in and finds you here, I might have to tell him how you didn't have enough work and volunteered to take some of mine."

"Just entertaining your guest, Stanislaski." But the use of the squad room's nickname for their captain had the men drifting reluctantly away.

"What can I do for you?"

"Well, I—"

"You're sitting on a homicide," he told her.

"Oh." She scooted off the desk. Without the stilettos, she was half a head shorter than he. Alex discovered he preferred it that way. "Sorry. I came by to thank you for straightening things out for me."

"That's what they pay me for. Straightening things out." He'd been certain she would rave a bit about being tossed into a cell, but she was smiling, friendly as a kindergarten teacher. Though he couldn't recall ever having a teacher who looked like her. Or smelled like her.

"Regardless, I appreciate it. My producer's very tolerant, but if it had gone much further, she would have been annoyed."

"Annoyed?" Alex repeated. He stripped off his jacket and tossed it onto his chair. "She'd have been annoyed to find out that one of her writers was out soliciting johns down at Twenty-third and Eleventh Avenue."

"Researching," Bess corrected, unoffended. "Darla— that's my producer—she gets these headaches. I gave her a whopper when I went on a job with a cat burglar."

"With a…" He let his words trail off and eased down on the spot on the desk she'd just vacated. "I don't think you want to tell me about that."

"Actually, he was a former cat burglar. Fascinating guy. I just had him show me how he'd break into my apartment." She frowned a little, remembering. "I guess he was a little rusty. The alarm—"

"Don't." Alex held up a hand. He was beginning to feel a headache coming on himself.

"That's old news, anyway." She waved it away with a cheerful gesture of her hands. "Do you have a first name, or do I just call you Officer?"

"It's Detective."

"Your first name is Detective?"

"No, my rank." He let out a sigh. "Alex."

"Alex. That's nice." She ran a fingertip over the strap of his harness. She wasn't being provocative; she wanted to know what it felt like. Once she knew him better, she was sure, she'd talk him into letting her try it on. "Well, Alex, I was wondering if you'd let me use you."

He'd been a cop for more than five years, and until this moment he hadn't thought anything could surprise him. But it took him three seconds to close his mouth. "I beg your pardon?"

"It's just that you're so perfect." She stepped closer. She really wanted to get a better look at his weapon—without being obvious about it.

She smelled like sunshine and sex. As he drew it in, Alex thought that combination would baffle any man. "I'm perfect?"

"Absolutely." She looked straight into his eyes and smiled. Her gaze was frank and assessing. She was studying him, the way a woman might study a dress in a showroom window. "You're exactly what I've been looking for."

Her eyes were pure green. No hint of gray or blue, no flecks of gold. There was a small dimple near her mouth. Only one. Nothing about that odd, sexy face was balanced. "What you're looking for?"

"I know you're busy, but I'd try not to take up too much of your time. An hour now and then."

"An hour?" He caught himself echoing her, and shook himself loose. "Listen, I appreciate—"

"You're not married, are you?"

"Married? No, but—"

"That makes it simpler. It just came to me last night when I was getting into bed."

God. He'd learned to appreciate women early. And he'd learned to juggle them skillfully—if he said so himself. He knew how to dodge, when to evade and when to sit back and enjoy. But with this one, all bets were off.

"Is this heavy?" she asked, fiddling with his harness.

"You get used to it. It's just there."

Her smile warmed, making him think of sunlight

again. "Perfect," she murmured. "I'd be willing to compensate you for your time, and your expertise."

"You'd be—" He wasn't certain if he was insulted or embarrassed. "Hold on, babe."

"Just think about it," Bess said quickly. "I know it's a lot to ask, but I have this problem with Matthew."

A brand-new emotion snuck in under his guard, and it was as green as her eyes. "Matthew? Who the hell is Matthew?"

"We call him Storm, actually. Lieutenant Storm Warfield, Millbrook PD."

Now he definitely had a headache. Alex rubbed his fingers against his temple. "Millbrook?"

"The fictional town of Millbrook, where the show's set. It's supposed to be somewhere in the Midwest. Storm's a cop. Personally, his life's a mess, but professionally, he's focused and intense and occasionally ruthless. In this new story line I'm working on, I want to concentrate on his police work, the routine, the frustrations."

"Wait." He'd always been quick, but it was taking him a minute to change gears. "You want me to help you with a story line?"

"Exactly. If you could just tell me how you think, how you go about solving a case, working with the system or around it. TV cops have to work around the system quite a bit, you know. It plays better than by-the-book."

He swore under his breath and rubbed his hands over his face. Damn it, his palms were sweaty. "You're a real case, McNee."

"You don't have to decide right now." She was also persistent. And she wondered if he had a spare gun strapped to his calf. One of those sexy-looking little chrome jobs. She'd seen that ploy in several movies. Still, she thought if she asked him that, she'd lose her edge. "I'm having a thing tonight." As she spoke, she dug into her huge bag for her notebook. "Eight o'clock until whenever. Bring a friend, if you like. Your partner, too. He seemed very sweet."

"He's adorable."

"Yeah." She ripped off the page and handed it to him. "I'd really like you to stop by."

He took the sheet, not bothering to remind her he already had her address. "Why?"

"Why not?" She beamed at him again.

Before he could list the reasons, he heard his name called.

"Alexi."

Alexi. Bess was already enchanted with the sound as she rolled the name over in her head. Different, exotic. Sexy. She was certain it suited him much more than the casual *Alex.*

Bess studied the woman bearing down on them. This wasn't one who'd be lost in a crowd, she mused. She was stunning, totally self-assured and very pregnant. Beside Bess, Alex pushed off the desk and sighed.

"Rachel."

"A moment of your time, Detective," Rachel said, flipping a glance over Bess before pinning Alex with a tawny stare. "To reacquaint you with civil rights."

"Your sister?" Bess surmised, beaming at both of them.

Alex sent her a considering frown. "How did you know that?"

"I'm really good with faces. Same bone structure,

same coloring, same mouth. You have to be brother and sister, or first cousins."

"Guilty," Rachel admitted. Though she would have liked to know what Alex was doing with the sharp-eyed redhead, she wasn't about to be swayed from her duties as a public defender. "Jesús Domingo, Alexi. Illegal search and seizure."

"Bull." Alex crossed his arms and leaned back against the desk.

"You had a search warrant?"

"Didn't need one. He invited us in."

"And invited you to poke through his belongings, I suppose."

"Nope." Alex grinned while Bess watched them bounce the verbal ball as though they were champion tennis players. "Jesús got sick. I offered to get him some water. He didn't object. I opened the freezer to get the poor guy some ice, and there it was. Two kilos. It'll all be in my report."

"That's lame, Alexi. You'll never get a conviction."

"Maybe. Maybe not. Talk to the DA."

"I intend to." Rachel shifted her briefcase and began to rub her belly in circular motions to soothe the baby, who seemed to be doing aerobics in her womb. "You had no probable cause."

"Sit down."

"I don't want to sit down."

"The baby does." He yanked over a chair and all but shoved her into it. "When are you going to knock this off?"

It did feel better to sit. Indescribably better. But she wasn't about to admit it. "The baby's not due for two months. I have plenty of time. We were discussing..."

"Rach." He laid a hand on her cheek, very gently. A shouted curse wouldn't have stopped her, but the small gesture did. "Don't make me worry about you."

"I'm perfectly fine."

"You shouldn't be here."

"I'm having a baby. It's not contagious. Now, about Domingo."

Alex gave a brief, pithy opinion on what could be done with Domingo. "Talk to the DA," he repeated. "Sitting down."

"She looks pretty strong to me," Bess commented. Two pair of eyes turned to her, one furious, the other thoughtful.

"Thank you. The men in my life are coddlers," Rachel explained. "Sweet, but annoying."

"Muldoon should take better care of you," Alex insisted.

"I don't need Zack to take care of me. And the fact is, between him and Nick, I'm barely allowed to brush my own teeth." She held out a hand to Bess. "Since my brother is too rude to introduce me, I'm Rachel Muldoon."

"Bess McNee. You're a lawyer?"

"That's right. I work for the public defender's office."

"Really?" Bess's thoughts began to perk. "What's it like to—"

Alex held up a hand. "Don't get her started. She'll pick your brain clean before you know she's had her fingers in it. Look, McNee—" he turned to Bess, determined not to be charmed by her easy smile "—we're a little busy here."

"Of course you are. I'm sorry." Obligingly she swung

her huge purse onto her shoulder. "We'll talk tonight. Nice to meet you, Rachel."

"Same here." Rachel ran her tongue over her teeth, and both she and Alex watched Bess weave her way out of the squad room. "Well, that was rude."

"It's the only way to handle her. Believe me."

"Hmm... She seems like an interesting woman. How did you meet her?"

"Don't ask." He sat back down on his desk, irked that the scent of sunshine and sex still lingered in the air.

"I can't believe we're doing this." Holly, Judd's pretty wife of eight months, was all but hopping out of her party shoes. "Wait until I tell everyone in the teachers' lounge where I spent the evening."

"Take it easy, honey." Judd tugged at the tie she'd insisted he wear. "It's just a party."

"Just a party?" As the elevator rode up, she fussed with her honey-brown hair. "I don't know about you two, but it isn't every day I get to eat canapés with ce-lebrities."

Ominously silent, Alex stayed hunched in his leather jacket. He didn't know what the hell he was doing here. His first mistake had been mentioning the invitation to Judd. No matter how insouciant Judd pretended to be, he'd been bursting at the seams when he called his wife. Alex had been swept along in their enthusiasm.

But he wasn't going to stay. Holly's sense of decorum might have insisted that she and Judd couldn't attend without him, but he'd already decided just how he'd play it. He'd go in, maybe have a beer and a couple of crack-ers. Then he'd slip out again. He'd be damned if he'd spend this rare free evening playing soap-opera groupie.

"Oh, my" was all Holly could say when the elevator doors opened.

The walls of the private foyer were splashed with a mural of the city. Times Square, Rockefeller Center, Harlem, Little Italy, Broadway. People seemed to be rushing along the walls, just as they did the streets below. It was as if the woman who lived here didn't want to miss one moment of the action.

The wide door to the main apartment was open, and music, laughter and conversation were pouring out, along with the scents of hot food and burning candles.

"Oh, my," Holly said again, dragging her husband along as she stepped inside.

From behind them, Alex scanned the room. It was huge, and it was packed with people. Draped in silk or cotton, clad in business suits and lush gowns, they stood elbow to elbow on the hardwood floor, lounged hip to hip on the sapphire cushions of the enormous circular conversation pit, sat knee to knee on the steps of a bronze circular staircase that led to an open loft where still more people leaned against a railing decked with naked cherubs.

Two huge windows let the lights of the city in. More partygoers sat on the pillow-plumped window seats, balancing plates and glasses on their laps.

Paintings were scattered over the ivory-toned walls. Vivid, frenetic modern art, mind-bending surrealism. There was enough color to make his head swim. Yet, through the crowd and the clashing tones, he saw her. Dancing seductively with a distinguished-looking man in a gray pin-striped suit.

She wore an excuse for a dress, the color of crushed purple grapes. He wondered, irritated, if she owned anything that covered those legs. This number certainly didn't. Nor did it cover much territory at all, the way it dipped to the waist in the back, skimmed above mid-thigh and left her shoulders bare, but for skinny, glittery straps. Multihued gemstones fell in a rope from her earlobes to those nicely sloped shoulders. Her feet were bare.

She looked, Alex thought as his stomach muscles twisted themselves into nasty knots, outrageously alluring.

"Oh, Lord, there's Jade. Oh, and Storm and Vicki. Dr. Carstairs, too." Holly's fingers dug into her husband's arm. "It's Amelia."

"Who?"

"'Secret Sins,' dummy." She gave Judd a playful punch. "The whole cast's here."

"That's not all." Because he remembered in time he was supposed to be jaded, Judd stopped himself from pointing and inclined his head. "That's Lawrence D. Strater dancing with our hostess. *The* L.D. Strater, of Strater Industries. The *Fortune 500*'s darling. The mayor's over in that corner, talking with Hannah Loy, the grand old lady of Broadway." His excitement began to hum in his voice as he continued to scan the room. "Man, there are enough luminaries in this room to light every borough in New York."

But Alex hadn't noticed. Furthermore, he didn't give a damn. His attention was focused on Bess. She'd stopped dancing, and had leaned up to whisper something in her partner's ear that made him laugh before he kissed her. Smack on the lips.

She kissed him back, too, her hands lightly intimate at his waist, before she turned and spotted the new arrivals. She waved, made her excuses, then scooted and dodged her way through the crowd toward them.

"You made it." She gave both Alex and Judd a friendly peck on the cheek before holding out both hands to Holly. "Nice to meet you."

"My wife, Holly, this is Bess McNee."

"Thanks for asking us." Holly caught herself starting to stutter, as she had the first time she faced a classroom of ten-year-olds. She flushed.

"My pleasure." Bess gave her hands a reassuring squeeze. "Let's get you something to eat and drink." She gestured toward a long table by the wall. Instead of the useless finger food and fancy, unrecognizable dishes Alex had expected, it was laden with big pots of spaghetti, mountains of garlic bread, and generous trays of antipasti.

"It's Italian night," she explained, grabbing a plate and heaping it high. "There's plenty of wine and beer, and a full bar." She handed the plate to Holly and began to dish up another. "The desserts are on the other side of the room. They're unbelievable." As she passed Judd a plate, she noted the gleam in Holly's eyes. "Would you like to meet some of the cast?"

"Oh, I…" The hell with sophistication. "Yes. I'd love it."

"Great. Excuse us. Help yourself, Alexi."

"This is really something," Judd said over a mouthful of spaghetti.

"Something," Alex agreed. Deciding to make the best of it, he fixed himself a plate.

He wasn't going to stay. But the food was great. In any case, he didn't have anything else to do. It didn't hurt to hang around and rub elbows with the fast and famous while he was helping himself to a good hot meal. It certainly made a change from his daily routine of wading through misery and bitterness.

After washing down spaghetti with some good red wine, he found himself a spot on a window seat where he could sit back and watch the show.

Bess dropped down beside him, clinked her glass against his. "Best seat in the house."

"Some house."

"Yeah, I like it. I'll show you the rest later, if you want." She broke off a tiny piece of the pastry on his plate and sampled it. "Great stuff."

"Yeah. You got a little...here." Before his good sense could take over, he rubbed a bit of the rich cream from her lip. Watching her, he licked it from the pad of his thumb. And tasted her. "It's not bad."

For a moment she wondered if the circuits in her brain had crossed. Something certainly had sent out a spark. She managed a small sound of agreement as she flicked her tongue to the corner of her mouth. And tasted him.

"Your, ah, partner's wife. Holly." Small talk, any talk, had always come easily to her. She wasn't sure why she was laboring now.

"What about her?"

"Who? Oh, right. Holly. She's nice. I can't imagine what it would be like to teach fifth-graders."

"I'm sure you'll ask her."

"I already did." At ease again, she smiled at him. Something about that sarcastic edge to his voice made her relax and enjoy. "Come on, Alexi. We may be in different professions, but both of them require a certain amount of curiosity about human nature. Aren't you sitting here right now wondering about all of these people, and what they're doing at my party?"

"Not as much as I'm wondering what *I'm* doing at your party." He swirled the wine in his glass before sipping. When he drank, his eyes stayed on hers. Watchful.

She liked that. She liked that very much, the way he could sit so still, energy humming from every pore, while he watched. While he waited. Bess was willing to admit that one of her biggest failings was being unable to wait for anything.

"You were curious," she told him.

"Some."

Her skirt hitched up another inch when she curled her legs up on the seat. "I'd be happy to tell you whatever you want to know, in exchange for your help. You see that guy over there, the gorgeous one with the blonde hanging on his biceps?"

Alex scanned, homed in. "Yeah. I wouldn't say he was gorgeous."

"You're not a woman. That's my detective, Storm Warfield, the black sheep of the snooty, disgustingly rich Warfield clan, the rebel, the volatile brother of the long-suffering Elana Warfield Stafford Carstairs. He's recently pulled himself out of the destructive affair with the wicked, wily Vicki. The blonde crawling up his chest. They're an item off-camera, but on, Storm is madly in love with the tragedy-prone and ethereal Jade, who is, of course, torn between her feelings for him and her misplaced loyalty to the maniacally clever and dastardly Brock Carstairs—half brother to Elana's stalwart husband Dr. Maxwell Carstairs. Max was once married to Jade's formerly conniving but now repentant sister, Flame, who was killed in a Peruvian earthquake soon after the birth of her son—who may or may not be her husband's child. Naturally, the body was never recovered."

"Either I've had too much wine, or you're making me dizzy."

Bess smiled and gave him a companionable pat on the thigh that sent his blood pressure soaring. "It's really not that complicated, once you know the players. But I want you for Storm."

Alex sent the actor a considering look. "I don't think he's my type."

"Your professional expertise, Detective. I need an informal technical advisor. My producer'd be happy to compensate you for your time—particularly since we've been number one in the ratings for the past nine months." Someone called her name, and Bess sent a quick wave. "Looks like it's going to start to thin out. Listen, can you hang around until I've finished playing hostess?"

She popped up and was gone before he could answer. After a moment, Alex set the rest of the dessert aside and rose. If he was going to see the party through, he might as well enjoy himself.

As she saw to the rest of her guests, Bess kept an eye on him. Once he decided to relax, she noted, he made the most of it. It didn't surprise her that he knew how to flirt, or that several women in the room made a point of wandering in his direction. Not even Lori— no pushover in the men department—was unaffected.

"So, that's the one who busted you?" Lori asked her, popping a plump olive into her mouth.

"What do you think?"

Lori chewed, savored, swallowed. "Yum-yum."

With a laugh, Bess chose a wedge of cheese. "I assume that's a comment on the man, not my buffet."

"You bet. And the best part is, he's not an actor."

"Still sore?" Bess murmured.

Lori shrugged, but her gaze cut over to Steven Marshall, alias Brock Carstairs. "I never give him, or his weenie little brain, a thought. No sensible woman would spend her life competing with an actor's ego for attention."

"Sense has nothing to do with it."

Lori looked away, because it hurt, more than she could bear to admit, to watch Steven while he was so busy ignoring her. "This from the queen of the bungled relationships."

"I don't bungle them, I enjoy them."

"I hasten to remind you that two of your former fiancés are in this room."

"It's a big party. Besides, I wasn't engaged to Lawrence."

"He gave you a ring with a rock the size of a Buick."

"A token of his esteem," Bess said blithely. "I never agreed to marry him. And Charlie and I..." She waved to Charles Stutman, esteemed playwright. "We were only engaged for a few months. We both agreed Gabrielle was perfect for him and parted the closest of friends."

"It was the first time I'd heard of a woman being best man at her former fiancé's wedding," Lori admitted. "I don't know how you do it. You don't angst over men, and they never toss blame your way when things fall apart."

"Because I end up being a pal." Bess's lips curved. For the briefest of moments, there was something wistful in the smile. "Not always a position a woman craves, but it seems to suit me."

"Going to be pals with the cop?"

Once again Bess found herself searching the remaining guests for Alex. She found him, dancing slow and close with a sultry brunette. "It would help if he'd bring himself to like me a little. I think it's going to take some work."

"I've never known you to fail. I've got to go. See you Monday."

"Okay." Bess was astute enough to glance over in Steven's direction as Lori left. She was also clear-sighted enough to see the expression of misery in his eyes as he watched Lori walk to the elevator.

People were much too hard on themselves, she thought with a sigh. Love, she was certain, was a complicated and painful process only if you wanted it to be. And she should know, she mused as she took another sip of wine. She had slipped painlessly in and out of love for years.

As she set the glass aside, Alex caught her eye. There was a quick, surprising tremor around her heart. But it was gone quickly as someone swept her up into a dance.

Chapter 3

"How often do you have one of these *things?*" Alex asked when he took Bess up on her offer of a last cup of cappuccino in her now empty and horribly cluttered apartment.

"Oh, when the mood strikes." The after-party wreckage didn't concern her. She and the cleaning team she'd hired would shovel it out sooner or later. Besides, she enjoyed this—the mess and debris, the spilled wine, the lingering scents. It was a testament to the fact that she, and a good many others, had enjoyed themselves.

"Want some cold spaghetti?" she asked him.

"No."

"I do." She unfolded herself from the corner section of the pit and wandered over to the buffet. "I didn't get a chance to eat much earlier—just what I could steal off other people's plates." She came back to stretch out on the cushions and twine pasta on her fork. "What did you think of Bonnie?"

"Who?"

"Bonnie. The brunette you were dancing with. The one who stuck her phone number in your pocket."

Remembering, Alex patted his shirt pocket. "Right. Bonnie. Very nice."

"Mmm…she is." As she agreed, Bess twined more pasta. She propped her feet on the coffee table, where they continued to keep the beat of the low-volume rock playing on the stereo. "I appreciate your staying."

"I've got some time."

"I still appreciate it. Let me run this by you, okay?" She continued to eat, rapidly working her way through a large plate full of food. "Jade's got a split personality due to an early-childhood trauma, which I won't go into."

"Thank God."

"Don't be snide—millions of viewers are panting for more. Anyway, Jade's alter ego, Josie, is the hooker— or will be, once we start taping that story line. Storm's nuts about Jade. It's difficult for him, as he's a very passionate sort of guy, and she's fragile at the moment."

"Because of Brock."

"You catch on. Anyway, he's wildly in love and miserably frustrated, and he's got a hot case to solve. The Millbrook Maniac."

"The—" Alex shut his eyes. "Oh, man."

"Hey, the press is always giving psychotics catchy little labels. Anyway, the Maniac's going around strangling women with a pink silk scarf. It's symbolic, but we won't get into that right now, either."

"I can't tell you how grateful I am."

She offered him a forkful of cold pasta. After a moment, he gave in and leaned closer to take it. "Now, the press is going to start hounding Storm," Bess continued. "And the brass will be on his case, too. His emotional life is a wreck. How does he separate it? How does he go about establishing a connection between the three— so far—victims? And when he realizes Jade may be in danger, how does he keep his personal feelings from clouding his professional judgement?"

"That's the kind of stuff you want?"

"For a start."

"Okay." He propped his feet beside hers. "First, you don't separate, not like you mean. The minute you have to think like a cop, that's what you are, that's how you think, and you've got no personal life until you can stop thinking like a cop again."

"Wait." Bess shoved the plate into his lap, then bounded up and hunted through a drawer until she came up with a notebook. She dropped onto the sofa again, curling up her legs this time, so that her knee lay against the side of his thigh. "Okay," she said, scribbling. "You're telling me that when you start on a case, or get a call or whatever, everything else just clicks off."

Since she seemed to be through eating, he set the plate on the coffee table. "It better click off."

"How?"

He shook his head. "There is no how. It just is. Look, cop work is mostly monotonous. It's routine, but it's the kind of routine you have to keep focused on. Make a mistake in the paperwork, and some slime gets bounced on a technicality."

"What about when you're on the street?"

"That's a routine, too, and you'd better keep your

head on that routine, if you want to go home in one piece. You can't start thinking about the fight you had with your woman, or the bills you can't pay, or the fact that your mother's sick. You think about now, right now, or you won't be able to fix any of those things later. You'll just be dead."

Her eyes flashed up to his. He said it so matter-of-factly. When she studied him, she saw that he thought of it that way. "What about fear?"

"You usually have about ten seconds to be afraid. So you take them."

"But what if the fear's for someone else? Someone you love?"

"Then you'd better put it aside and do what you've been trained to do. If you don't, you're no good to yourself or your partner, and you're a liability."

"So, it's cut-and-dried?"

He smiled a little. "Except on TV. You're asking me for feelings, McNee, intangibles."

"A cop's feelings," she told him. "I'd think they would be very tangible. Maybe a cop wouldn't be allowed to show his emotions on the job. An occasional flare-up, maybe, but then you'd have to suck it in and follow routine. And no matter how good you are, an arrest isn't always going to stick. The bad guy isn't always going to pay. That has to cause immeasurable frustration. And repressing that frustration..." Considering, she tapped her pencil against the pad. "See, I think of people as pressure cookers."

"Sure you do."

"No, really." That quick smile, the flash of the single dimple. "Whatever's inside, good or bad, has to have some means of release, or the lids blows." She shifted again, and her fingers nearly brushed his neck. She talked with them, he'd noted. With her hands, her eyes, her whole body. The woman simply didn't know how to be still. "What do you use to keep the lid on, Alexi?"

"I make sure I kick a couple of small dogs every morning."

She smiled with entirely too much understanding. "Too personal? Okay, we'll come back to it later."

"It's not personal." Damn it, she made him uncomfortable. As if he had an itch in the small of his back that he couldn't quite scratch. "I use the gym. Beat the crap out of a punching bag a few days a week. Lift too many weights. Sweat it out."

"That's great. Perfect." Grinning now, she cupped a hand over his biceps and squeezed. "Not too shabby. I guess it works." She flexed her own arm, inviting him to test the muscle. It was the gesture of a small boy on a playground, but Alex couldn't quite think of her that way. "I work out myself," she told him. "I'm addicted to it. But I can't seem to develop any upper-body strength."

He watched her eyes as he curled a hand over her arm and found a tough little muscle. "Your upper body looks fine."

"A compliment." Surprised that a reaction had leapt straight into her gut at the casual touch, she started to move her arm. He held on. It took some work to keep her smile from faltering. "What? You want to arm-wrestle, Detective?"

Her skin was like rose petals—smooth, fragrant. Experimenting, he skimmed his hand down to the curve of her elbow. She was smiling, he noted, and her eyes were lit with humor, but her pulse was racing. "A few years back I arm-wrestled my brother for his wife. I lost."

The idea was just absurd enough to catch her imagination. "Really? Is that how the Stanislaskis win their women?"

"Whatever works." Because he was tempted to explore more of that silky, exposed skin, he rose. He reminded himself that the uncomplicated Bonnie was more his style than the overinquisitive, oddly packaged Bess McNee. "I have to go."

Whatever had been humming between them was fading now. As Bess walked him to the door, she debated with herself whether she wanted to let those echoes fade or pump up the volume until she recognized the tune. "Stanislaski. Is that Polish, Russian, what?"

"We're Ukrainian."

"Ukrainian?" Intrigued, she watched him pull his jacket on. "From the southwest of the European Soviet Union, with the Carpathian Mountains in the west."

"Yeah." And through those mountains his family had escaped when he was no more than a baby. He felt a tug, a small one, as he often did when he thought of the country of his blood. "You've been there?"

"Only in spirit." Smiling, she straightened his jacket for him. "I minored in geography in college. I like reading about exotic places." She kept her hands on the front of his jacket, enjoying the feel of leather, the scent of it, and of him. Their bodies were close, more casual than intimate, but close. Looking into his eyes, those dark, uncannily focused eyes, she discovered she wanted to hear that tune again after all.

"Are you going to talk to me again?" she asked him.

His fingers itched to roam along that tantalizingly bare skin on her back. For reasons he couldn't have named, he kept his hands at his sides. "You know where to find me. If I've got the time and the answers, we'll talk."

"Thanks." Her lips curved as she rose on her toes so that their eyes and mouths were level. She leaned in slowly, an inch, then two, to touch her mouth to his. The kiss was soft and breezy. Either of his sisters might have said goodbye to him in precisely the same manner. But that cool and fleeting taste of her didn't make him feel brotherly.

She heard the humming in her head. A nice, quiet sound of easy pleasure. He tasted faintly of wine and spices, and his firm lips seemed to accept the gesture as it was meant—as one of affection and curiosity. Her lips were still curved when she dropped back on her heels.

"Good night, Alexi."

He nodded. He was fairly sure he could speak, but there was no point in taking the chance. Turning, he walked into the foyer and punched the elevator button. When he glanced back, she was still standing in the doorway. Smiling, she waved another goodbye and started to close the door.

It surprised them both when he whirled around and slapped a hand on it to keep it open. The fact that she took an automatic step in retreat surprised her further. But it was the look in his eyes, she thought, that made her feel like a rabbit caught in a rifle's cross hairs.

"Did you forget something?"

"Yeah." Very slowly, very deliberately, he slid his arms around her waist, ran his hand up her back, so that her eyes widened and her skin shivered. "I forgot I like to make my own moves."

Bess braced for the kind of wild assault that was in his eyes, and was surprised for the third time in as many minutes. He didn't swoop or crush, but eased her closer, degree by degree, until she was molded to him. His fingers cruised lazily up her back until they reached the nape of her neck, where they cupped and held. Still his mouth hovered above her.

His hand moved low, intimately, where skin gave way to silk. "Stand on your toes," he murmured.

"What?"

"Stand on your toes." This time, it was his lips that curved.

Dazed, she obeyed, then gave a strangled gasp when he increased the pressure on her back and pressed them center to center. His eyes stayed open as he moved his mouth to hers, brushing, nipping, then taking, in a dreamy kind of possession that had her own vision blurring.

The humming in her brain increased until it was a wall of sound, unrecognizable. She was deaf to everything else, even her own throaty moan as he dipped his tongue between her lips to seduce hers.

It was all slow-motion and soft-focus, but that didn't stop the heat from building. She could feel the little flames start to flare where she was pressed most intimately against him, then spread long, patient fingers of fire outward. Everywhere.

He never pushed, he never pressured, he savored, as a man might who had enjoyed a satisfying meal and was content to linger over a tasty dessert. Even knowing she was being sampled, tested, lazily consumed, she couldn't protest. For the first time in her life, Bess understood what it was to be helplessly seduced.

He hadn't meant to do this. He'd been thinking about doing just this for hours. However much pleasure it gave him to feel her curvy body melt against his, to hear those small, vulnerable sounds vibrating in her throat, to taste that dizzy passion on her lips, he knew he'd made a mistake.

She wasn't his type. And he was going to want more.

The instinct he'd been born with and then honed during his years on the force helped him to hold back that part of himself that, if let loose, could turn the evening into a disaster for both of them. Still, he lingered another moment, taking himself to the edge. When his system was churning with her, and his mind was clouded with visions of peeling her out of that swatch of a dress, he stepped back. He supported her by the elbows until her eyes fluttered open.

They were big and dazed. He clenched his teeth to fight back the urge to pull her to him again and finish what he'd started. But, however stunned and fragile she looked at the moment, Alex recognized a dangerous woman. He'd been a cop long enough to know when to face danger, and when to avoid it.

"You, ah…" Where was all her glib repartee? Bess wondered. It was a little difficult to think when she wasn't sure her head was still on her shoulders. "Well," she managed, and settled for that.

"Well." He let her go and added a cocky grin before he walked back to the elevator. Though his stance was relaxed, he was praying the elevator would come quickly, before he lost it and crawled back to her door. She was still there when the elevator rumbled open. Alex let out a quiet, relieved breath as he stepped inside and leaned against the back wall. "See you around, McNee," he said as the doors slid shut.

"Yeah." She stared at the mural-covered walls. "See you around."

* * *

"Holly hasn't been able to stop talking about that party." Judd was scarfing down a blueberry muffin as Alex cruised Broadway. "It made her queen of the teachers' lounge."

"I bet." Alex didn't want to think about Bess's party. He especially didn't want to think about what would be after the party. Work was what he needed to concentrate on, and right now work meant following up on the few slim leads they'd hassled out of Domingo.

"If Domingo's given it to us straight, Angie Horowitz was excited about a new john." Alex tapped his fingers against the steering wheel. "He'd hired her two Wednesdays running, dressed good, tipped big."

Judd nodded as he brushed muffin crumbs from his shirt. "And she was killed on a Wednesday. So was Rita Shaw. It's still pretty thin, Alex."

"So we make it thick." It continued to frustrate him that they'd wasted time interrogating the desk clerks at the two fleabag hotels where the bodies had been found. Like most in their profession, the clerks had seen nothing. Heard nothing. Knew nothing.

As for the ladies who worked the streets, however nervous they were, they weren't ready to trust a badge.

"Tomorrow's Wednesday," Judd said helpfully.

"I know what the hell tomorrow is. Do you do anything but eat?"

Judd unwrapped another muffin. "I got low blood sugar. If we're going to go back and look at the crime scene again, I need energy."

"What you need is—" Alex broke off as he glanced past Judd's profile and into the glaring lights of an all-night diner. He knew only one person with hair that shade of red. He began to swear, slowly, steadily, as he searched for a parking place.

"You really write for TV?" Rosalie asked.

Bess finished emptying a third container of nondairy product into her coffee. "That's right."

"I didn't think you were a sister." Interested as much in Bess as in the fifty dollars she'd been paid, Rosalie blew out smoke rings. "And you want to know what it's like to turn tricks."

"I want to know whatever you're comfortable telling me." Bess shoved her untouched coffee aside and leaned forward. "I'm not sitting in judgment or asking for confidences, Rosalie. I'd like your story, if you want to tell it. Or we can stick with generalities."

"You figure you can find out what's going on on the streets by putting on spandex and a wig, like you did the other night?"

"I found out a lot," Bess said with a smile. "I found out it's tough to stand in heels on concrete for hours at a time. That a woman has to lose her sense of self in order to do business. That you don't look at the faces. The faces don't matter—the money does. And what you do isn't a matter of intimacy, not even a matter of sex—for you—but a matter of control." She scooted her coffee back and took a sip. "Am I close?"

For a moment, Rosalie said nothing. "You're not as stupid as you look."

"Thanks. I'm always surprising people that way. Especially men."

"Yeah." For the first time, Rosalie smiled. Beneath the hard-edged cosmetics and the lines life had etched in her face, she was a striking woman, not yet thirty.

"I'll tell you this, girlfriend, the men who pay me see a body. They don't see a mind. But I got a mind, and I got a plan. I've been on the streets five years. I ain't going to be on them five more."

"What are you going to do? What do you want to do?"

"When I get enough saved up, I'm going South. Going to get me a trailer in Florida, and a straight job. Maybe selling clothes. I look real fine in good clothes." She crushed out her cigarette and lit another. "Lots of us have plans, but don't make it. I will. I'm clean," she said, and lifted her arms, turning them over. It took Bess a minute to realize Rosalie was saying she wasn't a user. "One more year, I'm gone. Less than that, if I hook onto a regular john with money. Angie did."

"Angie?" Bess flipped through her mental file. "Angie Horowitz? Isn't that the woman who was murdered?"

"Yeah." Rosalie moistened her lips before sucking in smoke. "She wasn't careful. I'm always careful."

"How can you be careful?"

"You keep yourself ready," Rosalie told her. "Angie, she liked to drink. She'd talk a john into buying a bottle. That's not being careful. And this guy, the rich one? He—"

"What the hell do you think you're doing?"

Both Rosalie and Bess looked up. Standing beside the scarred table was a tall man with thin shoulders. There was a cheroot clamped between his teeth, and a diamond winked on his finger. His face was moon-pale, with furious blue eyes. His hair was nearly as white, and slicked back, ending in a short ponytail.

"I'm having me a cup of coffee and a smoke, Bobby,"

Rosalie told him. But beneath the defiance, Bess recognized the trickle of fear.

"You get back on the street where you belong."

"Excuse me." Bess offered her best smile. "Bobby, is it?"

He cast his icy blue eyes on her. "You looking for work, sweetheart? I'll tell you right now, I don't tolerate any loafing."

"Thank you, but no, I'm not looking. Rosalie was just helping me with a small problem."

"She doesn't solve anyone's problems but mine." He jerked his head toward the street. "Move it."

Bess slid out of the booth but held her ground. "This is a public place, and we're having a conversation."

"You don't talk to anybody I don't tell you to talk to." Bobby gave Rosalie a hard shove toward the door.

Bess didn't think, simply reacted. If she detested anything, it was a bully. "Now just a damn minute." She grabbed his sleeve. He rounded on her. Other patrons put on their blinders when he pushed her into the table. Bess came up, fists clenched, just as Alex slammed through the door.

"One move, Bobby," he said tightly. "Just one move toward her."

Bobby brushed at his sleeve and shrugged. "I just came in for a cup of coffee. Isn't that right, Rosalie?"

"Yeah." Rosalie closed her hand over the business card Bess had slipped her. "We were just having some coffee."

But Alex's eyes were all for Bess. She didn't look pale and frightened. Her eyes were snapping, and her cheeks were flushed with fury. "Tell me you want to press charges."

"I'm sorry." With an effort, Bess relaxed her hands. "We were just having a conversation. Nice talking to you, Rosalie."

"Sure." She swaggered out, blowing smoke in Alex's face for effect.

"Take off."

Bobby moved his shoulders again, smirked. "The coffee's lousy here, anyway." He flicked a glance at Bess. "Next time, sweetheart."

Alex waited ten humming seconds after the door swung shut. Without a word, he stalked over to Bess and grabbed her by the arm and hustled her out the door.

"Look, if this is a knight-in-shining-armor routine, I appreciate it, but I don't need rescuing."

"You need a straitjacket."

With murder in his heart, he dragged her half a block.

"In the car," he snapped, opening the back door of the patrol car.

"A cab would be——"

He swore, put a hand on her head and shoved her into the back seat.

Resigned, Bess settled back. "Hi, Judd," she said as he took his place in the passenger seat in front. "How's Holly?"

"Great, thanks." He slanted a look toward his partner. "Ah, she really had a good time at your place."

"I'm glad. We'll have to do it again." Alex whipped out into traffic with enough force to have her slamming back against the seat. Without missing a beat, Bess crossed her legs. "Am I allowed to ask where we're going, or is this another bust?"

"I should be taking you to Bellevue, where you belong," Alex responded. "But I'm taking you home."

"Well, thanks for the lift."

His eyes flashed to hers in the rearview mirror. Her face was still flushed, and her irises were a sharp enough jade to slice to the bone, but she looked more miffed than upset. *Miffed,* he thought with a snort. Stupid word. It fit her perfectly.

"You're an idiot, McNee. And, like most idiots, you're dangerous."

"Oh, really?" She scooted up in the seat so that she could lean between him and Judd. "Just how do you figure that, smart guy?"

"Not only do you go back down to an area you have no business even knowing about—"

"Give me a break."

"But," he continued, "you sit there drinking coffee with a hooker, then pick a fight with her pimp. The kind of guy who'd as soon give a woman a black eye as wish her good-morning."

Bess poked a finger at his shoulder. "I didn't pick a fight with anyone, and if I had, it would be my business."

"That's why you're an idiot."

"Hey, Alex, ease off."

"Keep out of this," Alex and Bess snarled in unison.

"I'm not even here," Judd mumbled, scooting down in his seat.

"It so happens I was conducting an interview." Bess folded her arms on the seat so that she wouldn't give in to the nasty urge to twist Alex's ear. "In a public place," she added. "And you had no right to come bursting in and ruining everything before I'd finished."

"If I hadn't come bursting in, babe, you'd have had your nose broken again."

She scowled, wrinkling her undeniably crooked nose. "I can defend my nose, and anything else, just fine."

"Yeah, anyone can see you're a regular amazon. Ow!" He slapped at her hand and swore the air blue when she gave in and twisted his ear. "The minute I get you out of this car, I'm going to—"

"Uh, Alex?"

"I told you to keep out of it."

"I'm out," Judd assured him. "But you might want to take a look at the liquor store coming up at nine o'clock."

Still steaming, Alex did, then let out a heavy sigh. "Perfect. This makes it perfect. Call it in."

Bess watched, wide-eyed, as Judd radioed in an armed robbery in progress, gave their location and requested backup. Before she could shut her gaping mouth, Alex was swinging to the curb.

"You," he said, stabbing a finger in her face. "Stay in the car, or I swear I'll wring your neck."

"I'm not going anywhere," Bess assured him after she managed to swallow the large ball of fear lodged in her throat. But before the words were out, he and Judd were out of the car and drawing their weapons.

He'd already forgotten her, she realized as she stared at his profile. Before he and Judd had crossed the street, he'd put on his cop's mind and his cop's face. She'd seen hundreds of actors try to emulate that particular look. Some came close, she realized, but this was the real thing. It wasn't grim or fierce, but flat, almost blank.

Except for the eyes, she thought with a quick shudder. She'd had only one glimpse of his eyes, but it had been enough.

Life and death had been in them, and a potential for violence she would never have guessed at.

In the darkened car, she gripped her hands together and prayed.

He hadn't forgotten her. It infuriated him that he had to fight to tuck her into some back corner of his mind. There were innocent people in that store. A man and a woman. He could smell the fear while he was still three yards away.

But he broke his concentration long enough to glance back and make certain she was staying put.

He gestured Judd to one side of the door while he took the other. He didn't have time to worry that the rookie might freeze. Right now they were just two cops, and he had to believe Judd would go with him through the door.

The 9 mm felt warm in his hand. He'd already identified the weapons of the two perpetrators. One had a sawed-off shotgun, the other a wicked-looking .45. He could hear the woman crying, pleading not to be hurt. Alex ignored it. They would wait for backup as long as they could.

He shifted just enough to look inside.

Behind the counter, a woman of approximately sixty stood with her hands at her throat, weeping. A man of about the same age was emptying the cash register as fast as his trembling hands allowed. One of the gunmen grabbed a bottle off a shelf. He ripped off the top and guzzled. Swearing at the old man, he smashed the bottle on the counter and jabbed the broken glass toward his face.

Alex had seen the look before, and he knew they wouldn't be content with the money. "We're going in," he whispered to Judd. "You go low, go for the one on the right."

Pale, Judd nodded. "Say when."

"Don't fire your weapon unless you have to." Alex sucked in his breath and went through the door. "Police!" In the back of his mind he heard the sirens from the backup as the first gunman swung the shotgun in his direction. "Drop it!" he ordered, knowing it was useless. The woman was already screaming before the first shots were fired.

The shotgun blew out a bank of fluorescent lights as the force of Alex's bullet sent the man slamming backward. Alex was getting the second man in his sights when a bullet from the .45 slammed into a bottle inches above his head, spraying alcohol and glass. Judd fired, and stopped being a rookie.

Slowly, with the same blank look on his face, Alex came out of his crouch and studied his partner. Judd wasn't pale now. He was green. "You okay?"

"Yeah." After replacing his weapon, Judd rubbed the back of his hand over his mouth. There was a greasy knot in his stomach that was threatening to leap into his throat. "It was my first."

"I know. Go outside."

"I'm okay."

Alex gave him a nudge on the shoulder. His hand remained there a moment, surprisingly gentle. "Go outside anyway. Tell the backup to call an ambulance."

Bess was waiting beside the car when Alex came out some twenty minutes later. He looked the same, she thought. Just the same as he'd looked when he walked in. Then he lifted his head and looked at her, and she saw she was wrong.

His eyes hadn't looked so tired, so terribly tired, twenty minutes before.

"I told you to stay in the car."

"I did."

"Then get back in."

Gently she laid a hand on his arm. "Alexi, you made your point. I'll take a cab. You have things to do."

"I've done them." He skirted the car and yanked open the passenger door. She could almost feel his body vibrating, but when he spoke, his voice was firm, sharp. "Get in the damn car, Bess."

She didn't have the heart to argue, so she crossed over and complied. "What about Judd?"

"He's heading to the cop shop to file the report."

"Oh."

He let the silence hang for three blocks. It hadn't been his first, but he hadn't told Judd that the bright, shaky sickness didn't fade. It only turned inward, becoming anger, disgust, frustration. And you never stopped asking yourself why.

"Aren't you going to ask how it felt? What went through my mind? What happens next?"

"No." She said it quietly. "I don't have to ask when I can see. And it's easy enough to find out what happens next."

It wasn't what he wanted. He didn't want her to be understanding, or quietly agreeable, or to turn those damned sympathetic eyes on him. "Passing up a chance for grist for your mill? McNee, you surprise me. Or can't your TV cop blow away a couple of stoned perps?"

He was trying to hurt her. Well, she understood that,

Bess thought. It often helped to lash out when you were in pain. "I'm not sure I can fit it into any of our scheduled story lines, but who knows?"

His hands clenched on the wheel. "I don't want to see you down there again, understand? If I do, I swear I'll find a way to lock you up for a while."

"Don't threaten me, Detective. You had a rough night, and I'm willing to make allowances, but don't threaten me." Leaning back, she shut her eyes. "In fact, do us both a favor and don't talk to me at all."

He didn't, but when he pulled up at her building, the smoke from his anger was still hanging in the air. Satisfied, she slammed out of the car. She'd taken two steps when he caught up with her.

"Come here," he demanded, and hauled her against him. She tasted it, all the violence and pain and fury of what he'd done that night. What he'd had to do. There was no way for her to comfort. She wouldn't have dared. There was no way for her to protest. She couldn't have tried. Instead, she let the sizzling passion of the kiss sweep over her.

Just as abruptly, he let her go. He'd be trembling in a minute, and he knew it. God, he needed…something from her. Needed, but didn't want.

"Stay off my turf, McNee." He turned on his heel and left her standing on the sidewalk.

Chapter 4

"When it comes to murder," Bess mused, "I like a nice, quick-acting poison. Something exotic, I think."

Lori pursed her lips. "If we're going to do it, I really think he should be shot. Through the heart."

Shifting in her seat at the cluttered table, Bess scooped up a handful of sugared almonds. "Too ordinary. Reed's a sophisticated, sensuous cad. I think he should go out with more than just a bang." She munched and considered. "In fact, we could make it a slow, insidious poison—milk a few weeks of him wasting away."

"Nagging headaches, dizzy spells, loss of appetite," Lori put in.

"And chills. He really should have chills." Bess steepled her hands and imagined. "He gives this big cocktail party, see. You know how he likes to flaunt his power and money in the faces of all the people he's dumped on over the years."

Lori sighed. "That's why I love him."

"And why millions of viewers love to hate him. If we're going to take him out, let's do it big. They're all there at Reed's mansion.... Jade, who's never forgiven him for using her sister for his own evil ends. Elana, who's agonizing over the fact that Reed will use his secret file, distorting the information to discredit Max."

"Mmm..." Getting into the spirit, Lori gestured with her watered-down soft drink. "Brock, who's furious that with one phone call Reed can upset the delicate balance of the Tryson deal and cost Brock a fortune. And Miriam, of course."

"Of course. We haven't seen nearly enough of her lately. Reed's self-destructive ex-wife, who blames him for all her problems."

"Justifiably," Lori pointed out.

"Then there's Vicki, the woman scorned. Jeffrey, the cuckolded husband." She grinned. "And the rest of the usual suspects."

"Okay. What kind of poison?"

"Something rare," Bess mused. "Maybe Oriental. I'll work on it." She scribbled a reminder on a notepad. "So they all have a motive for killing him. Even the housekeeper, because he seduced her naive, innocent daughter, then cast her aside. Sometime during the party, we see a glass of champagne. The room's in shadows. Close-up on a small black vial. A hand pours a few drops into the glass."

"We'll see if it's a man or woman."

"The hand's gloved," Bess decided, then realized how ridiculous it would be to wear gloves at a cocktail party. "Okay, okay, we don't see it at the party. Before. There's this box, see? This ornately carved wooden box."

"And the gloved hand opens it. Candlelight flickers off the glass vial as the hand removes it from the bed of velvet."

"That's the ticket. We'll cut to that kind of thing three or four times during the week of the party. Let the audience know it's bad business for somebody."

"Meanwhile, Reed's playing everyone like puppets. Handing out his personal brand of misery, building the pressure to the boiling point, until it explodes on the night of the party."

"It'll be great," Bess assured her. "Throughout the evening, Reed's enjoying himself stirring up old fires, poking at sores. Miriam has too much to drink and gets sloppy and shrill. This provides the perfect distraction for our killer to doctor Reed's champagne. Because it's slow-acting, the symptoms don't begin to show right away. We have some fatigue, a little dizziness, some minor pain. Maybe a rash."

"I like a good rash," Lori agreed.

"By the time he kicks off, it'll be difficult for the cops to pinpoint the time and place when the poison was administered. We just might have the perfect crime."

"There is no perfect crime."

Both Bess and Lori glanced toward the doorway. Alex stood there, his hands tucked in his pockets. There was a half smile on his face, a result of his enjoyment at listening to them plotting a murder. "Besides, if your TV cop didn't figure it out, your viewers would be pretty disappointed."

"He'll figure it out." Bess reached for another almond as she watched him, her bare feet propped on the chair beside her. Alex discovered that the baggy slacks she wore effectively hid her legs but didn't stop him from thinking about them. "Did somebody call a cop?" she asked Lori.

"Not me." Well aware that three was most definitely a crowd, Lori rose. "Listen, I've got to make a call, and I think I'll run up and peek in on the taping. Nice to see you, Detective."

"Yeah." He shifted so that Lori could get through the door, but he didn't step inside. Instead, he glanced around, annoyed with himself for feeling so awkward. "Some place," he said at length.

Bess's lips curved. The room was hardly bigger than a closet and windowless. The table where she and Lori worked was covered with books, folders and papers, and dominated by a word processor that was still humming. Besides the table, there was one overstuffed chair, a small couch and two televisions.

"We call it home," Bess said, and tilted her head. "So, what brings you down to the dungeons, Alexi?"

The description was fairly apt. They were in the basement of the building that held the studios and production offices for "Secret Sins" and its network. He shrugged off her question with one of his own. "How long are you in for?"

"The duration, I hope." Casually she rubbed the ball of one foot over the instep of the other. "After the last Emmy, they did offer us an upstairs office with a view, but Lori and I are creatures of habit. Besides, who's going to come down here and peek over our shoulders while we write?" She recrossed her ankles. "Are you off-duty?"

"I took a couple hours' personal time."

"Oh." She drew the word out, thinking he looked very appealing when he was embarrassed. "Should I consider this a personal visit?"

"Yeah." He stepped inside, then regretted it. There wasn't enough room to wander around. "Listen, I just wanted to apologize."

It was probably very small of her, Bess thought, but, oh, she was enjoying this. "Generally or specifically?"

"Specifically." He shook his head when she held out the bowl of almonds. "After the robbery attempt, when I took you home. I was out of line."

"Okay." She set the bowl down and smiled at him. "We're dealing with your behavior during the last half hour of the evening."

His brows drew together. "Everything I said before that sticks. You had no business doing what you were doing, where you were doing it."

"Get back to the apology. I like that better."

"I took what I was feeling out on you, and I'm sorry." Figuring the worst was over, he sat on the edge of the table. "You didn't react the way I expected."

"Which was?"

"Scared, outraged, disgusted." He shrugged again. "I don't usually take women to armed robberies."

Now things were getting interesting. "Where *do* you take them?"

His gaze locked on hers. He knew when he was being teased, and he knew when it was good-natured. "To dinner, to the flicks, dancing. To bed."

"Well, armed robbery is probably more exciting. At least than the first three." She rose, placed her hands on his shoulders and kissed him lightly on the mouth. "No hard feelings." When his hands came to her hips and held her in place, she lifted a brow. "Was there something else?"

"I've been thinking about you."

"That could be good."

His lips twitched. "I haven't decided that yet. Maybe we could start with dinner."

"Start what?"

"Working our way to bed. That's where I want you."

"Oh." Her breath came out a little too quickly and not quite steady. It didn't help that his eyes were calm, amused and very confident. How, she wondered, had their positions been so neatly reversed? "That's certainly cutting to the chase."

"You said once that people in our professions observe people. What I've observed about you, McNee, is that you'd probably see through any flowers and moonbeams I might toss at you."

Slowly she ran her tongue over her teeth. "Depends on your pitching arm. The idea isn't without its appeal, Alexi, but I prefer taking certain aspects of my life—sex being one of them—in a cautious, gradual manner."

He grinned at her. "That could be good."

She had to laugh. "Meanwhile—" But he didn't let her scoot back.

"Meanwhile," he echoed, keeping his hands firm. "Have dinner with me. Just dinner."

Hadn't she told herself she wasn't going to get involved again, fall in love again? Oh, well. "I often enjoy just dinner."

"Tomorrow. I'm on tonight."

"Tomorrow's fine."

He nudged her an inch closer. "I'm making you nervous."

"No, you're not." Yes, he was.

"You're wriggling." He grinned again, surprised at how satisfying it was to know he'd unsettled her.

"I've got work, that's all."

"Me too. Why don't I come by about seven-thirty? My brother-in-law's got this place. I think you'll get a kick out of it."

"Lady clothes or real clothes?"

"What are you wearing now?"

She glanced down at her sweater and slacks. "Real ones."

"That'll do." He stood, then tilted her chin with a finger until they were eye-to-eye. "You have the oddest face," he said half to himself. "You should be ugly."

She laughed, unoffended. "I was. I've burned all pictures of me before the age of eighteen." Her dimple winked out as she smiled at him. "I imagine you were always gorgeous."

He winced, though he knew he should be used to having that term applied to him. "My sisters were gorgeous," he told her. "Are. My brother and I are ruggedly attractive."

"Ah, manly men."

"You got it."

"And you grew up surrounded by flocks of adoring females."

"We started with flocks and moved on to hordes."

Her eyes lit with amusement and curiosity. "What was it like to—"

He cut her off the most sensible way. He liked the quick little jolt her body gave before she settled into him. And the way her mouth softened, accepted. No pretenses here, he thought as she gave a quiet sigh and melted into the kiss. It was simple and easy, as basic as breathing.

If his system threatened to overcharge, he knew how to control it. Perhaps he drew the kiss out longer than he'd intended to, deepened it more than he had planned. But he was still in control. Maybe, for just a moment, he imagined what it would be like to lock the door, to sweep all those papers off the table and take her, fast and hot, on top of it.

But he wasn't a maniac. He reminded himself of that, even as his blood began to swim. A slow and gentle touch brought pleasure to both, and let a woman see that she was appreciated for everything she was.

"Dangerous," he murmured in Ukrainian as he slid his mouth from her. "Very dangerous woman."

"What?" She blinked at him with eyes that were arousingly unfocused and heavy. "What does that mean?"

He had to make a conscious effort to keep his hands gentle at her shoulders. "I said I have to go. Keep off the streets, McNee."

She called to him as he reached the doorway. "Detective." Her heart was thumping, her head was reeling, but she really hated not having the last word. For lack of anything better, she dredged up an old line from "Hill Street Blues." "Let's be careful out there."

Alone, she lowered herself into a chair, as carefully as an elderly aunt. Five minutes later, Lori found her in exactly the same spot, still staring into space.

"Uh-oh." One look had Lori dropping down beside her. With a shake of her head, she handed Bess a fresh soft drink. "I knew it. I knew this was going to happen the minute I saw that gorgeous cop at your party."

"It hasn't happened yet." Bess took a long drink. Funny, she hadn't realized how dry her throat had become. "I'm afraid it's going to, but it hasn't happened yet."

"You had that same look on your face when you fell for Charlie. And for Sean. And Miguel. Not to mention—"

"Then don't." Frowning, she focused on Lori. "Miguel? Are you certain? I was sure I had better taste."

"Miguel," Lori said ruthlessly. "Granted, you came to your senses within forty-eight hours, but the day after he took you to the opera you had the same stupid look on your face."

"We saw *Carmen*," Bess pointed out. "I don't think the look had anything to do with him. Besides, I'm not in love with Alexi, I'm just having dinner with him tomorrow."

"That's what you always say. Like with George."

Bess's shoulders straightened. "George was the sweetest man I've ever known. Being engaged to him taught me a lot about understanding and compassion."

"I know. You were understanding enough to be godmother to his firstborn."

"Well, after all, I did introduce him to Nancy."

"And he promptly dumped you and ran off with her."

"He didn't dump me. I wish you wouldn't hold that against him, Lori. Breaking our engagement was a mutual decision."

"And the best thing to happen to you. George was a wimp. A whiny wimp."

Because it was precisely true, Bess sighed. "He just needed a lot of emotional support."

"At least you never slept with him."

"He was saving himself."

They looked at each other and burst out laughing. Once she caught her breath, Bess shook her head. "I should never have told you that. It was indiscreet."

"Observation," Lori announced, and Bess gestured a go-ahead. "The cop isn't going to save himself."

"I know." Bess felt the warning flutter in her stomach. Thoughtfully she drew her finger down through the moisture on the bottle. "I'll cross that bridge when I come to it."

"Bess, you don't cross bridges, you burn them." Lori gave her hand a quick squeeze. "Don't get hurt."

There was a touch of regret in Bess's smile. "Do I ever?"

Alex liked the way she looked. It took a certain panache, he supposed, to be able to wear the jade-toned blouse with bright blue slacks, particularly if you were going to add hot-pink high-tops. But Bess pulled it off. Everything about her was vivid. He supposed that was why he'd gone into her office to apologize and ended up asking her out.

It was probably why he hadn't been able to get her, or the idea of taking her to bed, out of his mind since he'd met her.

For herself, Bess took one look at Zackary Muldoon's bar, Lower the Boom, and knew she had a relaxed, enjoyable evening in store. There was music from the juke box, a babble of voices, a medley of good, rich scents. The tangle of pear-shaped gemstones at her ears swung as she turned to Alex. "This is great. Is the food as good as it smells?"

"Better." He gave a wave in the general direction of the bar as he found them a table.

As usual, the bar was cluttered with people and thick with noise. Since his sister had married Zack, Alex had made a habit of dropping in once a week or so, and he knew most of the regulars by name. He grinned at the waitress who stopped at their table. "Hey, Lola. How's it going?"

"It'll do, cutie." Resting her tray on her hip, Lola gave Bess the once-over. Though less than ten years Alex's senior, Lola had taken a maternal interest in him. It wasn't often Alex brought a date into the bar, and Lola made it her business to check out his current lady. "So, what can I get you?"

"Tequila." Bess dropped her bag in the empty chair beside her with a thunk. "Straight up."

Alex only lifted a brow at Bess's choice. "Give me a beer, Lola. Rachel around?"

"Upstairs. And she better have her feet up." She gave the ceiling a scowl. "She'll probably sneak down here before the night's over. Can't keep her away from the boss."

"What's Rio's special tonight?"

"Paella." Her eyes lit with appreciation. She'd sampled some herself. "He's been driving Nick crazy, making him shell shrimp."

"You game for that?" Alex asked Bess.

"You bet." As Lola wandered off, Bess propped her chin on her hands. "So, who's the boss, who's Rio, and who's Nick?"

"Zack's the boss." He gestured toward the tall, broad-shouldered man working the bar. "Rio's the cook, this Jamaican giant who'll fix you the best meal this side of heaven. Nick's Zack's brother."

Bess nodded. She liked to know the players. "And Rachel's married to Zack." After a long study of the man behind the bar, she smiled. "Impressive. How'd she meet him?"

"She was Nick's PD after I busted him for attempted burglary."

Bess didn't blink or look shocked, she simply leaned a little closer. "What was he stealing?"

Alex was vaguely disappointed that he hadn't gotten a reaction. "Electronics—and doing a poor job of it. He was tangled up with a gang at the time. This was about a year and a half ago." Absently he toyed with the square-cut aquamarine on her finger, watching it catch the light. "Nick had some problems. Actually, he's Zack's stepbrother. Nick was still a kid when Zack went off and joined the navy and his mother died. Anyhow, when Zack came back a few years ago, his father was dying, and the kid was chin-deep in trouble."

"This is great." Bess beamed up at Lola as their drinks were served. "Thanks."

The smile did it. Lola sent Alex a look of approval before she swung by the bar to report to Zack.

"Don't stop now."

Alex lifted his mug of beer. He knew very well that Lola was giving Zack a sotto voce rundown of her impressions and opinions of his choice of companion. "You want to hear the whole thing?"

"Of course I do." Bess sprinkled salt on her wrist, licked it, then tossed back the tequila with all the flair of a Mexican bandit. While she sucked on the lime wedge Lola had brought with the drink, she grinned at Zack. "I like the zing."

"How many times can you do that and live?"

"I haven't tested it that far." The liquor left a nice trail of heat down her throat and into her stomach. "I did ten once, but I was younger then, and stupid. So keep going." She leaned forward again. "Zack came back after sailing the seven seas and found his brother in trouble."

"Well, Nick was tangled up with the Cobras..." Alex began. By the time their paella was served, he was enjoying himself. It always polished a man's ego to have a woman's complete and fascinated attention. "So that's how I ended up on the point of having an Irish-Ukrainian niece or nephew."

"Terrific. You've got a flair for storytelling, Alexi. Must be some Gypsy blood in there."

"Naturally."

She smiled at him. All he needed was a hoop of gold in one ear and a violin, she thought—but she was sure he wouldn't want to hear it. "It doesn't hurt that you have this wisp of an accent that peeks out now and then. Of course, your material's first-rate, too. I'm a sucker for happy endings. I can't have many of them in my field. Once we tie things up, we have to unravel them again, or we lose the audience."

"Why? I thought most people went for the happy ending."

"They do. But in soaps, a character loses the edge if he or she isn't dealing with some crisis or tragedy." She sampled the paella and sighed her satisfaction. "That's why Elana's been married twice, had amnesia, was sexually assaulted, had two miscarriages and a nervous breakdown, went temporarily blind, shot a former lover in self-defense, overcame a gambling addiction, had twins who were kidnapped by a psychotic nurse—and recovered them only after a long, heartrending and perilous search through the South American jungles." She took another glorious bite. "Not necessarily in that order."

Before Alex could ask who Elana was, Lola was setting down fresh drinks. "You watch 'Secret Sins'?" she asked Bess.

"Religiously. You?"

"Well, yeah." She shrugged, knowing there were several patrons in the bar who'd rag her about it. "I got hooked when I was in the hospital having my youngest. He's ten now. That was back when Elana was a first-year resident at Millbrook Memorial and in love with Jack Banner. He was a great character."

"One of the best," Bess agreed. "Brooding and self-destructive."

"I was really sorry when he died in that warehouse fire. I didn't think Elana would ever get over it."

"She's a tough lady," Bess commented.

"Had to be." When someone called her, Lola waved to them to wait. "If it hadn't been for her, Storm would never have gotten himself together and become the man he is today."

"You like Storm?"

"Oh, man, who wouldn't?" With a chuckle, Lola rolled her eyes. "The guy's every woman's fantasy, you know? I'm really pulling for him and Jade. They deserve some happiness, after everything they've been through. Jeez, all right, Harry, I'm on my way. Enjoy your dinner," she said to Bess, and hurried off.

Bess turned to Alex with a smile. "You look confused."

He only shook his head. "You two were talking about those characters as though they were real people."

"But they are," Bess told him, and scooped up some shrimp. "For an hour a day, five days a week. Didn't you ever believe in Batman, or Sam Spade? Scarlett O'Hara, Indiana Jones?"

"It's fiction."

"Good fiction creates its own reality. That's entertainment." Picking up the saltshaker, she grinned. "Come on, Alexi, even a cop needs to fantasize now and then."

He looked at her long enough to make her pulse dance. "I do my share."

Bess swallowed the tequila, but its zing paled beside the one that Alex's quiet statement had streaking through her. "You'll have to tell me about that sometime." She glanced around at the sound of piano music.

Against the far wall was a huge upright. A slimly built, sandy-haired young man was caressing blues out of the keys.

"That's Nick," Alex told her.

"Really?" Bess angled her chair around for a better look. "He's very good."

"Yeah. He talked Zack into putting a piano in the bar about a year ago. Rachel and Muldoon tried to get him to go back to school, get more training, but no dice."

"Some things can't be taught," Bess murmured.

"Looks like. Anyway, he still works in the kitchen with Rio, and comes out and plays when the mood strikes."

"And has every female in the joint mooning over him."

"He's just a kid," Alex said quickly—too quickly.

With her tongue in her cheek, Bess turned back. "Younger men have their own appeal to the experienced woman. In fact, right now Jessica is embroiled in a passionate affair with Tod—who's ten years her junior. The mail is running five to one in favor."

"We were talking about you."

She only smiled. "Were we?"

Zack walked over to slap Alex on the back. "How's the meal?"

"It's terrific." Bess held out a hand. "You're Zack? I'm Bess."

"Nice to see you." Zack kept a hand on Alex's shoulder after giving Bess's a quick squeeze. "You must be the Bess Rachel ran into down at the station."

"I must be. You have a great place here. Now that I've found it, I'll be back."

"That's what we like to hear." His blue eyes sparkled with friendly curiosity. "Alex doesn't bring his ladies around very often. He likes to keep us guessing."

She couldn't help but respond to the humor in Zack's eyes. "Is that so?"

"Ease off, Muldoon," Alex muttered.

"He's still sore at me for stealing his baby sister."

Alex sent him an arched look. "I just figured she had better taste." He lifted his beer. "Speaking of which." He gestured with the mug.

Bess saw Zack's eyes change and, recognizing love, her heart sighed. It didn't surprise her when Rachel came to the table.

"What's this?" Rachel demanded. "A party, and nobody invited me?"

"Sit," Zack and Alex said in unison.

"I'm tired of sitting." Ignoring them both, she turned

to Bess. "Nice to see you again." She took a deep, appreciative sniff. "Rio's paella. Incredible, isn't it?"

"Yes, it is. Alex was just telling me how the two of you met."

"Oh?" Rachel's brow lifted.

"Why don't you join us and give me your side of it?"

Twenty minutes later, Alex was forced to admit that Bess's casual friendliness had gotten Rachel to sit down and relax in a way neither he nor Zack would have been able to with their demanding concern.

For a woman who was so full of energy and verve, she had a knack for putting people at ease, he noted.

A gift for listening to details and asking just the right question. And for entertaining, he mused—effortlessly.

It didn't surprise him that she was able to talk music with Nick when he was called over to join them, or food with Rio when she asked to go back into the kitchen to compliment him on the meal. He wasn't surprised when she and Rachel made a date to meet for lunch the following week.

"I like your family," Bess stated as they settled into a cab.

"You've only met a fraction of it."

"Well, I like the ones I've met. How much more do you have?"

"My parents. Another sister, her husband, their three kids. A brother, his wife, and their kid. What about you?"

"Hmm?"

"Family."

"Oh. I was an only child. Do they all live in New York?"

"All but Natasha." He toyed with the curls at the nape of her neck. "You don't talk about yourself."

"Are you kidding?" She laughed, though she wanted to curl like a cat into the fingers brushing her skin. "I never stop talking."

"You ask questions. You talk about things, other people, your characters. But you don't talk about Bess."

She should have known a cop would notice what most people didn't. "We haven't had that many conversations," she pointed out. When she turned her head, her mouth was close to his. She wanted to kiss him, Bess thought. It wasn't merely to distract him. After all, she had nothing to hide. But she didn't speak, only moved her lips to his.

The fingers at the back of her neck tensed as he changed the angle of the kiss and the mood of it. It was light and friendly only for an instant. Then it darkened, deepened, lengthened. Mixed with the taste, the texture, were hints of what was to come.

There's a storm brewing, Bess thought dizzily. And, oh, she'd never been able to resist a storm.

Her heart was knocking by the time his lips moved to her temple. "You know how to change the subject, McNee."

"What subject?"

His hand slid to her throat, cupped there. He felt the pigeon beat of her rapid pulse. The rhythm of it was as seductive as jungle drums. "You. Now I'm only more curious."

"There's not that much to tell." Uneasy and confused by the sensation, she drew back as the cab pulled to the curb. "Looks like we're here." She slid across the seat while Alex paid the driver. Her knees were a little weak, she realized. Another first. Alexi Stanislaski was going to require some thought. "You don't have to walk me up," she said, surprised that it unnerved her to see the cab pull away and leave the two of them alone on the shadowy sidewalk.

"Which means you're not going to ask me in."

"No." She smiled a little, running her fingers up and down the strap of her bag. But she wanted to. It was amazing to her just how much she wanted to. "I think it would be smarter if I didn't."

He accepted that, because the choice had to be hers. And the prospect of changing her mind along the way was tremendously appealing. "We'll do this again."

"Yes."

He closed a hand over her restless one, brought it to his lips. "Soon."

She felt something, a small, vague ache centered in her heart. Confused by it, she slipped her hand away. "All right. Soon. Good night."

"Hold it." Before she could turn away, he took her face in his hands, held it there for a moment before lowering his mouth to hers.

The pressure was whisper-light, persuasive, invasive. Even as she responded, the kiss had that odd ache spreading. Helpless, she brought her hands to his wrists, clinging to them for balance. Though his mouth remained beautifully gentle, the pulse she felt beneath her fingers raced in time with her own.

Then he let her go, stepped back. His eyes stared into hers. "Good night," he said.

She managed a nod before hurrying inside.

There was something about Bess, Alex thought as he waited patiently for the light in her apartment to come on. Something. He'd just have to find out what it was.

Chapter 5

The last person Bess expected to see when she left her office a few days later was Rosalie. Even in the bustling crowds of midtown, the woman stood out. After a moment of blank surprise, Bess smiled and crossed the sidewalk.

"Hi. Were you waiting for me?"

"Yeah."

"You should have come in." Bess adjusted the weight of her bag and briefcase.

"I figured it would be better for you if I waited out here."

"Don't be silly…" Her words trailed off as she tried to see through and around Rosalie's huge tinted glasses. Those sunburst colors around the left eye weren't all cosmetics. Bess's friendly smile faded. "What happened to you?"

Rosalie shrugged. "Bobby. He was a little ticked off about the other night."

"That's despicable."

"I've had worse."

"Bastard." She said it between her teeth, but overlying her fury was a terrible sense of guilt. "I'm sorry. I'm so sorry. It was my fault."

"Ain't nobody's fault, girlfriend. Just the way things are."

"It's not the way they should be. And if I hadn't..." She let that go, knowing you could only go back and change things in scripts. "Do you want to go to the police? I'll go with you. We could—"

"Hell, no." Rosalie let out what passed for a laugh. "I'd get a lot worse than a sore eye if I tried that. And if you think there's a cop alive who gives a damn about a hooker with a black eye, you *are* as dumb as you look."

Alex would care, Bess thought. She refused to believe otherwise. "We'll do whatever you want."

Rosalie pulled out a cigarette, cocking her hip as she lit it. "Listen, you said you'd pay me to talk. I figure I can use the extra money. And I'm on my own time."

"All right." Ideas were beginning to stir. "How much do you average a night?"

As a matter of course, Rosalie started to inflate it, but found the lie stuck in her throat. "After Bobby takes his cut, about seventy-five. Maybe a hundred. Business isn't as good as it used to be."

"We'll talk." Distracted, Bess searched for a cab. "We'll never get a taxi at this hour," she mumbled. "I live uptown about twenty blocks. Do you mind walking?"

This time Rosalie laughed full and long. "Girl, walking the streets comes natural to me."

Once they reached Bess's apartment, Rosalie tipped down her shaded glasses and whistled. Unable to resist, she walked to one of the wide windows. She could see a swatch of the East River through other buildings. The sound of traffic was so muted, it was almost musical. A far cry from the clatter and roar she lived with every day.

"My, oh, my, you do live high."

"How about dinner?" Automatically Bess stepped out of her shoes. "We'll order in." Red meat, Bess thought. At the moment, she could have eaten it raw. "Sit down, I'll get us some wine."

Wine, Rosalie thought as she stretched out on the plump cushions of the pit. She figured that sounded just dandy. "You pay for all this just writing stuff?"

"Mostly." On impulse, Bess chose one of the best bottles in her wine rack. "You're not a vegetarian, are you?"

Rosalie snorted. "Get real."

"Good. I want a steak." After handing Rosalie a glass, she picked up the phone to order dinner.

"I can't pay for that."

"I'm buying," Bess assured her, and curled up on the couch. "I need a consultant, Rosalie." It was a risk, but so was breathing, she decided. "I'll give you five hundred a week."

Rosalie choked on the wine. "Five hundred, just to tell you about turning tricks?"

"No. I want more. I want why. I want you to tell me about the other women. What draws them in. What you're afraid of, what you're not. When I ask you a question, I'll want an answer." Her voice was brisk now, all business. "I'll know if you lie."

Rosalie's eyes were shrewd and steady. "You need all that for a TV show?"

"You'd be surprised." It had gone well beyond the show. The bruise on Rosalie's face grated on her. She had caused it, Bess reflected. She would find a way to fix it. "I'm buying a lot of your time for five hundred a week, Rosalie. You might want to take a little vacation from Bobby."

"What I do after I talk to you is for me to say."

"Absolutely. But if you decided you wanted to take a break from the streets, and if you needed a place to stay while you did, I could help you."

"Why?"

Bess smiled. "Why not? It wouldn't cost me any more."

Intrigued, Rosalie considered. "I'll think about it."

"Fine. We can get started right away." She rose to gather up pads, pencils, her tape recorder. "Remember, this is daytime TV, and we can only do so much. I'll have to filter down a great deal of what you tell me. Why don't I fill you in on the story line?"

Rosalie merely shrugged. "It's your nickel."

"Yes, it is." She settled down again, and was weaving the complex and overlapping relationships of Mill-brook—to Rosalie's confusion and fascination—when she heard the buzzer for her private elevator. Still talking, she walked over to release the security lock. "So, anyway, the Josie personality is dynamically opposed to Jade. The stronger she gets, the more confused and frightened Jade becomes. She doesn't remember where she's been when Josie comes out. And the lapses are getting longer."

"Sounds like the lady needs a shrink."

"Actually, she'll go to Elana—she's a psychiatrist— but that's down the road a bit. And under hypnosis— Ah, here's the food." At the elevator's ding, Bess opened the door. The smile froze on her face.

"Alexi."

"Don't you bother to ask who it is before you let someone come up?" He shook his head before he caught her chin in his hand and kissed her.

"Yes—that is, not when I'm expecting someone. What are you doing here?"

"Kissing you?" And, at that moment, she wasn't as responsive as he'd come to expect. Then it occurred to him that she'd said she was expecting someone. A man? A date? A lover? His eyes cooled as he stepped back. "I guess I should have called first."

"No. I mean, yes. That is…are you off tonight?"

"I go back on in a couple hours."

"Oh. Well." The buzzer sounded again.

"You could always tell him I'm the plumber."

Baffled, she stepped back inside to release the elevator. "Tell who what?"

"The guy on his way up."

"Why should I tell the delivery boy you're a plumber?"

"Delivery boy?" A sound inside the apartment had him edging closer. He wasn't jealous, damn it, he was just curious. "I guess you've already got company," he began, and pushed the door wider.

"Actually, I do." Giving up, Bess gestured him inside. "We were just about to have some dinner."

He looked over at the couch just as Rosalie stood.

Caught between them, Bess felt herself battered by double waves of hostility.

"What the hell is she doing here?"

"You called the cops," Rosalie said accusingly before Bess could answer. "You called the damn cops."

"No. No, I didn't."

Rosalie was already striding across the room. Bess knew that if the woman made it to the door she would have lost her chance. "Rosalie." She grabbed her arm. "I didn't call him."

"And why the hell *didn't* you?" Alex tossed back.

"Because it's none of your business." Still gripping Rosalie, Bess swirled on him. "This is my home, and she's my guest."

"And you're a bigger idiot than I thought."

Sizing up the situation, Rosalie relaxed fractionally. "You two got a thing?"

"Yes," Alex shot back.

"No," Bess snapped, then sighed. "Something in between the two," she mumbled. She snatched her wallet out of her bag as she heard the elevator ding. "Excuse me. That's dinner."

While she herded the delivery boy inside to set up the meal, Alex and Rosalie stood eyeing each other with mutual dislike and suspicion.

"What's the game, Rosalie?"

"No game." She flashed a smile that was as feral as a shark's. "I'm a paid consultant. Your lady hired me."

"The hell with that." He paused a moment, studying her bruised eye. "Bobby do that?"

Rosalie angled her chin. "I walked into a door."

"Sure you did." He did care. Bess might have been surprised at how much he cared. Rosalie certainly would have been stunned. But he also knew there were things that couldn't be fixed. "You'll want to watch your step."

"I don't make the same mistake twice."

He turned away from her, his hands balled into fists in his pockets. "McNee, I want to talk to you."

"Oh, just shut up." She didn't bother to look up as she counted out bills. "Can't you see I'm trying to figure the tip? There you go."

"Thanks, lady." The delivery boy tucked the bills away. "Enjoy your dinner."

"There's enough for three," Bess stated, turning toward Alex. "But you're not going to stay if you're rude."

"Rude?" The single word bounced off her ceiling. He was beside her in two strides. "You think it's rude for me to ask you if you've lost your mind when I walk in and find you've invited a hooker to dinner?"

Her eyes narrowed. "Out."

"Damn it, Bess…"

"I said out." She gave him a hefty shove toward the door. "We went on one date," she reminded him. "*One.* Maybe I entertained the idea of something more, but that gives you no right to come into my house and tell me what to do and who to talk with."

He grabbed her hand before she could push him again. "One has nothing to do with the other."

"You're right. Absolutely right. What I should have said is that I run my life, Detective." She snatched her hand away so that she could poke a finger at his chest. "Me. Alone. Get the picture?"

"Yeah." He wondered how she'd like a nice clip on that pointy little chin of hers. "I've got a picture for you." He hauled her up and kissed her hard. No gentle touch, no finesse. All steam heat. It lasted only seconds, but he succeeded in shocking her speechless. "Things change, McNee." Dark, furious eyes pinned her to the spot. "Get used to it."

With that, he stormed out, slamming the door behind him.

"Well." Bess took one breath, then another. Her throat felt scalded. "Of all the incredible nerve. Who the hell does he think he is, marching in here that way?" Hands on her hips, she spun to face Rosalie. "Did you see that?"

"Hard to miss it." Grinning, Rosalie snatched a french fry from a plate.

"If he thinks he's getting away with that—that *attitude*—he's very much mistaken."

"Man's nuts about you."

"Excuse me?"

"Girl, that was one lovesick puppy."

Bess snatched up her wine and gulped. "Don't be ridiculous. He was just showing off."

"Uh-huh. If I had me a man who looked at me like that, I'd do one of two things."

"Which are?"

"I'd either sit back and enjoy, or I'd run for my life."

Frowning, Bess sat down and picked up her fork. "I don't like to be pushed."

"Seems to me it depends on who's doing the pushing." She sat, as well, and dug right into her steak. "He sure is one fine-looking man—for a cop."

Bess stabbed at her salad. "I don't want to talk about him."

"You're paying the tab," Rosalie said agreeably.

With a grunt of assent, Bess tried to eat. Damn cop, she thought. He'd ruined her appetite.

* * *

There was something to be said for beating the hell out of inanimate objects. Alex had always found the therapy of a pair of boxing gloves and a punching bag immeasurably rewarding. With those so easily accessible, he could never figure out why so many people felt the need for a psychiatrist's couch.

Until recently.

Twenty minutes of sweating and pounding hadn't relieved his basic frustration. He often used the gym— in the middle of a difficult case, when one went wrong, when a good arrest turned sour in court. The same ingredients had worked equally well for him whenever he'd fought with family, or friends, or had female problems.

Not this time.

Whatever hold Bess McNee had on him, Alex couldn't seem to punch himself out of it.

"So much energy, so early."

The familiar voice had Alex blinking away the sweat that had dripped through his headband into his eyes. His brother Mikhail, and Alex's ten-month-old nephew, Griff, were standing hand in hand, grinning identical grins.

"Got your papa out early, did you, tough guy?" Alex swung Griff up for a smacking kiss.

Griff babbled out happily. The only word Alex could decipher in the odd foreign language of a toddler was *Mama*.

"Sydney's tired," Mikhail explained. "She has some wheeling and dealing keeping her up at night. This one's an early riser." He ruffled his son's hair. "So I thought we'd come down and lift weights. Right?"

Griff grinned and cocked his elbows. "Papa."

"Your muscle's bigger," Alex assured him.

"Hey, it's the Griff-man!" Rocky, the former light-weight who ran the gym, gave a whistle and held out his wiry arms. "Come see me, champ."

With a squeal of pleasure, Griff wiggled out of Alex's arms to toddle off on his almost steady legs. "Better watch out, Rock," Mikhail called out. "He's slippery."

"I can handle him." With the confidence of a four-time grandfather, he hefted Griff. "We got things to do," he told Mikhail. "Why don't you talk to your brother there and find out why this is the third time this week he's come in to pound on my equipment?"

"Nosy," Alex muttered. "He's worse than an old woman."

Mikhail tilted a brow when Alex went back to pounding the bag. "Speaking of women…"

"We weren't."

"Why do men come to such places as this unless it's to talk of women?" The music of the Ukraine flavored Mikhail's voice. Alex wondered if his brother knew how much he sounded like their father.

"To hit things," he retorted. "To talk dirty and to sweat."

"That, too. So, it is a woman, yes?"

"It's always a damn woman," Alex said between grit-ted teeth.

"This one's named Bess."

Alex's punch stopped in midswing. Turning, he used his forearm to swipe his brow. "How do you know about Bess?"

"Rachel tells me." Pleased, Mikhail grinned. "She also tells me that this Bess is not beautiful so much as unique, and that she's smart. This isn't your usual type, Alexi."

"She's nobody's type." Alex turned back to the bag, feinted with his right, then jabbed with his left. "Unique," he said with a snort. "That's her, all right. Her face. It was like God was distracted that day and mixed up the features for five different women. Her eyes are too big, her chin's pointed, her nose is crooked." His gloved fist plowed into the bag. "And she has skin like an angel. I touch it and my mouth waters."

"Mmm… I'll have to get a look at this one."

"I've sworn off," Alex told him between grunts. "I don't need the aggravation. She doesn't have all her circuits working at the same time. Maybe Rachel thinks she's smart because she went to college."

"Radcliffe," Mikhail supplied. "She had lunch with Rachel, and Rachel asked."

"Radcliffe?" Letting out a breath, Alex leaned against the bag. "It figures."

"She also told Rachel that the two of you had a… misunderstanding."

"I understood perfectly. Look, maybe she went to some fancy college, but you couldn't fill up a teaspoon with her common sense. I don't need to get involved with someone that flaky."

Mikhail's bark of laughter echoed through the gym. "This from a man who once dated Miss Lug Wrench."

"It was Miss Carburetor."

"Ah, that's different."

A smile twitched, and Alex punched halfheartedly at the bag. Working up a sweat hadn't relaxed him, but five minutes with Mikhail was doing the job. "Anyway, we're finished before we got started. And both better off."

"Undoubtedly you're right."

"I know I'm right. We'd always be coming at things from different angles. Hers is cross-eyed. She doesn't see anything the way she should."

"A difficult woman."

"Difficult." Alex held out his hands so that Mikhail could unlace his gloves. "That doesn't begin to describe her. She acts so mild and relaxed, you wouldn't think you could rile her with a cattle prod. Then you point out an obvious mistake, for her own good, and she jumps on you with both feet. Kicks you out of the house."

Mikhail tucked his tongue in his cheek. "You're better off without her."

"You're telling me." Alex tossed his gloves aside and flexed his hands. "Who needs unreasonable women?"

"Men."

"Yeah." With a sigh, Alex sent his brother a miserable look. "I want her so much I can't breathe."

"I know the feeling." He punched his brother's sweaty shoulder. "So go get her."

"Go get her," Alex repeated.

"Put her in her place."

A dangerous light, one Mikhail recognized, flickered in Alex's eyes. "Her place. Right."

"Hey!" Mikhail called out when his brother strode off. "The showers are that way."

"I'll catch one at the station. See you later."

"Later," Mikhail agreed. He wandered off to find his son, wondering how soon he would meet this unique, unreasonable woman without common sense.

She sounded perfect for his baby brother.

* * *

Bess was never at her best in the morning, and she suspected anyone who was. Her alarm was buzzing when she heard the pounding on her door. She'd been ignoring the first for nearly ten minutes, but the incessant knocking had her dragging herself out of bed.

Bleary-eyed, pulling a skimpy silk robe over an equally skimpy nightshirt, she stumbled to the door. "What the hell?" she demanded. "Is it a fire or what?"

"Or what," Alex told her when she yanked open the door.

Struggling to focus, she dragged a hand through her hair. The robe drooped off one shoulder. "How'd you get up here?"

"Flashed my badge for the security guard." After closing the door behind him, he looked his fill. There was a great deal to be said for a sleepy woman in rumpled white silk. "Get you up, McNee?"

"What time is it?" She turned away, following the scent from her coffeemaker, which was set to brew at 7:20 each morning. "What day is it?"

"Thursday." He followed her weaving progress through the living area and into a big white-and-navy kitchen. There was a huge arrangement of fresh orchids on the center island. Orchids in the kitchen, he thought. Only Bess. "About 7:30."

"In the morning?" Blindly she groped for a mug. "What are you doing here at 7:30 on a Thursday morning?"

"This." He spun her around. The taste of her mouth, warm and soft from sleep, had him groaning. Before she could think—he didn't want either of them to think— he slipped his tongue between her lips to seduce hers.

Her body went stiff, then melted, softening against his like candle wax touched by a flame.

Through the roaring of his blood, he heard the crash as the china mug she'd held slipped from her fingers and smashed on the tiles.

Was she still dreaming? Bess wondered. Her dreams had always been very vivid, but this… It wouldn't be possible to feel so much, need so desperately, in a dream.

And she could taste him. Really taste him. A mingling of man and desire and salty sweat. Delicious. His mouth was so hot, so unyielding, just as his hands were through the thin silk she wore.

She could feel the cool tiles beneath her feet, a shivery contrast to the heat roaring around her. Under her palms, his cheeks were rough, arousingly rough. And she heard her own voice, a muffled, confused sound, as she tried to say his name.

"I have to wake up," she managed when his mouth left hers to cruise over her throat. "I really have to."

"You are awake." He had to touch her—just once. However unfair his advantage, he had to. So he cupped her breasts in his hands, molding their firmness through the silk, brushing his thumbs, feather-light, over straining nipples. "See?"

She'd never been the swooning type, but she was afraid this would be a first. "I have to—" She gasped, for as she'd started to step back, he'd swept her up into his arms. A skitter of panic, completely unfamiliar, raced down her spine. "Alexi, don't."

He covered her mouth again, felt her trembling surrender. And knew he could. And could not. "Your feet are bare," he said, and set her on the counter. "I made you drop your cup."

Shaken, she stared down at the shards of broken crockery. "Oh."

"You have a broom?"

"A broom." She was awake now, wide-awake. But her mind was still mush. "Somewhere. Why?"

He was making her stupid, he realized, and grinned. "So I can clean it up before you cut yourself. Stay there." He walked to a likely-looking closet and located a dustpan and broom. Because he was a man whose mother had trained him well in such matters, he went about the sweeping job quickly and competently. "So, have you missed me?"

"I haven't given you a thought." She blew the hair out of her eyes. "Hardly."

"Me either." He dumped the shards into the trash, replaced the broom and dustpan. "How about some coffee?"

"Sure." Maybe that would help her regain her normal composure. As he poured, she caught a whiff of him over the homey morning aroma. "You smell like a locker room."

"Sorry. I was at the gym." When he handed her the coffee, she sat where she was and sipped. Half a cup later, she was able to take her first clear-eyed look at him.

He looked fabulous. Rough and sweaty and ready for action. The thick tangle of hair was falling over a faded gray sweatband. His face was unshaven, his NYPD T-shirt was ripped and darkened in a vee down the chest, his sweatpants were loose and frayed at the cuffs. When she lifted her gaze back to his, he smiled.

"Good morning, McNee."

"Good morning."

He skimmed a finger over her thigh. She was sensitive there, he noted. He could tell by the way her eyes darkened and the pulse in her throat picked up the beat. "I'm not apologizing this time."

"You should be."

"No. I'm right about this." He put a finger over her lips before she could speak. "Trust me. I'm a cop."

He could have all but seduced her in her own kitchen before her eyes were even open, but she had a point to make. Closing a hand over his wrist, she drew his hand away. "My personal decisions, whether they have to do with my professional or my private life, are just that. Personal. I've been making those decisions, right or wrong, for a long time. I don't intend to stop now."

"I'm not going to see you hurt."

"That's very sweet, Alexi." Softening a bit, she brushed a hand through his hair. "I don't intend to be hurt."

"You don't know what you're dealing with. Oh, you think you do," he continued, recognizing the look in her eyes. "But all you know is the surface. There are things that go on in the streets, every day, every night, that you have no conception of. You never will."

She couldn't argue, not with what she saw in his face. "Maybe not. I don't see what you see, or know what you know. Maybe I don't want to. My friendship with Rosalie—"

"Friendship?"

"Yes." The expression on her face dared him to contradict her. "I feel something for her—about her." With a helpless gesture, Bess set her cup aside. "I can't possibly explain it to you, Alexi. You're not a woman. I can help her. Don't tell me it's a fairy tale to believe I can save her from the streets and what she's chosen to be. I've gotten that advice already."

"From someone with at least half a brain," he surmised. "I had no idea this had gotten so out of hand. You said you wanted to talk to her for background stuff for your story."

"That's true enough." But Bess remembered the bruise on Rosalie's face too well. "Is it so impossible that I might be able to make a difference in her life? Has being a cop made you so hard you aren't willing to give someone a chance to change?"

He gripped her hands, hard. "This isn't about me."

"No," she said, and smiled. "It's not."

He swore and let go of her to pace to the coffee maker. "Okay, point taken. It's none of my business. But I'm going to ask for a promise."

"You can ask."

"Don't go out on the streets with her. Don't go anywhere near Bobby's territory."

She thought of the man with the silver hair and the vicious eyes. "That I can promise. Feel better?"

"I'm not through. Don't let her up here unless you're sure she's alone. Meet her down at your office, or in some public place."

"Really, Alexi…"

"Please."

She said nothing for a moment, and then, because she could see how much it had cost him to use that word, she relented. "All right." Bess scooted away from the counter, then opened the bread drawer. "Want a bagel?"

"Sure."

She popped two into the toaster oven before going to

the refrigerator for cream cheese. "There's something I should tell you."

"I'm hoping there's a lot of things."

With a puzzled smile, she turned back. "I'm sorry?"

"I want to know about this personal life of yours, McNee. I want to know all about you, then I want to take you to bed and make love with you until we both forget our own names."

"Ah…" It didn't seem to take more than one of those long, level looks of his to make her forget a great deal more than her name. "Anyway…"

"Anyway?" he repeated helpfully as the toaster oven dinged.

"I was going to tell you about Angie Horowitz."

The lazy smile vanished. His eyes went cool and flat. "What do you know about her?"

"Boy, it really does click off," Bess murmured. "I feel like I just stepped into one of those rooms with the two-way mirror and the rubber hoses."

"Angie Horowitz," he repeated. "What do you know about her?"

"I don't know much of anything, but I thought I should tell you what Rosalie told me." She got out plates, then began to spread the bagels generously. "She said that Angie was really happy to have hooked up with this one guy. He'd hired her a couple of times and slipped her some extra money. Treated her well, promised her some presents. In fact, he gave her this little pendant. A gold heart with a crack down the center."

Alex's face remained impassive. There had been a broken neck chain wrapped in Angie's hand when they found her, just as there had been with the first victim. That little detail had been kept out of the press. There hadn't been a heart, he thought now. But someone had broken the chain for a reason.

"She wore it all the time—according to Rosalie," Bess went on. "Rosalie also told me Mary Rodell had one just like it. She was the other victim, wasn't she?" she asked Alex. "She had it on the last time Rosalie saw her alive."

"Is that it?"

Bess was disappointed that he wasn't more pleased with the information. "There's a little more." Sulking a bit, she bit into her bagel. "Angie called the guy Jack, and she bragged to Rosalie that he was a real gentleman, and was built like…" She trailed off, cleared her throat, but her eyes were bright with humor, rather than embarrassment. "Women have colorful terms for certain things, just like men."

"I get the picture."

"He had a scar."

"What kind?"

"I don't know. A scar, on his hip. Angie told Rosalie he got upset when she asked him about it. That's all she told me, Alexi, but I figured the coincidence of the pendants, you might want to know about this guy."

"It never hurts." He gave her an easy smile, though his instincts were humming. "Probably nothing, but I'll look into it." He tugged on her hair. "Do yourself a favor, and don't tell Rosalie you passed this along to me."

"I'm softhearted, Detective. Not softheaded. She thinks you have a really nice butt—but you're still a cop."

He grimaced. "I don't think I like you discussing my anatomy with a—"

"Friend," she supplied, with a warning lift of her

brow. "I also had lunch with your sister. We discussed your nasty temperament."

"I heard." He stole her bagel. "Radcliffe, huh?"

"So?"

"So nothing. Want to go dancing with me?"

She debated with herself for almost a full second. "Okay. Tonight?"

"Can't. Tomorrow?"

It meant canceling dinner at Le Cirque with L.D. Strater. That debate took nearly half a second. "That's fine. Sexy or sedate?"

"Sexy. Definitely."

"Good. Why don't you come by around—" She glanced at the clock, stared, then yelped. "Damn it! Now I'm going to be late. I'll owe Lori twenty dollars if I'm late one more time this month." She began pushing Alex out of the kitchen. "It's all your fault. Now beat it, so I can throw on some clothes and get out of here."

"Since you're already late..." He had some very good moves. Even as she shoved him toward the door, he was turning to catch her close. "I can arrange it so you're a lot later."

"Smooth talker," she said with a laugh. "Take a hike."

"You've already lost twenty. I'm just offering to make it worth your while."

"I don't know how I can resist that incredibly romantic gesture, but somehow I find I have the strength."

"You want romance?" There was a gleam in his eyes as he headed for the door. "Tomorrow night. We'll just see how strong you are."

Chapter 6

After spending most of the morning kicking his heels in court, waiting to testify in an assault case, Alex returned to the station to find his partner hip-deep in paperwork. "The boss wants to see you," Judd said through a mouthful of chocolate bar.

"Right." Alex shrugged out of his jacket and dragged off his court-appearance tie. With his free hand, he picked up his pile of messages.

"I think he meant now," Judd said helpfully.

"I got it." As he passed Judd's desk, Alex peeked over his shoulder at the report in the typewriter. "Two *p's* in apprehend, Einstein."

Judd backspaced and scowled. "You sure?"

"Trust me." He swung through the squad room and knocked on Captain Trilwalter's glass door.

"Come."

Trilwalter glanced up. If Alex often thought he was swamped in paperwork, it was nothing compared to what surrounded his captain. Trilwalter's desk was heaped with it. The overflowing files, stacks of reports and correspondence gave Trilwalter a bookish, accountantlike look. This was enhanced by the half glasses perched on his long, narrow nose, the slightly balding head and the ruthlessly knotted knit tie.

But Alex knew better. Trilwalter was a cop down to the bone, and he might still be on the street but for the bullet that had damaged his left lung.

"You wanted to see me, Captain?"

"Stanislaski." Trilwalter crooked his finger, then pointed it, gesturing to Alex to come in and shut the door. He leaned back in his chair, folded his hands over his flat belly and scowled.

"What the hell is all this about soap operas?"

"Sir?"

"Soap operas," Trilwalter repeated. "I just had a call from the mayor."

Testing his ground, Alex nodded slowly. "The mayor called you about soap operas?"

"You look confused, Detective." A rare, and not entirely humor-filled, smile curved Trilwalter's mouth. "That makes two of us. The name McNee mean anything to you? Bess McNee?"

Alex closed his eyes a moment. "Oh, boy."

"Rings a bell, does it?"

"Yes, sir." Alex gave himself a brief moment to contemplate murder. "Miss McNee and I have a personal relationship. Sort of."

"I'm not interested in your personal relationship, sort of or otherwise. Unless they come across my desk."

"When I arrested her—"

"Arrested her?" Trilwalter held up one hand while he took off his glasses. Slowly, methodically, he massaged the bridge of his nose. "I don't think I have to know about that. No, I'm sure I don't."

Despite himself, Alex began to see the humor in it. "If I could say so, Captain, Bess tends to bring that kind of reaction out in a man."

"She's a writer?"

"Yes, sir. For 'Secret Sins.'"

Trilwalter lifted tired eyes. "'Secret Sins.' Apparently the mayor is quite a fan. Not only a fan, Detective, but an old chum of your Bess McNee's. *Old chum* was just how he put it."

Finding discretion in silence, Alex said nothing as Trilwalter rose. The captain walked to the watercooler wedged between two file cabinets in the corner of his office. He poured out a paper cupful and drank it down.

"His honor, the mayor, requests that Miss McNee be permitted to observe a day in your life, Detective."

Alex made a comment normally reserved for locker rooms and pool halls. Trilwalter nodded sagely.

"My sentiments exactly. However, one of the less appealing aspects of working this particular desk is playing politics. You lose, Detective."

"Captain, we're closing in on that robbery on Lexington. I've got a new lead on the hooker murders and a message on my desk from a snitch who could know something about that stiff we found down on East Twenty-third. How am I supposed to work with some ditzy woman hanging over my shoulder?"

"This is the ditzy woman you have a personal relationship with?"

Alex opened his mouth, then closed it again. How to explain Bess? "Sort of," he said at length. "Look, Captain, I already agreed to talk to McNee about police work, in general, now and again. I never agreed to specifics. I sure as hell don't want her riding shotgun while I work."

"A day in your life, Stanislaski." With that same grim smile, Trilwalter crushed his cup and tossed it. "Monday next, to be exact."

"Captain—"

"Deal with it," Trilwalter said. "And see that she stays out of trouble."

Dismissed, Alex stalked back to his desk. He was still muttering to himself when Judd wandered over with two cups of coffee.

"Problem?"

"Women," Alex said.

"Tell me about it." Because he'd been waiting all morning for the chance, Judd sat on the edge of Alex's desk. "Speaking of women, did you know that Bess was engaged to L.D. Strater?"

Alex's head snapped up. "What?"

"Used to be," Judd explained. "One of the teachers at Holly's school's a real gossip-gatherer. Reads all the tabloids and stuff. She was telling Holly how Strater and Bess were a thing a few months ago."

"Is that so?" Alex remembered how they'd danced together at her party. Kissed. His mouth flattened into a grim line as he lifted the cup.

"A real whirlwind sort of thing—according to my sources. Before that, she was engaged to Charles Stutman."

"Who the hell is that?"

"You know, the writer. He's got that hot play on Broadway now. *Dust to Dust.* Holly really wants to see it. I thought maybe Bess could wangle some tickets."

The sound Alex made was neither agreement nor denial. It was more of a growl.

"Then there was George Collaway—you know, the son of that big publisher? That was about three years ago, but he married someone else."

"The lady gets around," Alex said softly.

"Yeah, and in top circles. And, hey, Holly was really blown away when she found out that Bess was Roger K. McNee's daughter. You know, the camera guy."

"Camera guy?" Alex repeated, feeling a hole spreading in the pit of his stomach. "As in McNee-Holden?"

"Yeah. First camera I ever bought was a Holden 500. Use their film all the time, too. Hell, so does the department. Well." He straightened. "If you get a chance, maybe you could ask Bess about those tickets. It sure would mean a lot to Holly."

McNee-Holden. Alex ran the names over in his head while the noise of the squad room buzzed around him. For God's sake, he had one of their cameras himself. He'd bought their little red packs of film hundreds of times over the years. The department used their developing paper. He was pretty sure NASA did too.

Wasn't Bess just full of secrets!

So she was rich. Filthy rich. He picked up his messages again, telling himself it wasn't such a big deal. Wouldn't have been, he corrected silently, if she'd told him about it herself.

Engaged, he thought with a frown. Three times engaged. Shrugging, he picked up the phone. None of his business, he reminded himself as he punched in numbers. If she'd been married three times, it would be none of his business. He was taking her dancing, not on a honeymoon.

But it was a long time before he was able to shuffle her into a back corner of his mind and get on with his job.

Sexy, the man had said, Bess remembered, turning in front of her cheval glass. It looked as though she were going to oblige him.

Snug teal silk hugged every curve and ended abruptly at midthigh. Over the strapless, unadorned bodice, she wore a short, body jacket of fuchsia. Long, wand-shaped crystals dangled at her ears. After stepping into her heels, she gave her hair a last fluff.

She felt like dancing.

When her buzzer sounded, she grinned at her reflection. Leave it to a cop to be right on time. Grabbing her purse—a small one that bulged with what she considered the essentials—she hurried to the intercom.

"I'll come down. Hold on."

She found him on the sidewalk, looking perfect in gray slacks and a navy shirt. His hands were tucked in the pockets of his bomber jacket.

"Hi." She kissed him lightly, then tucked an arm through his. "Where are we going?"

It gave him a jolt, the way their eyes and mouths lined up. As they would if they were in bed. "Downtown," he said shortly, and steered her left toward the corner to catch a cab.

He couldn't have pleased her more with his choice of the noisy, crowded club. The moment she stepped inside, Bess's blood started to hum. The music was loud, the dancing in full swing. They squeezed up to the bar to wait for a table.

"Vodka, rocks," Alex ordered, raising his voice over the din.

"Two," Bess decided, and smiled at him. "I think I was here before, a few months ago."

"I wouldn't be surprised." Not his business, Alex reminded himself. Her background, the men in her life. None of it.

The hell it wasn't.

"It doesn't look like the kind of place Strater would bring you."

"L.D.?" Her eyes laughed. "No, not his style." She angled herself around. "I love to watch people dance, don't you? It's one of the few legal forms of exhibitionism in this country." When he handed her her drink, she murmured a thank-you. "Take that guy there." She gestured with the glass at a man who was strutting on the floor, thumbs in his belt loops, hips wiggling. "That's definitely one of the standard urban white male mating dances."

"Did you do a lot of dancing with Stutman?" Alex heard himself ask.

"Charlie?" She sampled the vodka, pursed her lips. "Not really. He was more into sitting in some smoky club listening to esoteric music that he could obsess to." Still scanning the crowd, she caught the eye of a man in black leather. He cocked a brow and started toward her. One hard look from Alex, and he veered away.

Bess chuckled into her glass. "That put him in his place." Rattling her ice, she grinned up at him. "Were you born with that talent, or did you have to develop it?"

Alex plucked the glass out of her hand and set it aside. "Let's dance."

Always willing to dance, Bess let him pull her onto the floor. But instead of bopping to the beat, he wrapped his arms around her. While legs flashed and arms waved around them, and the music rocked, they glided.

"Nice." Smiling into his eyes, she linked her arms around his neck. "I see why you like to make your own moves, Detective."

"I believe I promised you romance." He skimmed his lips over her jaw to her ear.

"Yes." Her breath came out slow and warm as she closed her eyes. "You did."

"I'm not sure what a woman like you considers romantic."

Her skin shivered under his lips. "This is a good start."

"It's tough." He drew away so that their lips were an inch apart. "It's tough for a cop to compete with tycoons and playwrights."

Her eyes were half-closed and dreamy through her lashes. "What are you talking about?"

"A couple of your former fiancés."

The lashes lifted fractionally. "What about them?"

"I wondered when you were going to mention them. Or the fact that your father runs one of the biggest conglomerates known to man. Or the little detail about your chum the mayor calling my captain."

They continued to dance as he spoke, but Bess could see the anger building in his eyes. "Do you want to take them as separate issues, or all in one piece?"

She was a cool one, he thought. He was feeling anything but cool. "Why don't we start with the mayor? You had no right."

"I didn't ask him to call, Alexi." She spoke carefully,

feeling the taut strength of his fingers at her waist. "We were having dinner, and—"

"You often have dinner with the mayor?"

"He's an old family friend," she said patiently. "I was telling him how helpful you'd been, and one thing led to another. I didn't know he'd called your captain until after it was done. I admit I liked the idea, and if it's caused you any trouble, I'm sorry."

"Great."

"My work's as important to me as yours is to you," she shot back, struggling with her own temper. "If you'd prefer, I can arrange to spend Monday observing another cop."

"You'll spend Monday where I can keep my eye on you."

"Fine. Excuse me." She broke away and worked her way through the crowd to the rest room. The music pulsed against the walls as she paced the small room, ignoring the chatter from the two women freshening their lipstick at the mirror. Losing her temper would be unproductive, she reminded herself. Better, much better, to handle this situation calmly, coolly.

When she was almost sure she could, she walked back out.

He was waiting for her. Taking her arm, he led her to a table in the rear, where they could talk without shouting.

"I think we should go. There's no use staying when you're so angry with me," she began, but he merely scraped back her chair.

"Sit."

She sat.

"When were you going to tell me about your family?"

"I don't see it as an issue." And that was true enough.

"Why should it be? This is only the second time we've gone out."

The look he sent her had her jiggling a foot under the table. "You know damn well there's more going on between us than a couple of dates."

"All right, yes, I do." She picked up her drink, then set it down again, untouched. "But that's not the point. You're acting as though I deliberately hid something from you, or lied. That's just not true."

He picked up the fresh drink he'd ordered. "So tell me now."

"What? Didn't you run a make on me?" His narrowed eyes gave her some small sense of satisfaction. "Okay, Detective, I'll fill you in since you're so interested. My family owns McNee-Holden, which, since its inception in 1873, has expanded from still cameras and film to movies, television, satellites, and all manner of things. Shall I have them send you a prospectus?"

"Don't get smart."

"I'm just warming up." She hooked an arm over the back of her chair. "My father heads the company, and my mother entertains and does good works. I'm an only child, who was born rather late in life to them. My father's name is Roger, and he enjoys a racketing good game of polo. My mother's name is Susan—never Sue or Susie—and she prefers a challenging rubber of bridge. What else would you like to know?"

Despite his temper, he wanted to take her hand and soothe her. "Damn it, Bess, it isn't an interrogation."

"Isn't it? Let me make it easy for you, Alexi. I was born in New York, spent the early part of my childhood on our estate on Long Island, in the care of a very British nanny I was extremely fond of, before going off to boarding school. Which I detested. This, however, left my mother free to pursue her many charitable causes, and my father free to pursue his business. We are not close. From time to time we did travel together, but I was not a pretty child, nor a tractable one, and my parents usually left my care up to the servants."

"Bess—"

"I'm not finished." Her eyes were hard and bright. "This isn't a poor-little-rich-girl story, Alexi. I wasn't neglected or unhappy. Since I had no more in common with my parents than they had with me, I was content to go my own way. They don't interfere, and we get along very well. Because I prefer making my own way, I don't trumpet the fact that I'm Roger K. McNee's little girl. I don't hide it, either—otherwise, I would have changed my name. It's simply a fact. Satisfied?"

He took her hand before she could rise. His voice was calm again, and too gentle to resist. "I wanted to know who you are. I have feelings for you, so it matters."

Slowly her hand relaxed under his. The hard gleam faded from her eyes. "I understand that someone with your background would feel that their family, who and what they came from, are part of what they are. I don't feel that way about myself."

"Where you come from means something, Bess."

"Where you are means more. What does your father do?"

"He's a carpenter."

"Why aren't you a carpenter?"

"Because it wasn't what I wanted." He drummed his fingers on the table as he studied her. "Your point," he acknowledged. "Look, I'm sorry I pushed. It was just weird hearing all this from Judd."

"From Judd?"

"He got it from Holly, who got it from some other teacher who reads the tabloids." Even as he said it, it struck him as ridiculous. He grinned.

"See?" Relaxed again, she leaned forward. "Life really is a soap opera."

"Yours is. *Three* ex-fiancés?"

"That depends on how you count." She took Alex's hand, because she liked the feel of it in hers. "I wasn't engaged to L.D. He did give me a ring, and I didn't have the heart to tell him it was ostentatious. But marriage wasn't discussed."

"One of the ten richest men in the country gave you an ostentatious ring, but marriage wasn't discussed?"

"That's right. He's a very nice man—a little pompous, sometimes, but who wouldn't be, with so many people ready to grovel? Can we get some chips or something?"

"Sure." He signaled to a waitress. "So you didn't want to marry him."

"I never thought about it." Since he asked, she did so now. "No, I don't think I would have liked it very much. He wouldn't have either. L.D. finds me amusing and a little unconventional. Being a tycoon isn't all fun and games, you know."

"If you say so."

She chuckled. "But he'd prefer a different type for his next wife." She dived in immediately when the waitress set baskets of chips and pretzels on the table. "I enjoyed being in love with him for a few weeks, but it wasn't the romance of the century."

"What about the other one, the writer?"

"Charlie." There was a trace of wistfulness now. "I

was really stuck on Charlie. He has this kind of glow about him. He's so interested in people, in emotions, in motivations." She gestured with half a pretzel. "The thing about Charlie is, he's good. Deep-down good. Entirely too good for me." She finished off the pretzel. "See, I do things like join Greenpeace. Charlie flies to Alaska to help clean up oil spills. He's committed. That's why Gabrielle is perfect for him."

"Gabrielle?"

"His wife. They met at a whale rally. They've been married almost two years now."

Alex was determined to get it right. "You were engaged to a married man?"

"No." Insulted, she poked out her lip. "Of course not. He got married after we were engaged—that is, after we weren't engaged anymore. Charlie would never cheat on Gabrielle. He's too decent."

"Sorry. My mistake." He considered changing the subject, but this one was just too fascinating. "How about George? Was he between Charlie and Strater?"

"No, George was before Charlie and after Troy. Practically in another life."

"Troy? There was another one?"

"Oh, you didn't know about him." She propped her chin on her hand. "I guess your source didn't dig back far enough. Troy was while I was in college, and we weren't engaged for very long. Only a couple of weeks. Hardly counts."

Alex picked up his drink again. "Hardly."

"Anyway, George was a mistake—though I'd never admit it to Lori. She gloats."

"George was a mistake? The others weren't?"

She shook her head. "Learning experiences. But

George, well… I was a little rash with him. I felt sorry for him, because he was always sure he was coming down with some terminal illness, and he'd been in therapy since kindergarten. We should never have gotten involved romantically. I was really relieved when he decided to marry Nancy instead."

"Is this like a hobby?" Alex asked after a moment.

"No, people plan hobbies. I never plan to fall in love. It just happens." Her smile was amused and tolerant. "It feels good, and when it's over, no one's hurt. It isn't a sexual thing, like with Vicki. She goes from man to man because of the sense of sexual power it gives her. I know most people think if you have a relationship with a man—particularly if you're engaged to him—you must be sleeping with him. But it's not always true."

"And if you're not engaged to him?"

Because the question demanded it, she met his eyes levelly. "Every situation has its own rules. I don't know what they are for this one yet."

"Things may get serious."

There was a slight pressure around her heart. "That's always a possibility."

"They're serious enough right now for me to ask if you're seeing anyone else."

She knew it was happening. Bess had never been able to prevent that slow, painless slide into love. "Are you asking me if I am, or are you asking me not to?"

It wasn't painless for him. It was terrifying. With what strength of will he had left, Alex held himself on that thin, shaky edge. "I'm asking you not to. And I'm telling you that I don't want anyone else. I can't even think of anyone else."

Her eyes were warm as she leaned over to touch her lips to his. "There is no one else."

He laid a hand on her cheek to keep her mouth on his for another moment. Even as he kissed her, he wondered how many other men had heard her say those same words.

He told himself he was a jealous idiot. With an effort, he managed to smother the feeling. Rising, he took her hands and pulled her to her feet.

"We're supposed to be dancing."

"So I was told. Alexi." Snuggling into love as she would have into a cozy robe, she cupped his face in her hands.

"What?"

"I'm just looking. I want to make sure you're not mad at me anymore."

"I'm not mad at you." To prove it, he kissed the tip of her crooked nose.

No, not angry, she thought, searching his eyes. But there was something else shadowed there. She couldn't quite identify it. "My middle name's Louisa."

With a half smile on his lips, he tilted his head. "Okay."

"I'm trying to think if there's something else you might want to know that I haven't told you." Needing to be close, she rested her cheek against his. "I really don't have any secrets."

He turned his face into her hair. God, what was she doing to him to tie him up in knots like this? He pulled her against him, wrapping his arms tight around her. "I know all I need to know," he said quietly. "We're going to have to figure out those rules, Bess. We're going to have to figure them out fast."

"Okay." She wasn't sure what was holding her back.

It would have been so easy to hurry out of the club with him, to go home and be with him. Her body was straining for him. And yet...

The first tremor of panic shocked her enough to have her pull back and smile, too brightly. She wasn't afraid, she assured herself. And she didn't need to overanalyze. When the time was right to move forward, she'd know it. That was all.

"Come on, Detective." Still smiling, she pulled him away from the table. "Let's see if you can keep up with me on the dance floor."

Chapter 7

Alex read over a particularly grisly autopsy report on half of a suspected murder-suicide, and tried to ignore the fact that Bess was sitting in a chair to his right, scribbling in her notebook. She was as good as her word, he was forced to admit. Though she did tend to mumble to herself now and again, she was quiet, unobtrusive, and once she'd realized he wouldn't answer her questions—much less acknowledge her presence—she'd directed them to Judd.

He couldn't say she was a problem. But, of course, she *was* a problem. She was there. And because she was there, he thought about her.

She'd even dressed quietly, in bone-colored slacks and a navy blazer. As if, he thought, the conservative clothes would help her fade into the background and make him forget she was bothering him. Fat chance, when he was aware of her in every cell.

"Here you go." Bess gave him a cup of coffee and a friendly smile. "You look like you could use it."

"Thanks." Cream, no sugar, he noted as he sipped. She'd remembered. Was that part of her appeal? he wondered. The fact that she absorbed those little details about people? "You must be getting bored."

Taking a chance, she sat on the edge of his desk. "Why?"

"Nothing much going on." He gestured to indicate the pile of paperwork. Maybe, just maybe, he could convince her she was wasting her time. "If you have your TV cop doing this, it isn't going to up your ratings."

"We'll want to show different aspects of his work." She broke a candy bar in half and offered Alex a share. "Like the fact that he'd have to concentrate and handle this sort of paperwork and detail in the middle of all this chaos."

He took a bite. "What chaos?"

She smiled again, jotting down notes. He didn't even see it any longer, she realized. Or hear it. All the noise, the movement, the rush. Dozens of little dramas had taken place that morning, fascinating her, unnoted by him.

"They brought a drug dealer in over there." She gestured with a nod as she continued to write. "Skinny guy in a white fedora and striped jacket, wearing a heavy dose of designer cologne."

"Pasquale," Alex said, noting the description. "So?"

"You saw him?"

"I smelled him." He shrugged. "Wasn't my collar."

Chuckling to herself, Bess crossed her legs and got comfortable. "A Korean shopkeeper came rushing in shouting about vandalism at his store. He was so excited he lost most of his English. They sent out for an interpreter."

"Yeah, it happens." What was her point? he wondered.

She only smiled and finished her chocolate. "Right after that, they brought in a woman who'd been knocked around by her boyfriend. She was sitting over there— defending him, even while her face was swelling. The detective at the far end had a fight with his wife over the phone. He forgot their anniversary."

"Must have been Rogers. He's always fighting with his wife." Impatience rippled back. "What's that got to do with anything?"

"Atmosphere," she told him. "You've stopped noticing it and become a part of it. It's interesting to see. And you're very organized," she added, licking chocolate from her thumb. "Not like Judd over there, with all his neat little piles, but in the way you spread things out and know just where to find the right piece of paper at the right time."

"I hate having you stare at me when I work." He slapped her hand away from the autopsy report.

"I know." Unoffended, she grinned. She leaned a little closer. There was something in her eyes besides humor, he noted. He wasn't sure if he'd ever seen desire and amusement merged in the same expression before. And he certainly hadn't realized how the combination could make a man's blood hum. "You look very sexy plowing your way through all this, gun strapped to your side, your hair all messed up from raking your fingers through it. That keen, dangerous look in your eyes."

Mortified, he shifted in his chair. "Cut it out, McNee."

"I like the way your eyes get all dark and intense

when you're taking down some important tidbit of information over the phone."

"For all you know, that was my dry cleaner."

"Uh-uh." She took his coffee to wash down the last bite of candy bar. "Tell me something, Alexi. Are you annoyed that I'm here, or are you nervous that I'm here?"

"Both." He rose. There must be something he had to do someplace else.

"That's what I thought." She hooked a finger around the strap of his holster. She wasn't afraid of the gun he wore. In fact, she was counting on talking him into letting her hold it one day. So that she could see how it felt. How he felt when he was forced to draw it. "You know, you haven't even kissed me."

"I'm not going to kiss you. Here."

She lifted her eyes, slowly. There was a definite dare in them. "Why not?"

"Because the next time I kiss you—" watching her, he slid a hand around her throat, his thumb caressing her collarbone, until her cocky smile faded away "—really kiss you, it's just going to be you and me. Alone. And I'm going to keep right on kissing you, and all sorts of other things, until there aren't any more rules. Any more reasons."

Was that what she wanted? She thought it was. Right now, when her skin was humming where his fingers lay, she thought it was exactly what she wanted. But there was something else, some complex mixture of yearning and fear, so unfamiliar it caused her to step back.

"What's wrong, McNee?" Delighted by her reaction, he let his hand slide down her shoulder and away. "Who's making who nervous now?"

"We're supposed to be working," she reminded him. "Not making each other nervous."

"Today, when I go off the clock, so do you."

"Stanislaski."

Alex's eyes stayed on hers another moment before flicking behind her. "Captain."

"Sorry to interrupt your social hour," he said sourly. "I need that report."

"Right here." Even as Alex was turning to reach for it, Bess was offering her hand to Trilwalter.

"Captain, it's so nice to meet you. I'm Bess McNee. I wanted to let you know how much I appreciate the department's cooperation today."

Trilwalter scowled at her a moment, then, remembering, stifled a sigh. "Right. You're the writer." A sneer twisted his mouth. "Soap operas."

"Yes, I am." Her smile made the fluorescents overhead dim. "I wonder...if I can have just a moment of your time? I know you're very busy, so I won't keep you."

He didn't want any part of her. He knew it, she knew it, and so did any of the cops hovering close enough to hear. But riding a desk had taught him that diplomacy was often his only weapon. Besides, once he made his feelings known, she'd be out of his hair and off finding another precinct to haunt.

"Why don't you come into my office, Ms. McNee?"

"Thank you." She shot a grin over her shoulder at Alex as she followed Trilwalter.

"You going to let her go in there alone?" Judd murmured.

"Yeah." Alex bit back a chuckle as he heard the glass

of Trilwalter's door rattle. "Oh, yeah. And I'm going to enjoy it."

Ten minutes later, Alex was surprised by a burst of laughter. Swiveling in his chair, he spotted Trilwalter leading Bess out of his office. The two of them were chuckling together like two old friends over a private joke.

"I'm going to remember that one, Bess."

"Just don't tell the mayor where you heard it."

"I know how to respect a source." Still smiling, he glanced over at a slack-jawed Alex. "Detective, you take care of Ms. McNee. Make sure she gets what she needs."

"Sir." He cut his eyes over to Bess. She merely batted her lashes, managing to look about as innocent as a smoking gun. "I have every intention of making certain Ms. McNee gets exactly what she needs."

Bess laid her hand in Trilwalter's. "Thank you again, Donald."

"My pleasure. Don't be a stranger."

"Donald?" Alex said, the moment the captain was out of earshot.

"Yes." Bess made a production out of brushing dust from her sleeve. "That is his name."

"We use several other names for him around here. What the hell did you do in there?"

"Why, we chatted. What else?"

Glancing over her shoulder, Alex noticed money changing hands. The odds had been even that Trilwalter would chew her up, then spit her out, within ten minutes. Since he'd lost twenty on the deal himself, Alex wasn't particularly pleased.

"Sit down and be quiet," he told her. "I've got work."

"Of course."

Before she could take her seat, his phone rang. "Stanislaski. Yeah." He listened a moment, then pulled out his notepad to scribble. "I hear you. You know how it works, Boomer. It depends on what it's worth." Nodding to himself, he replaced the pad. "Yeah, we'll talk. I'll be there. In ten."

When Alex hung up the phone and grabbed for his jacket, Bess was right behind him. "What is it?"

"I've got someplace to go. Judd, let's hit it."

"I'm going with you."

Alex didn't even glance back as he started out. He was already working on tucking her in some far corner of his mind. "Forget it."

"I'm going with you," she repeated, and snagged his arm. "That's the deal."

It surprised him when he tried to shake her off and she wouldn't shake. The lady had a good grip, he noted. "I didn't make any deal."

She could be just as tough and cold-blooded as he, she thought. She planted her feet, angled her chin. "Your captain did. I ride with you, Detective, wherever you may be going. A day in the life, remember?"

"Fine." Frustration vibrated through him as he stared her down. "You ride—and you stay in the car. No way you're scaring off my snitch."

"Want me to drive?" Judd offered as they headed down the steps to the garage.

"No." Alex's answer was flat and left no room for argument. Judd sent Bess a good-natured shrug. Then, because Alex made no move to do so, he opened the back door of their nondescript unmarked car for her.

"Where are we going?" Bess asked, determined to be pleasant.

"To talk to the scum of the earth," Alex shot back as he pulled out of the garage.

"Sounds fascinating," Bess said, and meant it.

She didn't think she'd ever been in this part of town before. Many of the shop windows were boarded up. Those still in business were grubbier than usual. People still walked as though they were in a hurry, but it didn't look as if they had anyplace to go.

Funny, she thought, how Alex seemed to blend with the surroundings. It wasn't simply the jeans and battered jacket he wore, or the hair he'd deliberately mussed. It was a look in the eyes, a set of the body, a twist of the mouth. No one would look twice at him, she thought. Or if they bothered, they wouldn't see a cop, they'd see another street tough obviously on the edge of his luck.

Taking her cue from him, she pulled out her bag of cosmetics, darkening her mouth, adding just a little too much eyeliner and shadow. She tried a couple of bored looks in the mirror of her compact and decided to tease up her hair.

Alex glanced back at her and scowled. "What the hell are you doing to your face?"

"Getting into character," she said blithely. "Just like you. Are we going to bust somebody?"

He only turned away and muttered.

Just his luck, he thought. He wanted to slip into Boomer's joint unobtrusively, and he was stuck with a redhead who thought they were playing cops and robbers.

Unoffended, Bess put away her mirror and scanned the area. Parking wasn't a problem here. Bess decided that if anyone left his car unattended in this neighborhood for above ten minutes, he'd come back and be lucky to find a hubcap.

Alex swung over the curb and swore. He couldn't leave her in the car here, damn it. Any of the hustlers or junkies on the streets would take one look, then eat her alive.

"You listen to me." He turned, leaning over the seat to make his point. "Stay close to me, and keep your mouth shut. No questions, no comments."

"All right, but where—"

"No questions." He slammed out of his door, then waited for her. With his hand firm on her arm, he hauled her to the sidewalk. "If you step out of line, I swear, I'll slap the cuffs on you."

"Romantic, isn't he?" she said to Judd. "Just sends shivers down my spine."

"Keep a lid on it, McNee," Alex told her, refusing to be amused. He pulled her through a grimy door into an airless shop.

It took her a minute to get her bearings in the dim light. There were shelves and shelves crowded with dusty merchandise. Radios, picture frames, kitchenware. A tuba. A huge glass display counter with a diagonal crack across it dominated one wall. Security glass ran to the ceiling. Cutting through it was a window, like a bank teller's, studded with bars.

"A pawnshop," Bess said, with such obvious delight that Alex snarled at her.

"One word about atmosphere, I'll clobber you."

But she was already dragging out her notebook. "Go ahead, do what you have to do. You won't even know I'm here."

Sure, he thought. How would anyone know she was

there, simply because that sunshine scent of hers cut right through the grime and must? He stepped up to the counter just as a scrawny man in a loose white shirt came through the rear door.

"Stanislaski."

"Boomer. What have you got for me?"

Grinning, Boomer passed a hand over his heavily greased black hair. "Come on, I got some good stuff, and you know I make a point of cooperating with the law. But a man's got to make a living."

"You make one ripping off every poor slob who walks through the door."

"Aw, now you hurt my feelings." Boomer's pale blue eyes glittered. "Rookie?" he asked, nodding at Judd.

"He used to be."

After an appraising look, Boomer glanced over at Bess. She was busy poking through his merchandise. "Looks like I got me a customer. Hang on."

"She's with me." Alex shot him a knife-edged look that forestalled any questions. "Just forget she's here."

Boomer had already appraised the trio of rings on Bess's right hand, and the blue topaz drops at her ears. He sighed his disappointment. "You're the boss, Stanislaski. But listen, I like to be discreet."

Alex leaned on the counter, like a man ready to shoot the bull for hours. His voice was soft, and deadly. "Jerk my chain, Boomer, and I'm going to have to come down here and take a hard look at what you keep in that back room."

"Stock. Just stock." But he grinned. He didn't have any illusions about Alex. Boomer knew when he was detested, but he also knew they had an agreement of sorts. And, thus far, it had been advantageous to both of them. "I got something on those hookers that got sliced up."

Though his expression didn't change, though he didn't move a muscle, Alex went on alert. "What kind of something?"

Boomer merely smiled and rubbed his thumb and forefinger together. When Alex drew out a twenty, it disappeared quickly through the bars. "Twenty more, if you like what I have to say."

"If it's worth it, you'll get it."

"You know I trust you." Smelling of hair grease and sweat, Boomer leaned closer. "Word on the street is you're looking for some high roller. Guy's name's Jack."

"So far I'm not impressed."

"Just building up to it, pal. The first one that was wasted? She was one of Big Ed's wives. I recognized her from the newspaper picture. Now, she was fine-looking. Not that I ever used her services."

"Turn the page, Boomer."

"Okay, okay." He shot a grin at Judd. "He don't like conversation. I heard both those unfortunate ladies were in possession of a certain piece of jewelry."

"You've got good ears."

"Man in my position hears things. It so happens I had a young lady come in just yesterday. She had a certain piece of jewelry she wanted to exchange." Opening a drawer, Boomer pulled out a thin gold chain. Dangling from it was a heart, cracked down the center. When Alex held out a hand, Boomer shook his head. "I gave her twenty for it."

Saying nothing, Alex pulled another bill out of his wallet.

"Seems to me I'm entitled to a certain amount of profit."

Eyes steady, Alex pulled the twenty back an inch. "You're entitled to go in and answer a bunch of nasty questions down at the cop shop."

With a shrug, Boomer exchanged the bill for the heart. He'd only given ten for it, in any case. "She wasn't much more than a kid," Boomer added. "Eighteen, maybe twenty at a stretch. Still pretty. Bottle blonde, blue eyes. Little mole right here." He tapped beside his left eyebrow.

"Got an address?"

"Well, now…"

"Twenty for the address, Boomer." Alex's tone told the man to take it. "That's it."

Satisfied, Boomer named a hotel a few blocks away. "Signed her name Crystal," he added, wanting to keep the partnership intact. "Crystal LaRue. Figure she made it up."

"Let's check it out," he said to Judd, then tapped Bess on the shoulder. She was apparently absorbed in an ugly brass lamp in the shape of a rearing horse. "Let's go."

"In a minute." She turned a smile on Boomer. "How much?"

"Oh, for you—"

"Forget it." Alex was dragging her to the door.

"I want to buy—"

"It's ugly."

Annoyed at the loss, but pleased to have recorded the entire conversation, she sighed. "That's the point." But she climbed meekly into the car and began to scribble her impressions in her book.

Cramped shop. Very dirty. Mostly junk. Excellent place for props. Proprietor a complete sleaze. Alexi in complete control of exchange—a kind of game-playing. Quietly disgusted but willing to use the tools at hand.

By the time she'd finished scribbling, Alex was pulling to the curb again.

"Same rules," he said to Bess as they climbed out of the car.

"Absolutely." Lips pursed, she studied the crumbling hotel. She recognized it as a rent-by-the-hour special. "Is this where she lives?"

"Who?"

"The girl you were talking about." She lifted a brow. "I have ears, too, Alexi."

He should have known. "As long as you keep your mouth shut."

"There's no need to be rude," she told him as they started in. "Tell you what, just to show there's no hard feelings, I'll buy you both lunch."

"Great." Judd gallantly opened the door for her.

"You're so easy," Alex muttered to his partner as they entered the filthy lobby.

"Hey, we gotta eat sometime."

He hated to bring her in here, Alex realized. Into this dirty place that smelled of garbage and moldy dreams. How could she be so unaffected by it? he wondered, then struggled to put thoughts of her aside as he approached the desk clerk.

"You got a Crystal LaRue?"

The clerk peered over his newspaper. There was an unfiltered cigarette dangling from the corner of his mouth and total disinterest in his eyes. "Don't ask for names."

Alex merely pulled out his badge, flashed it. "Blonde, about eighteen. Good-looking. A beauty mark beside her eyebrow. Working girl."

"Don't ask what they do for a living, neither." With a shrug, the clerk went back to his paper. "Two-twelve."

"She in?"

"Haven't seen her go out."

With Bess trailing behind, they started up the steps. To entertain herself, she read the various tenants' suggestions and statements that were scrawled on the walls.

There was a screaming match in progress behind one of the doors on the first floor. Someone was banging on the wall from a neighboring room and demanding—in colorful terms—that the two opponents quiet down.

A bag of garbage had spilled on the stairs between the second and first floors. It had gone very ripe.

Alex rapped on the door of 212, waited. He rapped again and called out. "Crystal. Need to talk to you."

With a glance at Judd, Alex tried the door. The knob turned easily. "In a place like this, you'd think she'd lock it," Judd commented.

"And wire it with explosives," Alex added. He slipped out his gun, and Judd did the same. "Stay in the hall," he ordered Bess without looking at her. They went through the door, guns at the ready.

She did exactly what she was told. But that didn't stop her from seeing. Crystal hadn't gone out, and she wouldn't be walking the streets again. As the door hung open, Bess stared at what was sprawled across the sagging mattress inside. The stench of blood—and worse—streamed through the open doorway.

Death. Violent death. She had written about it, discussed it, watched gleefully as it was acted out for the cameras.

But she'd never seen it face-to-face. Had never known how completely a human being could be turned into a thing.

From far away, she heard Alex swear, over and over, but she could only stare, frozen, until his body blocked her view. He had his hands on her shoulders, squeezing. God, she was cold, Bess thought. She'd never been so cold.

"I want you to go downstairs."

She managed to lift her gaze from his chin to his eyes. The iced fury in them had her shivering. "What?"

He nearly swore again. She was white as a sheet, and her pupils had contracted until they were hardly bigger than the point of a pin. "Go downstairs, Bess." He tried to rub the chill out of her arms, knowing he couldn't. "Are you listening to me?" he said, his voice quiet, gentle.

"Yes." She moistened her lips, pressed them together. "I'm sorry, yes."

"Go down, stay in the lobby. Don't say anything, don't do anything, until Judd or I come down. Okay?" He gave her a little shake, and wondered what he would do if she folded on him. "Okay?"

She took one shaky breath, then nodded. "She's... so young." With an effort, she swallowed the sickness that kept threatening to rise in her throat. "I'm all right. Don't worry about me. I'm all right," she repeated, then turned away to go downstairs.

"She shouldn't have seen this," Judd said. His own stomach was quivering.

"Nobody should see this." Banking down on every emotion, Alex closed the door at his back.

She stuck it out, refusing to budge when Judd came down to drive her home. After finding an old chair, she settled into a corner while the business of death went on around her. From her vantage point, she watched them come and go—forensics, the police photographer, the morgue.

Detached, she studied the people who crowded in, asking questions, making comments, being shuffled out again by blank-faced cops.

There was grief in her for a girl she hadn't known, a fury at the waste of a life. But she remained. Not because of the job. Because of Alex.

He was angry with her. She understood it, and didn't question it. When they were finished at the scene, she rode in silence in the back of the car. Back at the station, she took the same chair she'd had that morning.

Hours went by, endlessly long. At one point she slipped out and bought Alex and Judd sandwiches from a deli. After a time, he went into another room. She followed, still silent, noted a board with pictures tacked to it. Horrible pictures.

She looked away from them, took a chair and listened while Alex and other detectives discussed the latest murder and the ongoing investigation.

Later, she rode with him back to the pawnshop. Waited patiently while he questioned Boomer again. Waited longer while he and Judd returned to the motel to reinterview the clerk, the tenants.

Like them, she learned little about Crystal LaRue. Her name had been Kathy Segal, and she'd once lived in

Wisconsin. It had been hard, terribly hard, for Bess to listen when Alex tracked down and notified her parents. Hard, too, to understand from Alex's end of the conversation that they didn't care. For them, their daughter had already been dead.

She'd been nobody's girl. She'd worked the streets on her own. Two months after she moved into the tiny little room with the sagging mattress, she had died there. No one had known her. No one had wanted to know her.

No one had cared.

Alex couldn't talk to Bess. It was impossible for him. Intolerable. He shared this part of his life with no one who mattered to him. It was true that his sister Rachel saw some of it as a public defender but as far as Alex was concerned that was too much. Perhaps that was why he kept all the pieces he could away from the rest of his family and loved ones.

He hated remembering the look on Bess's face as she'd stood in that doorway. There should have been a way to protect her from that, to shield her from her own stubbornness.

But he hadn't protected her, he hadn't shielded her, though that was precisely what he had sworn to do for people he'd never met from the first day he'd worn a badge. Yet for her, for the woman he was—God, yes, the woman he was in love with—he'd opened the door himself and let her in.

So he didn't talk to her, not even when it was time to turn it off and go home. And in the silence, his anger built and swelled and clawed at his guts. He found the words when he stepped into her apartment and closed the door.

"Did you get enough?"

Bess was in no mood to fight. Her emotions, always close to the surface, had been wrung dry by what she'd seen and heard that day. She would let him yell, if that was what he needed, but she was tired, she was aching, and her heart went out to him.

"Let me get you a drink," she said quietly, but he snagged her arm and whirled her back.

"Is it all in your notes?" That cold, terribly controlled fury swiped out at her. "Can you find a way to use it to entertain those millions of daytime viewers?"

"I'm sorry." It was all she could think of. "Alexi, I'm so sorry." She took a deep breath. "I want a brandy. I'll get us both one."

"Fine. A nice, civilized brandy is just what we need."

She walked away to choose a bottle from an old lacquered cabinet. "I don't know what you want me to say." Very carefully, very deliberately, she poured two snifters. "I'll apologize for choosing today to do this, if that helps. I'll apologize for making it more difficult for you by being there when this happened." She brought the snifter to him, but he didn't take it. "Right now, I'd be willing to say anything you'd like to hear."

He couldn't get beyond it, no matter what she said. He couldn't get beyond knowing he'd opened the door on the kind of horror she'd never be able to forget. "You had no business being there. You had no business seeing any of that."

With a sigh, she set both snifters aside. Maybe brandy wouldn't help after all. "You were there. You saw it."

His eyes flashed white heat. "It's my damn job."

"I know." She lifted a hand to his cheek, soothing. "I know."

Compelled, he grabbed her wrist, held tight a moment before he turned away. "I don't want you touched by it. I don't want you touched by it ever again."

"I can't promise that." Because it was her way, she wrapped her arms around his waist, rested her cheek against his back. He was rigid as steel, unyielding as granite. "Not if you want something between us."

"It's because I do want something between us."

"Alexi." So many emotions, she thought. Always before it had been easy to sort them out, to drift with them. But this time... It had been a long, hard day, she reminded herself. There would be time to think later. "If what you want is someone you can tuck in a comfortable corner, it isn't me. What you do is part of what you are." When he turned, she brushed her hands over his cheeks again, refusing to let him retreat. "You want me to say I was appalled by what I saw in that room? I was. I was appalled by the cruelty of it, sickened by the terrible, terrible waste."

That sliced at him, a long, thin blade through the heart. "I shouldn't have let you go with me. That part of my life isn't ever going to be part of yours."

"Stop." The sorrow that had paled her face hardened into determination. "Do you think that because I write fantasy I don't know anything about the real world? You're wrong. I know, it just doesn't overwhelm my life. And I know that what you faced today you may face tomorrow. Or worse. I know that every time you walk out the door you may not come back." The quick lick of fear reminded her to slow down and speak carefully. "What you are makes that a very real possibility. But I won't let that overwhelm me, either. Because there's nothing about you I'd change."

For a moment, he simply stared at her, a hundred different feelings fighting for control inside him. Then, slowly, he lowered his brow to hers and shut his eyes. "I don't know what to say to you."

"You don't have to say anything. We don't have to talk at all."

He knew what she was offering, even before she tilted her head and touched her lips to his. He wanted it, and her. More than anything, he wanted to steep himself in her until the rest of the world went away.

He took his hands through her hair, letting his fingers toy with those loose, vivid curls. "We haven't come up with those rules."

Her lips curved, slanted over his. "We'll figure them out later."

He murmured his agreement, drawing her closer. "I want you. I need to be with you. I think I'd go crazy if I couldn't be with you tonight."

"I'm here. Right here."

"Bess." His mouth moved from hers to skim along those sharp cheekbones. "I'm in love with you."

She felt her heart stutter. That was the only way she could describe this sensation she'd never experienced before. "Alexi—"

"Don't." He closed his mouth over hers again. "Don't say it. It comes too easy to you. Just come to bed." He buried his face against her neck. "For God's sake, let me take you to bed."

Chapter 8

Hurt. Oh, she'd read the stories and the poetry, watched the movies. She'd even written the scenes. But she'd never believed that love and pain existed together, could twine into one clenched fist to batter the soul.

Yet his words had hurt her—immeasurably—even as her heart opened to give and accept.

This time it was different. How could she possibly explain that to him, when she was still groping for the answers herself? And what good were words now, when there was so much need?

A touch would be enough, she promised herself as they swayed toward the steps. Tonight would be enough, and tomorrow all the aches would only be memories.

His mouth came back to hers, restless, insistent, as they began the climb. The first helpless sigh caught in her throat as he pulled her close and aroused her unbearably with a long, sumptuous meeting of lips.

Her fingers trembled when she tugged at his jacket. Had they ever trembled for a man before? she wondered. No. And as the leather slid away, leaving her free to grip those magnificent shoulders, she knew that none of this had happened before. Not the trembling, not the raw scrape of nerves, not the sting of bright tears, not the sweet, slow throb of her blood.

This was the first time for so many things.

He didn't know how much longer he could perform the simple act of drawing breath in and out of his lungs. Not when her body was shivering against his. Not when he could hear those small, desperately needy sounds in her throat. The staircase seemed to stretch interminably. With a muffled oath, he swept her up into his arms.

Her eyes met his, and though her heart seemed ready to burst, she managed to smile. She knew he needed smiles tonight. "And I said you weren't romantic."

"I have my moments."

Shaky, she nuzzled her face into the curve of his neck. "I'm awfully glad I'm here for this one."

"Keep it up," he said in a strained voice as she ran nibbling kisses from throat to ear, "and I'll do something really romantic, like falling on my face and dropping you."

"Oh, I trust you, Detective." She caught the lobe of his ear in her teeth and felt the quick jerk of reaction. "Completely."

With his heart roaring in his head, he reached the top. She was teasing his jawline now, making little murmurs of approval as she sampled his flesh. He headed for the first door. "This better be the bedroom."

"Mmm-hmm…" While she worked her way to his mouth, her fingers were busy unbuttoning his shirt.

He recognized her scent first. Even as he passed through the doorway, it wrapped its alluring woman's fingers around him. That cheerful, sexy fragrance hung in the air, the result, no doubt, of spilled powder and an unstoppered bottle of perfume. Her clothes were a colorful mess of silk blouses, bright cotton pants, tangled hose. His quick scan passed over a life-size stuffed ostrich, a pair of thriving ficus trees flanking the wide window, and a collection of antique bottles, elegant in jewel colors, before he focused on the bed.

It was a long, wide ocean of cool blue sheets, topped by a lush mountain of vivid-toned pillows. All satins and silks.

Because his mouth was beginning to water, he took one long, slow breath. But the air, so fragrant, burned his lungs. "That looks big enough for six close friends."

"I like a lot of room." Even as his stomach quivered at the images that evoked, she was continuing. "I used to fall out of bed a lot when I was a kid."

"Is that how you broke your nose?"

"No. But I chipped a tooth once."

He set her down beside the bed, pleased that her arms stayed linked around his neck. "I think we can probably keep from falling out of this one. If we work on it."

She raised up on her toes, just a little, just enough to bring them eye-to-eye. "I'm willing to risk it."

Determined to steady himself, he kissed her brow, her cheeks. "Let me take my gun off."

He stripped off the holster, set it on the floor. With fingers that were suddenly numb and awkward, she reached for the buttons of her blazer.

"No." It was that one quick flash of nerves in her eyes that had settled his own. He closed his hands over hers. "Let me." He unfastened buttons, then took his hands slowly up her sides, his thumbs just brushing her breasts. "You're shaking."

"I know."

Watching her, he slid the jacket from her shoulders. "Are you afraid of me?"

"No." She couldn't swallow. "Of this, a little. It's silly."

He toyed with the first button of her blouse, then the second. Her skin quivered as his knuckle skimmed over it. "I like it."

"That's good." She tried to laugh, but only managed one trembling breath. "Because I can't seem to stop."

"There's plenty of time to relax." The blouse slipped away, and desire curled its powerful fist in his stomach. Midnight-blue silk shimmered in the dimming light, gleaming against ivory skin. "There's no hurry."

"I—" Her head fell back as he traced a finger over the silk. Gently, so gently, over the swell of her breasts, as though hers was the first body he'd touched. The only one he wanted to touch. "God, Alexi…"

"I've spent a lot of time imagining this. Step out of your shoes," he suggested while he unhooked her slacks. In a daze, she obeyed as the slacks slithered down her legs. "I'm going to spend a lot more time enjoying it. I want all of you." Lazily, testingly, he ran a finger under the lace cut high on her thigh. Ah, the skin there was like rose petals dewed with morning. Her eyes went wide and dark; her body quaked. "All of you," he repeated.

She couldn't move. Every muscle in her body had turned to water. Hot, rushing water. She couldn't speak, not when so many emotions clogged her throat. As she stood swaying, helplessly seduced, he watched her.

Touched her. Clever fingers brushing, stroking, exploring. He trailed them up her arms, slid them over her shoulders. Then back to silk, until her body burned like fever.

His eyes never left hers. Even when he kissed her, lightly, tormenting her hungry lips with the barest of tastes, his eyes stayed open and aware.

"You're making me crazy." Her voice hitched out through trembling lips.

"I know. I want to."

He caught her wrists when she reached for him, then ran their tangled fingers over her, so that she felt her own response to him, inside and out, as he touched his mouth to hers again. Patiently, erotically, he deepened the kiss, until her hands went limp and her pulse thundered. Then he brought her hands up, spread them over his chest. Together they spread his open shirt apart. With his mouth still clinging to hers, he tugged it off. His heart gave a quick, hard lurch as her hands, hot and eager, raced over him.

Yanking her close, he took off his shoes. His skin was already damp when he fumbled for the snap of his jeans.

"I want you under me." He tore his mouth from hers to savor her throat. "I want to feel you move under me."

They lowered to the bed, rolled once, then twice, over silk. He used every ounce of control, every degree of will, to keep himself from plunging into her and taking the quick, desperate release his body craved. His mind, his soul, wanted more than that.

She seemed smaller like this. Slighter. It helped him remember that passion could outstrip tenderness. So, while the blood pounded and burned in his veins, he loved her slowly.

She discovered that a woman could drown willingly in sweetness. She knew there was a gun on the floor beside them and that he had used it at least once to kill. But the hands that moved over her were those of a gentle man. One who cared. She rested a palm on his cheek as she floated away on the kiss. One who loved.

Who loved her.

Staggered by the knowledge, she poured everything she had into the kiss, needing to show him that whatever he felt was returned, equally. Then his mouth slid from hers to trail down her throat, over her shoulder. All thought, all reason, skittered away.

In a warm, slippery pool of silk and satin, he showed her what it was to ache for someone. To yearn for the sharp, thin point of pain the poets call ecstasy. Her hips arched under his, desperately offering. But he only continued that tormenting journey over her with teasing lips and gentle hands.

When his tongue flicked under the line of lace that clung tenuously to her breasts, she moaned, pressing an urgent hand to the back of his head. The taste there—honey, dampened by her arousal—nearly unraveled the taut knot of his control. So he pleased them both, closing a greedy mouth over that firm, scented swell.

Gasping out with pleasure, she bucked under him, straining for more, her nails digging heedlessly into his back as she whimpered and struggled for what was just out of reach. Maddened by her response, he brought his mouth to hers again, crushing her lips as he slithered a hand down to cup the heat between her thighs. Prayers and pleas trembled on her tongue, but before she could voice them, he slipped under the silk to stroke.

The unbearable pleasure shattered. Fractured lights, whirling colors, spun behind her eyes to blind her. She heard herself cry out; his name was nearly a sob. Then there was his groan, a sound of sweet satisfaction as her body went limp in release.

Never before. Her hands slid away from him, boneless. Sweet Lord, never like this. She felt weak, wrecked, weepy. As her breath sobbed out, as her eyes fluttered closed, they both knew that her mind, her body, were totally his for the taking.

He'd never felt stronger. Her wild response, her absolute surrender, filled him with a kind of intense power he'd never experienced before. Silk rustled against silk as he drew the teddy down, tossed it aside. Her skin, slick with passion, glowed in the shadows. He touched where he chose, watching, fascinated, as his own hands molded her. Gold against ivory. He tasted wherever he liked, feeling her muscles quiver involuntarily as he traced openmouthed kisses over her rib cage, down to her stomach. Heat to heat.

Then, wanting that instant of sheer pleasure again, he drove her up a second time, shuddering himself as her body convulsed and flowed with the crest of the wave.

At last, unable to wait a moment longer, he slipped inside that hot, moist sheath. Her groan of stunned delight echoed his own.

Slowly, as in a dream, her arms lifted to wrap around him. She rose to meet him, to take him deep. They moved gently at first, treasuring the intimacy, willing to prolong it. But need outpaced them, driving them faster, until, thrust for thrust, they sprinted toward the final crest.

His hand fisted in her hair as the last link of control snapped clean. Her name exploded from his lips like an oath as he emptied himself into her.

She wondered how she could ever have thought herself experienced. While it was true she hadn't been with as many men as some thought, she hadn't come to Alexi an innocent.

Yet things had happened tonight that had never happened before. And, because she was a woman who understood herself well, she knew that nothing she had experienced here would happen again—unless it was with him.

Relaxed now, she rubbed her cheek over his chest, content to remain as she'd been since he rolled over and dragged her across him. Tucked in the cocoon of his arms, she felt as cozy as a cat, and she arched lazily as he ran a hand down her spine.

"Will you tell me again?" she asked.

"What?"

She pressed her lips against him, feeling his heart beating strong and fast beneath them. "What every woman wants to hear."

"I love you." When she lifted her head, he laid a hand gently over her lips. He knew it would hurt to hear her say it, when she didn't mean it as he did.

Suddenly she was glad it was dark, and he couldn't see the smile fade away from her face. "Even after this," she said carefully, "you don't want me to love you back."

More than anything, he thought. More than life. "Let's just leave things as they are." He traced her face with a fingertip, enjoying those odd angles. "Tell me how you broke your nose."

She was silent a moment, gathering her composure. She couldn't offer what he didn't want to take. "Fist-fight."

He chuckled and drew her back to cuddle, instinctively soothing the tension out of her. "I should have figured."

She made an effort to relax against him. There was time to convince him. Hadn't he said they had plenty of time? "At boarding school," she added. "I was twelve and homely as a duck. Too skinny, funny hair, dumb face."

"I like your face. And your hair." His hand cupped her breast comfortably. "And your body."

"You didn't know me when I was twelve. When you're odd in any way, you're a target."

"I know."

Interested, she lifted her head again. "Do you?"

"I didn't learn English until I was five. Before my father's business got off the ground, times were rough." He turned his face into her hair to breathe in the scent. "I was this little Ukrainian kid, wearing my brother's hand-me-downs. And back then, Soviets weren't particularly popular with Americans."

"Well, you made such great villains." She kissed his cheek, comforting the small boy he'd been. "It must have been difficult for you."

"I had the family. We had each other. School was a little rugged at first. Name-calling, playground scuffles. Even some of the parents weren't too keen on having their kids play with the Russkie. No point in trying to explain we were Ukrainian." He shifted, tangled his legs with hers. "So, after a few black eyes and bloody noses, I earned a reputation for being tough. After a while, we kind of got absorbed into the neighborhood."

"What neighborhood?"

"Brooklyn. My parents still live there. Same house." With a shake of his head, he drew back. He could make her out now in the dark, could see the way her eyes were smiling at him. "How come we're talking about me, when I asked you about your nose?"

"I like hearing it."

"There was a fistfight," he said, prompting her.

Bess sighed. "One of those girl cliques," she began. "You know the type. The cool kids, all hair and teeth and attitude. I was the nerd they liked to pick on."

"You were never a nerd."

"I was a *champion* nerd. Gawky, top of the class academically, socially inept."

"You?"

There was such pure disbelief in the tone, she laughed. "Which of those descriptions don't you buy, Alexi?"

He considered a moment. "Any of them."

"I guess I'm two-thirds flattered and one-third insulted. I was tall for my age and skinny. A very late bloomer in the bosom and hips department."

"You might have bloomed slow," he began, proving his point with a sweep of his hand, "but you bloomed very well."

"Thank you. My mind, however, had developed quite nicely. Straight *A*'s."

"No kidding?" He grinned in the dark. "And you were the kid who always trashed the grading curve for the rest of us."

"That's the idea. Added to that, I was more comfortable with a book, or thinking, than I was tittering. Young girls do a lot of tittering. Because I was hard-headed, I automatically took a dislike to anything that was popular or fashionable at the time. As a result, I took a lot of flak. Bess the Mess, that sort of thing."

She paused long enough to shift some pillows. "Anyway, we had this history exam coming up. One of the cool kids—her name was Dawn Gallagher... Heart-shaped face, perfect features, long, flowing blond hair. You get the picture."

"Prom-queen type."

"Exactly. She was flunking big-time and wanted me to let her copy from my paper. She'd made my life adolescent hell, and she figured if she was nice to me for a couple of days, let me stand within five feet of her, maybe sit at the same lunch table, I'd be so grateful, I'd let her."

"But you hung tough."

"I don't cheat for anybody. The upshot was, she flunked the exam, and her parents were called to the school for a conference. Dawn retaliated by pinching me whenever I got too close, getting into my room and breaking my things, stealing my books. Small-time terrorism. One day on the basketball court—"

"You shot hoop?"

"Team captain. I was an athletic nerd," she explained. "Anyway, she tripped me. If that wasn't bad enough, she had a few friends on the other team. They elbowed the hell out of me during the game. I had bruises everywhere."

An immediate flood of resentment had him tightening his hold. "Little bitches."

Pleased with the support, she cuddled closer. "It

was an epiphany for me. Suddenly I saw that pacifism, while morally sound, could get you trampled into dust. I waited for Dawn outside the science lab one day. We started out with words—I've always been good at them. We progressed to pushing and shoving and drew quite a crowd. She swung first. I didn't expect it, and she bopped me right on the nose. Let me tell you, Detective, pain can be a great motivator."

"Separates the nerds from the toughs."

"You got it. It took three of them to pull me off her, but before they did, I'd blackened her baby-blues, split her Cupid's-bow mouth and loosened several of her pearly-whites."

"Good for you, McNee."

"It was good," she said with a sigh. "In fact, it felt so good, I've had to be careful with my temper ever since. I didn't just want to hurt her, you see. I wanted to mangle her."

He took her hand, curled it into a fist and raised it to his lips. "I'll have to watch my step. Did you take much heat?"

"We both got suspended. My parents were appalled and embarrassed enough by my behavior to cancel my summer plans and switch me to another school."

"But—" He cut himself off. Not every family was as supportive as his.

"It was the best thing that could have happened to me," she told him. "I started off with a clean slate. I was still ugly, but I knew how to handle myself."

Even if she didn't realize she was carrying around some emotional scars, he did. He rolled over her, cupping her face in his hands. "Listen, McNee, you're beautiful."

Amused, she grinned. "Sure I am."

He didn't smile. In the dim light, his eyes were very intense. "I said, you're beautiful. Why else haven't I been able to get you out of my mind since the first time I saw you?"

"Intriguing," she corrected. "Unusual."

"Gorgeous," he murmured, and watched her blink in surprise. "Ivory for skin, fire for hair, jade for eyes. And these." He traced a fingertip over a sprinkling of freckles. "Gold dust."

"You've already gotten me into bed, Alexi," she said lightly. She had to speak lightly, or she'd humiliate herself with tears. "But the flattery is appreciated." With a grin, she linked her arms around his neck. "But haven't you heard the one about actions speaking louder than words?"

He arched a brow. "If you insist."

"Oh, I do," she murmured, as his mouth came down to hers. "I absolutely do."

With her bag slapping hard against her hip, Bess raced into the office, ten minutes late. "I have a good excuse," she called to Lori.

Her perpetually prompt partner was standing by the coffeepot, her back to the door. "It's all right. I'm running behind myself."

"You?" Bess dropped her bag, stretched her shoulders. She might have skipped her workout that morning, but she was feeling as limber as a snake. "What is it, a national holiday?" She crossed to the pot herself, chattering as she poured a cup. "Well, I'd save my excuse for another time, but I can hardly stand not to tell you." She lifted shining eyes, then stopped after one look at Lori's face. "What is it, honey?"

"It's nothing." After giving herself a shake, Lori sipped her coffee. "It's just that Steven caught me on my way in."

"Did he say something to upset you?"

"He said he loved me." She pressed her lips together. She'd be damned if she'd cry over him again. "The sonofabitch."

"Let's sit down." Bess curled a comforting arm around Lori's shoulder. "You might not want to hear this, but I think he means it."

"He doesn't even know what it means." Furious, Lori dashed one rogue tear away. "I'm not going to let him do this to me again. Get me believing, get me all churned up, just so he can back off when things get serious. Let him have the fantasy life. I've got reality."

Because she'd been waiting for an opening just like this, Bess crouched down in front of her. "Which is?"

"A job, paying your bills—"

"Boring," Bess finished, and Lori's brimming eyes flashed.

"Then I'm boring."

"No, you're not." Sighing, Bess set her coffee aside and took one of Lori's hands. "Maybe you're afraid to take risks, but that doesn't make you boring. And I know you want more out of life than a job and a good credit rating."

"What's wrong with those things?"

"Nothing, as long as that's not all you have. Lori, I know you're still in love with him."

"That's my problem."

"His, too. He's miserable without you."

Suddenly weary, Lori rubbed her fingers between her

brows. "He's the one who broke things off. He said he didn't want complications, a long-term commitment."

"He was wrong. I'd bet the bank that he knows he's wrong. Why don't you just talk to him?"

"I don't know if I can." She squeezed her eyes tight. "It hurts."

An odd light flickered in Bess's eyes. "Is that how you know it's real? When it hurts?"

"It's one of the top symptoms." She opened her eyes again. This time, there was a trace of hope mixed with the tears. "Do you really think he's unhappy?"

"I know he is. Just talk, Lori. Hear each other out."

"Maybe." She gave Bess's hand a quick squeeze, then reached for her coffee again. "I wasn't going to dump this on you first thing."

"What are pals for?"

"Well, pal, we'd better get to work, or a lot of people will be out of a job."

"Great. I've been playing with the dialogue in that scene between Storm and Jade. We want to bump up the sexual tension."

Lori was already nodding and booting up the computer. "You're the dialogue champ," she began, then glanced up. "So why were you late?"

"It's not important. We've got them running into each other at the station house. The long look first, then—"

"Bess, you're only making me more curious. Get it out of the way, or I won't be able to work."

"Okay." She was all but bursting to tell, in any case. "I was with Alexi."

"I thought that was yesterday."

"It was." Bess's smile spread. "And last night. And

this morning. Oh, Lori, it's incredible. I've never felt this way about anyone."

"Right." She started to pick up her reading glasses, then looked up again. For a moment, she did nothing but study Bess's face. "Say that again."

"I've never felt this way about anyone."

"Good grief." On a quick huff of breath, Lori sat back. "I think you mean it."

"It's different." With a half laugh, Bess pressed a hand to her cheek. "It's scary, and it hurts, and sometimes I look at him and I can't even breathe. I'm so afraid he might take a good look at me and realize his mistake." She let her hand drop away. "It's supposed to be easy."

"No." Slowly Lori shook her head. "That was always *your* mistake. It's supposed to be hard, and scary and real."

"There's this clutching around my heart."

"Yeah."

"And...and..." Frustrated, Bess turned, scooting around a chair so that she could pace the length of the table. "And my stomach's all tied up in knots one minute. The next I feel so happy I can hardly bear it. When we were together last night..." No way to describe it, she thought. No possible way. "Lori, I swear, no one's ever made me feel like that. And this morning, when I woke up beside him, I didn't know whether to laugh or cry."

Lori rose, held out a hand. "Congratulations, McNee. You've finally made it."

"Looks that way." With a laugh, she threw her arms around Lori and squeezed. "Why didn't you ever tell me how it feels?"

"It's something you have to experience firsthand. How about him?"

"He loves me." She felt foolish and weepy. Digging through her bag she found a tattered tissue. "He told me. He looked at me, and he told me. But—"

"Oh-oh."

"He doesn't want me to tell him how I feel." Hissing a breath through her teeth, she pressed a hand to her stomach. "Oh, God, it hurts. It hurts everywhere when I realize he doesn't trust me enough. He thinks it's like all the other times. Why shouldn't he? But I want him to know it's not—and I don't know how."

"He only has to look at you."

"It's not enough." Calmer now, Bess blew her nose. "Everything's different this time. I guess I have to prove myself. I do love him, Lori."

"I can see that. I wasn't sure I ever would." Touched, she lifted a hand to Bess's hair. "You could take your own advice, and talk to him."

"We have talked. But he doesn't want to hear this, at least not yet. He wants things to stay as they are."

Lori lifted her brows. "What do you want?"

"For him to be happy." She chuckled and stuffed the mangled tissue back in her purse. "That makes me sound like a wimp. You know I'm not."

"Who knows you better? It only makes you sound like a woman in the first dizzy stages of love."

Bess gave her a watery smile. "Does it get worse or better?"

"Both."

"That's good news. Well, while it's getting worse and better, I'll have time to show him how I feel." She picked up her coffee, then set it aside again. "Lori, there's one more thing."

"What could be bigger?" Lori demanded.

"Alexi wants me to have dinner with his family on Sunday."

After a quick gurgle of laughter, Lori's eyes widened. "He's taking you home to Mother?"

"And Father," Bess put in. "And brothers and sisters and nieces and nephews. A couple times a month they have a big family dinner on Sunday."

"Obviously the man is crazy about you."

"He is. I know he is." Then she shut her eyes and dropped into a chair. "His family is enormously important to him. You can hear it every time he mentions one of them." She grabbed another tissue and began to tear it to shreds. "I want to meet them. Really. But what if they don't like me?"

"You have got it bad. Take it from me, you just be the Bess McNee we all know and love, and they'll be crazy about you, too."

"But what if—"

"What if you pull yourself together?" This time Lori picked up her glasses, perched them on her nose. "Put some of this angst into Storm and Jade's heartbreak. Millions of viewers will thank you."

After a deep breath, Bess nodded. "Okay, okay. That might work. And if we don't get the morning session out of the way, we won't be ready when Rosalie comes in at noon for a consulting session."

"Your deal, sister." Frowning, Lori gestured with a pencil. "That particular lady makes me nervous."

"Don't worry about Rosalie. I know what I'm doing."

"How many times have I heard that?"

But Bess only smiled and let her mind drift. "Okay. Storm and Jade." She closed her eyes, envisioned the scene. "So, they run into each other at the station…"

Chapter 9

"And then," Bess continued as she zipped through traffic, "Jade turns back, devastated, and says, 'But what you want isn't always what you need.' Music swells, fade out."

"It's not that I'm not fascinated by the twists and turns of those people in Holbrook…"

"Millbrook."

"Right." Alex winced as she cut off a sedan. "I just wish you'd watch the road. It would be really embarrassing if you got a ticket while I was in the car with you."

"I'm not speeding." Frowning, she glanced down at her speedometer. "Hardly."

She handled the five-speed like a seasoned veteran of the Indianapolis 500, Alex thought. And at the moment she was treating the other, innocent drivers on the road like competitors. "Maybe you could find a home in one lane and stay there."

"Killjoy." But she did as he asked. "I hardly ever get to drive. I love it."

He had to smile. The wind whipping in through the open sunroof was blowing her hair everywhere. "I'd never have guessed."

"The last time I had a chance was when L.D. and I went to some fancy do on Long Island." She checked her mirror and, unable to resist, shot into the next lane. "One trip with me and he insisted on taking his car and driver every damn place." She sent Alex a smile, then sobered instantly when she saw his expression. "I'm sorry."

"For what?"

"For bringing him up."

"I didn't say anything."

No, he hadn't said anything, she admitted. A man didn't have to say a word when his eyes could go that cold. Her hands tightened on the wheel. Now she stared straight ahead.

"He was a friend, Alexi. That's all he ever was. I didn't…" She took a long, careful breath. "I never slept with him."

"I didn't ask one way or the other," he said coolly.

"Maybe you should. One minute you want to know all there is about me, and the next you don't. I think—"

"I think you're driving too fast again." He reached over and brushed his knuckles down her cheek. "And you should relax. Okay?"

"Okay." But her fingers remained tight on the wheel. "I'd like—sometime—for us to talk about it."

"Sometime." Damn it, didn't she realize he didn't want to talk about the other men who'd been part of her life? He didn't want to think about them. Especially now, now that he was in love, and he knew what it was like to be with her.

He knew the sound of that little sigh she made when she turned toward him in the night. The way her eyes stayed unfocused and heavy, long after she awakened in the morning. He knew she liked her showers too hot and too long. And that she smelled so good because she rubbed some fragrant cream all over before she'd even dried off.

She was always losing things. An earring, a scribbled note, money. She never counted her change, and she always overtipped.

He knew those things, was coming to treasure them. Why should he talk about other men who had come to know them?

"Turn here."

"Hmm?"

"I said turn..." He trailed off with a huff of breath as she breezed by the exit. "Okay, take the next one, and we'll double back."

"The next what?"

"Turn, McNee." He reached over and gave her hair a quick tug. "Take the next turn, which means you have to get over in the right lane."

"Oh." She did, punching the gas and handily cutting off another car. At the rude blast of its horn, she only lifted a hand and waved.

"He wasn't being friendly," Alex pointed out—after he took his hands from in front of his eyes.

"I know. But that's no reason for me to be rude, too."

"Some people consider cutting off another driver rude."

"No. That's an adventure."

Somehow they made it without mishap. But the moment she'd squeezed into a parking place two doors down from his parents' row house, he held out his hand. "Keys."

Sulking, she jingled them in her hand. "I didn't get a ticket."

"Probably because there wasn't a traffic cop brave enough to pull you over. Let's have them, McNee. I've had enough adventure for one day."

"You just want to drive." Her eyes narrowed suspiciously. "It's a man thing."

"It's a survival thing." He plucked them from her hand. "I just want to live." Not that he was going to object to handling the natty little Mercedes. But he decided against bringing that up as they climbed out of opposite doors.

"Pretty neighborhood," she commented, taking in the trees and freshly painted house trim and flowering plants, the scatter of kids riding over the uneven sidewalk on bikes and skateboards.

A few of them called out to Alex. Bess found herself being given the once-over by a group of teenage boys before they sent hoots and whistles and thumbs-up signs in Alex's direction.

"Ah, the first stamp of approval." But she rubbed her damp palm surreptitiously against her skirt before taking his hand. "Did you used to ride bikes along the sidewalk?"

"Sure."

Battling nerves, she strolled with him toward the house. "And sit on the curb in the summer and lie about girls?"

"I didn't have to lie," he told her with a wicked grin.

He glanced up the steps as the door opened and Mikhail came out, Griff on his hip.

"You're late again." He started down, jiggling Griff. "She missed the turn."

"He's always late." Mikhail smiled. "You're Bess."

"Yes. Hello." She held out a hand and found that his was hard as rock. Griff had already leaned over to give Alex a kiss, and now, still puckered, he leaned toward Bess. Laughing, she pressed her mouth to his. "And hello to you, too, handsome."

"Griff likes the ladies," Mikhail told her. "Takes after his uncle."

"Don't start," Alex muttered.

Mikhail ignored him and continued to study Bess until she was fighting the need to squirm. "Do I have dirt on my face, or what?"

"No, sorry." He shifted his gaze to his brother. "You're improving, Alexi," he said in Ukrainian. "This one is well worth a few sweaty mornings in the gym."

"Tak." He skimmed a hand down to the nape of Bess's neck. "If you tell her about that, I'll strangle you in your sleep."

Mikhail's grin flashed. The resemblance was startling, Bess thought. Those wild, dark looks, that simmering sexuality. And the child had the looks, as well, she realized. Lord help the women of the twenty-first century.

"Guy talk?" she asked.

"Bad manners," Mikhail said apologetically, deciding he liked not only her unusual looks, but the intelligence in her eyes, as well. Yes, indeed, he thought, Alex was definitely improving. "I was complimenting my brother on his taste. Take her in, Alex. Griff wants to watch the kids ride awhile."

"Sydney?" he asked as he mounted the steps.

"She's here, but she's tired."

"She works too hard."

"There is that." The grin spread again. "And she's pregnant."

Alex stopped, turned. "Yeah?" He went down the steps again to catch Mikhail and Griff in a bear hug. "It's good?"

"It's great. We want our children close, our family big."

"You're off to the right start." He grabbed Bess's hand as Mikhail lifted Griff onto his shoulders and crossed the street. Griff was clapping his hands and shouting toddler gibberish to the other kids. "I'm still trying to get used to him being a papa, and now he's going to have another."

She'd forgotten her nerves. Perhaps the child's sweet, unaffected kiss had done it. She slipped an arm around Alex's waist. "Come on, Uncle Alex. I want to meet the rest of them."

"They're loud," he warned as they started back up the door.

"I like loud."

"They can be nosy."

"So can I."

At the door, he took both of her hands. He'd brought women into his home before, but it had never been important. This was vital. "I love you, Bess." Before she could speak, he kissed her, then pushed open the door.

They certainly were loud, Bess discovered. No one seemed to mind if everyone talked at once, or if the big, droopy-eared dog barked and raced around the living room to hide behind chairs. And they were nosy, though they were charming with it. She'd hardly had a chance to get her bearings before she was sitting next to Alex's father, Yuri, and being cagily interrogated.

"So you write stories for TV." He nodded his big, shaggy head approvingly. "You have brains."

"A few." She smiled up at Zack when he offered her a glass of wine.

"Rachel says more than a few." He sent his wife a wink as she sat with her hands folded over her enormous belly. "She's been watching your show."

"Oh, yeah?"

"I admit I was curious." Rachel wanted to shift to get comfortable, but she knew it was useless. "After we met, I taped it a couple of times. Then, when I gave in to Zack's hounding me about taking maternity leave, I realized how easy it is to get hooked. I'm not sure I've got all the characters straight yet, but it's amazingly entertaining. Nick's caught it with me." She glanced at her brother-in-law.

To his credit, Nick didn't blush, but he did squirm. "I was just keeping you company." He might have come a long way from trying to prove his manhood with gangs like the Cobras, but even at nearly twenty-one, he wasn't quite secure enough to admit he'd gotten caught up in the "Secret Sins" of Millbrook. He shrugged, shook back his shaggy blond hair, then caught the quick grins of his family. "It wasn't like I was really watching." His green eyes glinted with humor. "Except for the babes."

"That's what they all say." Bess smiled back, enjoying him. Too bad he wasn't an actor, she thought. Those brooding good looks—tough, with just a hint of vulnerability beneath—would shine on-screen. "So, who's your type, Nick? LuAnne, our sensitive ingenue with the big, weepy eyes, who suffers in silence, or the scheming Brooke, who uses her sexuality to destroy any man who crosses her?"

Considering, he ran his tongue around his teeth. "Actually, I go for Jade. I've got this thing for older women."

Zack caught him in a headlock.

"Hey." Nick laughed, not bothering to try to free himself. "We're having a conversation here. I'm trying to make time with Alex's lady."

"Kill him in the other room, will you?" Alex said easily. "We have to eat in here."

"I watch your show many times," Nadia said as she popped in from the kitchen. Alex's mother's handsome face was flushed pink from oven heat. "I like it."

"Well, that Vicki's not hard to watch." Zack stood behind his wife now, rubbing her shoulders.

"Men always go for the cheap floozies," Rachel put in. "How about you, Alex? Caught any 'Secret Sins'?"

"No." Not that he'd admit. "McNee keeps me up on what's happening in Millbrook."

"It must be hard." Sydney, looking pale but blissfully relaxed in her corner of the couch, sipped her ginger ale. "The pace."

"It's murder." Bess grinned. "I love it."

"So, how is it you meet Alexi?" Yuri asked.

"He arrested me."

There was a moment of silence, while Alex aimed a killing look at Bess. Then a burst of laughter that sent the dog careening around the room again.

"Did I miss a joke?" Mikhail demanded as he swung through the door with Griff.

"No." Rachel chuckled again while her brother sat

on the arm of the couch, beside his wife. "But I have a feeling it's going to be a good one. Come on, Bess, this I have to hear."

She told them, while Alex interrupted a half-dozen times to disagree or correct or put in his own perspective. Even as they sat at the big old table to enjoy Nadia's pot roast, they were shouting with laughter or calling out questions.

"He put you in a cell, but you still go out with him." This from Mikhail.

"Well." Bess ran her tongue over her teeth. "He is kind of cute."

With a hearty laugh, Yuri slapped his son on the back. "The ladies, they always say so."

Alex scooped up potatoes. "Thanks, Papa."

"Is good to be attractive to women." He wiggled his brows at his wife. "Then, when you pick one, she is helpless to resist."

"I picked you," Nadia told him, passing biscuits to Nick. "You were very slow. Like a bear with, ah…" She struggled for the right word. "Soft brains." She ignored Yuri's snort of objection. "He did not come to court me. So I courted him."

"Every time I turn, there she is. In my way." When he looked at his wife, Bess saw memories and more in his eyes. "There was no prettier girl in the village than Nadia. Then she was mine."

"I liked your big hands and shy eyes," she told him. Her smile was quick and lovely. "Soon you were not so shy. But my boys," she added, turning the smile on Bess, "they were never shy with the girls."

"Why waste time?" On impulse, Alex put a hand on Bess's cheek and turned her face to his. Her smile was puzzled. Then surprise shot into her eyes as he covered her mouth with his. Not a quick, friendly kiss, this, but a searing one that made her head buzz.

She had no way of knowing that he'd never kissed a woman not of his family at his mother's table. Nor that by doing so, he was telling those he loved that this was *the* woman.

As the table erupted with applause, Bess cleared her throat. "No," she managed. "Not a bit shy."

Nadia blinked back tears and raised her glass. She understood what her son had told her and felt the bittersweet pleasure that came from knowing the last of her children had given his heart. "Welcome," she said to Bess.

A little confused, Bess reached for her glass as all the others were lifted. "Thank you." She sipped, relieved when the chattering started again.

How easy to fall in love with them, she realized. All of them were so warm, so open, so comfortable with each other. Her parents would never have had such a sweetly intimate conversation at the table. Nor had they ever embraced her with the verve and passion both Yuri and Nadia showed their children.

Was this what she'd been missing all of those years? Bess wondered. Had lacking something like this caused her to be so socially clumsy as a child, and, making up for it, so socially active as an adult?

Still, what she had had, and what she hadn't, had forged her into what she was, so she couldn't regret it. Well, perhaps a little, she mused, falling unknowingly into the family tradition by sneaking the dog bits of food under the table. It was hard not to regret it a little when you saw how lovely it could be to be part of such a solid whole.

Absorbing everything, she glanced around the table. And found Mikhail's eyes on her. This time she smiled. "You're doing it again," she told him.

"Yes. I want to carve you."

"I beg your pardon?"

"Your face." He reached out to take it in his hand. The conversation continued around them, as if he handled women at the dinner table regularly. "Very fascinating. Mahogany would be best."

Amused, she sat patiently while he turned her face this way and that. "Is this a joke?"

"Mikhail never jokes about his work," Sydney commented, coaxing one more green bean into her son. "I'm just surprised it's taken him so long to demand you sit for him."

"Sit?" She shook her head, and then her eyes widened as it all came together. "Oh, of course. Stanislaski. The artist. I've seen your work. Lusted after it, actually."

"You will sit for me, and I'll give you a piece. You'll choose it."

"I could hardly turn down an offer like that."

"Good." Satisfied, he went back to his meal. "She's very beautiful," he said to Alex, in such an offhand way that Bess laughed.

"I'd say that Stanislaski taste runs to the odd, but your wife proves me wrong."

Mikhail brushed a hand over Sydney's halo of auburn hair, stroked a finger down her classically lovely face. "There are different kinds of beauty. You'll come to the studio next week."

"Don't bother to argue." Sydney caught Mikhail's hand, squeezed it. "It won't do you a bit of good."

At the other end of the table, Rachel winced. Nadia leaned closer, spoke gently. "How far apart?"

Rachel gave a little sigh. "Eight, ten minutes. They're very mild yet."

"What's mild?" Zack glanced at her, and then his mouth all but dropped to his knees. "Oh, God, now? *Now?*"

"Not this very minute." She would be calm, Rachel told herself and took a deep, cleansing breath to prove it. "I think you have time for some of Mama's cream cake."

"She's in labor." He gaped across the table at his equally panicked brother.

"We're not ready here." Nick stumbled to his feet. "We're ready back at home. I'm supposed to call the doctor, but I don't have the number."

"Mama does," Rachel assured her husband's younger brother. Then she lifted a hand to her husband's. "Take it easy, Muldoon. There's plenty of time."

"Time, hell. We're going now. Shouldn't we go now?" Zack demanded of Nadia.

She smiled and nodded. "It would be best for you, Zack."

"But, Mama—"

Rachel's protest was cut off by Nadia's gentle flow of Ukrainian, the gist of which had a great deal to do with placating frightened husbands.

"She should put her feet up," Mikhail announced. "This helped you, yes?"

"Yes," Sydney agreed. "But I think we should wait until she gets to the hospital."

"Nine-one-one." Alex shoved away from the table and sprang to his feet. "I'll call."

"Oh, sit down." Rachel waved an annoyed hand at him. "I don't need a cop."

"An ambulance," he insisted.

"I'm not sick, I'm in labor."

"I take her in the truck." Yuri was already up, prepared to lift his baby girl into his big arms. "We get there very fast."

While the men began to argue in a mixture of languages, Nadia rose quietly and went into the kitchen to call Rachel's obstetrician.

"I've already been through this," Mikhail was saying to Alex. "I know how to handle it."

"Ha." Their father pushed them both aside and pounded a fist on his broad chest. "Me, four times. You know nothing."

"We don't have the tape recorder or the music." Nick ran a hand through his flow of sandy hair. He was desperately afraid he'd be sick. Though no one was listening to him, he continued to babble. "The video camera. We've got to get the video camera."

"Honey, you want some water? You want some juice?" When she yelped, Zack turned dead white. "Another one? It hasn't been ten minutes, has it?"

"You're breaking my hand." Rachel shook it free and sent a pleading look to Sydney.

"Okay, guys, back off." The steel under velvet that made Sydney a successful businesswoman snapped into her voice. "Alex, go upstairs and get your sister a pillow for the ride. Yuri, go start the truck. That's a very good idea. Nick, you, Mikhail and Griff go back to your apartment and get what Rachel needs. We'll meet you at the hospital."

"How do you get there?" Mikhail demanded.

"I have a car." Bess was watching the family drama with fascinated eyes. "We can fit three in a pinch."

"Wonderful." Dispersing the troops with all the flair of a general, Sydney gave her husband a kiss and a shove. "Get going. Zack and Nadia will ride with Yuri and Rachel. I'll go with Alex and Bess."

As the next contraction hit, Rachel began to breathe slowly, steadily. "Sorry," she said to Bess in between breaths, "to put you out."

"No problem." She had to bite her tongue to prevent herself asking what it felt like to go into labor at a family dinner. There'd be time for that later.

"I called the doctor, and Natasha." Nadia came back into the room, pleased that Sydney had organized the troops. "Natasha and her family are coming."

"We should go." Zack helped Rachel to her feet and swallowed hard. "Shouldn't we go?"

By the time they arrived at the hospital, Sydney and Bess were the best of friends. It was difficult to be otherwise, when they'd been crammed together in one seat while Alex drove like a madman back to Manhattan.

They talked about clothes, a few mutual friends they'd discovered, and the Stanislaski men. Sydney agreed that it was very forbearing of Bess not to mention the quality of Alex's driving, after he'd been so critical of hers.

By the time they found their way to the maternity level, Rachel was already settled in a birthing room,

Zack had gotten over the first stages of panic, and Yuri was patting a pocket full of cigars.

"She's in the early stages," Nadia explained to them in the corridor. "Company is good for her."

Alex strode straight through the door, but Bess hung back. "I don't want to intrude," she said to Nadia.

"This is not intrusion. This is family." Nadia cocked her head. "Are you uneasy with childbirth?"

"Oh, no. I couldn't be, after I've written so many."

Alex poked his head back out. "How'd you research that, McNee?"

"I did rounds with an obstetrician." Her dimple winked out. "And found a few mothers-to-be who didn't object to having me hang around during labor and delivery. Have you ever seen one?"

"No." His eyes changed. Just like a man. "They, ah, show us films, just in case, but I've never been at ground zero."

"It's pretty great." She laughed, perfectly able to read his thoughts. "Don't worry. I'll hold your hand."

They passed the time in the big, airy birthing room telling stories, giving advice, joking with Zack once Mikhail and Nick arrived with Rachel's things. Griff was happily settled in with Zack's cook, Rio, so there was little to do but wait.

When Rachel felt like walking, they took turns leading her around the corridors, rubbing her back, making small talk to take her mind off the discomfort between contractions.

"I can see your mind working," Alex murmured to Bess. "'How can I use this?'"

"It's ingrained." She murmured her thanks when he passed her his cold drink. "Your family," she said, glancing around the room. "I've never known anyone like them. My parents—they'd be appalled to be expected to take part in something like this."

"It's our baby, too."

She smiled and lifted a hand to his cheek. "That's what I mean. You're all very special."

"I'm glad you're here." As he leaned over to kiss her, Yuri slapped him on the back.

"Now all my children make babies but you." He wiggled his brows at Bess. "You start soon, yes?"

"Papa..." Not sure how to take Bess's chuckle, Alex rose and spoke, firmly and quietly, in his mother tongue. "When I decide to make babies, I'll let you know."

"What decide?" Yuri gestured toward Bess. "She's the one you want, isn't she?"

"Yes."

Now Yuri gestured expansively with both hands. "Then?"

"I have my reasons for waiting. They're my reasons."

Though the shake of Yuri's head was a gesture of sadness, there was a twinkle in his eye. "How is it all my children are so stubborn?"

"How is it my papa is so nosy?"

With a laugh, Yuri embraced Alex and kissed both his cheeks. "Go take this pretty girl for a walk, steal some kisses. Your sister will be some time yet."

"That's advice I'll take." He reached for Bess's hand and pulled her to her feet. "Come on, let's get some air."

"Alexi." Bess had to quicken her pace to keep up with him. "Don't be angry with him. He didn't mean to embarrass you."

"Yes, he did, but I'm not angry with him."

"What were you two rattling on about?"

He punched the button for the elevator. "You know, I don't think I'll teach you any Ukrainian. It comes in too handy."

"But it's—"

"Rude," he finished for her, grinning. "I know."

By the time they came back again, Alex had taken his father's advice to heart. Bess's head was still spinning when they walked past the waiting room. It was Alex who spotted Nick, pacing and smoking in the smoking lounge like the cliché expectant daddy.

"How's it going, kid?"

"It's been an awfully long time." Nick's hand shook a bit as he lifted the cigarette to his lips. "I mean, Sydney was only in a couple of hours for Griff. It's getting really intense, and Rachel kicked me and the camera out. How come they don't do something?"

"I don't know a lot about it," Alex mused. "But I think babies come when they're ready."

"It's only been a little more than six hours." Bess moved in to soothe, touched that Nick should have such deep concern for his sister-in-law.

"Feels like six days," Zack commented as he staggered in. He plucked the cigarette from Nick's hand and took a deep drag. "She's swearing at me. I know what some of those names are now, even if they aren't in English."

"That's a good sign," Bess assured him. "It means things are moving along."

"She swore at the doctor, too." With a sigh, he passed the cigarette back to Nick. "But she didn't take a swing at *him*."

"If she missed," Alex commented, "she must be in really bad shape."

Wincing, Zack rubbed his shoulder. "She didn't. I'd better get back."

"Let's go give him some support," Alex began, but then he spotted a woman rushing off the elevator. "Tash!"

"Oh, Alex!"

Bess watched the woman fly into the waiting room, Gypsy hair flowing. There was concern in her eyes and laughter on her lips as she swung into Alex's arms.

"Alexi, how is Rachel?"

"Swearing at her doctor and punching Zack."

"Ah." She relaxed instantly. "That's good. Nick." She held out a hand for his. "Don't look so worried. Your niece or nephew will be along soon. Spence is parking the car. We were going to leave the children, but they were so disappointed, we brought them. Freddie's looking forward to seeing you."

Nick brightened a bit. "How's she doing?"

"She's taller than me now, and so pretty. Alex, where's Rachel?"

"I'll take you. Oh, this is Bess."

"Bess?" Natasha turned, one hand still on her brother's arm. Of course, she'd heard about Bess. West Virginia might be a fair distance from New York, but family business traveled fast on phone wires. "I'm sorry. I didn't realize."

"That's all right. You've got a lot on your mind." And then Bess said the first thing that came to hers. "What fabulous genes you all have."

Natasha's brows lifted. Then, below them, her eyes lit with laughter. "Rachel said I would like you. I hope we have time to talk before we leave town. I'm sorry to rush off."

"Don't worry about it. I think Nick and I'll go to the cafeteria, rustle up some food for this group."

Three hours later, Bess had delivered sandwiches and coffee, bounced Natasha's youngest daughter, Katie, on her knee and introduced herself to Spence Kimball and helped him entertain his very cranky son. She'd met Freddie and noted that the pretty, pixielike teenager was deep in puppy love with Nick.

As time dragged on, she added her support when Mikhail pressured his very tired wife to rest in the waiting room, took a few minutes to interrogate some nurses to help her beef up some hospital scenes and soothed Alex's nerves as his sister's labor reached the final stages.

"It won't be much longer."

"That's what they said an hour ago."

They were standing in the waiting room. Alex refused to sit. After a yawn and a good stretch, Bess wrapped her arms around him.

"She's fully dilated, and the baby was crowning. The last glance I had of the fetal monitor showed a really strong heartbeat. A fast one. I think it's a girl."

"How do you know so much?"

"Research." She settled her head on his shoulder. "I was figuring earlier that I've delivered twelve babies, including one set of twins. In a matter of speaking."

When her voice slurred, he tipped up her chin. "You're asleep on your feet, McNee. I should have sent you home."

"You couldn't have pried me away."

No, that was true, he realized. It was just one more aspect to her beauty. "I owe you."

"Then pay up." She lifted her mouth, sighing into the kiss.

"Mama." Though he'd enjoyed watching his brother, Mikhail shot to his feet when he spotted his parents in the doorway.

"We have a new member of the family." There were tears in Nadia's eyes and in Yuri's as he stood with his arm tight around his wife.

"What is it?" Nick and Alex demanded together.

"You will come see. They bring the baby to the glass in a moment."

"Rachel is resting." Yuri dashed away a tear. "You will kiss her good-night soon."

They trooped out together, to wait by the nursery window for the first glimpse.

"I'm an uncle," Nick said to Freddie. The girl's cheeks turned pink as he gave her a hard hug. "Hey, there's Zack." He kept his arm around her as his brother walked forward, holding a tiny bundle. The bundle was squalling, and Zack was grinning from ear to ear.

He held the baby up. Atop the curling black hair was a bright pink bow.

"It's a girl," Alex murmured, and held Bess hard against him. "She's beautiful."

"Man" was the best Nick could do. "Oh, man." Overcome for a moment, he glanced down and found himself looking at Freddie, who was still tucked under his arm. He drew back, brushed a fingertip along her cheek and caught a tear on the tip. "What's this?"

"It's just so sweet." Freddie's eyelashes were spiky and her eyes swam as she looked up at him. He thought for a moment—an uncomfortable moment—that it would be easy to drown in those eyes.

"Yeah, it's great." He let out a careful breath. She was his cousin, he reminded himself. Well, a kind of cousin. And she was hardly more than a kid. "I, ah, don't have a handkerchief or anything."

"It's all right." Freddie felt a drop roll down her cheek, but she didn't mind. After all, these were the very best kind of tears. "Do *you* ever think about having babies?" she asked with disarming candor.

"Having—" Nick would have stepped back then, way back, but the family was crowding him in. "No," he said firmly, and made himself look away from her damp, glowing face. "No way."

"I do." She sighed and let her head rest against his arm.

Mikhail was whispering something to Sydney that had her nodding and wiping away tears. Behind Freddie, Natasha shifted Katie in her arms and turned to her husband. He had one hand on Freddie's shoulder, and his sleeping son lay curved on his own.

"Every one is a miracle."

He bent his head to kiss her damp cheeks. "Just say the word anytime you decide you'd like another miracle of our own."

"I am a man blessed." Yuri grabbed the closest body. It happened to be Bess's, and she found herself whirled in a circle. "Two grandsons. Now three granddaughters." He tossed Bess up. She came down laughing, gripping his shoulders.

"Congratulations." She pleased him enormously by kissing him firmly on the mouth. "Grandpapa."

"It's a good day." He reached in his pocket. "Have a cigar."

Chapter 10

Rosalie considered herself an excellent judge of people, and she had already decided Bess was one strange lady. But she kept coming back.

Sure, the money was good, Rosalie thought as she sat drinking a diet soda in Bess's basement office. And for a woman with a retirement plan, that had to be number one. Yet it was more than making an extra buck that kept her taking the trip up and across town several days each week. More, too, that kept her hanging around after they finished what Bess liked to call 'consulting sessions.'

Rosalie was human enough to get a charge out of being connected, however remotely, to the entertainment world. She couldn't deny that she'd been excited, awed and impressed when she watched a couple of tapings.

But there was another factor, a much more basic one. Rosalie enjoyed Bess's company.

Besides being a strange lady, Bess had class. Rosalie didn't figure a person had to possess class to recognize it in another. Class wasn't just a matter of pedigree— though she'd discovered Bess had one. It was more than having an old lady in the DAR, or an old man in *Who's Who*. It was hazier than that. Though Rosalie couldn't quite come up with the terms she wanted, she had recognized in Bess those rare and often nebulous qualities, grace and compassion.

She was procrastinating over taking the trip back downtown by dawdling over her drink. Bess didn't seem to mind if Rosalie hung around while she worked. In the few weeks since they'd hooked up, Rosalie had noted that Bess worked hard and long. Harder, in Rosalie's opinion, than she herself, or any of the other ladies in her profession. Certainly Bess's hours were longer.

It amused Rosalie to compare the two. In fact, she and Bess had gotten into a very interesting discussion on the similarities and differences between Bess's selling her mind and Rosalie her body.

What a kick that had been, Rosalie thought now, while Bess typed and mumbled. Philosophical discussions weren't the norm in Rosalie's world.

The simple term she had not quite grasped for their relationship was *friendship*. They had become friends.

"How late you gonna work?" Rosalie asked, and Bess glanced up absently from the computer screen.

"Oh...not much longer." Her eyes were still slightly unfocused when she blew her hair away from them. Brock was on the verge of seducing Jessica. "I just had this idea for a little twist on a scene for tomorrow." She smiled then. It was quick, and a little wicked. "Of course, several members of the cast are going to want to murder me when I toss this at them in the morning. But that's show biz."

Rosalie took a drag on her cigarette. "What time did you get in here this morning?"

"Today? About nine-thirty. I was…" She thought of Alex. "Running a little late."

Lips pursed, Rosalie looked at the fake designer watch on her wrist. "And it's after seven now." Her grin flashed. "Girlfriend, you'd only put in half that many hours in my line of work."

"Yeah, but I get to sit down." Bess rubbed at the dull ache in the back of her neck. She really was going to have to work on her posture. "Hungry?" she asked. "Want to order something in?"

With a little tug of regret, Rosalie stabbed out the cigarette. "No. I gotta get to work, too."

"You could take the night off." Casually Bess ran a finger lightly over the keyboard. "Maybe we could catch a movie."

Chuckling, Rosalie dug in her purse for a mirror to check her makeup. "You said you weren't going to try to reform me."

"I lied." Bess sat back in her chair while Rosalie painted her mouth bloodred. She'd tried very hard not to pontificate, not to pressure, not to preach. And thought she had succeeded. But she hadn't tried not to care. That would have been useless. "I really worry about you. Especially since the last murder."

The odd twisting in Rosalie's stomach had her shifting her eyes from her compact mirror to Bess. She couldn't remember if anyone had ever worried about her before. Certainly not in years. "Didn't I tell you I could take care of myself?"

"Yes, but—"

"No buts about it, honey." With a second dip into her purse, Rosalie pulled out a stiletto. One flick of the wrist, and the long, razor-sharp blade zipped out. "What I can't handle, this can."

Bess managed to close her mouth, but her eyes stayed riveted to the knife. In the overhead lights, it gleamed silver, bright as sudden death. She couldn't say it was elegant. But it was fascinating, deathly fascinating. "Can I?"

With a shrug of her shoulders, Rosalie passed the weapon to her. "Don't mess with the blade," she warned. "It's as sharp as it looks."

Bess took a good grip on the handle, twisting her wrist this way and that, like a fencer. She wondered if Jade/Josie might carry one. She was already imagining a scene where the tormented Jade found the knife— maybe with the blade smeared with blood—in one of her practical handbags. No, her briefcase. Better.

"Have you ever—"

"Not yet." Rosalie held out a hand to take it back. "But there's always a first time." She pressed the button, and the blade whisked away again. "So don't lose any sleep over me." After dropping the weapon back into her bag, she took out an atomizer and sprayed scent generously on her skin. The air bloomed with roses. "Couple more months, I'll have enough put away. I'm going to be spending the winter in the Florida sunshine while you slog through dirty snow." She rose, tugging her tight off-the-shoulder top provocatively down, so that the rise of her breasts swelled invitingly over it. "See you around."

"Wait." Bess scrambled through her own purse and

came up with her mini recorder. "If it won't bother your ethics, I thought you might use this." At Rosalie's wry glance, Bess's cheeks heated. "I don't mean to record that part. Just the streets, conversations with the other women, maybe a couple of, ah…transactions."

"You're the boss." Taking the recorder, Rosalie slipped it away.

"Be careful," Bess added, though she knew Rosalie would laugh.

She did, sending a last cocky look over her bare shoulder. "Girlfriend, I'm always careful."

Still chuckling, Rosalie headed down the narrow corridor toward the freight elevator. She was already picturing the way Bess's eyes would pop out when she listened to the tape and discovered that her "consultant" had recorded *everything*. The prospect of pulling such a fine joke had her grinning as the doors slid open. Her amusement died a quick death when Alex walked off.

While they eyed each other with mutual suspicion, Alex pressed two fingers to the Door Open button. "How's the moonlighting going, Rosalie?"

"It passes the time."

When she started past him, he raised an arm to block the elevator opening. "What do you know about Crystal LaRue?"

"I know she's dead." Rosalie fisted a hand on her hip, cocked it. "Something else you want?"

Alex let her see that her snide invitation only amused him. "What do you know about her before she was dead?"

"Nothing." She would have given him the same answer if she'd been Crystal's most intimate friend, but as it was, she was telling the simple truth. "I never met her. Heard she was new, didn't have a man yet."

"Now, I heard that, too," Alex said conversationally. "And I heard that Bobby wanted to make her one of his wives."

"Maybe. Bobby likes to start them young."

Alex struggled with his disgust. She'd been seventeen, he thought. A runaway who hadn't known the rules and would never have a chance to learn them. "Did Bobby roust her, put on the pressure?"

"Can't say."

"Can't say? Or won't?"

Rosalie opened the hand on her hip and began to drum her fingers there. "Listen, I don't know what Bobby did. I've been keeping out of his way lately."

Saying nothing, Alex studied her face. The bruising had faded. "Seems to me Bess is paying you enough that you could stay out of his way altogether."

"That's my business."

"And hers," Alex said evenly. "I don't want him finding out about this sideline of yours and going after her." His eyes were cold and passionless. "Then I'd have to kill him."

"You think I'd turn Bobby on to her?" Arrogance was sidelined as fury snapped into Rosalie's voice. "I *owe* her."

"What?"

"Respect," she said, with an innate and graceful dignity that had Alex softening. "She had me eat at her table. She even said I could stay in her extra bedroom. Like a guest." Her lips thinned at Alex's expression. "Don't sweat it, honey. I didn't take her up on it. Sure, she's paying me, and maybe you don't think that's any different than me taking money from some slob off the street. But she treats me like somebody. Not some *thing,* some*body.*" Embarrassed by her own vehemence, she shrugged. "She doesn't have the sense not to."

"She's got sense, all right. Not all good." Alex's lips twitched, even as Rosalie's did. "Maybe she hasn't gone so wrong here. I just don't want her hurt."

"Neither do I." Rosalie tapped a scarlet nail on his chest. "You got a bad case, cop. Stars in your eyes." The little wisp of envy came and went, almost unnoticed. "Make sure you keep them in hers, or you'll answer to me."

His grin flashed before he could prevent it. The charm of it nearly had Rosalie changing her mind about cops. "Yes, ma'am." Like Bess, he wanted to say something that would stop her from going back on the streets. Unlike Bess, he accepted that there was nothing that would do it.

"Maybe I see why she's so stuck on you." When he moved his blocking arm, she stepped into the elevator, turned. "You be good to her, Stanislaski. She deserves good."

The elevator doors clunked shut. Alex stood studying them a moment before he turned and wandered down the corridor to find Bess.

She was bent over the keys, rapping out a machine-gun fire of words onto the monitor. Her fingers moved like lightning, but her eyes were far away. In Millbrook, he thought, smiling to himself.

She had her legs crossed under her, up on the chair. The way her shoulders were hunched, he imagined her muscles would complain loudly the moment she came back to earth.

She was wearing a skirt again, a little leather number in bold blue that was hiked high up on her thighs. The hot-pink blouse she'd tucked into it should have clashed with her hair, but it didn't. The blouse looked like silk and was carelessly shoved up to her elbows. A half-dozen gold bracelets clanged at her wrist as she worked. Rings flashed on her fingers, and the big Gypsy hoops she wore at her ears peeked out of her tousled hair.

His heart ached with love for her. And his loins… Alex let out a little breath. He wanted, quite simply, to devour her. Inch by delicious inch.

What the hell was he going to do, he wondered, when she tried to slither out of his life? He was sure she would, as she'd done with others before. He could lock her up, carry her off. He could beg or threaten. He already knew he would do whatever he had to in order to keep her in his life.

What had ever made him think he would one day find some nice, pretty woman with simple tastes and a quiet style? Someone who would be content to sit home while he worked his crazy hours? Who would have and help him raise the houseful of children he so badly wanted?

With Bess, nothing was simple, nothing was quiet. She would never be content to sit home but would badger him incessantly, picking at him until he gave in and talked about the darker aspects of his work, those pieces of his life that he wanted to keep locked away from everyone who mattered. As for children… He didn't know how the devil to get and keep a ring on her finger, much less ask her to help make a family.

Being in love with her left him helpless, made him

stupid, brought him a kind of fear he'd never faced as a cop. Not fear for his life. Fear for his heart.

He could only take his own advice and leave things as they were. Handle each day until she was so used to him she'd want to stay.

As he watched, she stopped typing, lifted a hand to her neck for a quick, impatient rub. Her skirt hiked higher as she shifted. It took all his control not to lick his lips. She punched a few buttons, had the machine clicking. A moment later, the printer beside her began to hum.

With a smile on his face and lust in his heart, Alex closed the door quietly at his back. Locked it.

She jumped like a rabbit when his hands came down on her shoulders. "Didn't anyone ever teach you to sit in a chair?"

"Alexi." She pressed a hand to her galloping heart. "You scared— Oh…" Her sigh was long and heartfelt as he massaged away the aches. "That's wonderful."

"You're going to do permanent damage if you keep sitting like that all day."

"I was planning on soaking in a hot tub for two or three days." She leaned into his hands.

"Where's Lori?"

"She wasn't feeling too terrific." As the printer continued to rattle, Bess closed her eyes. "I told her I was leaving, too. Then I snuck back. I wanted to make a few changes for tomorrow." She brought her hand up to one of his, skimming her fingers over it to the wrist. "You said you might have to work late."

"Lead fizzled. We'll work on tracing the heart necklace down, but that's better during business hours."

"Trace it down?"

"Hit the jewelers," he explained, "see if we can track down to when it was bought. Long shot, but…"

"Do you think the heart has a personal meaning for him?"

"Like some woman broke his heart, so he gives them a symbol of it before he whacks them?" He gave a little grunt as he continued to knead her muscles. "It's a little too obvious to dismiss. Psychiatric profile figures him as sexually inadequate on a normal level, so he pays for women to perform. He wants them and detests himself for that, as much as he detests them for being available. The fact that he goes through a short courtship routine shows that—" He broke off as she reached for a pad. "Hold on, McNee." He gave her shoulders a hard squeeze. "I don't know how you do it. One minute I'm thinking about getting you out of these clothes and the next you've got me talking about a case." He pressed a kiss to the top of her head. "No notes."

Her fingers retreated from the pad, but with obvious reluctance. "I like hearing you talk about your work. I want you to be able to talk to me about anything."

"Apparently I can. Even the stuff I don't want you to hear. I've got a problem with you, Bess. You won't let me tuck you into that nice safe corner where I want you to be."

"You only think that's where you want me to be." Smiling, she tugged his hand around so that she could kiss it. "You like me right where I am." Turning his hand over, she pressed her lips to his palm. "I'm going to stay there."

She felt his fingers tense, then relax slowly as he spread them over her cheek. "I was watching you while you worked."

A rippling thrill raced through her at the words and at the shimmer of desire she heard in them. "Were you?"

"And thinking." His hands slid down over her breasts, sampled their weight, molded them. "Fantasizing."

Her head fell back against the chair. Her breathing quickened. "About?"

"The things I'd like to do with you." Through layers of silk, he caught her nipples, tugging gently. "To you."

When she tried to shift in the chair to face him, he increased the pressure, held her still. Her dazzled eyes focused on the monitor. She could still see the ghost of herself there, and his hands moving. Sliding. Stroking.

Impossibly erotic to see, and to feel. Dry-mouthed, she watched his fingers undo her buttons and saw the dark shadow of his hair as he pressed a hot mouth to her throat. She lifted a hand, hooked it around his neck as she tilted her head to offer more.

"I can shut down in thirty seconds."

He bit her lightly, just above the collarbone. "I'm not going to give you a chance to shut down."

She laughed shakily, even as she lifted her other arm to capture him in a reverse embrace. "I meant the computer."

He would have laughed himself, but he'd stopped breathing. "I know what you meant."

"But I—" He slipped a hand under her skirt, and it was so sudden, so searing. Before she could gasp out in shock, he had driven her ruthlessly to the peak.

"I watched you." Each word burned his throat as she poured into his hand. "I wanted you." Half demented, he whipped her up again, pressing his face into her neck as her body shuddered. "Do you remember the first time I found you here?"

"What?" She couldn't remember her own name. There was only this need he was ruthlessly building inside her again. "Alexi, please. Come home with me. I need—" This time she cried out as the third high, hard wave swamped her.

"I wanted you then." In one violent move, he spun her chair around and dragged her to her feet, and her already weakened system went limp at what she read in his face. "Let me show you exactly what I wanted."

This wasn't the smooth and patient lover of the night before. This man with the fierce eyes and bruising hands wouldn't cuddle her and whisper exotic endearments. This was the warrior she'd only glimpsed. He would plunder. Whether or not she was ready, he was showing her that dark, reckless side of him that he kept so tightly controlled.

In the moment when he stared at her, the look in his eyes hot and concentrated, she understood that excitement took a twist into the primitive when it carried a touch of fear.

He fisted a hand in her hair and yanked her against him. His body was like rock, vibrating from deep within, as if from an erupting volcano. For that moment, there was only the strength and the fury of the inevitable.

His mouth burned over hers, his tongue diving deep, while his free hand tugged the snap of her skirt free. He wanted her flesh, craved it. That heated silk, those alluring curves and taut muscles. Time and place had lost all impact. There was only here. Only now. Only her.

Shivery fingers of fear ran up her spine. She hadn't known what it was to be wanted this way. It was so huge, so violent, so glorious. Before, he had given her more than she had ever dreamed of. Now, he seemed compelled to give her more than she had ever *dared* dream.

Beside them, the printer stopped its practical clatter and dropped into a hum. The low, waiting sound was drowned out by the thundering of her heart. The bright working lights overhead seemed to dim as he took her hips and pressed her hard against him.

"You make a war inside me," he muttered as his teeth scraped roughly down her throat. "There's no end to it. No peace from it. Say my name. I want to hear you say my name."

"Alexi." When his lips crushed down on hers again, he felt her breathe it, warm, into his mouth. "Take me. Now."

The wild need slammed into her so that her mouth was as turbulent, her hands as frantic. Dozens of tiny explosions burst inside her body, merging into one huge tumult of sensation that battered, bruised and bewitched. She was all but sobbing with it as she tugged and pulled at his clothes.

She was quivering for him. Couldn't stop. The power and pressure growing inside her was all but unbearable. And the heat, the furnace blast of heat, had her skin slicked and her head spinning. Glorying in it, she brought her mouth to his bare shoulder, savoring the taste of flesh. His busy, bruising hands had her bearing down with teeth and nails. His breath hissed in her ear as she reached down to curl impatient fingers around him.

Confused and tangled phrases whirled in his mind. He heard them burst from his lips to hang on the thick air as he fought to catch his breath. On an oath, he gripped her shoulders and hauled her back.

Her face was flushed, her eyes were glowing. He'd marked that ivory skin. He could see where his fingers had pressed, where his roughened cheeks had scraped. But the part of him that would have been shocked by his lack of care was far overshadowed by a dark and desperate desire to conquer, to consume. To mate.

He saw them now as brands, signs that made her his. Only his.

With a jerk of his head, he tossed his hair back. The way it swayed and settled had new emotion burning her throat. Naked, muscles bunched as if to fight, he looked so magnificent he dazzled her eyes.

Then he looked at her, and the smile that had nearly formed on her face froze into wonder.

"No one makes you feel like this but me."

His accent had thickened, and the sound of it sent chills along her heated skin. She could only shake her head.

"No one touches you like me." He took his hands from her shoulders and gripped the bodice of her chemise. "No one has you, ever again, but me."

"Alexi—"

But he shook his head. He could feel her heart pounding under his hands, and his own chest was heaving. "Understand me. You're mine now." Her eyes widened with shock as he jerked his hands and ripped the chemise in half. "All of you."

He pushed her back against the table, watching the play of stunned excitement over her face. Yes, he wanted to excite her. And shock her. Stagger her.

His fingers dug into her hips as he lifted her. He was

braced, straining like a stallion at the bit. "Hold on to me," he demanded, but her fluttering hands slid off his sweat-slick arms. His breath heaved out, his fingers dug into her smooth, taut flesh. "Hold!"

She met his eyes then, and felt that wild whip of power. Drunk on it, she gripped his hair and wrapped her legs around him. When he plunged inside her, her body arched back, absorbing that first rocketing flash of heat. It was like being consumed from the inside out.

She felt the cool surface of the table against her back first, then his weight on her. Greedy for more, she tightened around him, matching his fast, frantic rhythm, dragging his mouth back to hers so that they could echo the intimacy with their tongues.

He lost himself. There was only her now, and the need to possess her. The desperate craving to be possessed by her. Images reeled through his brain, all dark and sharp-edged, until he thought he would go mad.

And went mad.

In a frenzy of movement, he dragged her farther onto the table, crushing papers, knocking aside empty cups, scattering pencils. He couldn't take his eyes from her face, the way her eyes clouded, like fog over moss, the way her lips trembled with each gasping breath. There was a bloom on her skin now, a rose under glass. He was hammering himself into her, empowered by a rabid fury of emotion that had its razor-tipped fingers around his throat.

Too much, she thought frantically. Never enough. The harsh overhead lights fractured into rainbows that blinded her eyes. They seemed to arch around his head, but she didn't think of angels. His eyes were so dark, so fiercely focused. Even as her own grew leaden, she refused to close them.

Oh, to watch him wanting her. Taking her.

She couldn't understand the words he murmured, over and over again. But she understood what was in those eyes. They were tearing each other apart, and they couldn't stop. The animal had taken over, and it had diamond-sharp claws and jagged teeth.

There was nothing left but the sound of their mixed labored breathing, the solid slap of flesh against flesh, and the heady scent of hot, desperate sex.

She felt his body go rigid, felt the rippling muscles in the arms she gripped turn to stone. He groaned out her name as his eyes sharpened like daggers. When he poured himself into her, she cried out in triumph, then again in wonder as he drove her over that crumbling edge with him.

The strength that had screamed through him switched off like a light, and he collapsed, panting, his full weight on her. Fighting for breath, he wallowed in her hair, drawing in the scent of it and the fragrance they'd made together. He couldn't find his center, the focus that was so vital for survival. He no longer had one without her.

God, he could feel her vibrating beneath him, shuddering from the aftershocks. And there were tears mixed with the dew of sweat on her face.

With breath still burning his lungs, he levered himself on his elbows and shook his head to try to clear it. At the movement, she made a small, whimpering sound in her throat that both aroused and dismayed. Trying to find the gentleness that had always been so easy for him, he shifted their positions and began to stroke her hair, her shoulders, her back.

Murmuring apologies, he cradled her like a child. "*Milaya*, I'm sorry. I hurt you. I must have hurt you. Don't cry."

"I'm not crying." But, of course, she was. He could feel the tears fall even as she ran kisses over his face and throat. "Just tell me you love me. Please tell me you love me."

"I love you. Shh." He covered her mouth tenderly with his. "You know I love you."

"I love you." She pressed those wet, shaky kisses to his cheeks, to his jaw. "You have to believe that I love you."

A hot fist clenched in his gut, but he kept his hands gentle. "Just let me hold you."

Tearing up again, she pressed her face to his shoulder. "Even now you don't believe me. Alexi, what more can I do?"

"I believe you." But they both knew he said it only to comfort. "You belong to me. I believe that."

"You're everything I want." She relaxed against him, satisfied that he would take that much.

"No more tears?"

"No."

He tilted her chin up to search her face. "How badly did I hurt you?"

"I don't think the results will be in for days." She smiled a little. "How badly did I hurt you?"

His eyes narrowed, and her smile widened. "You're not…upset?"

"About what?"

"I was an animal." With a hand that had yet to steady,

he brushed her tumbled hair out of her face. "I took you on a table like a lunatic."

"I know." After one long, satisfied sigh, she slid her body lazily over his. "It was wonderful."

"Yes?" Guilt began to turn to pride. "You liked it?"

After being so thoroughly ravished, it wasn't difficult to stroke his ego. "It was like being dragged off by some barbarian. I couldn't even understand what you were saying. It was exciting." She kissed his cheek. "Frightening." And the other. "It was also the most erotic experience of my life."

"You were crying."

"Alexi." She touched a hand to his face. "You didn't just overpower me. You overwhelmed me. No one's ever made me feel more wanted. More irresistible."

"I can't resist you, but I'm sorry I put bruises on you."

"I don't mind—under the circumstances." After another luxurious sigh, she glanced around the room. "I don't know how I'll ever work in here again, though."

Now he grinned, wickedly. "Maybe it'll inspire you."

"There is that." She shifted to straddle him and watched his sleepy eyes skim down to her breasts and back. Possibilities, she thought. There were definite possibilities in that look. "Being a cop, I imagine you've been through arduous physical training."

The possibilities had occurred to him, as well. "Absolutely."

"And you'd probably have amazing recuperative powers."

His brow lifted. "Under the right conditions."

"Good." To be certain she created them, she ran her hands over his still-gleaming chest.

With a half laugh, he caught her wrists. "McNee, wouldn't you rather pick this up in bed?"

For an answer, she leaned over, letting her lips hover a breath away from his. The tip of her tongue darted out to trace the shape of his mouth, to dip teasingly inside, then retreat. Slowly, she tilted her head. Softly, she tasted his lips. Achingly, achingly, she deepened the kiss.

"Does that give you a clue, Detective?"

Chapter 11

"I can't believe you want to spend the best part of a Saturday morning in a sweaty gym." Alex was stalling, even as he walked with Bess up the iron steps that led to Rocky's.

"It's your sweaty gym," Bess said, and kissed him.

The past few days had been almost like a honeymoon, she thought. If she took out the hours they'd both been at work. But they'd made the most of what time they'd had together, snuggling on the couch in her place, cooking a meal in his, wrestling in bed in both.

She was starting to hope that he believed she loved him. And, once he did, she wanted nothing more than for them to take that next step. The step that would lead to an authentic honeymoon, with all the trimmings.

"You picked me up at my gym yesterday," she pointed out.

"That wasn't a gym." There was the faintest trace of a masculine sneer in his voice. "That was an exercise palace. Fancy lighting, piped-in music. All those mirrors."

"At least I'll be able to see when my butt starts to drop."

He gave it a friendly pat. "I'll let you know."

"Do, and die," she said smartly, and pushed through the frosted glass doors.

She immediately thought of every bad boxing film she'd ever seen. The huge room echoed with grunts and slaps and thumps. It smelled of mildew and sweat and… She took a testing sniff and decided she didn't want to know what else. There were exposed pipes along the ceilings and walls, and there was a hardwood floor that looked as though it had been gouged by spikes. The boxing ring that was set up in one corner was already occupied by two compact, dancing men in tiny shorts who were trying to pop each other in the eye.

A trio of punching bags hung at strategic points. A half-naked man with a body like a cement truck was currently trying to whip the tar out of one of them.

Weights were being employed as well. She watched tendons bulge and muscles bunch.

They didn't worry about mirrors and lighting here. Nor did she spot any of the high-tech equipment she was accustomed to. This was down-and-dirty—squat, sweat and punch. She sincerely doubted there would be a juice bar in the vicinity, either.

"Had enough?" Alex asked. He was obviously amused at the thought of her stripping down to her leotard and having a go with the boys.

Bess closed her mouth, then answered his grin with a cool stare. "I haven't even started yet."

It was his turn to drop his jaw when she peeled off her sweatshirt. Beneath she wore a snug, low-cut crop top in zigzagging stripes of green and purple. As she shimmied out of her baggy street shorts, he shoved the discarded shirt in front of her.

"Come on, Bess, put your clothes on. Sweet Lord." The bottom half was worse. Over formfitting tights she had on a teeny strip of spandex that covered little more than a G-string. "You can't wear that in here."

"Is it illegal?" She bent over to stuff her sweats into her gym bag and heard the heavy thump of weights as they were dropped. Maintaining position, she turned her head and smiled at the pop-eyed man staring at her.

The catcalls and whistles started immediately, the sound swelling and bouncing off the cinder-block walls. Alex was very much afraid there would be a riot—one he was likely to incite himself. "Damn it, put something on before I have to kill somebody."

"They look harmless." She straightened again and lifted her arms to tie the short curls at the nape of her neck into a stubby ponytail. "Anyway, I came to work out." With a challenging grin, she flexed a muscle. "How much can you bench-press?"

"McNee, don't you dare—" He broke off with an oath as she blithely strolled across the room to chat with the weightlifter. The two hundred pounds of muscle began to babble like a teenager. Alex had no choice but to send out a warning snarl, much as a guard dog might to a pack of encroaching wolves, before he went after her.

She pulled it off, of course. He should have known she would. The men started out drooling, kicked over into laughing and finally wound up competing with each other to show her the proper way to perform squat lifts, chin-ups and leg curls.

Before an hour was over, she'd been shown pictures of wives and children, listened to sob stories over sweethearts and stopped being ogled—unless it was at a discreet distance.

"You sure you want to do this?" Alex asked again, tapping his gloved hands together.

"Absolutely." She smiled at Rocky as he himself laced up her gloves. "I couldn't leave without one sparring match."

"You watch out for his left—it's a good one," Rocky advised her. "Kid could've been a contender if he hadn't wanted to be a cop."

She winked at Rocky. "I've got fast feet. He won't lay a glove on me."

Two of her new admirers held open the ropes for her so that she could step into the ring. Enjoying the sensation, she adjusted her padded helmet. "Aren't we supposed to wear those funny retainers?"

"The what— Oh, mouth guards?" He couldn't resist, and he leaned over and kissed her to an accompaniment of hoots. "Baby, I'm not going to hit you." In a friendly gesture, he tapped his gloves to hers. "Okay, put your hands up." When she did, lifting them toward the ceiling, he rolled his eyes. "It's not an arrest, McNee." Patiently he adjusted her hands until they were in a defensive position.

"Now, you want to guard, see? Keep your left up, keep it up. If I come in like this—" he did a slow-motion jab at her jaw "—you block, jab back. That's it."

"And I fake with my left," she said, and did so.

"If you want." Lord, she was sweet. "Now try for

here." He tapped his own chin. "Go ahead, you don't have to pull it." When she punched halfheartedly, he shook his head. "No, you punch like a girl. Put your body behind it. Pretend I'm Dawn Gallagher."

Her eyes lit, and she swung full-out, only to come up solidly against his block. "Hey, that's good." Impressed, she swung again. "But I've got to move around, right? Fake you out with my grace and fancy footwork."

She did a quick boogie that had the onlookers clapping and Alex grinning at her. "You got style. Let's work on it."

He was enjoying himself, showing her the moves. And it certainly didn't hurt for a woman living in the city to learn how to defend herself with something more than an ammonia-filled water pistol.

"It's fun." She ducked her head as he'd shown her and tried two quick jabs with her left.

"Always room for another flyweight," Rocky called out to her. "Come on, Bess, body blow."

Chuckling, she aimed for Alex's midsection and dodged his light tap toward her chin. "You look so cute in gym shorts," she murmured.

"Don't try to distract me."

"Well, you do." She danced around him again, and, laughing, he turned toward her.

"Okay, that ought to—" He ended on a grunt when she connected hard with his jaw and set him down on his butt.

"Oh, God." She crouched instantly, battering his face with her gloves as she tried to stroke it. "Oh, Alexi, I'm sorry. Did I hurt you?"

He wiggled his jaw, sending her a dark look. "Right

cross," he muttered as men climbed through the ropes to cheer and hold Bess's arms in the air.

"I'm really sorry," Bess said again as they started down the iron steps. But she was fingering the little bit of tarnished metal Rocky had pinned—with some ceremony—to her sweatshirt. "You said not to pull my punches."

"I know what I said." He'd be lucky if he didn't have a bruise, Alex thought. And how the hell would he explain that? "You only got through because I was finished."

She ran her tongue over her teeth and stepped outside. "Uh-huh."

"Don't get smart with me, McNee." He snatched her up and swung her around. "Or I'll demand a rematch."

Wildly in love, she tossed her arms around his neck. "Anytime."

"Oh, yeah? How about…" He trailed off with a grimace as his beeper sounded. "Sorry."

"It's all right." She only sighed a little as he tracked down a phone and called in. As she stood beside him, watching his face, listening to his terse comments, she realized that their plans for a picnic in the park and some casual shopping were about to go bust.

"You have your cop's face on," she said when he hung up. "Do you have to go in?"

"Yeah." But he didn't tell her they'd found another victim. It was bad enough that he was spoiling their plans for the day. "It's probably going to take a while. I'm really sorry, Bess."

"Look." She framed his face with her hands. "I understand. This is part of it."

He brought those hands to his lips. "I..." But he didn't tell her he loved her, because she would echo the words, and it made him nervous to hear them. "I appreciate it," he said instead. "And I'll make it up to you."

"Tell you what—why don't I finish up what I have to do, then stop by the market? I'll make dinner. Something that won't spoil if it has to be warmed up a couple of times."

Though his mind was already drifting away from her, he managed a pained smile. "You're going to cook."

"I'm not that bad. I'm not," she insisted with a bit of a huff when he grinned. "I only burned the potatoes the other night because you kept distracting me."

"I guess it's the least I can do." He kissed her lightly once, then again, longer. "I'll try to call."

"If you can." She waved him off, then stood watching while he jogged down into the subway. With a quick laugh, she spun around, hugging herself.

She felt just like a cop's wife.

"I hope you don't mind me dropping by."

"Of course not." Rachel took a look at the bulging shopping bags in Bess's hands. "Been busy?"

"Whenever I get started with that little plastic card, I can't seem to stop." She dumped her purchases inside the apartment door. "You look wonderful. How can you look wonderful less than a week after going through childbirth?"

"Strong genes." Pleased in general, and with Bess in particular, Rachel kissed her on both cheeks. "Come sit down."

"Thanks. I— Oops." She dipped into the bag and pulled out a gold-foiled candy box. "For Mom."

"Oh." Rachel's eyes took on the glow a woman's get when she looks at a lover—or a five-pound box of exclusive chocolates. "I think you just became my best friend."

Chuckling, Bess dug into the bags again. "Well, I know that people tend to drop by with baby gifts." She held out a box wrapped in snowy white with bright red lollipops scattered over it. "And, though I couldn't resist the tradition, I figured you deserved something really sinful for yourself."

"I do." Rachel tucked the baby box under her other arm. "It's really sweet of you, Bess, and unnecessary. You and Alex already brought Brenna that wonderful stuffed dragon."

"That was from us. This is from me. It's a girl thing. I saw this tiny little white organdy dress with all these flounces and little pink bows and I couldn't resist."

Rachel's new-mother's heart melted. "Really?"

"I figure in another year she might want to wear motorcycle boots, so this may be your only chance to play dress-up."

"I swore that whatever I had, I wouldn't make sexist decisions in dress or attitude." She sighed over the box. "White organdy?"

"Six flounces. I counted."

"I can't wait to put her in it."

"Ah, company." Mikhail strode out of the bedroom with Brenna tucked in his arm. "Hello, Aunt Bess." He kissed both of her cheeks, then her mouth.

"You said you wouldn't wake her up." This from Rachel, who was already leaning over to coo.

"I didn't. Exactly. What's this?" Recognizing the gold foil box, he flipped it open and dived in.

"Mine," Rachel said in a huff. "If you eat more than one, I'll break your fingers."

"She was always greedy," he said over the first piece. "Where's Alexi?"

"He got called in."

"Good. Now you have time to sit down. I'll sketch you."

"Now?" Womanlike, Bess lifted a hand to her hair. "I'm not exactly dressed for it."

"I want your face." Obviously well used to making himself at home, he opened the drawer on an end table and rummaged for a pad. "Perhaps I'll do your body later. It's a good one."

Her laugh was quick. "Thanks."

"You might as well cooperate," Rachel told her, and crossed over to take the baby. "Once the artist in him takes over, you haven't got a chance."

"I'm flattered, really."

"There's no reason to be," he said absently as he unearthed a suitable pencil. "You have the face you were born with."

"Thank God that's not always true."

That caught his interest. "You had it fixed?"

"No. I just sort of grew into it."

"Not there," he told her before Bess could sit. "Over there, closer to the window, in the light. Rachel, when do I get the drink you promised me?"

"On its way." She stopped nuzzling Brenna long enough to look up. "What can I get you, Bess?"

"Anything cold—and a shot at holding the baby."

"I can accommodate you on both counts." Rachel laid her daughter gently in Bess's arms. "She hardly ever cries. And I think her eyes may stay blue. Like Zack's."

"She's a beauty." Bess leaned down to brush her lips over the curling dark hair and to draw in the indescribably sweet scent of baby. "Like all of you."

"Move," Mikhail ordered his sister. "You're in my way."

Shooting off a mild Ukrainian insult, she headed for the kitchen.

"Talk if you like." Mikhail gestured with his pencil, and began to sketch.

"It's one of my best things." She'd already forgotten to be self-conscious. "Where's Sydney and Griff?"

"Griff has the sniffles." The pencil was moving with quick, deft strokes over the pad. "Sydney fusses over him, but she says *I'm* fussing over him and sends me out on errands."

"Which he does by coming by and plaguing me," Rachel called out.

"She's happy to see me," Mikhail said. "Because she's lonely, with Zack and Nick over checking on the progress of the new apartment."

"Oh, that's right, you're moving." Comfortable, Bess tucked up her legs. "Alexi mentioned it."

"We need a bigger place. Of course, it was supposed to be ready a month ago, but things never run on time. I'll miss this one," she said, coming back in with a tray of cold drinks. "And having Nick underfoot. But I imagine he'll like having this place to himself."

Bess reached for her drink with her free hand, gently jiggling the baby with the other. "I guess he had as big a crush on you as Freddie has on him."

For a moment, Rachel only stared. Then she let out her breath in a quiet laugh. "Alex said you saw things."

"Just part of the job."

Rachel didn't consider herself a slouch in the reading-people department. "So, how big a crush do you have on Alexi?"

"The biggest." Bess smiled and rubbed her cheek over Brenna's. "He thinks I'm flighty. Fickle. But I'm not. Not with him."

"Why would he think that?"

"I have a varied track record. But it's different with him." When Bess lowered her head to murmur to the baby, Rachel glanced at her brother. They exchanged a great deal without uttering a word. "It makes me envy people like your sister, Natasha," Bess went on. "Those three beautiful children, a husband who after years together still looks at her as if he can't believe she belongs to him. Work she loves. I envy all that."

"You'd like a family?"

"I never had one."

Rachel knew it was the lawyer in her, but she couldn't help moving along the line of questioning. "Does it bother you that he's a cop?"

"Bother me?" Bess's brows lifted in surprise. "No. Do you mean, will I worry? I suppose I will. But it's not something I could change, or that I want to change. I love who he is."

"He's making you sad," Mikhail said quietly.

"No." Bess's denial was quick enough to startle the dozing baby. She soothed her automatically as she shook her head. "No, of course he isn't."

"I see what's in your eyes."

He would, she realized, and felt the warmth creep into her cheeks. "It's only that I know he doesn't trust me—my feelings. Or, I suppose, the endurance of my feelings. It's not his fault."

"He was always one to pick things apart." There was brotherly disgust in Mikhail's voice. "Never one to take anything on faith. I'll speak to him."

"Oh, no." This time, she laughed. "He'd be furious with both of us. All that Slavic pride and male ego."

Instantly Mikhail's eyes narrowed. "What's wrong with that?"

"Nothing." She grinned at Rachel. "Not a thing. I'll just wear him down in my own way. In fact, I'm going to start tonight. I'm cooking dinner. I thought maybe I could call your mother, find out if he has a favorite dish."

"I can tell you that," Rachel offered. "Anything."

"Well, that certainly widens my choices. Do you think she'd mind if I called her, asked for some pointers? My kitchen skills are moderate at best."

"She'd love it." Rachel smiled to herself, knowing her mother would hang up the phone and immediately start planning the wedding.

It was after midnight when Alex let himself into Bess's apartment with the key she'd given him. He was punchy with fatigue, and his head was buzzing from too much coffee. Those were usual things, as much a part of his work as filing reports or following a lead. But the sick weight in his stomach was something new.

He would have to tell her.

She'd left the television on. In an old black-and-white movie a woman screamed in abject terror and fled down a moonlit beach. As he shrugged out of his jacket, Alex moved across the room to switch it off. Before he reached the set, he saw her, curled on the couch.

She'd waited for him. The sweetness of that speared

through him as he crouched beside her. For so many years now, he'd come home alone, to no one. Gently he brushed the dark red curls from her cheek and replaced them with his lips. She stirred, murmuring. Her eyes fluttered open.

"I'm just going to carry you into bed," he whispered. "Go back to sleep."

"Alexi." She lifted a hand to rub over the cheek he hadn't shaved that morning. Her voice was thick with sleep, her eyes glazed with it. "What time is it?"

"It's late. You should have gone to bed."

She made a vague sound of disagreement and pushed up on one elbow. "I was waiting up, but the movie was so bad." Her laugh was groggy, and she rubbed her eyes like a child. "It zapped me." She circled her shoulders before leaning forward to kiss him. "You had a long day, Detective."

"Yeah." And maybe, because she was half-asleep, he could put off the rest. "So have you. I'll cart you in."

"No, I'm okay." She sat up, yawning. "Did you eat something?"

"I caught a sandwich. I'm really sorry, I tried to call."

"And got the machine," she said with a rueful nod. "Because I'd forgotten the paprika and had to run back out to the market."

"You cooked?" The idea both touched him and accented his guilt.

"I amazed myself." It felt good to settle against him when he joined her on the couch and slipped an arm around her. Cozy, right, and wonderfully simple. "Your mother's recipe for chicken and dumplings—Hungarian-style."

"Csirke paprikas?" Normally it would have made his mouth water. "That's a lot of work."

"It was a culinary adventure—and the cleaning lady will probably quit on Monday, after one look at the kitchen." She laughed up at him, then scrubbed her knuckles over his cheek when she caught the look in his eyes. "Don't worry. It'll heat up just fine for tomorrow's lunch. Then again..." She snuggled closer. "If you're feeling really guilty, I'll take you up on that ride to the bedroom—and whatever else you can think of."

But instead of chuckling and scooping her up, he pushed away to pace to the television and snap it off. "We have to talk."

His tone had nerves skittering in her stomach, but she nodded. "All right."

He thought it might be best—for both of them—if they had some of the brandy she had offered him during an earlier crisis. Trying out the words in his head, he walked to the lacquered cabinet.

"It's bad," she murmured, and pressed her lips together, hard. Her first thought was that he had changed his mind about her. That he had finally taken that good look she'd been afraid of and realized his mistake.

"It's bad," he concurred, then brought the snifters to the couch. "Here. Drink a little."

"It's all right. I don't make scenes."

He tilted the brandy toward her lips himself. "Just a little, *milaya.*"

She closed her eyes and did as he asked. He couldn't say that sweet word to her in that loving tone if he'd changed his mind. "Okay." A deep breath, and she opened her eyes again.

"There was another murder last night."

"Oh, Alexi." Instantly the image of Crystal LaRue's mangled body flashed behind her eyes. "Oh, God." She caught his hand in hers and squeezed. "Last night?"

"The desk clerk found her this morning. They had an arrangement. She only used that room for work, and he was ticked that she hadn't checked out and slipped him his usual tip." He was taking it slow, deliberately, so that the general horror would pass before he hit her with the specifics. Again he tipped the brandy up to her lips. "She'd rented the room three times last night. He caught a glimpse of the third john when they went up, so we've had him looking over mug shots most of the day."

"You'll catch him."

"Oh, yeah. There's no doubt about it this time. He didn't find the guy in the books, but he gave the police artist a fair description. We'll be broadcasting it. This time we should have his blood type, too. DNA. Couple of other things."

"You'll have him soon."

"Not soon enough. Bess, the woman…" His fingers tightened on hers, but he told her the worst as gently as he knew how. "It was Rosalie."

She only stared, and he watched, helpless, as the color simply slid out of her face. "No." She was tugging her hand from his, but he only held tighter. "You're wrong. You made a mistake. I just saw her. I just talked to her a couple of days ago."

"There's no mistake." His voice toughened, for her sake. "I ID'd her myself. Rechecked that with prints, and the desk clerk's ID. Bess, it was Rosalie."

The moan came out brokenly as she wrapped her arms around herself and began to rock. "Don't," she said when he tried to gather her close. "Don't, don't, don't."

She sprang up, needing the distance, desperate to find something to do with the helpless rage that was building inside her. "She didn't have to die. It isn't right. It isn't right for her to die like that."

"It's never right."

It was his tone, the cool detachment of it, that had her whirling on him. "But she was just a hooker. Don't get involved, right? Don't feel anything. Isn't that what you told me?"

He went very still, as if she'd pulled a gun and taken aim. "I guess I did."

"I wanted to help her, but you told me I couldn't. You told me it was a waste of my time and energy. And you were right, weren't you, Alexi? How fine it must be to always be so right."

He took the blow. What else could he do? "Why don't you sit down, Bess? You'll make yourself sick."

She wanted to break something, to smash it—but nothing was precious enough. "I *cared,* damn you. I cared about her. She wasn't just a story line to me. She was a person. All she wanted was to go south, buy a trailer." When her breath began to hitch, she covered her mouth with her hands. "She shouldn't have died like that."

"I wish I could change it." The bitter sense of failure turned his voice to ice. "I wish to God I could." Before he realized the glass was leaving his hand, he was heaving the snifter against the wall. "How do you know what I felt when I walked into that filthy room and found her like that? How the hell do you know what it's like to face it and know you couldn't stop it? She was a person to me, too."

"I'm sorry." The tears that spilled over now spilled for all of them. "Alexi, I'm sorry."

"For what?" He tossed back. "It was the truth."

"Facts. Not truth." He'd tried to soften the blow, to cushion her when his own emotions were raw. He'd needed to comfort. His eyes had been dazed with fatigue and pain and the kind of grief she might never understand, but he'd needed to shield her. And she hadn't allowed it. "Hold me, please. I need you to hold me."

For a moment she was afraid he wouldn't move. Then he crossed to her. Though his arms were rigid with tension, they came around her.

"I didn't mean to hurt you," she murmured, but he only shook his head and stroked her hair. Grieving, she turned her face into his throat. "I wanted to make it a lie somehow. To make you wrong so it could all be wrong." She squeezed her eyes closed and held tight. "She was somebody."

He stared blankly over her shoulder as he remembered one of the last things Rosalie had said to him. *She treats me like somebody.* "I know."

"You'll catch him," she said fiercely.

"We'll catch him. We'll put him away. He won't hurt anybody else." Though her words still scraped against him, he rocked her. He would tell her the rest and hoped it helped. "She had a knife."

"I saw it. She showed me."

"She used it. I don't know how bad she hurt him, but she put up a hell of a fight. It's recorded."

"Recorded?" Eyes dull with shock, she leaned back. "My God. The tape. I gave her my mini recorder."

"I figured as much. For whatever consolation it is,

the fact that you did give it to her, and she decided to use it, is going to make a difference. A big one."

"You heard them," she said through dry lips. "You heard—"

"We got everything, from the deal on the street until...the end. Don't ask me, Bess." He lifted a hand to cup her face. "Even if I could tell you what was on the tape, I wouldn't."

"I wasn't going to ask. I don't think I could bear to know what happened in that room."

Calmer now, he searched her face. "I've only got a few hours. I have to go in first thing in the morning. Do you want me to stay with you tonight, or would you rather I go?"

She'd hurt him more than she'd realized. Perhaps the only way she could heal the wound was to admit, and to show him, that she needed comfort. Needed it from him. Drawing him close, she laid her head on his shoulder.

"I want you with me, Alexi. Always. And tonight— I don't think I'd make it through tonight without you."

She began to cry then. Alex picked her up and carried her to the couch, where they could lie down and grieve together.

Chapter 12

Judd flexed his hand on the steering wheel as he turned on West Seventy-sixth. He wasn't nervous this time. He was eager. The idea of bringing Wilson J. Tremayne III—a U.S. senator's grandson—in for questioning in the murders of four women had him chafing at the bit.

They had him, Judd thought. He knew they had the creep. The artist's sketch, the blood type, the voiceprint. It had been quick work on that, he mused. Flavored with luck. Bess's tape had been one of those twisted aspects of police work that never failed to fascinate him.

It was Trilwalter who'd identified Tremayne from the sketch. Judd remembered that the boss had taken a long, hard look at the artist's rendering and then ordered Alex to the newspaper morgue. The desk clerk had picked the reprint of Tremayne's newspaper picture from a choice of five.

From there, Alex had used a connection at one of the local television stations and had finessed a videotape of Tremayne campaigning for his grandfather. The lab boys had jumped right on it, and had matched the voice to the one on Bess's tape.

It still made him queasy to think about what had been on that tape, but that was something he didn't want to show to Alex. Just as he knew better than to let Alex spot his eagerness now.

"So," he said casually, "you think the Yankees have got a shot this year?"

Alex didn't even glance over. He could all but taste his partner's excitement. "When a cop starts licking his lips, he forgets things. Miranda rights, probable cause, makes all kinds of little procedural mistakes that help slime ooze out of courtrooms and back onto the street."

Judd clenched his jaw. "I'm not licking my lips."

"Malloy, you'll be drooling any minute." Alex looked over at the beautiful old building while Judd hunted up a parking space. The Gothic touches appealed to him, as did the tall, narrow windows and the scattering of terrace gardens. Tremayne lived on the top floor, in a plush two-level condo with a view of the park and a uniformed doorman downstairs.

He came and went as he pleased, wearing his Italian suits and his Swiss watch.

And four women were dead.

"Don't take it personally," Alex said when they got out of the car. "Stanislaski's rule number five."

But Judd was getting good, very good, at reading his partner. "You want him as bad as I do."

Alex looked over, his eyes meeting, then locking on Judd's. There wasn't eagerness in them or excitement or even satisfaction. They were all cold fury. "So let's go get the bastard."

They flashed their badges for the doorman, then rode partway up in the elevator with a plump middle-aged woman and her yipping schnauzer. Alex glanced up and spotted the security camera in the corner. It might come in handy, he thought. The DA would have to subpoena the tapes for the nights of the murders. If they were dated and timed, so much the better. But, if not, they would still show Tremayne going and coming.

The schnauzer got off at four. They continued on to eight. Side by side, they approached 8B.

Though the door was thick, Alex could hear the strains of an aria from *Aida* coming from the apartment. He'd never cared much for opera, but he'd liked this particular one. He wondered if it would be spoiled for him now. He rang the buzzer.

He had to ring it a second time before Tremayne answered. Alex recognized him. It was almost as though they were old friends now that Alex had pored over the newspaper shots and stories, the videotape. And, of course, he knew his voice. Knew it when it was calm, when it was amused and when it was darkly, sickly, thrilled.

Dressed in a thick velour robe that matched his china-blue eyes, Tremayne stood dripping, rubbing a thick monogrammed towel over his fair hair.

"Wilson J. Tremayne?"

"That's right." Tremayne glanced pleasantly from face to face. He didn't have the street sense to smell cop. "I'm afraid you've caught me at a bad time."

"Yes, sir." Never taking his eyes off Tremayne's, Alex took out his badge. "Detectives Stanislaski and Malloy."

"Detectives?" Tremayne's voice was bland, only mildly curious, but Alex saw the flicker. "Don't tell me my secretary forgot to pay my parking tickets again."

"You'll have to get dressed, Mr. Tremayne." Still watching, Alex replaced his shield. "We'd like you to come with us."

"With you?" Tremayne eased backward a step. Judd noted that his hand eased down toward the doorknob, closed over it. Knuckles whitened. "I'm afraid that would be very inconvenient. I have a dinner engagement."

"You'll want to cancel that," Alex said. "This may take a while."

"Detective—?"

"Stanislaski."

"Ah, Stanislaski. Do you know who I am?"

Because it suited him, because he wanted it, Alex let Tremayne see the knowledge. "I know exactly who you are, Jack." Alex allowed himself one quick flash of pleasure at the fear that leaped into Tremayne's eyes. "We're going downtown, Mr. Tremayne. Your presence is requested for questioning on the murders of four women. Mary Rodell." His voice grew quieter, more dangerous, on each name. "Angie Horowitz, Crystal LaRue and Rosalie Hood. You're free to call your attorney."

"This is absurd."

Alex slapped a hand on the door before Tremayne could slam it shut. "We can take you in as you are—and give your neighbors a thrill. Or you can get dressed."

Alex saw the quick panic and was braced even as Tremayne turned to run. He knew better—sure he did—but it felt so damn good to body-slam the man up against that silk-papered wall. A small, delicate statue tipped from its niche and bounced on the carpet. When he hauled Tremayne up by the lapels, he saw the gold chain, the dangling heart with a crack running through it that was the twin of the one they had in evidence. And he saw the fresh white bandage that neatly covered the wounds Rosalie had inflicted as she fought for her life.

"Give me a reason." Alex leaned in close. "I'd love it."

"I'll have your badges." Tears began to leak out of Tremayne's eyes as he slid to the floor. "My grandfather will have your badges."

In disgust, Alex stood over him. "Go find him some pants," he said to Judd. "I'll read him his rights."

With a nod, Judd started for the bedroom. "Don't take it personally, Stanislaski."

Alex glanced over with something that was almost a smile. "Kiss off, Malloy."

They had him cold, Alex thought as he turned into Bess's building. They could call out every fancy lawyer on the East Coast, and it wouldn't mean a damn thing. The physical evidence was overwhelming—particularly since they'd found the murder weapon in the nightstand drawer.

Opportunity was unlikely to be a problem, and as for motive—he'd leave that up to the shrinks. Undoubtedly they'd cop an insanity plea. Maybe they'd even pull it off. One way or the other, he was off the streets.

It went a long way toward easing the bitterness he'd felt over Rosalie's death. He hoped it helped Bess with her grief.

He'd nearly called her from the station, but he'd wanted to tell her face-to-face. As he waited for the elevator, he shifted the bunch of lilacs he held. Maybe it was a weird time to bring her flowers, but he thought she needed them.

Stepping into the car, he tucked a hand in his pocket and felt the jeweler's box. It was even a weirder time to propose marriage. But he knew he needed it.

It scared him just how much he'd come to depend on having her with him. To talk to him, to listen to him, to make him laugh. To make love with him. He knew he was rushing things, but he justified it by assuring himself that if he got her to marry him quickly enough, she wouldn't have time to change her mind.

She believed she was in love with him. After they were committed, emotionally and legally, he would take as much time as necessary to make certain it was true.

The elevator opened, and Alex dug for his keys. They'd order in tonight, he decided. Put on some music, light some candles. He grimaced as he fit the key into the lock. No, she'd probably had that routine before, and he'd be damned if he'd follow someone else's pattern. He'd have to think of something else.

He opened the door with his arms full of nodding lilacs, his mind racing to think of some clever, inno-vative way to ask Bess to be his wife. The color went out of his face and turned his eyes to midnight. He felt something slam into his chest. It was like being shot.

She was standing in the center of the room, her laughter just fading away. In another man's arms, her mouth just retreating from another man's lips.

"Charlie, I—" She heard the sound of the door and turned. The bright, beaming smile on her face froze, then faded away like the laughter. "Alexi."

"I guess I should have knocked." His voice was dead calm. Viciously calm.

"No, of course not." There were butterflies in her stomach, and their wings were razor-sharp. "Charlie, this is Alexi. I've told you about him."

"Sure. Think I met you at Bess's last party." Lanky, long-haired and obviously oblivious to the tension throbbing in the air, he gave Bess's shoulders a squeeze. "She gives the best."

Alex set the flowers aside. One fragile bloom fell from the table and was ignored. "So I've heard."

"Well, I've got to be going." Charlie bent to give Bess another kiss. Alex's hands clenched. "You won't let me down?"

"Of course not." She worked up a smile, grateful that Charlie was too preoccupied to sense the falseness of it. "You know how happy I am for you, Charlie. I'll be in touch."

He went out cheerfully, calling out a last farewell before he shut the door. In the silence, Alex noticed the music for the first time. Violins and flutes whispered out of her stereo. Very romantic, he thought, and his teeth clenched like his fists.

"Well." Her eyes were burning dry, though her heart was weeping. "I can see I should explain." She walked over to the wine she'd poured for Charlie and topped off her glass. "I can also see that you've already made up your mind, so explanations would be pointless."

"You move fast, Bess."

She was glad she had her back to him for a moment. Very glad, because her hand trembled as she lifted the wine. "Do you think so, Alexi?"

"Or maybe you've been seeing him all along."

"You can say that?" Now she turned, and the first

flashes of anger burst through her. "You can stand there and say that to me?"

"What the hell do you expect me to say?" he shot back. He didn't go near her. Didn't dare. "I walk in here and find you with him. A little music, a nice bottle of wine." He wished he had been shot. It couldn't possibly hurt more than this bite of betrayal. "Do you think I'm an idiot?"

"No. No, I don't." She needed to sit, but she locked her knees straight. "But I must be to have been so careless as to have an assignation here when you were bound to find me out." Her eyes were like glass as she toasted him. "Caught me."

He took a step forward, stopped himself. "Are you going to tell me you didn't sleep with him?"

In the thrum of silence, the flutes sang. "No, I'm not going to tell you that. I'm not ashamed that I once cared enough for a very good man to be intimate with him. I'd tell you that I haven't been with Charlie or anyone else since I met you, but the evidence is against me, isn't it, Detective?"

She was so tired, Bess thought, so terribly tired, and the scent of the lilacs made her want to weep. Rosalie's funeral had been that morning, and she'd quietly made the arrangements herself. She'd gone alone, without mentioning it to Alex. But she'd needed him.

"You let him kiss you."

"Yes, I let him kiss me. I've let lots of men kiss me. Isn't that the problem?" She set down the wine before she could do something rash, like tossing it to the floor. "You didn't come to me a virgin, Alexi, nor did I expect you to. That's one of the big differences between us."

"There's a bigger difference between a virgin and a—"

He broke off, appalled with himself. He wouldn't have meant it. Stumbling, horrified apologies whirled through his head. But he could see by the way her head jerked up, the way her color drained, that there would be no taking back even the unsaid.

"I think," she said in an odd voice, "you'd better go."

"We haven't finished."

"I don't want you here. Even a whore can choose."

His face was as pale as hers. "Bess, I didn't mean that. I could never mean that. I want to understand—"

"No, you don't." She cut him off, her voice so thick with tears that she had to fight for every word. "You never wanted to understand, Alexi. You never wanted to hear the one thing I needed you to believe. Now the only thing you need to understand is that I don't want to see you again."

He felt something rip apart in his gut. "You can't have that."

"If you don't leave now, I'll call Security. I'll call your captain, I'll call the mayor." Desperation was rising like a flood. "Whatever it takes to keep you away from me."

His eyes narrowed, sharpened. "You can call God Almighty. It won't stop me."

"Maybe this will." She gripped her hands tightly together and looked just over his shoulder. "I don't love you, I don't want you, I don't need you. It was fun while it lasted, but the game's over. You can let yourself out."

She turned away and walked quickly up the stairs. There had been hurt in his eyes. If there had been anger, she knew, he would have come after her, but there had been hurt, and she made it to the bedroom alone. With her hands over her face, she waited, biting back sobs, until she heard the door close downstairs. With a sound of mourning, she lowered herself to the floor and tasted her own tears. They were bitter.

Impatient and unsympathetic, Mikhail paced the floor of Alex's sparsely furnished apartment. "You don't answer your phone," he was saying. "You don't return messages." He kicked a discarded shirt aside. The apartment was a shambles. "Lucky for you I came instead of Mama. She'd box your ears for living like a pig."

"I gave the staff the month off." With the concentrated care of the nearly drunk, Alex poured another glass of vodka from the half-empty bottle on the table.

"And drinking alone in the middle of the day."

"So, join me." Alex gestured carelessly toward the kitchen, where dishes were piled high. "Bound to be a clean glass somewhere."

Mikhail washed one out before coming back to the table. He sat, poured. "What is this, Alexi?"

"Celebration. My day off." Alex took a swallow and waited for the vodka to join the rest swimming through his system. "I caught the bad guy." With a half laugh, he toasted himself. "And lost the girl."

Mikhail drummed his fingers on the table as he drank. It was no less than he'd expected. "You fought with Bess?"

"Fought?" Lips pursed, Alex studied the clear, potent liquid in his glass. "I don't know that's the term, exactly. Found her with another man."

Mikhail's glass froze halfway to his lips. "You're wrong."

"Nope." Alex reached for the bottle with an almost steady hand. "Walked in and found her lip-locked to this guy she used to be engaged to. Bess has this hobby of getting engaged."

Mikhail merely shook his head. Something was not quite right with this picture. "Did you kill him?"

"Thought about it." Before he drank again, Alex ran his tongue over his teeth. Good, he thought. They were nearly numb. The rest would follow. "Too damn bad I'm a cop."

"What was her explanation?"

"Didn't give me one. Got pissed, is all." He set the glass down so that he could use both hands to rub his face.

"Because you accused without trusting."

"I didn't accuse," Alex shot back, then pressed his fingers to his burning eyes. "I didn't have to. What I didn't say was unforgivable. She tossed me out on my ear, but not before she told me she didn't love me anyway."

"She lies." Before Alex could lift his glass again, Mikhail grabbed his wrist. "I tell you, she lies. A few days ago she visited Rachel and the baby. I made her sit for me and sketched her while she talked of you. There's no mistaking what I saw in her eyes, Alexi. You're blind if you haven't seen it yourself."

He had seen it, and the pain of remembering what he'd seen clawed through him so that he stumbled to his feet as if to escape it. "She falls in love easily."

"So? There is love, and love. How many times have you taken the fall?"

"This is the first."

"For this kind, yes. There were others."

"They were different."

"Ah." Patient and amused, Mikhail held up a finger.

"So it's okay for you to play with love until you find the truth, but it's not okay for Bess."

"It's—" Put that way, it was tough to argue with. Especially when his head was reeling. "Damn it, I was jealous. I have a right to be jealous."

"You have a right to make an ass of yourself, too." Pleased, now that he knew it could be fixed, Mikhail kicked back and crossed his booted feet. "Did you?"

"Big-time." Alex swayed, then sat down heavily. "I was going to ask her to marry me, Mik. I had the ring in my pocket and these stupid lilacs. I was scared to death she'd say yes. More scared that she'd say no." He propped his spinning head in his hands. "What the hell was she doing kissing that son of a bitch?"

"Maybe if you had asked nicely, she would have told you."

With a lopsided grin, Alex turned his bleary eyes on his brother. "Would you have asked nicely?"

"No, I would have broken his arms, maybe his legs, too. Then I would have asked." With a sigh, Mikhail patted Alex's shoulder. "But that is me. You were always more impulsive."

"We could go find him." Alex considered and, warming to the idea, leaned over to give Mikhail a sloppy hug. "We'll go beat him up together. Like old times."

"We'll try something different." Rising, Mikhail hauled Alex to his feet.

"Where we going?"

"I'm going to put you in a cold shower until your head's clear."

Alex staggered and linked an arm around his brother's neck. "What for?"

"So you can go find your woman and grovel."

Unsure of his footing, Alex stared at the tilting floor. "I don't wanna grovel."

"Yes, you do. It's best to get used to it before you marry her. I have more experience in this."

"Oh, yeah?" Enjoying the idea of his big brother crawling at Sydney's feet, he grinned as Mikhail thrust him, fully clothed, into the shower. "Can I watch next time?"

"No." With immense satisfaction, Mikhail turned the cold water on full and listened to his brother's pained shout bounce viciously on the tiles. "This is a very good start," he decided.

"You son of a bitch." They were both laughing when Alex grabbed Mikhail in a headlock and dragged him under the spray.

He was nearly sober by the time he walked into Bess's office, but he wasn't laughing. It was hard to laugh when your throat was thick with nerves.

He was going to be reasonable, he promised himself. They would discuss the entire matter like civilized adults. And if she didn't give him the right answers, he'd strangle her. He could always arrest himself afterward.

But he saw only Lori sitting at the keyboard, frantically typing. "I'll have the damn changes by six," she called out. Her brow was furrowed in concentration as she glanced up. Her eyes frosted over.

"What the hell do you want?"

"I need to see Bess."

"You're out of luck." Nobody hurt her friend and got away with it. Nobody. "She's not here."

"Where?"

She offered an anatomically impossible suggestion,

offered it so coolly he nearly smiled. But it wasn't enough. She leapt up and slammed the door shut. Locked it. "Sit down, buster, I've got an earful for you."

"Tell me where she is."

"When hell freezes over. Do you know what you did to her?" She took the flat of her hand to push him back. "Why didn't you just cut out her heart and slice it into little pieces while you were at it?"

"What *I* did?" He jammed his hands into his pockets so he wouldn't shove her back. "I'm the one who walked in and found her snuggled up to that pretty-faced playwright."

"You don't know what you found."

"Then why don't you tell me?"

She'd die first. "You don't know her at all, do you? You didn't have a clue how lucky you were. She's the most loving, most generous, most unselfish person I've ever known. She'd have crawled through broken glass for you." Afraid she'd do something violent if she didn't move, Lori began to pace. "I was so happy when she told me about you. I could see how much in love she was. Really in love. She wasn't just taking you under her wing until she could find someone for you."

"Find someone for me?"

"What do you think she did with all those other men who were dazzled by her?" Lori tossed back. "Oh, she'd try to talk herself into being in love, and thinking they loved her back, and the whole time she'd listen to their problems like some den mother. Then she'd steer them in the direction of some woman she'd decided was perfect for them. She was usually right."

"She was going to marry—"

"She was never going to marry anyone. Whenever

she said yes, it was because she couldn't bear to hurt anyone's feelings. And, okay, because she always wanted to have someone she could count on. But however loyal, however sensitive, she is to other people's feelings, she's not stupid. She'd tell herself she was going to get married, then she'd go into overdrive finding the guy a substitute."

"Substitute? Why—?" But Lori wasn't ready to let him get a word in.

"Not that she ever calculated it that way. But after you watched it happen a couple of times, you saw the pattern. But you…" She whirled back to him. "You broke the pattern. She needed you. You made her cry." Angry tears glazed Lori's own eyes. "Not once did I ever see her cry over any man. She'd just slip seamlessly into the my-pal-Bess category, and everyone was happy. But she's cried buckets over you."

He felt sick, and small, and he was beginning to understand a great deal about groveling. "Tell me where she is. Please."

"Why the hell should I?"

"I love her."

She wanted to snarl at him for daring to say so, but she recognized the same misery in his eyes she'd seen in her friend's. "Charlie was—"

"No." He shook his head quickly. "It doesn't matter." What did matter was trust, and it was time he gave it. "I don't need to know. I just need her."

With a sigh, Lori fingered the square-cut diamond on her left hand. Bess had pushed her into taking the right step with Steven. She could only hope she was doing the same in return. "If you hurt her again, Alex—"

"I won't." Then he sighed. "I don't want to hurt her again, but I probably will."

She weakened, because it was exactly the thing a man in love would say. "I sent her home. She wasn't in any shape to work."

"Dyakuyu."

"What?"

"Thanks."

She hated feeling this way. The only way Bess could get from one day to the next was by telling herself it would get better. It had to get better.

But she didn't believe it.

She hadn't had the heart to throw out the lilacs. She'd tried to. She'd even stood holding them over the trash can, weeping like a fool. But the thought of parting with them had been too much. Now she tormented herself with the fragile scent whenever she came downstairs.

She thought about taking a trip—anywhere. She certainly had the vacation time coming, but it didn't seem fair to leave Lori in the lurch, especially since Lori had added wedding plans to her work load.

A lot of good she was doing Lori, or the show, this way, she thought. But the problems of the people in Millbrook seemed terribly petty when compared to hers. Too bad she couldn't write herself out of this one, she thought, as she stood in the kitchen, trying to talk herself into fixing something to eat.

Well, she'd certainly made the grade, Bess told herself, and pressed her fingers against her swollen eyes. She'd fallen in love and had her heart broken. Great research for the next troubled relationship she invented for the television audience.

The hell with food. She was going to go up to bed and will herself to sleep. Tomorrow she would find some way to put her life back together.

When she stepped out of the kitchen, what was left of her life shattered at her feet.

He was standing by the table, one hand brushing over the lilacs. All he did was look at her, turn his head and look, and she nearly crumpled to her knees.

"What are you doing here?" The pain made her voice razor-sharp.

"I still have my key." He lowered his hand slowly. Her eyes were still puffy from her last bout of tears, and there were smudges of fatigue under them. Nothing that had been said to him, nothing he'd said to himself, had lashed more sharply.

"You didn't have to bring it by." If composure was all she had left, she would cling to it. "You could have dropped it in the mail. But thanks." Her smile was so cold it hurt her jaw. "If that's all, I'm in a hurry. I was just on my way up to change before I go out."

"You can't look at me when you lie." He said it half to himself, remembering how her eyes had drifted away from his face when she said she didn't love him.

She forced her gaze back to his, held it steady. "What do you want, Alexi?"

"A great many things. Maybe too many things. But first, for you to forgive me."

Her face crumpled at that. She put a hand up to cover it, knowing it was too late. "Leave me alone."

"*Milaya,* let me—"

"Don't." She cringed away, crossing her arms over herself in self-defense, and his hands stopped an inch away. There was an odd catch in his breath as he drew them back and let them fall to his sides.

"I won't touch you." His voice was quiet and strained. "Please, let me say what I've come to say."

"What else could there be?" She turned away. "I know what you think of me. You made that clear."

"What I did was hurt you and make a fool of myself."

"Oh, yes, you hurt me." She was still trembling from it. "But not just that last time. You hurt me every time you pulled back when I needed to tell you how much I loved you. I thought, I won't let it matter, because he'll have to see it. God, he'll have to see it, because it's right there every time I look at him. Every time I think about him. And he loves me. He wants me. In my whole life, no one wanted me. Not really."

"Bess."

She jerked away from his hands. "My parents," she began, turning back. "How many times I heard them say to each other, 'Where did she come from?' As if I was some stray pet that had wandered in by mistake."

When she began to roam the room, her shoulders still hunched protectively, he said nothing. How could he tell her he was sorry he'd opened up old wounds, and sorry, as well, that it had taken that to have her reveal those smothered feelings to him?

"I handled it." Those stiff shoulders jerked as she tried to shrug it off. "What else could I do? It wasn't their fault, really. They've always been so perfect, in their way, and I could never be. Not for them. Not even for you."

"Do you think that's what I want?"

She glanced back then. The tears had dried up. There was no point in them. "I don't know what you want,

Alexi. I only know it keeps circling around. I went from my parents into school. Those awful teenage years, when all the girls were so bright and pretty, and falling in and out of love. No one wanted me. Oh, I had friends. Somewhere along the line I'd learned that if you didn't try so hard, if you just relaxed and acted naturally, that there were a lot of people who'd like you for what you were. But there was never anyone to love. There has never been anybody to love until you."

"There's never going to be anyone else." He waited until she turned back. "I love you, Bess. Please, give me another chance."

"It won't work." She rubbed at her drying tears with the heel of her hand. "I thought it would, I wanted it to. I was so sure love would be enough. But it's not. Not without hope. Certainly not without faith."

The calm way she said it had panic streaking through him. "Do you want me to crawl?" He ignored her defensive retreat and gripped her arms. "Then I will. You're not going to push me out of your life because I was stupid, because I was afraid. I won't let you."

Was this how a man crawled? she wondered. With his eyes flashing fire and his voice booming? "And the next time you see me kissing an old friend?"

"I won't care." With a sound of disgust, he released her to stalk the room. "I will care. I'll kill the next one who touches you."

"Then New York would be littered with bodies." It should be funny, she thought. Why wasn't it funny? "I can't change what I am for you, Alexi. I wouldn't ask you to change for me."

"No, you wouldn't." He scrubbed his hands over his face and struggled to find some balance. "I know a kiss between friends is harmless, Bess. I'm not quite that big a fool. But the other night, when I walked in—"

"You assumed I was betraying you."

"I don't know what I assumed." It was as honest as he could get. "When I saw you, I felt… It was all feeling," he said carefully. "So I didn't think. In my heart, in my head, I know better than to assume anything. One of my own rules that I broke. There were reasons." Calmer now, he walked back and took her hands. "We'd just finished the bust, and I was wired from it. I knew I'd tell you about it, all about it. I'd gone beyond trying to separate that part of my life—any part of it—from you. It was going to upset you to think about it, because of Rosalie. I knew that, too. Damn it, I knew you'd gone to that funeral alone, and I felt like the lowest kind of creep for letting you."

He was prying her heart open again, inch by inch. "I didn't think you knew."

"I knew." His voice was flat. All he could think was how desperately he wanted to hold her. "You leave notes everywhere. All these pieces of paper scattered around, with scribbling on them about dry-cleaning and dialogue and appointments. I saw the one about the flowers you'd ordered for her, and the directions to the cemetery." He looked down at their hands. "If things hadn't been moving so fast in the investigation, I would have taken the time. I would have tried to."

That she didn't doubt. "It was more important to me that you catch the man who killed her than that you go stand over her grave."

"I wasn't with you," he said, more slowly. "And I wanted to be. And when I got here, I wanted to…" This was hardly the time to bring up the ring in his pocket.

"I was churned up about a lot of things, Bess. My response was way out of line, and I'll apologize for it as often as you like. But I'd like you to hear me out."

"It's all right." She gave his hands a squeeze, hoping he'd release hers. He didn't. "Alexi, Charlie was here because—"

"I don't need to know." Now he let her hands go to bring his own to her face. He wanted her to see what was in his eyes. "You don't have to explain yourself to me. You don't have to change yourself for me."

She felt something move inside her heart and was afraid to believe it was healing. "I'd rather clear the air. I was too angry to do it before. He came by to tell me that Gabrielle was expecting. He was like a little boy at Christmas, and he wanted to share his good news with a friend. And to ask me if I'd be godmother—even though it's seven and a half months down the road."

He lowered his brow to hers. "You should have slugged me, McNee." When he moved his mouth toward hers, he felt her retreat. Patiently he stroked his thumbs over her temples. "Just once," he murmured and tasted her lips.

He didn't mean to deepen the kiss, didn't mean to crush her against him and hold her so tightly neither of them could breathe. But he couldn't stop himself until he felt her body shake with a fresh bout of tears.

"Don't. Please don't." He pressed his face into her hair and rocked her. "I'll break apart."

Turning her face into his shoulder, she fought back the worst of the tears. "I didn't want you to come back. I didn't want to feel this again."

He deserved that, he thought as he squeezed his eyes tight. "You were right to send me away. I want a chance to prove to you that you're right to let me back in." He brushed a hand through her hair. "You're so good at listening, Bess. I have to ask you to listen to me now."

"You don't need to apologize again." She could do nothing but love him, she realized, and, drawing back, she managed a smile. "And I can't let you back in, because you were always here."

Her words brought a pressure to his chest. He pressed their joined hands against it to try to ease it away. "Just that easy?"

"It's not easy." She supposed it would never be easy. "It's just the way it is."

"Mikhail said I would grovel," he murmured. "Bess, you humble me."

"Let's put it behind us." She drew a deep breath, then kissed both his cheeks as a sign of peace. "I'm good at fresh starts."

"No." Taking her hand, he pulled her to the couch. "I like our other start. We don't need a new one, only to play this one out. Sit." He pulled her down with him, keeping her hand close to his heart. "You explained, now I will. I was afraid to believe in you. No woman has ever meant what you mean, and I let myself imagine that you'd be with me forever. Just as I let myself imagine that you'd turn away. And because I was more afraid of the second, it seemed more real."

"It's hard to be afraid." She turned her cheek to his hand. "I know."

"You don't know all." He glanced away, toward the flowers subtly scenting the room. "You kept the lilacs."

"I tried not to." She smiled again. "But they were so beautiful."

"I brought you something besides lilacs that day." He

reached into his pocket and drew out the box. Her hand went limp in his. He watched her lips tremble apart. "I don't think it's ostentatious." When she only continued to stare, he shifted. "That was a joke."

"Okay." The two syllables came out in a whisper. "Are you—are you going to let me see it?"

For an answer, he opened the box himself. Inside was a gold band set with a rainbow of gems. He knew what they were only because he'd asked the jeweler to identify each of them. The amethyst, the peridot, the blue topaz, the citrine.

"I know it's not traditional," he said when she remained silent. "But it reminded me of you, and I wanted—hell, I wanted something no one else would have thought to give you."

"No one has," she managed, barely breathing. "No one would."

"If you don't like it, we can look for something else."

She was afraid she would cry again and knew it would do neither of them any good. "It's lovely. Beautiful." She managed to tear her gaze from it. "You bought me this before? You had it with you the other night? You were going to give it to me, then you walked in and saw me with Charlie." Laughing, she lifted a hand to her cheek. "I'm surprised you didn't gun us both down. I couldn't have written it better myself."

"Then you forgive me?"

She already had, but since he was looking so nervous, she nodded. "Anyone with such good taste deserves a second chance."

"I bought this days ago, but it took me a while to work up the nerve. Facing a junkie with an Uzi seemed easier." But he was into it now, and he was going to finish. "My idea was to pressure you to accept it, then push for a quick wedding so you wouldn't change your mind. But that was wrong." He closed the box, and was encouraged by Bess's quick gasp of dismay. "It was stupid, and it showed a lack of faith in both of us. I'm sorry."

"I— You—" She let out a frustrated breath. "I don't mind."

"Of course you do," he said. "It was calculating, even devious, when a proposal of marriage should be romantic. So, when we're both ready, I'll ask you properly."

Her face fell. "When we're both ready?"

"I don't want to push you when you might be feeling a little vulnerable. Especially since a long engagement is out. So I'll give you time."

"Time," she echoed, ready to scream.

"It's fair." He waited a beat. "Okay, I'm ready."

Before she could laugh, he was down on one knee. "What are you doing?"

"A proper proposal of marriage." He nearly launched into his humble little speech. Instead, his eyes darkened when she continued to laugh. "You don't want one."

"Damn right I want one. But I want you up here." She took his hand to tug him back to the couch so that they were at eye level with each other. "I want you to look me right in the eye."

"Okay, then I get something I want, too."

"Name it."

"I want to hear you say it." He caught her hand, brought it to his cheek. "I want very much to hear you say it. I need to hear the words from you."

"I love you, Alexi." For the first time, she said the words smiling, knowing they would be taken as they were meant. "I'm going to love you forever."

He turned his face so that his lips pressed into her palm. Taking the ring out of the box, he slipped it onto her finger. It shot out a rainbow of color. As he linked his fingers with hers, he lifted his head. "Be my family." He shook his head before she could speak and felt himself stumble. "I meant to be romantic. Let me—"

"No." Overwhelmed, she laid a hand over his lips. "That was perfect. Don't change it. Don't change anything."

"Then say yes."

"Yes." She threw her arms around him and laughed. "Oh, yes...."

* * * * *

THE PERFECT
NEIGHBOR

To all my cyberpals who've touched my heart
with so many smiles.

Chapter 1

"So...have you talked to him yet?"

"Hmm?" Cybil Campbell continued to work at her drawing board, diligently sectioning off the paper with the skill of long habit. "Who am I talking to?"

There was a long and gusty sigh—one that had Cybil fighting to keep her lips from twitching. She knew her first-floor neighbor Jody Myers well—and understood exactly what *him* she was referring to.

"The gorgeous Mr. Mysterious in 3B, Cyb. Come on, he moved in a week ago and hasn't said a word to anyone. But you're right across the hall. We need some details here."

"I've been pretty busy." Cybil flicked a glance up, watching Jody, with her expressive brown eyes and mop of dusky-blond hair, energetically pace around the studio. "Hardly noticed him."

Jody's first response was a snort. "Get real. You notice everything."

Jody wandered to the drawing board, hung over Cybil's shoulder, then wrinkled her nose. Nothing much interesting about a bunch of blue lines. She liked it better when Cybil started sketching in the sections.

"He doesn't even have a name on the mailbox yet. And nobody ever sees him leave the building during the day. Not even Mrs. Wolinsky, and nobody gets by her."

"Maybe he's a vampire."

"Wow." Intrigued with the idea, Jody pursed her pretty lips. "Would that be cool or what?"

"Too cool," Cybil agreed, and continued to prep her drawing, as Jody danced around the studio and chattered like a magpie.

It never bothered Cybil to have company while she worked. The fact was, she enjoyed it. She'd never been one for isolation and quiet. It was the reason she was happy living in New York, happy to be settled into a small building with a handful of unapologetically nosy neighbors.

Such things not only satisfied her on a personal level, they were grist for her professional mill.

And of all the occupants of the old, converted warehouse, Jody Myers was Cybil's favorite. Three years earlier when Cybil had moved in, Jody had been an energetic newlywed who fervently believed that everyone should be as blissfully happy as she herself was.

Meaning, Cybil mused, married.

Now the mother of the seriously adorable eight-month-old Charlie, Jody was only more committed to her cause. And Cybil knew she herself was Jody's primary objective.

"Haven't you even run into him in the hall?" Jody wanted to know.

"Not yet." Idly, Cybil picked up a pencil, tapped it against her full-to-pouty bottom lip. Her long-lidded eyes were the green of a clear sea at twilight, and might have been exotic or sultry if they weren't almost always shimmering with humor.

"Actually, Mrs. Wolinsky's losing her touch. I have seen him leave the building during the day—which rules out vampire status."

"You have?" Instantly caught, Jody dragged a rolling stool over to the drawing board. "When? Where? How?"

"When—dawn. Where? Heading east on Grand. How? Insomnia." Getting into the spirit, Cybil swiveled on her stool. Her eyes danced with amusement. "Woke up early, and I kept thinking about the brownies left over from the party the other night."

"Atomic brownies," Jody agreed.

"Yeah, so I couldn't get back to sleep until I ate one. Since I was up anyhow, I came in here to work awhile and ended up just standing at the window. I saw him go out. You can't miss him. He must be six-four. And those shoulders..."

Both women rolled their eyes in appreciation.

"Anyway, he was carrying a gym bag and wearing black jeans and a black sweatshirt, so my deduction was he was heading to the gym to work out. You don't get those shoulders by lying around eating chips and drinking beer all day."

"Aha!" Jody speared a finger in the air. "You *are* interested."

"I'm not dead, Jody. The man is dangerously gorgeous, and you add that air of mystery along with a tight butt..." Her hands, rarely still, spread wide. "What's a girl to do but wonder?"

"Why wonder? Why don't you go knock on his door, take him some cookies or something. Welcome him to the neighborhood. Then you can find out what he does in there all day, if he's single, what he does for a living. If he's single. What—" She broke off, head lifting in alert. "That's Charlie waking up."

"I didn't hear a thing." Cybil turned her head, aiming an ear toward the doorway, listened, shrugged. "I swear, Jody, since you gave birth you have ears like a bat."

"I'm going to change him and take him for a walk. Want to come?"

"No, can't. I've got to work."

"I'll see you tonight, then. Dinner's at seven."

"Right." Cybil managed to smile as Jody dashed off to retrieve Charlie from the bedroom where she'd put him down for a nap.

Dinner at seven. With Jody's tedious and annoying cousin Frank. When, Cybil asked herself, was she going to develop a backbone and tell Jody to stop trying to fix her up?

Probably, she decided, about the same time she told Mrs. Wolinsky the same thing. And Mr. Peebles on the first floor, and her dry cleaner. What was this obsession with the people in her life to find her a man?

She was twenty-four, single and happy. Not that she didn't want a family one day. And maybe a nice house out in the burbs somewhere with a yard for the kids. And the dog. There'd have to be a dog. But that was for some time or other. She liked her life right now very much, thanks.

Resting her elbows on her drawing board, she propped

her chin on her fists and gave in enough to stare out the window and allow herself to daydream. Must be spring, she mused, that was making her feel so restless and full of nervous energy.

She reconsidered going for that walk with Jody and Charlie, after all, but then heard her friend call out a goodbye and slam the door behind her.

So much for that.

Work, she reminded herself, and swiveled back to begin sketching in the first section of her comic strip, "Friends and Neighbors."

She had a steady and clever hand for drawing and had come by it naturally. Her mother was a successful, internationally respected artist; her father, the reclusive genius behind the long-running "Macintosh" comic strip. Together, they had given her and her siblings a love of art, a sense of the ridiculous and a solid foundation.

Cybil had known, even when she'd left the security of their home in Maine, she'd be welcomed back if New York rejected her.

But it hadn't.

For over three years now her strip had grown in popularity. She was proud of it, proud of the simplicity, warmth and humor she was able to create with everyday characters in everyday situations. She didn't attempt to mimic her father's irony or his often sharp political satires. For her, it was life that made her laugh. Being stuck in line at the movies, finding the right pair of shoes, surviving yet another blind date.

While many saw her Emily as autobiographical, Cybil saw her as a marvelous well of ideas but never recognized the reflection. After all, Emily was a statuesque blonde who had miserable luck holding a job and worse luck with men.

Cybil herself was a brunette of average height with a successful career. As for men, well, they weren't enough of a priority for her to worry about luck one way or the other.

A scowl marred her expression, narrowing her light-green eyes as she caught herself tapping her pencil rather than using it. She just couldn't seem to concentrate. She scooped her fingers through her short cap of brandy-brown hair, pursed her softly sculpted mouth and shrugged. Maybe what she needed was a short break, a snack. Perhaps a little chocolate would get the juices flowing.

She pushed back, tucking her pencil behind her ear in an absentminded habit she'd been trying to break since childhood, left the sun-drenched studio and headed downstairs.

Her apartment was wonderfully open; aside from the studio space, that had been the main reason she'd snapped it up so quickly. A long service bar separated the kitchen from the living area, leaving the lower level all one area. Tall windows let in light and the street noises that had kept her awake and thrilled for weeks after her arrival in the city.

She moved well, another trait inherited from her mother. What her father called the Grandeau Grace. She had long limbs that had been suited to the ballet lessons she'd begged for as a child—then grown tired of. Barefoot, she padded into the kitchen, opened the refrigerator and considered.

She could whip something interesting up, she mused. She'd had cooking lessons, too—and hadn't become bored with them until she'd outdistanced her instructor in creativity.

Then she heard it and sighed. The music carried through the old walls, across the short hallway outside her door. Sad and sexy, she mused, the quiet sob of the alto sax. Mr. Mysterious in 3B didn't play every day, but she'd come to wish he would.

It always stirred her, those long liquid notes and the swirl of emotion behind them.

A struggling musician? she wondered. Hoping to find his break in New York. Brokenhearted, no doubt, she continued, weaving one of her scenarios for him as she began to take out ingredients. A woman behind it, of course. Some cold-blooded redhead who'd caught him under her spell, stripped his soul, then crushed his still-throbbing heart under her four-inch Italian heel.

A few days before, she'd invented a different lifestyle for him, one where he'd run away from his filthy rich and abusive family as a boy of sixteen. Had survived on the streets by playing on street corners in New Orleans—one of her favorite cities—then had worked his way north as that same vicious family—headed by an insane uncle—scoured the country for him.

She hadn't quite worked out why they were scouring, but it wasn't really important. He was on the run and comforted only by his music.

Or he was a government agent working undercover.

An international jewel thief, hiding from a government agent.

A serial killer trolling for his next victim.

She laughed at herself, then looked down at the ingredients she'd lined up without thinking. Whatever he was, she realized with another laugh, apparently it looked like she was making him those cookies.

His name was Preston McQuinn. He wouldn't have considered himself particularly mysterious. Just private. It was that ingrained need for privacy that had plopped him down in the heart of one of the world's busiest cities.

Temporarily, he mused, as he slipped his sax back into its case. Just temporarily. In another couple of months, the rehab would be completed on his house on Connecticut's rocky coast. Some called it his fortress, and that was fine with him. A man could be blissfully alone for weeks at a time in a fortress. And no one got in unless the gates were lifted.

He started back upstairs, leaving behind the nearly empty living room. He only used it to play—the acoustics were dandy—or to work out if he didn't feel like going to the gym a couple of blocks away.

The second floor was where he lived—temporarily, he thought again. And all he needed in this way station was a bed, a dresser, the right lighting and a desk sturdy enough to hold his laptop, monitor and the paperwork that they often generated.

He wouldn't have had a phone, but his agent had forced a cell phone on him and had pleaded with him to keep it on.

He did—unless he didn't feel like it.

Preston sat at the desk, pleased that the little turn with his sax had cleared out the cobwebs. Mandy, his agent, was busy chewing on her inch-long nails over the progress of his latest play. He could have told her to spare the enamel. It would be done when it was done, and not a minute before.

The trouble with success, he thought, was that it became its own entity. Once you did something people liked, they wanted you to do it again—only faster and bigger. Preston didn't give a damn about what people wanted. They could break down the doors of the theater to see his next play, give him another Pulitzer, toss him another Tony and bring him money by the truckloads. Or they could stay away in droves, critically bomb the work and demand their money back.

It was the work that mattered. And it only had to matter to him.

Financially, he was secure, always had been. Mandy said that was part of his problem. Without the need or desire for money to keep him hungry, he was arrogant and aloof from his audience. Then again, she also said that was what made him a genius. Because he simply didn't give a damn.

He sat in the big room, a tall, muscular man with disordered hair the color of a well-fed mink's pelt. Eyes of cool blue scanned the words already typed. His mouth was firm and unsmiling, his face narrow, rawboned and carelessly handsome.

He tuned out the street sounds that seemed to batter against the windows day and night, and let himself slip back into the soul of the man he'd created inside the clever little computer. A man struggling desperately to survive his own desires.

The harsh sound of his buzzer made him swear as he felt himself sucked back into that empty room. He considered snarling and waiting it out, then weighed in human nature and decided the intruder would probably keep coming back until he dispatched them once and for all.

Probably the eagle-eyed old woman from the ground floor, Preston decided as he started down. She'd already tried to snag him twice when he'd headed out to the club in the evening. He was good at evading, but it was becoming a nuisance. Smarter to hit her face-on with a few rude remarks and let her huff away to gossip about him.

But when he checked the peephole, he didn't see the tidy woman with her bright bird's eyes, but a pretty brunette with hair short as a boy's and big green eyes.

From across the hall, he realized, and wondered what the hell she could want. He'd figured since she'd left him alone for nearly a week, she intended to keep right on doing so. Which made her, in his mind, the perfect neighbor.

Annoyed that she'd spoiled it, he opened the door, leaned against it. "Yeah?"

"Hi." Oh, yes, indeed, Cybil thought, he was even better when you got a good close-up look at the face. "I'm Cybil Campbell. 3A?" She offered a bright, friendly smile and gestured to her own door.

He only lifted an intriguingly winged eyebrow. "Yeah?"

A man of few words, she decided and continued to smile—though she wished his eyes would flicker away just long enough for her to crane her neck and see beyond him into the apartment. She couldn't very well try it when he was focused on her, without appearing to be prying. Which, of course, she wasn't. Really.

"I heard you playing a while ago. I work at home and sound travels."

If she was here to bitch about the noise, she was out of luck, Preston mused. He played when he felt like playing. He continued to study her coolly—the pert, slightly turned-up nose; the sensuously ripe mouth; the long narrow feet with sassily painted pink toes.

"I usually forget to turn the stereo on while I'm working," she went on cheerfully, making him notice a tiny dimple that winked off and on beside her mouth. "So it's nice to hear you play. Ralph and Sissy were into Vivaldi big-time. Which is fine, really, but monotonous when that's all you hear. They used to live in your place, Ralph and Sissy," she explained, waving a hand toward his apartment. "They moved to White Plains after Ralph had an affair with a clerk at Saks. Well, he didn't really have an affair, but he was thinking about it, and Sissy said it was move out of the city or she'd scalp him in a divorce. Mrs. Wolinsky gives them six months, but I don't know, I think they might make it. Anyway..."

She held out the pretty yellow plate with a small mountain of chocolate-chip cookies heaped on it, covered by clear pink plastic wrap. "I brought you some cookies."

He glanced down at them, giving her a very brief window of opportunity to sneak a peek around him and see his empty living room.

The poor guy couldn't even afford a couch, she thought. Then his unsmiling blue eyes flicked back to hers.

"Why?"

"Why what?"

"Why did you bring me cookies?"

"Oh, well, I was baking them. Sometimes I cook to clear out my head when I can't seem to concentrate on work. Most often it's baking that does it for me. And if

I keep them all, I'll just eat them all and hate myself."
The dimple kept fluttering. "Don't you like cookies?"

"I've got nothing against them."

"Well then, enjoy." She pushed them into his hands.
"And welcome to the building. If you need anything
I'm usually around." Again she gestured vaguely with
pretty, slim-fingered hands. "And if you want to find
out who's who around here, I can fill you in. I've lived
here a few years now, and I know everybody."

"I won't." He stepped back and shut the door in her
face.

Cybil stood where she was a moment, stunned speechless by the abrupt dismissal. She was fairly certain that
she'd lived for twenty-four years without ever having
had a door shut in her face, and now that she'd had the
experience, she decided she didn't care for it.

She caught herself before she could pound on his
door and demand her cookies back. She wouldn't sink
that low, she told herself, turning sharply on her heel
and marching back to her own door.

Now she knew the mysterious Mr. Mysterious was
insanely attractive, built like a god and as rude as a
cranky two-year-old who needed a swat on the butt
and a nap. Well, that was fine, just fine. She could stay
out of his way.

She didn't slam her door—figuring he'd hear it and
smirk with that go-to-hell mouth of his. But when she
was safely inside, she turned to the door and indulged
in a juvenile exhibition of making faces, sticking out
her tongue and wagging her fingers from her ears.

It made her feel marginally better.

But the bottom line was the man had her cookies,

her favorite dessert plate, her very rare animosity. And she still didn't know his name.

Preston didn't regret his actions. Not for a minute. He calculated his studied rudeness would keep his terminally pert neighbor with the turned-up nose and sexy pink toenails out of his hair during his stay across the hall. The last thing he needed was the local welcoming committee rolling up at his door, especially when it was led by a bubbly motormouth brunette with eyes like a fairy.

Damn it, in New York, people were supposed to ignore their neighbors. He was pretty sure it was a city ordinance, and if not, it should be.

Just his luck, he thought, that she was single—he had no doubt that if she'd had a husband she'd have poured out all his virtues and delights. That she worked at home and would therefore be easy to trip over whenever he headed out was just another black mark.

And that she made, hands-down, the best chocolate-chip cookies in the known universe was close to unforgivable.

He'd managed to ignore them while he worked. Preston McQuinn could ignore a nuclear holocaust if the words were pumping. But when he surfaced, he started to think about them lying in his kitchen on their chirpy yellow plate.

He thought about them while he showered, while he dressed, while he eased out the kinks brought on by hours sitting in one spot with posture his third-grade teacher, Sister Mary Joseph, had termed deplorable.

So when he went down for what he considered a well-earned beer, he eyed the plate on the counter. He'd popped the top, took a thoughtful drink. So what if he had a couple? he mused. Tossing them in the trash wasn't necessary—he'd given perky Cybil the heave-ho.

She was going to want her party plate back, he imagined. He might as well sample the wares before he dumped the plate outside her door.

So he ate one. Grunted in approval. Ate a second and blew out a breath of pure appreciation.

And when he'd consumed nearly two dozen, he cursed.

Like a damn drug, he thought, feeling slightly ill and definitely sluggish. He stared at the near-empty plate with a combination of self-disgust and greed. With what scraps of willpower he had left, he dumped the remaining cookies in a plastic bowl, then crossed the room to get his sax.

He was going to walk around the block a few times before he headed to the club.

When he opened the door he heard her stomping up the stairs. Wincing, he drew back, leaving his door open only a crack. He could hear that mile-a-minute voice of hers going, which had him lifting a brow when he saw she was alone.

"Never again," she muttered. "I don't care if she sticks bamboo shoots under my nails, holds a hot poker to my eye. I will never, ever, go through that torture again in this lifetime. That's it. Over, done."

She'd changed her clothes, Preston noted, and was wearing snug black pants with a tailored black blazer, offsetting them with a shirt the color of ripe strawberries and long dangles at her ears.

She kept talking to herself as she opened a purse the size of a postage stamp. "Life's too short to be bored witless for two precious hours of it. She will not do this to me again. I know how to say no. I just have to practice, that's all. Where the bloody hell are my keys?"

The sound of the door opening behind her made her jump, spin around. Preston noted that the dangles in her ears didn't match and wondered if it was a fashion statement or carelessness. Since she apparently couldn't find her keys in a bag smaller than the palm of his hand, he opted for the latter.

She looked flushed, flustered and fresh. And smelled even better than her cookies. And because he noticed, she only irritated him more.

"Hold on," he said simply, then turned back into his apartment to get her plate.

Cybil had no intention of holding on, and finally found her key where it had decided to hide in the narrow inner pocket of the bag—where she'd put it so she'd know just where it was when she needed it.

But he beat her. He strode out of his apartment, letting the door slam at his back. He carried his saxophone case in one hand and her plate in the other.

"Here." He wasn't going to ask her what had put that sulky look on her sea-fairy face. He had no doubt that she'd tell him, for the next half hour.

"You're welcome," she snapped, snatching it from him. Because her head was throbbing after two hours of listening to Jody's cousin Frank's monotone account of the vagaries of the stock market, she decided she'd give Mr. Mysterious a piece of her mind while the mood was on her.

"Look, buddy, you don't want to be friends, that's just fine. I don't need any more friends," she said, swinging the plate for emphasis. "I have so many now I can't take another on until one moves out of the country. But there's no excuse for behaving like a snot, either. All I did was introduce myself and give you some damn cookies."

His lips wanted to twitch, but he controlled it. "Damn good cookies," he said before he could stop himself, then immediately regretted it as the temper in her eyes switched to amusement.

"Oh, really?"

"Yeah." He walked away, leaving her reluctantly intrigued and completely baffled.

So she followed impulse, one of her favorite hobbies. After unlocking her door quickly, she stuck the plate on the table inside, locked up again, then, trying to keep her footsteps muffled, set off to follow him.

It would be a great strip gag for Emily, she thought, and handled right could play out for weeks.

Of course she'd have to make Emily wild about the guy, Cybil decided as she tried to tiptoe and race down the steps at the same time. It wouldn't just be normal, perfectly acceptable curiosity but dreamy-eyed obsession.

Breathless with the excitement of the chase, her mind whirling with possibilities, Cybil rushed out the front door, looked quickly right and left.

He was already halfway down the block. Long stride, she thought, and, grinning, started after him.

Emily, of course, would be sort of skulking, then jumping behind lampposts; or flattening herself against walls in case he turned around and—

Nearly yelping, Cybil jumped behind a lamppost as the object of the chase sent an absent glance over his shoulder. With a hand over her heart, Cybil dared a peek and watched him turn the corner.

Annoyed that she'd worn heels instead of flats to dinner, she sucked in a breath and made the dash to the corner.

He walked for twenty minutes, until her feet were screaming and her initial rush of excitement was draining fast. Did the man just wander the streets with his saxophone every night? she wondered.

Maybe he wasn't just rude. Maybe he was crazy. He'd been recently released from the asylum—that's why he didn't know how to relate to people in the normal way.

His filthy rich and abusive family had caught him, locked him up so that he couldn't claim his rightful inheritance from his beloved grandmother—who had died under suspicious circumstances and had left him her entire fortune. And all those years of being imprisoned by the corrupt psychiatrist had warped his mind.

Yes, that would be exactly what Emily would cook up in her head—and she'd be certain her tender care, her unqualified love, would cure him. Then all the friends and neighbors would try to talk her out of it—even as she dragged them into her schemes.

And before it was over Mr. Mysterious would—

She pulled up short as he walked into a small, dingy club called Delta's.

Finally, she thought, and skimmed back her hair. Now all she had to do was slip inside, find a dark corner and see what happened next.

Chapter 2

The place smelled of whiskey and smoke. Not really offensive, Cybil thought. More…atmospheric. It was dimly lit, with a pale-blue light illuminating a stingy stage. Round tables hardly bigger than pie plates were crammed together, and though most of them were occupied, the noise level was muted.

She decided people talked in whispers in such places, planning liaisons, affairs, or enjoying those already made.

At a thick wooden bar on the side wall, patrons loitered on stools and huddled over their drinks as if protecting the contents from invaders.

It was, she decided, the kind of club that belonged in a black-and-white movie from the forties. The kind where the heroine wore long, slinky dresses, dark-red lipstick with a sweep of her platinum hair falling sulkily over her left eye as she stood on the stage under a single key light, torching her way through songs about the men who'd done her wrong.

And while she did, the man who wanted her, and had done her wrong, brooded into his whiskey with his world-weary eyes shadowed by the brim of his fedora.

In other words, she thought with a smile, it was perfect.

Hoping to go unnoticed, she scooted along the rear wall and found a table and, sitting, watched him through a haze of smoke and whiskey fumes.

He wore black. Jeans with a T-shirt tucked into the waistband. He'd already taken off the leather jacket he'd put on against the evening chill. The woman he was speaking with was gorgeous, Black and outfitted in a hot red jumpsuit that hugged every curvaceous inch. She had to be six feet tall, Cybil mused, and when she threw back her beautiful head and laughed, the full rich sound rocked through the room.

For the first time Cybil saw him smile. No, not just smile, she thought, transfixed by the lightning transformation of that stern and handsome face. That hot punch of grin, the hammer-blow power of it, couldn't be called anything as tame as a smile.

It was full of fun and affection and sly humor. It made her rest her chin on her fisted hands and grin in response.

She imagined he and the beautiful Amazon were lovers, was certain of it when the woman grabbed his face in her hands and kissed him lavishly. Of course, Cybil thought, a man like that—with all those secrets and heartaches—would have a lover, and they would meet in a dim, smoky bar where the music was dreamy and sad.

Finding it wonderfully romantic, she sighed.

Onstage, Delta gave Preston's cheeks an affectionate pinch. "So now you got women following you, sugar lips?"

"She's a lunatic."

"You want me to bounce her out?"

"No." He didn't glance back but could feel those big green eyes on him. "I'm pretty sure she's a harmless lunatic."

Delta's tawny eyes glittered with amusement. "Then I'll just check her out. Woman starts stalking my sugar lips, I gotta see what's she made of, right, André?"

The skinny black man at the piano stopped noodling keys long enough to smile up at her out of a face as battered and worn as the old spinet he played. "That you do, Delta. Don't hurt her, now—she's just a little thing. You ready to blow?" he asked Preston.

"You start. I'll catch up."

As Delta glided offstage, André's long, narrow fingers began to make magic. Preston let the mood of it slide into him; then, closing his eyes, let the music come.

It took him away. It cleared his head of the words and the people and the scenes that often crowded his head. When he played like this, there was nothing but the music, and the aching pleasure of making it.

He'd once told Delta it was like sex. It dragged something out of you, put something back. And when it was over, it was always too soon.

In the back, Cybil drifted into it, slid down into those low, bluesy notes, rose up with the sudden wailing sobs.

It was different, she thought, watching him play than just hearing it through the walls. Watching him, there was more power, more heartbreak, more of that subtle sexual pull.

It was music to weep by. To make love to. To dream on.

It caught her, focused her on the stage so she didn't see Delta moving toward her table.

"What's your pleasure, little sister?"

"Hmm." Distracted, Cybil glanced up, smiled vaguely. "It's wonderful. The music. It makes my heart hurt."

Delta lifted a brow. The girl had a bright and pretty face, she mused. Didn't look much like a lunatic with that tipped nose and those long-lidded eyes. "You drinking or just taking up space?"

"Oh." Of course, Cybil realized, a place like this needed to sell drinks. "It's whiskey music," she said with another smile. "I'll have a whiskey."

Delta's brow only arched higher. "You don't look old enough to be ordering whiskey, little sister."

Cybil didn't bother to sigh. It was an opinion she heard constantly. She flipped open her purse, pulled out her driver's license.

Delta took it, studied it. "All right, Cybil Angela Campbell, I'll get your whiskey."

"Thanks." Content, Cybil rested her chin on her fists again and just listened. It surprised her when Delta came back not with one glass of whiskey but two, then folded that glamorous body into the chair next to her.

"So, what are you doing in a place like this, young Cybil? You got a Rainbow Room face."

Cybil opened her mouth, then realized she could hardly say she'd followed her mysterious neighbor all over Soho. "I don't live far from here. I suppose I just followed an impulse." She lifted the whiskey, gestured with it to the stage. "I'm glad I did," she said, then drank.

Delta's lips pursed. The girl might look like a varsity cheerleader, but she drank her whiskey like a man. "You go wandering around the streets alone at night, somebody's going to eat you up, little sister."

Cybil's eyes gleamed over the rim of her glass. "Oh, I don't think so. Big sister."

Considering, Delta nodded. "Maybe, maybe not. Delta Pardue." She touched her glass to Cybil's. "This is my place."

"I like your place, Delta."

"Maybe, maybe not." Delta let loose that rich laugh again. "But you sure like my man there. You've had your pretty cat's-eyes on him since you came in."

Thoughtfully, Cybil swirled her whiskey while she debated how to play it. Though she had no doubt she could handle herself on the streets—or anywhere else, for that matter—Delta outweighed her by at least thirty pounds. And as she'd said, it was her place. Her man. No point in making a potential new friend want to rip out her lungs at their first meeting.

"He's very attractive," Cybil said casually. "It's hard not to look. So I'll keep looking if it's all the same to you. I doubt his eyes are going to wander when he's got someone like you in focus."

Delta's teeth flashed in a brilliant grin. "Maybe you can take care of yourself, after all. You're a smart girl, aren't you?"

Cybil chuckled into her whiskey. "Oh, yeah. I am. And I do like your place. I like it a lot. How long have you owned it, Delta?"

"This? Two years here."

"And before? It's New Orleans I'm hearing in your voice, isn't it?"

Delta inclined her head. "You got good ears."

"I do, actually, for dialects, but yours is one I couldn't miss. I have family in New Orleans. My mother grew up there."

"I don't know any Campbells—what's your mama's maiden name?"

"Grandeau."

Delta eased back. "I know Grandeaus, many Grandeaus. Are you kin to Miss Adelaide?"

"Great-aunt."

"Grand lady."

Cybil snorted, drank. "Stuffy, irritating and cold as winter. The twins and I—my brother and sister—used to think she was a witch of the wicked sort."

"She has power, but it only comes from money and a name. Grandeau, eh? Who's your mama?"

"Geneviève Grandeau Campbell, the artist."

"Miss Gennie." Delta set her whiskey down so that she could rear back and thump a hand to her heart as she rocked with laughter. "Miss Gennie's little girl comes into my place. Oh, the world is a wonderful thing."

"You know my mother?"

"My mama cleaned house for your *grandmère,* little sister."

"Mazie? You're Mazie's daughter? Oh." Instantly bonded, Cybil grabbed Delta's hand. "My mother talked about Mazie all the time. We visited her once when I was a little girl. She gave us beignets, fresh and wonderful. We sat on the front porch and had lemonade, and my father did a sketch of her."

"She put it in her parlor and was very proud. I was in the city when your family came. I was working. My mama, she talked of that visit for weeks after. She had a place deep in her heart for Miss Gennie."

"Wait until I tell them I met you. How is your mother, Delta?"

"She died last year."

"Oh." Cybil laid her other hand over Delta's, cupping it warmly. "I'm so sorry."

"She lived a good life, died sleeping, so died a good death. Your mama and your daddy, they came to the funeral. They sat in the church. They stood at the grave. You come from good people, young Cybil."

"Yes, I do. So do you."

Preston didn't know how to figure it. There was Delta, a woman he considered the most sane of anyone he knew, huddled together with the pretty, crazy woman, apparently already the fastest of friends. Sharing whiskey, laughs. Holding hands the way women do.

For more than an hour they sat together in the back of the room. Now and then, Cybil would begin what could only have been one of her chattering monologues, her hands gesturing, her face mobile. Delta would lean back and laugh, or lean forward, shaking her head in amazement.

"Look at that, André." Preston leaned on the piano.

André wiggled his fingers loose, then lit a cigarette. "Like a couple of hens in the coop. That's a pretty girl there, my man. Got sparkle to her."

"I hate sparkle," Preston muttered, and no longer in the mood to play, tucked his sax in the case. "Catch you next time."

"I'll be here."

He thought he should just walk out, but he was just a little irritated to have his good friend getting chummy with his lunatic. Besides, it would give him some satisfaction to let his nosy neighbor know he was onto her.

But when he stopped by the table, Cybil only glanced up and smiled at him. "Hi. Aren't you going to play anymore? It was wonderful."

"You followed me."

"I know. It was rude. But I'm so glad I did. I loved listening, and I might never have met Delta otherwise. We were just—"

"Don't do it again," he said shortly, and stalked to the door.

"Ooooh, he's plenty pissed off," Delta said with a chuckle. "Got that ice in his eyes, chills down to the bone."

"I should apologize," Cybil said as she bolted to her feet. "I don't want him angry with you."

"Me? He's—"

"I'll come back soon." She dropped a kiss on Delta's cheek, making the woman blink in surprise. "Don't worry, I'll smooth things over."

When she dashed out, Delta simply stared after her, then let out one of her long laughs. "Little sister, you got no idea what you're in for. Then again," she mused, "neither does sugar lips."

Outside, Cybil dashed down the sidewalk. "Hey!" she shouted at his retreating back, then cursed herself for not having the sense to ask Delta what the man's name was. "Hey!" Risking a twisted ankle, she switched from jog to run and managed to catch up.

"I'm sorry," she began, tugging on the sleeve of his jacket. "Really. It's completely my fault."

"Who said it wasn't?"

"I shouldn't have followed you. It was impulse. I have such a problem resisting impulse—always have—and I was irritated because of that idiot Frank and…well, that doesn't matter. I only wanted to—could you slow down a little?"

"No."

Cybil rolled her eyes. "All right, all right, you wish I'd get run over by a truck, but there's no need to be upset with Delta. We just started talking and we found out that her mother used to work for my grandmother, and she—Delta, I mean—knows my parents and some of my Grandeau cousins, so we hit it off."

He did stop now, to simply stare at her. "Of all the gin joints in all the towns in all the world," he muttered, and made her laugh.

"I had to follow you into that one and make pals with your girlfriend. Sorry."

"My girlfriend? Delta?"

And to Cybil's amazement, the man could laugh. Really laugh, with a wonderful baritone rumble that melted all the ice and made her sigh in delight.

"Does Delta look like anyone's *girl*friend? Man, you are from Mars."

"It's just an expression. I didn't want to be presumptive and call her your lover."

His eyes were still warm with amusement as he stared down at her. "That's a happy thought, kid, but the guy I was just jamming with happens to be her husband, and a friend of mine."

"The skinny man at the piano? Really?" Pursing her

lips, Cybil thought about it, found it charming and romantic. "Isn't that lovely?"

Preston only shook his head and started walking again.

"What I meant was," Cybil continued—he'd just known she couldn't possibly be finished—as she hurried along beside him, "I'm sure she came back to check me out, you know? To make sure I wasn't going to hassle you, and then, well, one thing led to another. I don't want you to be annoyed with her."

"I'm not annoyed with her. You, on the other hand, have gone so far beyond being an annoyance I can't find the word."

Her mouth fell into a pout. "Well, I'm sorry, and I'll certainly make it a point to leave you alone, since that's apparently what you like best."

Her perky nose went up in the air, and she sailed across the street in the opposite direction from their building.

Preston stood there a moment, watching her scissor those very pretty legs down the opposite sidewalk. Then, with a shrug, he turned the corner, telling himself he was glad to be rid of her. It wasn't his concern if she wandered around alone at night. She wouldn't have been out walking around on those silly, skinny heels if she hadn't followed him in the first place.

He wasn't going to worry about it.

And swearing, he turned around, headed back. He was going to make sure she got home, that was all. Back inside, where he could wash any responsibility for her welfare off his hands and forget her.

He was still the best part of a crosstown block away when he saw it happen. The man slid out of the shadows, made his grab and had Cybil letting out an ear-piercing scream as she struggled. Preston dumped his case, sprinted forward with his fists already clenched.

Then skidded to an amazed halt as Cybil not only broke free but doubled her attacker over with a hard knee to the groin, knocked him flat with a perfect uppercut.

"I only had ten lousy dollars in here. Ten lousy dollars, you jerk!" She was shouting by the time Preston gathered his wits and rushed up beside her. "If you'd needed money, why didn't you just ask!"

"You hurt?"

"Yes, damn it. And it's your fault. I wouldn't have hit him so hard if I hadn't been mad at you."

Noting that she was nursing the knuckles on her right hand, Preston grabbed it by the wrist. "Let's see. Wiggle your fingers."

"Go away."

"Come on, wiggle."

"Hey!" The shout came from a woman hanging out an open window across the street. "You want I should call the cops?"

"Yes." Cybil snapped the word back as she wiggled her fingers and Preston probed, then blew out a steadying breath. "Yes, please. Thanks."

"Polite little victim, aren't you?" Preston muttered. "Nothing's broken. You might want to get it X-rayed anyway."

"Thanks so much, Dr. Doom." She jerked her hand away, kept her chin lifted and gestured with her uninjured hand in what Preston thought of as a grandly regal gesture. "You can go. I'm just fine."

As the man sprawled on the sidewalk began to moan

and stir, Preston set a foot on his throat. "I think I'll just stick around. Why don't you go get my sax for me. I dropped it back there when I still believed the Big Bad Wolf ate Red Riding Hood."

She nearly told him to go get it himself, then decided if she had to hit the jerk on the sidewalk again, she'd hurt herself as much as him. With stiff dignity, she walked down the block, picked up the case and carried it back.

"Thank you," she said.

"For what?"

"For the thought."

"Don't mention it." Preston added a bit more weight when the man on the ground began to curse.

When the squad car pulled up ten minutes later, he stepped back. Cybil wasn't having any trouble giving the cops the details, and Preston harbored the hope that he could just slide away and stay out of it. The hope died as one of the uniforms turned to him.

"Did you see what happened here?"

Preston sighed. "Yeah."

And that was why it was nearly 2:00 a.m. before he trooped up the steps with Cybil toward their respective apartments. He still had the unappealing taste of police station coffee in his mouth and a low-grade headache on the brew.

"It was kind of exciting, wasn't it? All those cops and bad guys. It was hard to tell one from the other in the detective bureau. Well, you could because the detectives have to wear ties. I wonder why. It was nice of them to show me around. You should have come. The interrogation rooms look just the way you imagine they would. Dark and creepy."

He was certain she had to be the only person on the planet who could find a sunny side to being mugged.

"I'm wired," she announced. "Aren't you wired? Want some cookies? I still have plenty."

He nearly ignored her as he dug out his keys, then his stomach reminded him he hadn't eaten anything for the past eight hours. And her cookies were a minor miracle.

"Maybe."

"Great." She unlocked her door, left it open, stepping out of her shoes as she walked to the kitchen. "You can come in," she called out. "I'll put them on a plate for you so you can take them back and eat them in your own den, but there's no point in waiting in the hall."

He stepped in, leaving the door open behind him. He should have known her place would be bright and cheerful, full of cute and classy little accents. With his hands in his pockets, he wandered around, tuning out her bubbling chatter while she transferred cookies from a canister in the shape of a maniacally grinning cow to the same bright-yellow plate she'd used before.

"You talk too much."

"I know." She skimmed a hand over her spiky bangs. "Especially when I'm nervous or wired up."

"Are you ever otherwise?"

"Now and then."

He noted a scatter of framed photos, several pairs of earrings, another shoe, a romance novel and the scent of apple blossoms. Each suited her, he thought, as perfectly as the next. Then he paused in front of a framed copy of a comic strip on the wall.

"'Friends and Neighbors,'" he mused, then studied the signature under the last section. It read simply, Cybil. "This you?"

She glanced over. "Yes. That's my strip. I don't imagine you spend much time reading the comics, do you?"

Knowing a dig when he heard one, he looked back over his shoulder. It must have been the late hour, he decided, after a long day that made her look so fresh and pretty and appealing. "Grant Campbell—'Macintosh'—that your old man?"

"He's not old, but yes, he's my father."

The Campbells, Preston mused, meant the MacGregors. And wasn't that a coincidence? He moved over to stand on the opposite side of the counter and help himself to the cookies she was arranging in a stylish circular pattern.

"I like the edge to his work."

"I'm sure he'll appreciate that." Because he was reaching for another cookie, Cybil smiled. "Want some milk?"

"No. Got a beer?"

"With cookies?" She grimaced but turned to her refrigerator. Preston had a chance to see it was well stocked as she bent down—which gave him a chance to appreciate just what snug black slacks could do for a perky woman's excellent butt—and retrieved a bottle of Beck's Dark.

"This do? It's what Chuck likes."

"Chuck has good taste. Boyfriend?"

She smirked, getting out a pilsner glass before he could tell her he'd just take the bottle. "I suppose that indicates that I'm the type to have *boy*friends, but no. He's Jody's husband. Jody and Chuck Myers, just below you in 2B. I was out to dinner with them tonight, and Jody's excessively boring cousin Frank."

"Is that what you were muttering about when you came home?"

"Was I muttering?" She frowned, then leaned on the counter and ate one of his cookies. Muttering was another habit she kept trying to break. "Probably. It's the third time Jody's roped me into a date with Frank. He's a stockbroker. Thirty-five, single, handsome if you like that lantern-jawed, chiseled-brow sort. He drives a BMW coupe, has an apartment on the Upper East Side, a summer place in the Hamptons, wears Armani suits, enjoys French-provincial cuisine and has perfect teeth."

Amused despite himself, Preston washed down cookies with cold beer. "So why aren't you married and looking for a nice split-level in Westchester?"

"Ah, you've just voiced my friend Jody's dream. And I'll tell you why." She wagged a cookie, then bit in. "One, I don't want to get married or move to Westchester. Two, and really more to the point, I would rather be strapped to an anthill than strapped to Frank."

"What's wrong with him?"

"He bores me," she said, then winced. "That's so unkind."

"Why? Sounds honest to me."

"It is honest." She picked up another cookie, ate it with only a little guilt. "He's really a very nice man, but I don't think he's read a book in the last five years or seen a movie. A few selected films, perhaps, but not a movie. Then he critiques them."

"I don't even know him, and I'm already bored."

That made her laugh and reach for another cookie. "He's been known to check out his grooming in the back of his spoon at the dinner table—just to make sure he's still perfect—and he can spend the rest of his life, and yours, talking about annuities and stock futures. And all that aside, he kisses like a fish."

"Really." He forgot he'd wanted to grab a handful of cookies and get out. "And how is that exactly?"

"You know." She made an *O* with her mouth, then laughed. "You can imagine how a fish kisses, which I suppose they don't, but if they did. I nearly escaped without having the experience tonight, then Jody got in the way."

"And it doesn't occur to you to say no?"

"Of course it occurs to me." Her grin was quick and completely self-deprecating. "I just can't seem to get it out in time. Jody loves me, and for reasons that continue to elude me, she loves Frank. She's sure we'd make a wonderful couple. You know how it is when someone you care about puts that kind of benign pressure on you."

"No. I don't."

She tilted her head. Remembering his empty living room. No furniture, and now no family. "That's too bad. As inconvenient as it may be from time to time, I wouldn't trade it for anything."

"How's the hand?" he asked when he saw her rubbing her knuckles.

"Oh. A little sore still. It'll probably give me some trouble working tomorrow. But I should be able to turn the experience into a good strip."

"I can't see Emily laying a mugger out on his ass."

Cybil's face glowed on a grin. "You *do* read it."

"Now and again." She was entirely too pretty, he thought suddenly. Entirely too bright. And it was abruptly too tempting to find out if she tasted the same way.

That's what happened, Preston supposed, when you hung around eating homemade cookies in the middle of the night with a woman who made her living looking at the light side of life.

"You don't have your father's edge or your mother's artistic genius, but you have a nice little talent for the absurd."

She let out a half laugh. "Well, thank you so much for that unsolicited critique."

"No problem." He picked up the plate. "Thanks for the cookies."

She narrowed her eyes as he headed for the door. Well, he was going to see just how much of a talent she had for the absurd in some upcoming strips, she decided.

"Hey."

He paused, glanced back. "Hey, what?"

"You got a name, apartment 3B?"

"Yeah, I've got a name, 3A. It's McQuinn." He balanced his beer and his plate, and shut the door between them.

Chapter 3

When scenes and people filled her head, Cybil could work until her fingers cramped and refused to hold pencil or brush.

She spent the next day fueled on cookies and the diet soft drinks she liked to pretend balanced out the cookie calories. On paper, section by section, Emily and her friend Cari—who over the last couple of years had taken on several Jody-like attributes—plotted and planned on how to discover the secrets of the Mr. Mysterious.

She was going to call him "Quinn," but not for several installments.

For three days she rarely left her drawing board. Jody had a key, so it wasn't necessary to run down and let her in every time she dropped over for a visit. And Jody was always happy enough to dash down to open the door for Mrs. Wolinsky or one of the other neighbors who stopped by.

At one point on the third evening, enough people were in the apartment to have put together a small, informal party while Cybil remained coloring in her big Sunday strip.

Someone had turned on the stereo. Music blared, but it didn't distract her. Laughter and conversation rose up the stairs, and there was a shout of greeting as someone else dropped in.

She smelled popcorn, and wondered idly if anyone would bring her some.

Leaning back, she studied her work. No, she didn't have her father's edge, she acknowledged, or her mother's genius. But all in all, she did indeed have a "nice little talent."

She had a quick and clever hand at drawing. She could paint—quite well, really, she mused—if the mood was right. The strip gave her an arena for her own brand of social commentary.

Perhaps she didn't dig into sore spots or turn a sarcastic pencil toward politics, but her work made people laugh. It gave them company in the morning over their hurried cup of coffee or along with a lazy Sunday breakfast.

More than anything, she thought as she signed her name, it made her happy.

If McQuinn in 3B thought his careless comment insulted her, he was wrong. She was more than content with her nice little talent.

Flushed with the success of three days' intense work, she picked up the phone as it rang and all but sang into it. "Hello?"

"Well, well, there's a cheery lass."

"Grandpa!" Cybil leaned back in her chair and

stretched cramped muscles. "Yes, I'm a cheery lass, and there's no one I'd rather talk to than you."

Technically, Daniel MacGregor wasn't her grandfather, but that had never stopped either of them from thinking of him as such. Love ignored technicalities.

"Is that so? Then why haven't you called me or your grandmother? You know how she worries about you down there in that big city all alone."

"Alone?" Amused, she held out the phone so the sounds of the party downstairs would travel through the receiver to Hyannis Port. "It doesn't feel as if I'm ever alone."

"You've got the place full of people again?"

"So it seems. How are you? How is everyone? Tell me everything."

She settled back, happy to chat with him about family, her aunts and uncles, her cousins, the babies.

She listened and laughed, added her own comments, and was pleased when he told her there was a family gathering in the works for the summer.

"Wonderful. I can't wait to see everyone again. It's been too long since Ian and Naomi's wedding last fall. I miss you."

"Well then, why do you have to wait until summer? We're right here, after all."

"Maybe I'll surprise you."

"I called with one for you. I'll wager you haven't heard as yet that little Naomi's expecting. We'll have another bairn under the Christmas tree this year."

"Oh, Grandpa, that's wonderful. I'll call them tonight. And with Darcy and Mac ready to have theirs any day, we'll have lots of babies to cuddle this Christmas."

"For a young woman so fond of babes, you ought to be busy making your own."

It was an old theme and made her grin. "But my cousins are doing such a fine job of it."

"Hah! That they are, but that doesn't mean you can shirk your duty, little girl. You may be a Campbell by birth, but you've got some MacGregor in your heart."

"Well, I could always give in and marry Frank."

"The one with the fish mouth?"

"No, he just kisses like a fish. Then again…yeah, the one with the fish mouth. We could make you some guppies."

"Bah. You need a man, not a trout in an Italian suit. A man with more on his mind than dollars and cents, with an understanding of art, with enough of a serious nature to keep you out of trouble."

"I keep myself out of trouble," she reminded him, but decided it was best not to mention the mugging incident. "Besides, Grandma won't let me have you, so I'll just have to pine away here in the big, bad city."

He let out a bark of a laugh. "All the men in that city, you ought to be able to find one to suit you. You get out and about, don't you? You're not sitting there all day writing your funny papers."

"Just lately, but I hit a hot streak here and needed to run with it. There's this new guy across the hall. Kind of surly and standoffish. No, actually, let's just say it straight. He's rude and abrupt. I think he's out of work, except he plays the sax sometimes in this little club a few blocks from here. He's just the perfect new neighbor for Emily."

"Is that so?"

"He stays inside his apartment all day, doesn't talk to anyone. His name's McQuinn."

"If he doesn't talk to anyone, how do you know his name?"

"Grandpa." She allowed herself a smug smile. "Have you ever known me to fail getting anyone to talk to me if I put my mind to it? Not that he's the chatty sort even when you prime his pump with cookies, but I wheedled his name out of him."

"And how does he look to you, little girl?"

"He looks good, very, very good. He's going to drive Emily crazy."

"Is he, now?" Daniel said, and laughed with delight.

When he'd gotten all that he needed to know out of his honorary granddaughter, Daniel made his next call. He hummed to himself, examined his nails, buffed them on his shirt, then grinned fiercely when Preston answered the phone with an impatient, "Yeah, what?"

"Ah, you've such a sweet nature to you, McQuinn. It warms my heart."

"Mr. MacGregor." There was no mistaking that booming Scottish burr. In an abrupt shift of mood, Preston smiled warmly and pushed away from his computer.

"Right you are. And how are you settling in to the apartment there?"

"Well enough. I have to thank you again for letting me use it while my house is a construction zone. I'd never have been able to work with all those people around." He scowled at the wall as the noise from across the hall battered against it. "Not that it's much better here tonight. My neighbor seems to be celebrating something."

"Cybil? She's my granddaughter, you know. Sociable child."

"You're telling me. I didn't realize she was your granddaughter."

"Well, in a roundabout way. You ought to shake yourself loose, boy, and join the party."

"No, thanks." He'd rather drink drain cleaner. "I think half the population of Soho's crammed in there. This building of yours, Mr. MacGregor, is full of people who'd rather talk than eat. Your granddaughter appears to be the leader."

"Friendly girl. It comforts me to know you're across the hall for a bit. You're a sensible sort, McQuinn. I don't mind imposing by asking you to keep an eye on her. She can be naive, if you get my meaning. I worry about her."

Preston had the image of her flattening a mugger with the speed and precision of a lightweight boxer and smiled to himself. "I wouldn't worry."

"Well, I won't knowing you're close by. Pretty young thing like Cybil…she is a pretty thing, isn't she?"

"Cute as a button."

"Smart, too. And responsible, for all it seems like she's fluttering through life. You can't be a dim-witted flutterer and produce a popular comic strip day after day, now can you? Got to be creative, artistic and practical enough to meet deadlines. But you know about that sort of business, don't you? Writing plays isn't an easy business."

"No." Preston rubbed his eyes, gritty from fighting with work that refused to run smooth. "It's not."

"But you've a gift, McQuinn, a rare one. I admire that."

"It's been feeling like a curse lately. But I appreciate it."

"You should get yourself out, take your mind off it. Kiss a pretty girl. Not that I know much about writing—though I've two grandchildren who make their living from it, and damn well, too. You should make the most of being right there in the city before you take yourself back and lock the doors on your house."

"Maybe I will."

"Oh, and McQuinn, you'll do me the favor of not mentioning to Cybil that I asked you to mind her a bit? She'd get huffy over it. But her grandmother worries herself sick over that girl."

"She won't hear it from me," Preston promised.

Since the noise was going to drive him crazy, Preston took himself off. He played at the club but found it didn't quite get him past the thoughts that jangled in his brain.

It was too easy to imagine Cybil sitting at the table in the back, her chin on her fists, her lips curved, her eyes dreamy.

She'd invaded one of his more well-guarded vaults, and he resented it bitterly.

Delta's was one of his escapes. There were times he'd drive into the city from Connecticut just to slip onto the stage with André and play until all the tension of the day dissolved into, then out of, the music.

He could drive home again or, if the hour grew too late, just drop down on the cot in Delta's back room and sleep until morning.

No one bothered him at the club or expected more than he wanted to give.

But now that Cybil had been here, he'd started to

look at that back table, and wondered if she'd slip in again. To watch him with those big green eyes.

"My man," André said as he stopped to take a long drink from the water glass he kept on his beloved piano. "You ain't just playing the blues tonight. You got 'em."

"Yeah. Looks like."

"Usually a woman tangled up there when a man's got that look about him."

Preston shook his head, scowling as he lifted the sax to his lips. "No. No woman. It's work."

André merely pursed his lips as Preston sent out music that throbbed like a pulse. "You say so, brother. If you say so."

He got home at three, prepared to beat on Cybil's door and demand quiet. It was a letdown to arrive and discover the party was over. There wasn't a sound coming from her apartment.

He let himself in, locked up, then told himself he'd take advantage of the peace. After brewing a pot of coffee strong enough to dance on, he settled back at his machine, back into his play, back into the minds of characters who were destroying their lives because they couldn't reach their own hearts.

The sun was up when he stopped, when the sudden rush of energy that had flooded him drained out again. He decided it was the first solid work he'd managed in nearly a week, and celebrated by falling facedown and fully dressed into bed.

And there he dreamed.

Of a pretty face framed by a fringe of glossy brown hair, offset by long-lidded and enormous eyes the color of willow fronds. Of a voice that bubbled like a brook.

Why does everything have to be so serious? she asked him, laughing as she slid her arms up his chest, linked them around his neck.

Because life's a serious business.

That's only one-half of one of the coins. There are lots and lots of coins. Aren't you going to dance with me?

He already was. They were in Delta's, and though it was empty, the music was playing, low and sultry.

I'm not going to keep my eye on you. I can't afford it. But you already are.

The top of her head reached his chin. When she tilted her head back, flicked her tongue lazily over his jaw, he felt the rush of his own blood.

That's not all you want to keep on me, is it?

I don't want you.

There was that laugh, light as air, frothy as champagne. *What's the point of lying,* she asked him, *in your own dreams? You can do anything you want to me in dreams. It won't matter.*

I don't want you, he said again, even as he pulled her to the floor.

He awoke, sweating, tangled in sheets, appalled, amazed, and finally when his head started to clear, amused.

The woman was a menace, he decided, and the only thing that had reflected any sort of reality in the painfully erotic dream was that he didn't want her.

He rubbed his hands over his face, glanced at the watch still on his wrist. Since it was after four in the afternoon, he judged he'd gotten the first decent eight hours of sleep he'd had in nearly a week. So what if it was at the wrong end of the time scale?

He trooped down to the kitchen, drank the dregs of

the coffee and rooted out the only bagel that still looked edible. He was going to have to break down and buy some food.

He spent an hour working out, mechanically lifting weights, reminding his body it wasn't built to simply sit at a keyboard. Pleased that the sweat he'd worked up this time had nothing to do with sexual fantasies, he spent another twenty minutes indulging in a hot shower, and shaved for the first time in three—or maybe it was four—days.

He thought he might take himself out for a decent meal—which would be a nice change of pace. Then he'd face the tedium and low-grade horror of going to the market. Dressed and feeling remarkably clearheaded and cheerful, he opened his door.

Cybil dropped the hand she'd lifted to ring his buzzer. "Thank God you're home."

His mood wavered as his thought zoomed right back to the dream, and the barroom floor. "What?"

"You have to do me a favor."

"No, I don't."

"It's an emergency." She grabbed his arm before he could walk by. "It's life and death. My life and very possibly Mrs. Wolinsky's nephew Johnny's death. Because one of us is going to die if I have to go out with him, which is why I told her I had a date tonight."

"And you think this interests me because…"

"Oh, don't be surly now, McQuinn, I'm a desperate woman. Look, she didn't give me time to think. I'm a terrible liar. I mean, I just don't lie very often, so I'm bad at it. She kept asking who I was going out with, and I couldn't think of anybody, so I said you."

Because she'd meant it when she'd told him she was desperate, she darted in front of him to block his path.

"Kid, let me point out one simple fact. This isn't my problem."

"No, it's mine, I know it, and I would have made something better up if she hadn't caught me when I was working and thinking of something else." She lifted her hands, pushed them through her hair and had it standing in spikes. "She's going to be watching, don't you see? She's going to know if we don't go out of here together."

She whirled away to pace and rap her knuckles against her temples as if to stimulate thought. "Look, all you have to do is walk out of here with me, give an appearance of a nice, casual date. We'll go have a cup of coffee or something, spend a couple of hours, then come back—because she'll know if we don't come back together, too. She knows everything. I'll give you a hundred dollars."

That stopped him. The basic absurdity of it pulled him up short at the head of the stairs. "You'll pay me to go out with you?"

"It's not exactly like that—but close enough. I know you can use the money, and it's only fair to compensate you for your time. A hundred dollars, McQuinn, for a couple hours, and I'll buy the coffee."

He leaned back against the wall, studying her. It was just ridiculous enough to appeal to a sense of the absurd he'd all but forgotten he had. "No pie?"

Her laugh erupted on a gush of relief. "Pie? You want pie? You got pie."

"Where's the C note?"

"The…oh, the money. Hold on."

She dashed back into her apartment. He could hear her running up the steps, slamming around.

"Just let me fix myself up a little," she called out.

"Meter's running, kid."

"Okay, okay. Where the hell is my...ah! Two minutes, two minutes. I don't want her to tell me I'd hold on to a man if I'd just put on lipstick."

He had to give her credit. When she said two minutes, she meant it. She ran back out, her feet in another pair of those skinny heels, her lips slicked with deep pink and earrings dangling. Mismatched again, he noted as she handed him a crisp hundred-dollar bill.

"I really appreciate this. I know how foolish it must seem. I can't stand to hurt her feelings, that's all."

"Her feelings are worth a hundred bucks to you, it's your business." Entertained, he stuffed the bill in his back pocket. "Let's go. I'm hungry."

"Oh, do you want dinner? I can spring for a meal. There's a diner just down the street. Good pasta. Okay, now. Pretend you don't know she's keeping her eye out for us," she murmured as they walked to the entrance. "Just look natural. Hold my hand, will you?"

"Why?"

"Oh, for heaven's sake." She snatched his hand, linked her fingers firmly with his, then shot him a bright smile. "We're going on a date, our first. Try to look like we're enjoying ourselves."

"You only gave me a hundred," he reminded her, surprised when she laughed.

"God, you're a hard man, 3B. A really hard man. Let's get you a hot meal and see if it improves your mood."

It did. But it would have taken a stronger man than

he to hold out against an enormous, family-style bowl of spaghetti and meatballs and Cybil's sunny disposition.

"It's great, isn't it?" She watched him plow through the food with pleasure. Poor man, she thought, probably hasn't had a decent meal in weeks. "I always eat too much when I come here. They give you enough for six starving teenagers with each serving. Then I end up taking home the rest and eating too much the next day. You can save me from that and take mine home with you."

"Fine." He topped off their glasses of Chianti.

"You know, I bet there are dozens of clubs downtown that would be thrilled to hire you to play."

"Huh?"

"Your sax."

She smiled at him, luring him to look at her mouth, that flickering dimple, and wonder again.

"You're so good. I can't imagine you won't find steady work really soon."

Amused, he lifted his wine. She thought he was an out-of-work musician. Fine, then. Why not? "Gigs come and they go."

"Do you work private parties?" Inspired, she leaned on the table. "I know a lot of people—someone's always having a party."

"I bet they are, in your little world."

"I could give your name out if you like. Do you mind traveling?"

"Where am I going?"

"Some of my relatives own hotels. Atlantic City's not far. I don't suppose you have a car."

He had a snazzy new Porsche stored in a downtown garage. "Not on me."

She laughed, nibbled on bread. "Well, it's not difficult to get from New York to Atlantic City."

As entertaining as it was, he thought it wise to steer off awhile. "Cybil, I don't need anyone to manage my life."

"Terrible habit of mine." Unoffended, she broke the bread in half and offered him part. "I get involved. Then I'm annoyed when other people do the same to me. Like Mrs. Wolinsky, the current president of Let's Find Cybil a Nice Young Man Club. It drives me crazy."

"Because you don't want a nice young man."

"Oh, I suppose I will, eventually. Coming from a big family sort of predisposes you—or me, anyway—into wanting one of your own. But there's lots of time for that. I like living in the city, doing what I want when I want. I'd hate to keep regular hours, which is why nothing ever stuck before cartooning. Not that it isn't work or doesn't take discipline, but it's my work and my time. Like your music, I guess."

"I guess." His work was very rarely a pleasure—as hers seemed to be. But his music was.

"McQuinn." Smiling, she nudged her bowl to the side, thinking it would make him a very nice meal later in the week. "How often do you really rip loose and come up with more than, oh, say, three declarative sentences in a row during a conversation?"

He ate the last half of his last meatball, studied her. "I like November. I talk a lot in November. It's the kind of transitory month that makes me feel philosophical."

"Three on the button, and clever, too." She laughed at him. "You have a sly sense of humor in there, don't you?" Sitting back, she sighed lustily. "Want dessert?"

"Damn right."

"Okay, but don't order the tiramisu, because then I'd be forced to beg you for a bite, then two, then I'd end up stealing half of it and go into a coma."

Keeping his eyes on hers, he signaled for the waitress with the casual authority of a man used to giving orders. It made Cybil's brow crease.

"Tiramisu," he told the waitress. "Two forks," and made Cybil weak with laughter. "I want to see if putting you into a coma actually shuts you up."

"Won't." She patted her chest as the last laugh bubbled out. "I even talk in my sleep. My sister used to threaten to put a pillow over my head."

"I think I'd like your sister."

"Adria's gorgeous—probably just your type, too. Cool and sophisticated and brilliant. She runs an art gallery in Portsmith."

Preston decided they might as well finish off the wine. It was a very nice Chianti, he mused, which probably explained why he was feeling more relaxed than he had in weeks. Months, he corrected. Maybe years. "So, are you going to fix me up with her?"

"She might go for you," Cybil considered, eyeing him over her glass and enjoying the happy little buzz the wine had given her. "You're great-looking in a sort of rough, I-don't-give-a-damn way. You play a musical instrument, which would appeal to her love and appreciation of the arts. And you're too nasty to treat her like royalty. Too many men do."

"Do they?" he murmured, realizing that his talkative dinner companion was well on her way to being plowed.

"She's so beautiful. They can't help it. Worse, she's irritated when they're dazzled by the way she looks, so she ends up tossing them back. She'd probably end up breaking your heart," she added, gesturing with her glass. "But it might be good for you."

"I don't have a heart," he said when the waitress brought their dessert. "I thought you'd figured that out."

"Sure you do." With a sigh of surrender, Cybil picked up her fork, scooped up the first bite and tasted with a long moan of pleasure. "You've just got it wrapped in armor so nobody can bayonet it again. God, isn't this wonderful? Don't let me eat any more than this one bite, okay?"

But he was staring at her, amazed that the little lunatic across the hall had zeroed in on him so accurately, so casually, when those who claimed to love him had never come close.

"Why do you say that?"

"Say what? Didn't I tell you not to let me eat any more of this. Are you a sadist?"

"Never mind." Deciding to let it go, he yanked the plate out of her reach. "Mine," he said simply. And proceeded to eat the rest.

He only had to poke her once with his fork to hold her off.

"Well, I had fun." Cybil tucked her arm through his as they walked back toward their building. "Really. That was so much more entertaining than an evening trying to keep Johnny from sliding his hand up my skirt."

For some reason, the image irritated him, but Preston merely glanced down. "You're not wearing a skirt."

"I know. I wasn't sure I could get out of the date, and this was my automatic defense system."

The breezy saffron-colored slacks struck him abruptly as more sexy than defensive. "So why don't you just break Johnny's face like you did the mugger's the other night?"

"Because Mrs. Wolinsky adores him, and I'd never be able to tell her that the apple of her eye has hands like an ape."

"I think that's a mixed metaphor, but I get the picture. You're a pushover."

"Am not."

"Are so," he said before he caught himself and fell too deeply into the childish game. "You let your friend Joanie—"

"Jody."

"Right, push her cousin on you, and the old lady downstairs sticks you with her nephew with the fast hands, and God knows how many other friends you have dumping their cast-off relatives in your lap. All because you can't just say butt out."

"They mean well."

"They're meddling with your life. It doesn't matter what they mean."

"Oh, I don't know." She blew out a breath and smiled at a young couple strolling on the opposite side of the street. "Take my grandfather. Well, he's not really my grandfather if you get picky, which we don't. He's my dad's sister Shelby's father-in-law. And on my mother's side, she's cousin to the spouses of his other two children. It's a little complicated, if you get picky."

"Which you don't."

"Exactly. There's all this convoluted family connection between Daniel and Anna MacGregor and my parents, so why niggle? My aunt Shelby married their son Alan MacGregor—you might have heard of him. He used to live in the White House."

"The name rings a distant bell."

"And my mother, the former Genviève Grandeau, is a cousin of Justin and Diana Blade—siblings—who married, respectively, Daniel and Anna's other two children, Serena and Caine MacGregor. So Daniel and Anna are Grandpa and Grandma. Is that clear?"

"Yes, I can follow that, but I've forgotten the entire point of the exercise."

"Me, too." She laughed in delight, then had to tighten her grip before she overbalanced. "A little too much wine," she explained. "Anyway, let me think… Yes, I have it. Meddling. We were talking about meddling, which my grandfather—who would be Daniel Mac-Gregor—is the uncontested world champ at. When it comes to matchmaking, he knows no peer. I'm telling you, McQuinn, the man is a wizard. I have…"

She had to stop, use her fingers to count. "Um, I think it's seven cousins so far he's managed to match up, marry off. He's terrifying."

"What do you mean 'match up'?"

"He just sort of finds the right person for them— don't ask me how—then he works out a way to put them together, let nature take its course, and before you know it, you've got wedding bells and bassinets. He just told me my cousin Ian and his wife are expecting their first. They were married last fall. The man's batting a thousand."

"Does anyone tell him to butt out?"

"Oh, constantly." She tipped up her head and grinned. "He just doesn't pay attention. I figure he's going to work on Adria or Mel next—give my brother, Matthew, time to season."

"What about you?"

"Oh, I'm too slick for him. I know his canny tricks, and I'm not going to fall in love for years. What about you? Ever been there?"

"Where would that be?"

"Love, McQuinn, don't be dense."

"It's not a place—it's a situation. And there's nothing there."

"Oh, I think there will be," she said dreamily. "Eventually."

For the second time, she pulled up short. "Oh, damn. That's Johnny's car. He's come in from New Jersey, after all. Damn, damn, damn. Okay, here's the plan."

She whirled around, shook her head clear when it spun. "I should never have had that last glass of wine, but I'm still master of my fate."

"You bet you are, kid."

"Enough to know you call me 'kid' so you can feel superior and aloof, but that's beside the point. We're just going to stroll on down a few more feet until we're right in front of her window. Very natural, okay?"

"That's a tough one, but I'll see what I can do."

"I just love that nasty streak of sarcasm. Okay, this is fine, this is good. Now, we're going to stand right here, because she's watching, I promise. Any minute you'll see her curtains twitch. Look for it."

Because it seemed harmless, and he was starting to enjoy the way she held on to him, he flicked a glance over her head. "Right on cue. So?"

"You're going to have to kiss me."

His gaze shot back to hers. "Am I?"

"And you're going to have to make it look good. If you do it right, she'll figure Johnny's a lost cause—for a while, anyway. And I'll give you another fifty."

He ran his tongue around his teeth. She had her face tipped back and looked as appealing as a single rose-bud in a garden of thorns. "You're going to pay me fifty bucks to kiss you."

"Like a bonus. This could send Johnny back to Jersey for good. Just think of it as being onstage. Doesn't have to mean anything. Is she still watching?"

"Yeah." But he wasn't looking at the window now, and didn't have a clue.

"Great. Good. Make it count, okay. Romantic. Just slide your arms around me, then lean down and—"

"I know how to kiss a woman, Cybil."

"Of course you do. No offense meant whatsoever. But this should be choreographed so that—"

He decided the only way to shut her up was to get on with it, and to get on with it his way. He didn't slide his arms around her—he yanked her against him, and nearly off her feet. He had one glimpse of those big green eyes widening in shock, before his mouth crushed down on hers and sent the next babbling words sliding down her throat.

He was right. That was her last dizzy thought. He was absolutely right. He did know how to kiss a woman.

She had to grab on to his shoulders. Had to rise up to her toes.

She had to moan.

Her head was spinning in fast, giddy circles. Her heart had flipped straight into her throat to block any chance of air. It made her feel helpless, lost, shaky as his mouth pumped heat like a furnace into her body.

And his mouth was so hard, so hard, and stunningly hungry. What else could she do but let him feed?

It was like the dream, he thought. Only better. Much,

much better. Her taste hadn't been so unique in his imagination. Her body hadn't trembled with quick, hard little shock waves. Her hands hadn't clawed their way up into his hair to fist while she moaned pure pleasure into his mouth.

He yanked her back, but only to see if her eyes had gone dark, if heat had climbed into her cheeks the way he felt it climb through his system. She only stared at him, her breath coming short and fast through parted lips, her hands still clutched in his hair.

"Next one's on me," he murmured, and took her under again.

A horn blasted. Someone cursed. There was a rush of displaced air from a passing car. Someone shoved an apartment window open and let out a stream of blistering rock music and the acrid smell of burned dinner.

She might have been on a deserted island with crystal-blue waves crashing at her feet.

When he drew her away the second time, he did so slowly, with his hands skimming down from her shoulders to her elbows, then back in a gesture that stopped only a hint short of a caress. It gave her enough time to feel her head revolve once, like a slow-motion merry-go-round, before it settled weakly on her shoulders.

He wanted to lap her up on the spot, every inch of that flushed, lovely skin. To devour her innate—and, to him, misplaced—cheerfulness that shone out of her like sunlight. He wanted all that impossible, unflagging energy under him, over him, open to him.

And he had no doubt that once he had, he'd leave them both bitter.

Now the hands that lingered on her shoulders eased

her back off her toes. Steadied her. Released her. "I think that ought to do it."

"Do it?" she echoed, staring up at him.

"Satisfy Mrs. Wolinsky."

"Mrs. Wolinsky?" Absolutely blank, she shook her head. "Oh. Oh, yeah." She blew out a long breath and decided her system might settle sometime before the end of the next decade. "If it doesn't it's hopeless. You're awfully good at it, McQuinn."

A reluctant smile flitted around his mouth. The woman was damn near irresistible, he thought, and, taking her arm, turned her toward the front of the building. "You're not half-bad at it yourself, kid."

Chapter 4

Cybil sang as she worked, belting out a duet with Aretha Franklin. Behind her, the open window welcomed the cool April breeze and the amazing noise that was the downtown streets in brilliant sunshine.

The stream of light was no sunnier than her mood.

Turning to the mirror on the wall beside her, she tried to work her face into a state of shock to help her with a character expression. But all she could do was grin.

She'd been kissed before. She'd been held by and against a man before. As far as she was concerned comparing all her other experiences to that stunning sidewalk embrace with the man across the hall was like pitting a firecracker against a nuclear attack.

One hissed, popped and was momentarily entertaining. The other detonated and changed the landscape for centuries.

It had left her marvelously dizzy for hours.

She loved the sensation, adored every moment of that giddy, slack-muscled, purely feminine rush. Could there be anything more wonderful than feeling weak and strong, foolish and wise, confused and aware all at the same time?

And all she had to do was close her eyes, let her mind wander back, to feel it all over again.

She wondered what he was thinking, what he was feeling. No one could be unaffected by an experience of that…magnitude. And after all, he'd been right there with her at ground zero. A man couldn't kiss a woman like that and not suffer some potent residual effects.

Suffering, Cybil decided, as her body tingled, was highly underrated.

She chuckled; she sighed; then, bending over her work, sang with Aretha about the joys of feeling like a natural woman.

"God, Cyb, it's freezing in here!"

Cybil looked up, beamed. "Hi, Jody. Hi, sweet Charlie."

The baby gave her a sleepy-eyed smile as Jody strode to the window with him cocked on her hip. "You're sitting in front of an open window. It can't be more than sixty degrees out there." With a little grunt, Jody shoved the window closed.

"I was feeling kind of warm." Cybil set her pencil aside to stroke Charlie's pudgy cheek. "It's miraculous, isn't it, that men start out this way? As pretty little babies? Then they…wow, boy do they grow up into something else."

"Yeah." Puzzled, Jody frowned, examined her friend's somewhat glassy eyes. "You look funny. Are you okay?"

Jody laid a maternal hand on Cybil's forehead. "No fever. Stick out your tongue."

Cybil obeyed, crossing her eyes as she did and making Charlie bubble with laughter. "I'm not sick. I'm fabulous. I feel like a million after taxes."

"Hmm." Unconvinced, Jody pursed her lips. "I'm going to put Charlie down for his morning nap. He's zonked. Then I'll get us some coffee and you can tell me what's going on."

"Sure. Um-hmm." Dreaming again, Cybil picked up a red pen and began to doodle pretty little hearts on scrap paper.

Since that was fun, she drew larger ones, sketching Preston's face inside one.

He had a great one, she mused. Hard mouth, cool eyes, very strong features set off by that thick, dark hair. But that mouth softened a bit when he smiled. And his eyes weren't cool when he laughed.

She loved making him laugh. He always sounded just a little out of practice. She could help him with that, she mused, drawing his face again with the warmth of laughter added. After all, one of her nice little talents was making people laugh.

And after she'd helped him find some steady work, he wouldn't have so much to worry about.

She'd get him some work, make certain that he ate regular meals—she was always cooking too much for one person anyway—and she was sure she could find someone who had a secondhand sofa they were willing to part with on the cheap.

She knew enough people to start the ball rolling here and there for him. He'd feel better, wouldn't he, once he was more settled in, more secure? It wouldn't be like meddling. That was her grandfather's territory. She would just be helping out a neighbor.

A gorgeous, sexy neighbor who could kiss a woman straight into the paradise of delirium.

Of course that wouldn't be why she was doing it. Cybil shook herself, turned the scraps of paper over a little guiltily. She'd helped Mr. Peebles find a good podiatrist, hadn't she? And nobody would consider him a cool-eyed Adonis with great hands, would they?

Of course not.

She was just being a good neighbor. And if there were any other…benefits, well, so what?

Satisfied with her plans, she folded her legs under her and got back to work.

Jody settled the baby, thinking as she always did when she tucked him in that he was the most beautiful child ever to grace the planet. When his heavy eyes shut, his blanket was smoothed and his favorite teddy bear left on guard, she trotted downstairs to turn down the music.

As at home in Cybil's kitchen as her own, she poured morning coffee into two thick yellow mugs, sniffed out a couple of cranberry muffins, then loaded up a tray.

The midmorning ritual was one of her favorite parts of the day.

In the past few years, Cybil had become as close as a sister to her. Closer, Jody thought, wrinkling her nose. Her own sisters were always bragging about their husbands, their kids, their houses—when anyone could see her Chuck and her Charlie were miles superior. But Cybil listened. Cybil had held her hand through the difficult decision to quit her job and stay home with the baby full-time. It had been Cybil who'd stood by during those early days when she and Chuck had been panicked over every burp and sniffle Charlie had made.

There was no better friend in the world. Which was why Jody was determined to see Cybil blissfully happy.

She carried the tray up, set it on the table, then handed Cybil her mug.

"Thanks, Jody."

"Great strip this morning. I can't believe Emily decking herself out in a trench coat and fedora and tailing Mr. Mysterious all over Soho. Where does she get this stuff?"

"She's a creature of impulse and drama." Cybil broke off a piece of a muffin. It was usual for them to discuss Emily and the other characters as separate people. "And she's nosy. She just has to know."

"What about you? Did you find out anything yet about our Mr. Mysterious?"

"Yeah." Cybil said it on a sigh. "His name's McQuinn."

"I heard that." Instantly alert, Jody jabbed out a finger. "You sighed."

"No, I was just breathing."

"Uh-uh, you sighed. What gives?"

"Well, actually…" She was dying to talk about it. "We sort of went out last night."

"Went out? Like a date?" Quickly, Jody pulled over a chair, sat, leaned close. "Where, how, when? Details, Cyb."

"Okay. So." Cybil swiveled so they were face-to-face. "You know how Mrs. Wolinsky's always trying to fix me up with her nephew?"

"Not again?" Jody rolled her dark eyes. "Why can't she see you two are totally wrong for each other?"

Vast affection prevented Cybil from mentioning that it might be the same selective blindness that prevented Jody from seeing the flaws in the Cybil-Frank match.

"She just loves him. But anyway, she'd cooked up another date for me for last night, and I just couldn't face it. You have to swear you won't tell her —or anyone."

"Except Chuck."

"Husbands are excluded from the vow of silence in this case. I told her I already had a date—with McQuinn."

"You had a date with 3B?"

"No, I just told her I did because I was flustered. You know how I start babbling when I lie."

"You should practice." Nodding, Jody bit into a muffin. "You'd get better at it."

"Maybe. So after I tell her, I realize she's going to be looking for us to leave together, and I have to cut some kind of deal with McQuinn to go along with it. I gave him a hundred and bought him dinner."

"You paid him." Jody's eyes widened, then narrowed in speculation. "That's brilliant. The whole time I was dating—especially during that drought period I told you about my sophomore year in college? I never thought about just offering a guy some money to have dinner with me. How'd you settle on the hundred? Do you think that's, like, the going rate?"

"It seemed right. He's not working regularly, you know. And I figured he could use the money and a hot meal. We had a good time," she added with a new smile. "Really good. Just spaghetti and conversation. Well, mostly one-sided conversation, as McQuinn doesn't say a lot."

"McQuinn." Jody let the name roll over her tongue. "Still sounds mysterious. You don't know his first name."

"It never came up. Anyway, it gets better. We're walking back. I think I loosened him up, Jody. He really seemed relaxed, almost friendly. Then I see Johnny Wolinsky's car, and I panicked. I'm figuring she's not going to stop trying to shove him at me unless she thinks I've got a guy. So I cut another deal with McQuinn and offered him fifty bucks to kiss me."

Jody pursed her lips, then sipped coffee. "I think you should've said that was included in the hundred."

"No, we'd already defined terms, and there wasn't time to renegotiate. She was looking out the window. So he did, right there on the sidewalk."

"Wow." Jody grabbed the rest of her muffin. "What move did he use?"

"He just sort of *yanked* me against him."

"Oh, man. The yank. I really like the yank."

"Then I was plastered there, up on my toes because he's tall."

"Yeah." Jody chewed, licked crumbs off her lips. "He's tall. And built."

"Really built, Jody. I mean the man is like a rock."

"Oh, God." On the moan, Jody rubbed her stomach. "Wow. Okay, so you're plastered up there, on your toes. What next?"

"Then he just…swooped."

"Oh-oh, the yank and swoop." Crumbs scattered as Jody waved her hands. "It's a classic. Hardly any guy can really pull it off, though. Chuck did on date six.

That's how we ended up back at my apartment, eating Chinese in bed."

"McQuinn pulled it off. He really, really pulled it off. Then, while my head was exploding, he yanked me back, just looked at me."

"Man. Man."

"Then he just…did it all again."

"A double." Near tears with vicarious excitement, Jody gripped Cybil's hand. "You got a double. There are women who go all their lives without a double. Dreaming of, yes, but never achieving the double yank and swoop."

"It was my first," Cybil confessed. "It…was…*great!*"

"Okay, okay, just the kiss part, okay? Just the lips and tongues and teeth thing. How was that?"

"It was very hot."

"Oh… I'm going to have to open the window. I'm starting to sweat."

She jumped up, shoved up the window and took a deep gulp of air. "So, it was hot. Very hot. Keep going."

"It was like being, well, devoured. When your system just goes…" At a loss, she lifted her hands, wiggled them wildly. "And your head's circling around about a foot above your shoulders, and… I don't know how to describe it."

"You've got to." Desperate, Jody squeezed Cybil's shoulders. "I'm on the edge here. Try this—on the one-to-ten scale, where did it hit?"

Cybil closed her eyes. "There is no scale."

"There's always a scale—you can say off the scale, but there's always a scale."

"No, Jody, there is no scale."

Eyeing Cybil, Jody stepped back. "The no scale is an urban myth."

"It exists," Cybil said soberly. "The no scale exists, my friend, and has now been documented."

"Sweet Lord. I have to sit down." She did so, her eyes never leaving Cybil's face. "You experienced a no scale. I believe you, Cyb. Thousands wouldn't. Millions would scoff, but I believe you."

"I knew I could count on you."

"You know what this means, don't you? He's ruined you for anything less. Even a ten won't satisfy you now. You'll always be looking for the next no scale."

"I've thought of that." Considering, Cybil picked up her pencil to tap. "I believe it's possible to live a full and happy life, hitting with some regularity between seven and ten, even after this experience. Man goes to the moon, Jody. Travels through space and time, finds himself on another world, but only briefly. He must come back to earth and live."

"That's so wise," Jody murmured, and had to dig a tissue out of her pocket. "So brave."

"Thank you. But in the meantime," Cybil added with a grin, "there's no harm in knocking on the door across the hall from time to time."

Because she didn't want to appear overanxious, Cybil put in a full morning's work. She didn't break until after two, when she thought her neighbor might enjoy sharing a cup of coffee, maybe a nice walk in the April sunshine.

He really had to get out of that apartment more, she decided. Take advantage of all the city had to offer. She imagined him brooding behind his locked door, worried about his lack of employment, the bills.

She was certain she could help him with that. There was no reason she couldn't put a buzz in a few ears and get him a few gigs to tide him over.

She heard the sax begin to weep as she stood in her bedroom fussing with her makeup. It made her tingle again, the low, sexy throb of it.

He deserved a break, something to take that cynical gleam out of his eyes. Something that would prove to him life was full of surprises. She wanted to help him. There was a quality about him—an underlying unhappiness she was driven to smooth away.

After all, she'd made him laugh. She'd helped him relax. If she could do it once, she could do it again. She badly wanted to see him laugh again, to hear that sardonic edge to his voice when he made some pithy comment, to see that grin flash when she said or did something that got through his cynical shield.

And if they lit a few sexual sparks between them while she was at it, what was wrong with that?

She was on her way downstairs, and singing again, when the buzzer from the entrance door sounded on her intercom.

"Yes?"

"I'm looking for McQuinn. 3A?"

"No, he's 3B."

"Well, damn it. Why doesn't he answer?"

"Oh, he probably doesn't hear you. He's practicing."

"Buzz me in, will you, sweetie? I'm his agent and I'm running way behind."

"His agent." Cybil perked up. If he had an agent, Cybil wanted to meet her. She'd already thought of half a dozen names to pass on for possible jobs. "Sure. Come on up."

She released the door, then opened her own and waited.

The woman who stepped out of the little-used elevator looked very professional, very successful, Cybil noted with some surprise, in her snazzy power suit of drop-dead red. She was thin and wiry, with a sharp-featured face, dark-blue eyes that were snapping with annoyance and an incredibly fabulous mane of streaked blond hair.

She moved with the precision of a bullet and carried a leather briefcase that Cybil estimated cost the equivalent of a month's rent on a good uptown apartment.

So, she mused, why was her client scrambling for work if his agent could afford designer duds and pricey accessories?

"3A?"

"Yes, I'm Cybil."

"Amanda Dresher. Thanks, Cybil. Our boy here isn't answering his phone, and apparently forgot we had a one o'clock at the Four Seasons."

"The Four Seasons?" Baffled, Cybil stared. "On Park?"

"Is there another?" With a laugh, Mandy pressed the buzzer on 3B and—knowing her prey—held it down. "Our Preston's loaded with talent, but he's my biggest pain in the butt."

"Preston." It only took a minute for the confusion to form, settle, then clear away. "Preston McQuinn." She let out a shaky breath that was equal parts betrayal and mortification. *"A Tangle of Souls."*

"That's our boy," Mandy said cheerfully. "Come on,

come on, McQuinn, answer the damn door. I thought when he decided to stay in the city for a couple months I'd be able to keep better track of him. But it's still an obstacle course. Ah, here we go."

They both heard the bad-tempered snick of locks being turned. Then he yanked open the door. "What the hell do you... Mandy?"

"You missed lunch," she snapped. "You're not answering the phone."

"I forgot lunch. The phone didn't ring."

"Did you charge the battery?"

"Probably not." He stood where he was, staring across the hall to where Cybil watched him with wounded eyes in a pale face. "Come on in. Just give me a minute."

"I've already given you an hour." She tossed a glance over her shoulder as she walked inside. "Thanks for buzzing me up, sweetie."

"No problem. No problem at all." Then Cybil looked Preston dead in the eye. "You bastard," she said quietly, and closed her door.

"Don't you have any place to sit in here?" Mandy complained behind him.

"No. Yes. Upstairs. Damn it," he muttered, despising the slide of guilt. Doing his best to shrug it off, he closed his door. "I don't use the space down here much."

"No kidding. So who's the kid across the hall?" she asked as she set her briefcase on the kitchen counter.

"Nobody. Campbell, Cybil Campbell."

"I thought she looked familiar. 'Friends and Neighbors.' I know her agent. He's crazy about her. Claims she's the only ego-proof, neurosis-free client he's ever had. Never whines, doesn't miss deadlines, never demands coddling, and is currently making him a fat pile of money on the sales of her trade books and calendars, plus the merchandising tie-ins."

She sent Preston a baleful look. "I wonder what it's like to have a neurosis-free client who remembers lunch dates and sends me gifts on my birthday."

"The neuroses are part of the package, but I'm sorry about lunch."

Annoyance faded into concern. "What's up, Preston? You look ragged out. Is the play stalled?"

"No, it's moving. Better than I expected. I just didn't get a lot of sleep."

"Out playing your horn till all hours again?"

"No." Thinking of the woman in 3A, he thought. Pacing the floor. Wanting the woman in 3A. The woman who now, undoubtedly, considered him a slightly lower life-form than slime.

"Just a bad night, Mandy."

"Okay." Because as irritated as he could make her, she cared about him. She crossed the room to give his tensed shoulders a brisk rub. "But you owe me lunch. How about some coffee?"

"There's some on the stove. It was fresh at six this morning."

"Let's start over, then. I'll make it." She moved behind the counter. After she had the coffee going, she poked into the cupboards. She considered Preston's welfare part of her job.

"God, McQuinn, are you on a hunger strike? There's nothing in here but potato-chip crumbs and what once might have been cracked-wheat bread and is now a science project."

"I didn't make it to the market yesterday." Again his

gaze flicked to the door and his mind to Cybil. "Mostly I call in dinner."

"On the phone you don't answer?"

"I'll recharge the battery, Mandy."

"See that you do. If you'd remembered sooner, we'd be sitting in the Four Seasons right now, drinking Cristal to celebrate." She grinned as she leaned on the counter toward him. "I closed the deal, Preston. *A Tangle of Souls* is going to be a major motion picture. You got the producers you wanted, the director you wanted and the option to do the screenplay yourself. All that plus a tidy little fee."

She gave him an amount in seven figures.

"I don't want them to screw it up," was Preston's first reaction.

"Leave it to you." Mandy sighed. "If there's a downside, you find it. So do the screenplay."

"No." He shook his head, walking to the window to try to absorb the news. A film would change the intimacy the play had achieved in the theater. But it would also take his work to millions. And the work mattered to him.

"I don't want to go back there, Mandy. Not that deep."

She poured two cups of coffee and joined him at the window. "Supervisory capacity. Consultant?"

"Yeah, that works for me. Fix it, will you?"

"I can do that. Now, if you'll stop turning cartwheels and dancing on the ceiling, we can talk about your work in progress."

Her dry tone got through, made his lips twitch. He set his coffee on the windowsill, turned and took her sharp-boned face in his hands. "You're the best, and certainly the most patient agent in the business."

"You're so right. I hope you're as proud of yourself as I am. Are you going to call your family?"

"Let me sit on it a couple days."

"It's going to hit the trades, Preston. You don't want them to hear about it that way."

"No, you're right. I'll call them." Finally, he smiled. "After I charge the phone. Why don't I clean up and take you out for that champagne."

"Why don't you. Oh, one more thing," she added as he started for the stairs. "Pretty Miss 3A? Are you going to tell me what's going on between you?"

"I'm not sure there's anything to tell," he murmured.

He still wasn't sure when he knocked on her door later that evening. But he knew he had to answer for that look he'd put in her eyes.

Not that it had been any of her business in the first place, he reminded himself. He hadn't asked her to come nosing around. In fact he'd done everything to discourage her.

Until last night, he thought, and hissed out a breath.

Bad judgment, he decided. It had just been bad judgment. He shouldn't have followed impulse and gone along with her. Shouldn't have compounded the mistake by enjoying himself.

Or by kissing her.

Which he wouldn't have done, his mind circled back, if she hadn't asked him to.

When she pulled open the door, he was ready with an apology. "Look, I'm sorry," he began, delivering it with an impatient edge of annoyance. "But it was none of your business anyway. Let's just straighten this out."

He started to step in, coming up short when she slapped a hand on his chest.

"I don't want you in here."

"For God's sake. You started it. Maybe I let it get out of hand, but—"

"Started what?"

"This," he snapped, furious at the sudden lack of words, hating the kicked-puppy look in her eyes.

"All right, I started it. I should never have brought you cookies. That was devious of me. I shouldn't have worried that you didn't have a job, shouldn't have bought you a decent meal because I thought you couldn't afford it on your own."

"Damn it, Cybil."

"You let me think that. You let me believe you were some poor, out-of-work musician, and I'm sure you had a few private laughs over it. The brilliant, award-winning playwright Preston McQuinn, author of the stunning, emotionally wrenching *A Tangle of Souls*. But I bet you're surprised I even know your work. A bubblehead like me."

She shoved him back a step. "What would a fluffy comic-strip writer know about real art, after all? About serious theater, about *literature*? Why shouldn't you have a few laughs at my expense? You narrow-minded, arrogant creep." Her voice broke when she'd promised herself she wouldn't let it. "I was only trying to help you."

"I didn't ask for your help. I didn't want it." He could see she was close to tears. The closer she got, the more furious he became. He knew how women used tears to destroy a man. He wouldn't let it happen. "My work's my own business."

"Your work's produced on Broadway. That makes it public business," she shot back. "And that has nothing to do with pretending to be a sax player."

"I play the damn sax because I like to play the damn sax. I didn't pretend to be anything. You assumed."

"You let me assume."

"What if I did? I moved in here for a little peace and quiet. To be left alone. The next thing I know you're bringing me cookies, then you're following me and I'm spending half the night in the police station. Then you're asking me to go out so you can slip by a seventy-year-old woman because you don't have the guts to tell her to butt out of your personal life. And you top it off by offering me fifty dollars to kiss you."

Humiliation had the first tear spilling over, trailing slowly down her cheek and making his stomach clench. "Don't." The order whipped out of him. "Don't start that."

"Don't cry when you humiliate me? When you make me feel stupid and ridiculous and ashamed?" She didn't bother to dash the tears away but simply looked at him out of unapologetically drenched eyes. "Sorry, I don't work that way. I cry when someone hurts me."

"You brought it on yourself." He had to say it, was desperate to believe it. And escaped by stalking to his own door.

"You have the facts, Preston," she said quietly. "You have them all in an accurate row. But you've missed the feelings behind them. I brought you cookies because I thought you could use a friend. I've already apologized for following you, but I'll apologize again."

"I don't want—"

"I'm not finished," she said with such quiet dignity

he felt one more wave of guilt. "I took you to dinner because I didn't want to hurt a very nice woman, and I thought you might be hungry. I enjoyed being with you, and I felt something when you kissed me. I thought you did, too. So you're right." She nodded coolly, even as another tear slid down her cheek. "I did bring it all on myself. I suppose you save all your emotions for your work, and can't find the way to let them into your life. I'm sorry for you. And I'm sorry I trod on your sacred ground. I won't do it again."

Before he could think of how to respond, she shut her door. He heard her locks slide into place with quick, deliberate clicks. Turning, he let himself in to his own apartment, followed her example by closing, then locking, the door behind him.

He had what he wanted, he told himself. Solitude. Quiet. She wouldn't come knocking on his door again to interrupt his thoughts, to distract him, to tangle him up in feelings and conversations he didn't want. In feelings he didn't know what to do with.

And he stood, exhausted by the storm and sick of himself, staring at an empty room.

Chapter 5

He couldn't sleep, except in patches. And the patches were riddled with dreams. In them he would find himself wrapped around Cybil. His back in a corner, up against a wall, at the edge of a cliff.

It always seemed as if she'd maneuvered him there, where there was nowhere to go but to her.

And when he did, the dreams became brutally erotic, so that when he managed to rip himself from them, he found himself aroused, furious and filled with the memory, the taste, of her in his mouth.

He couldn't eat, found himself picking at food when he bothered with it at all. Nothing satisfied him; everything reminded him of that simple meal they'd shared a few nights before.

He lived on coffee until his nerves jangled and his stomach burned in protest.

But he could work. It seemed he could always flow into a story, into his people, when his emotions were pumped. It was painful to tear those feelings out of his own heart and have the characters he created gobble them greedily up. But he relished the exchange, even fed on it.

He remembered what Cybil had said before she'd closed the door on him—that he used all his emotions in his work and didn't know how to let them into his life.

She was right, and it was better that way. There were, to his mind, very few people he could trust with feelings. His parents, his sister—though his need to fulfill their expectations of and for him was a double-edged sword.

Then Delta and André, those rare friends he allowed himself and who expected no more from him than what he wanted himself.

Mandy, who pushed him when he needed pushing, listened when he needed to unburden and somehow managed to care about him even when he didn't.

He didn't want a woman digging her way into his heart. Not again. He'd learned his lesson there, and had kept any and all applicants since Pamela out of that vulnerable territory.

She'd cured him, he thought, with lies, deceptions, betrayals. A man could learn a good deal at the tender age of twenty-five that held him in good stead for the duration. Since he'd stopped believing in love, he never wasted time looking for it.

But he couldn't stop thinking of Cybil.

He'd heard her go out several times in the last three days. He'd been distracted more than once by the laughter and voices and music from her apartment.

She wasn't suffering, he reminded himself. So why was he?

It was guilt, he decided. He'd hurt her and it had been neither necessary nor intentional. He'd been charmed by her; reluctantly, but charmed nonetheless. He hadn't meant to make her feel foolish, to bruise her feelings. Tears could still rip at him, even knowing how false and sly they could be when they slid down a woman's cheek.

But they hadn't looked false or sly on Cybil, he remembered. They'd looked as natural as rain.

He wasn't going to resolve the problem—his problem, he thought—until he'd settled with her. He hadn't apologized well; he could admit that. So he'd apologize again now that she'd had some time to get those emotions of hers she was so free with under some control.

There was no reason for them to be enemies, after all. She was the granddaughter of a man he admired and respected. He doubted Daniel MacGregor would return the compliment if he learned that Preston McQuinn had made his little girl cry.

And, Preston realized, Daniel MacGregor's opinion mattered to him.

So, a little voice nagged at him, did Cybil's.

That was why he was pacing the living area of his apartment instead of working. He'd heard her go out, again, but hadn't been quite quick enough to get downstairs and into the hall before she'd gone.

He could wait her out, Preston thought. She had to come back sometime. And when she did, he'd head her off and offer her a very civilized apology. It was blatantly obvious the woman had a soft heart. She'd have to forgive him. Once she had, they could go back to being neighbors.

There was the matter of the hundred dollars, as well, which instead of amusing him as it had initially, now made him feel nasty.

He was sure she'd be ready to laugh the whole thing off now. How long could that kind of cheerful nature hold a grudge?

He would have been surprised to find out just how long, and how well, if he'd seen Cybil's face as she rode the elevator up to the third floor.

It annoyed her, outrageously, that she had to pass the man's door to get to her own. It infuriated her that doing so made her think of him, remember how stupid she'd been—and how much more stupid he'd made her feel.

She shifted the weight of the two bags of groceries she carried in either arm and tried to dig out her key so she wouldn't have to linger in the hallway a second longer than necessary.

The elevator gave its usual announcing thud when it reached her floor. She was still searching for the elusive key when she stepped off.

Her teeth set when she saw him, and her eyes went frosty.

"Cybil." He'd never seen her eyes cold, and the chill of them threw him off rhythm. "Ah, let me give you a hand with those."

"I don't need a hand, thank you." She could only pray to grow a third one, rapidly, that could find her bloody keys.

"Yes, you do, if you're going to keep rooting around in that purse."

He tried a smile, then scowled as they played tug-of-war with one of her bags. In the end he just wrenched it out of her grip. "Look, damn it, I said I was sorry.

How many times do I have to say it before you get out of this snit you're in?"

"Go to hell," she shot back. "How many times do I have to say it before you start to feel the heat?"

She finally snagged the key, jabbed it into the lock. "Give me my groceries."

"I'll take them in for you."

"I said give me the damn bag." They were back to tugging, until she hissed out a breath. "Keep them, then."

She shoved open the door, but before she could slam it in his face, he'd shoved it open again and pushed his way inside. Their eyes met, both narrowed, and he thought he caught a glint of violence in hers.

"Don't even think about it," he warned her. "I'm not an underweight mugger."

She thought she could still do some damage but decided it would only make him seem more important than she'd determined he would be. Instead, she turned on the heel of her pink suede sneakers, dumped her bag on the counter. When he did the same, she nodded briskly.

"Thanks. Now you've delivered them. Want a tip?"

"Very funny. Let's just settle this first." He reached in his pocket, where he'd folded the hundred-dollar bill she'd given him. "Here."

She flicked the money a disinterested glance. "I'm not taking it back. You earned it."

"I'm not keeping your money over what turned out to be a bad joke."

"Bad joke!" The ice in her eyes turned to sharp green flames. "Is that what it was? Well, ha-ha. Now that you bring it up, I owe you another fifty, don't I?"

That hit the mark, had his jaw clenching as she

grabbed up her purse. "Don't push it, Cybil. Take the money back."

"No."

"I said take the damn money." He grabbed her wrist, yanked her around and crumpled the bill into her palm. "Now…" Then watched in astonishment as she ripped a hundred dollars into confetti.

"There, problem solved."

"That," he said on what he hoped was a calming breath, "was amazingly stupid."

"Stupid? Well, why break pattern? You can go now," she said.

Her voice was so suddenly regal, so completely princess to peon, he nearly blinked. "Very good, very effective," he murmured. "The lady-of-the-manor tone was so utterly unexpected."

Her next suggestion, delivered in the same haughty tone, was also utterly unexpected, to the point, and made him blink.

"That works, too," he acknowledged. "And I don't think you meant that in a romantic sense."

She simply turned, stalked around the counter and began to put away her groceries. If insults and swearing didn't work, perhaps ignoring him would.

It might have if he hadn't seen her fingers tremble as she pushed a box into the cupboard. And seeing it, he felt everything inside him fade but the guilt.

"Cybil, I'm sorry." He watched her hand hesitate, then grab a soup can and shove it away. "It took on a life of its own, and I didn't do anything to stop it. I should have."

"You didn't have to lie to me. I'd have left you alone."

"I didn't lie—or didn't start out to. But I let you assume something other than the truth. I want my privacy. I need it."

"You've got it. I'm not the one who just bullied his way into someone's apartment."

"No, you're not." He stuck his hands in his pockets, dragged them out again and laid them on the counter. "I hurt you, and I didn't have to. I'm sorry for it."

She closed her eyes as she felt the gate she'd sworn to keep locked on her heart creak open. "Why did you?"

"Because I thought it would keep you on your own side of the hall. Because you were a little too appealing for comfort. And because part of me got a kick out of you wanting to help me find work."

He saw her shoulders draw up at that and winced. "I didn't mean it that way. Cybil, how could I not be amused when you offered me a hundred dollars to have dinner with you? A hundred dollars so you could spare an old woman's feelings and get some out-of-work sax player a hot meal. It was…sweet. That's not a word that comes easy to me."

"It's humiliating," she muttered, and grabbed the second bag and began shoving produce into the fridge.

"Don't let it be." He took a chance and walked around the counter so they both stood in the kitchen. "It only backfired because the timing was off, and that's my fault. If I'd told you who I was over dinner, as I should have, you'd have laughed about it. Instead, I made you cry, and I can't stand knowing that."

She stood where she was, staring into the refrigerator. She hadn't expected him to care, for it to matter to him. But it did. She simply couldn't hold out against a caring heart.

Drawing a deep breath, she told herself they would start fresh. Try for casual friends. "Want a beer?"

Every knot in his shoulders loosened. "Oh, yeah."

"Figured." She reached in for a bottle, disposed of the top, reached for a glass. "I haven't heard you talk so much at one time since I met you." When she turned, offering the beer, her eyes were smiling. "You must be dry."

"Thanks."

Her dimple fluttered. "But I'm out of cookies."

"You could always make some more."

"Maybe." She turned away to deal with the groceries. "But I was thinking about baking a pie." Tossing a look over her shoulder, she lifted a brow. "We never did have that pie."

"No, we didn't."

Too appealing for comfort, he thought again. She was wearing an oversize cotton shirt, plain white. Leggings the color of summer skies, those silly shoes.

Since she'd been marketing, he doubted that the just-under-the-smoldering-point perfume had been dabbed on to please anyone but herself, and had no idea why she would wear two gold hoops in one ear and a single diamond stud in the other.

But it all combined into one fascinating package.

When she turned back to reach into the bag again, he took her wrist with his free hand. "Are we on level ground now?"

"Looks like."

"Then there's something else." He set the beer down. "I dream about you."

Now it was her mouth that went dry. And her stomach erupted with the crazed flapping of a hundred wings. "What?"

"I dream about you," he repeated, and stepped forward until her back was against the refrigerator. Her back against the wall this time, he thought. Not his. "About being with you, touching you." Watching her face, he skimmed his fingertips over the tops of her breasts. "And I wake up tasting you."

"Oh, God."

"You said you felt something when I kissed you, and thought I did, too." With his eyes still on hers, he ran his hands down her sides to her hips. "You were right."

Weak at the knees, she swallowed. Hard. "I was?"

"Yeah. And I want to feel it again."

She strained back as he leaned forward. "Wait!"

His mouth paused a breath from hers. "Why?"

And her mind went blank. "I don't know."

His lips curved in one of his rare smiles. "Stop me when you do," he suggested, then captured her.

It was the same. She was sure it wouldn't be, couldn't be the same fast, hot spin of heart and mind and body. But all those parts of her seemed to have been waiting, and poised to leap. Jody was right, she thought dimly. He'd ruined her.

Bright, fresh, soft as a sunbeam. She was all those things. Warm, sweet, generous. All the things he'd forgotten to need were trembling in his arms.

And he wanted them, wanted her with a quick punch of greed he hadn't expected.

On an oath, he savaged her throat. "Here. Right here."

"No." It was the last thing she'd expected to hear come out of her own mouth when his hands were making her ache for more. Even as the need roared in her blood she said it again. "No. Wait."

He lifted his head, kept eyes that had gone the color of a storm at sea on hers. "Why?"

"Because I…" Her head fell back on a moan when his hands, slow and firm, stroked up her body, awakening every pore.

"I want you." His thumbs circled her breasts, over them. "You want me."

"Yes, but—" Her hands opened and closed on his shoulders as she fought off a new spurt of longing. "There are a few things I don't let myself do on impulse. I'm really sorry to say this is one of them."

She opened her eyes again, let out one more shaky breath. How closely he watched her, she realized. How sharply, even with desire clouding his mind. He could step back from it, look through it, and measure.

"It's not a game, Preston."

He lifted a brow, surprised that she'd understood his thoughts so clearly. "No? No," he decided, because he believed her. "You wouldn't be good at that kind of game, would you?"

Someone had been, she thought, and was suddenly, brutally sorry for him. "I don't know. I've never played it."

He stepped back, shrugged and seemed completely in control again while her system continued to jangle. Unconsciously, she lifted her fingertips to her throat where his mouth had aroused dozens of raw nerves.

"I need time before I share myself that way. Making love is a gift and shouldn't be given thoughtlessly."

Her words touched him and, for reasons he couldn't understand, settled him. "It often is."

"Not for me." She shook her head. "Not from me."

Because he had a sudden urge to stroke her cheek,

he hooked his thumbs in his front pockets. Better not to touch again, he reasoned. Not quite yet. "And telling me that is supposed to make me content to step back?"

"Telling you that is supposed to make you understand why I said no, when I want to say yes. When we both know you could make me say yes."

Heat flicked into his eyes. "That's a dangerous kind of honesty you have there."

"You need the truth." She didn't believe she'd ever known anyone who needed it more. "And I don't lie to men I'm planning to be intimate with."

He stepped forward again, watched her lips tremble on a strangled breath. He could make her say yes... and the power of that was heady. Using it, he realized, would damage something he wasn't completely sure he believed existed.

"You need time," he said. "You got an estimate on that?"

Her breath shuddered out again. "Right now it feels like five minutes ago. But..." She managed a weak laugh when his lips curved. "I can't really say, except you'll be the first to know."

"Maybe we could shave a couple of days off it," he murmured, and indulged himself by leaning down to rub his lips over hers.

Hoping it would focus her, she kept her eyes open. But her vision went blurry at the edges. "Um, yes, that's probably going to work."

"Let's shoot for a week," he murmured, deepening the kiss degree by degree until she went limp.

When he stepped back, she pressed a hand to her heart. "Fortnight. I've always liked that word, haven't you? We could try for a fortnight."

The last thing he'd expected to do when buffeted by desire was laugh. "I think we'll save that one for later."

"Right, good. Smart." She concentrated on breathing as he turned and picked up his beer. "Well, I have all this…" She gestured vaguely.

"Food?" he suggested. Delighted by her bewilderment.

"Food, yes. I have all this food. I thought I'd fix some…"

He waited a beat while she pressed her hand to her temple and frowned at the stove. "Dinner?"

"That's it. Ha. Dinner. Funny how words just skip out of reach sometimes. I'm going to fix dinner." She blew out a breath. "Would you like to stay for dinner?"

He sipped his beer, leaned back against the counter. "Can I watch you cook?"

"Sure. You can sit there and maybe slice vegetables or something."

"Okay." Because the idea had amazing appeal, he skirted the counter to sit on a stool. "You cook a lot?"

"Yes, I guess. I really like to cook. It's an adventurous process, all the ingredients, heat, timing, the mix of smells and textures and tastes."

"So…do you ever cook naked?"

She paused in the act of sniffing a glossy red pepper. Giggling, she set it on the counter between them. "McQuinn, you made a joke." She put a hand over his, squeezed. "I'm so proud."

"No, I didn't. That was a perfectly serious question."

When she laughed, leaned over to grab his face and kiss him noisily on the mouth, he wouldn't have recognized his own foolish grin. "So do you?"

"Never when I'm sautéing chicken. Which is what I'm about to do."

"That's all right. I have an excellent imagination."

She laughed again; then, catching the wicked gleam in his eyes, cleared her throat. "I think I want some wine. Do you want wine?" He only lifted his nearly full glass of beer. "Oh, yeah."

She took a bottle of white out of the refrigerator, then turned back, giggling again. "You're going to have to stop that."

"Stop what?"

"Stop making me think I'm naked. Go put on some music," she ordered, waving a hand toward the living area. "Maybe open a window, because it's really hot in here, and give me a minute to clear the lust out of my head so I can think of something else to talk about."

"You never have trouble talking."

"You consider that an insult," she said as he slid off the stool. "I don't. I'm a conversation connoisseur."

"Is that the current term for chatterbox?"

"Well, you're just full of wit and humor tonight, aren't you?" And nothing could have pleased her more.

"Must be the company," he murmured, then cocked a brow as he flipped through her CDs. "You have decent taste in music."

"You were expecting otherwise?"

"I wasn't expecting Fats Waller, Aretha, B.B. King. Of course, you've got plenty of chirpy stuff in here, too."

"What's wrong with chirpy music?"

In answer, he held up a CD of *The Partridge Family's Greatest Hits*. "I rest my case."

"Excuse me, but that was given to me by a very dear friend, and it happens to be a classic."

"A classic what?"

"Obviously, you have no appreciation for nostalgia

and have failed to recognize the sly, underlying social commentary of David Cassidy's rendition of 'I Think I Love You,' or the desperate sexual motivation that permeates the mood of 'Doesn't Somebody Want To Be Wanted.' But I'd be happy to discuss them with you."

"I bet you actually know the lyrics."

She managed to swallow the chuckle and began to wash the vegetables. "Naturally. During a brief, shining period in my youth, *I* was in a band."

"Right." He settled on B.B.

"Lead vocals and rhythm guitar. The Turbos." She smiled as he walked back to the counter. "Jesse—lead guitar—was into cars."

"You play guitar."

"Yes. Well, I played the guitar. A hot red Fender, which I imagine my mother still has in my old room— along with my toe shoes, my chemistry set, the sketches I made when I was going to be a fashion designer and the books I collected on animal husbandry before I realized that if I became a vet, I'd have to euthanize animals as well as play with them."

She laid a cutting board on the counter, selected the proper knife from her block. "They were all quests."

Fascinating, he thought. The woman was absolutely fascinating. "Fender guitars and toe shoes were quests?"

"I couldn't make up my mind what I wanted to be. Everything I tried was so much fun at first, then it was just work. Do you know how to slice peppers?"

"No. Don't you consider what you do now work, of a sort?"

She sighed and began to slice the peppers herself. "Yes, and it's not of a sort, either. It's a lot of work, but it's still fun. Don't you enjoy writing?"

"Rarely."

She looked up again. "Then why do you do it?"

"It won't let me do anything else. It's my only quest."

She nodded, switching to fat, white mushrooms. "It's like that for my mother. She never wanted to do anything but paint. Sometimes, when I watch her working, I can see how painful it is for her to have a vision and to have to pull out all her skills to transfer what she wants to communicate to canvas. But when she's finished, when it's right, she glows. The satisfaction, maybe even the shock of seeing what she's capable of doing, I suppose. It would be like that for you."

She glanced up, saw him studying her speculatively. "It always surprises you when I understand something other than what's right on the surface, doesn't it?"

He grabbed her hand before she could turn away. "If it does, it only means I'm the one who doesn't understand you. I'm likely to keep offending you until I do."

"I'm ridiculously easy to understand."

"No, that's what I thought. I was wrong. You're a maze, Cybil. With dozens of twists and turns and unexpected angles."

Her smile bloomed slowly, beautifully. "That's the nicest thing you've ever said to me."

"I'm not a nice man. You'd be smart to boot me out, lock your door and keep it that way."

"Being smart, I've figured that out for myself already. However…" Gently, she laid a hand to his cheek. "You seem to be my new quest."

"Until it stops being fun and just becomes work?"

His eyes were so serious, she thought. And he was so ready to believe the worst. "McQuinn, you're already work, and you're still sitting in my kitchen." She smiled again. "Do you know how to slice carrots into pencil sticks?"

"I don't have a clue."

"Then watch and learn. Next time you're going to have to carry your weight." She peeled a carrot clean with a few quick, experienced strokes, then flicked a glance up at him. "Am I still naked?"

"Do you want to be?"

She laughed and picked up her neglected wine.

It took a long time to cook a simple meal when you were distracted by conversation, by lingering looks, by seductive touches.

It took a long time to eat a simple meal when you were sliding lazily into love with the man across from you.

She recognized the signs—the erratic beating of the heart, the bubbling in the blood that was desire. When those were tangled so silkily around dreamy smiles and soft sighs, love was definitely a short trip away.

She wondered what it would be like when she reached it.

It took a long time to say good-night when you were floating on deep, dark kisses in the doorway.

And longer still to sleep when your body ached and your mind was full of dreams.

When she heard the faint drift of his music, she smiled and let it lull her to sleep.

Chapter 6

With his hair still wet from his morning shower, Preston sat at his own kitchen counter on one of Cybil's stools she'd insisted he borrow. He scanned the paper as he ate cold cereal and bananas because Cybil had pushed both on him once she'd gotten a look at his cupboards.

Even a kitchen klutz—which apparently meant him—could manage to pour milk onto cold cereal and slice a banana, she'd told him.

He'd decided against taking offense, though he didn't think he was quite as clumsy in the kitchen as she did. He'd managed to put a salad together, hadn't he? While she'd done something incredible and marvelous to a couple of pork chops.

The woman was one hell of a cook, he mused, and was rapidly spoiling his appetite for the quick slap-together sandwiches he often lived on.

It didn't seem to bother her that they hadn't gone out to dinner since that first meal she'd cooked for him. He imagined she would, before much longer, tire of preparing the evening meal and demand a restaurant.

People generally got itchy for a change of pace when the novelty wore off and routines became ruts.

And he supposed they already had a kind of routine. They kept to their separate corners during the day. Well, except for the couple of times she'd dropped by and persuaded him to go out. To the market, just for a walk, to buy a lamp.

He glanced back toward his living room, frowning at the whimsical bronze frog holding up a triangular-shaped lamp shade. He still wasn't sure how she'd talked him into buying such a thing, or into paying Mrs. Wolinsky for a secondhand recliner she'd wanted to get rid of.

And rightfully so, he decided. Who the hell wanted a green-and-yellow plaid recliner in their living room?

But somehow he had one—which despite its hideous looks was amazingly comfortable.

Of course if you had a chair and a lamp you needed a table. His was a sturdy Chippendale in desperate need of refinishing—and as Cybil had pointed out—a bargain because of it.

She just happened to have a friend who refinished furniture as a hobby, and would put him in touch.

She also just happened to have a friend who was a florist, which explained why there was a vase of cheerful yellow daisies on Preston's kitchen counter.

Another friend—of which Preston had decided she had a legion—painted New York street scenes and sold them on the sidewalk, and couldn't he use a couple of paintings to brighten up the walls?

He'd told her he didn't want to brighten anything, but there were now three very decent original watercolors on his wall.

She was already making noises about rugs.

He didn't know how she worked it, Preston thought, shaking his head as he went back to his breakfast. She just kept talking until you were pulling out your wallet or holding out your hand.

But they kept out of each other's way.

Well, there had been Saturday afternoon, when she'd invaded with buckets and mops and brooms and God knows what. If he was going to live in a place, she'd told him, at least it could be clean. And somehow he'd ended up spending three hours of a rainy afternoon, when he should have been writing, scrubbing floors and chasing down dust.

Then again, he'd nearly gotten her into bed. Very nearly gotten her there, he remembered, when she'd stood in speechless shock at the state of his bedroom.

She'd gotten her voice back quickly enough and had launched into a lecture. He should have more respect for his workplace if not for his sleeping area, since they seemed to be one in the same. Why the hell did he keep the curtains drawn over the windows? Did he like caves? Did he have a religious objection to doing laundry?

He'd grabbed her out of self-defense and had stopped her mouth in the most satisfying of ways.

And if they hadn't tripped over a small mountain of laundry on the way to the bed, he doubted they'd have ended the afternoon with a trip to the cleaners.

Still, there were advantages, he thought. He appreciated a clean space, even though he rarely noticed a messy one. He liked tumbling into bed on freshly laundered sheets—though he would have preferred to tumble on them with Cybil. And it was hard to complain when you opened a cupboard and found actual food.

Even the sexual frustration was working for him. The writing was pouring out of it, and out of him. Maybe the play had taken a turn on him, focusing now more on a female character, one with a shining naiveté and enthusiasm. A woman alive with energy and optimism. And one who'd be seduced by and damaged by a man who had none of those things inside him. A man who wouldn't be able to stop himself from taking them from her, then leaving her shattered.

He saw the parallels well enough between what he created and what was, but he refused to worry about it.

He sipped his coffee, reminding himself to ask Cybil why his always tasted faintly of swamp water, and turned to the comic section to see what she'd been up to.

He skimmed it, frowned, then went back to the first section and read it again.

She was already at work, her window open, because spring had decided to be kind. A lovely warm breeze wafted through along with the chaos of street noise.

After her sheet of paper was set and scaled, she set her T-square back in its place in the custom-built tool area she'd designed to suit herself. She tilted her head, facing the first blank section. It was double the size of what would appear in the dailies in a couple of weeks. She already had it in her mind—the setup, the situation and the punch line that would comprise those five windows and give the readership their morning chuckle over coffee.

The elusive Mr. Mysterious, now known as Quinn, huddled in his dim cave, writing the Great American Novel. Sexy, cranky, irresistible Quinn, so serious, so intense in his own little world he was completely unaware that Emily was crouched on his fire escape, peering through the narrow chink of his perpetually drawn curtains, struggling to read his work in progress through a pair of binoculars.

Amused at herself—because in her own way Cybil knew her subtle little probes and questions on how his play was going were the more civilized version of her counterpart's voyeurism—she settled down to lightly sketch her professional interpretation of the man across the hall.

She exaggerated ruthlessly, his good points and his bad. The tall, muscular body, the ruggedly chiseled looks, the cool eyes. His rudeness, his humor and his perpetual bafflement with the world Emily lived in.

Poor guy, she thought, he doesn't have a clue what to do with her.

When the buzzer sounded, she tucked her pencil behind her ear, thinking Jody had forgotten her key.

She stopped to top off her coffee cup on the way. "Just hang on. Coming."

Then she opened the door and experienced one more rapid meltdown. His hair was just a little damp and he wasn't wearing a shirt. Boy, oh, boy, just look at those pecs, she thought, and barely resisted licking her lips.

His jeans were faded, his feet bare, and his face—his face was so wonderfully serious and sober.

"Hi." She managed to make it sound bright and easy

while she pictured herself biting him. "You run out of soap in the shower? Need to borrow some?"

"What? No." He'd forgotten he was only half-dressed. "I want to ask you about this," he continued, lifting the paper.

"Sure, come on in." It would be safe, she told herself. Jody would be there any minute and stop her from jumping Preston. "Why don't you get some coffee and come up? I'm working and it's rolling pretty well."

"I don't want to interrupt, but—"

"Not much does," she said cheerfully over her shoulder as she started up the stairs. "There's cinnamon bagels if you want one."

"No." Hell, he thought, and ended up pouring a cup of coffee and taking a bagel, after all.

He hadn't been upstairs before, since he'd never come over when she was working. He tormented himself by glancing into her bedroom, studying the big bed with its bold blue cover and sumptuous mountain of jewel-toned pillows, the slim rods of the white iron headboard where he could imagine trapping her hands under his as he finally did everything he wanted with her. To her.

It smelled of her, fresh, female, with seductive undertones of vanilla.

She kept rose petals in a bowl, a book beside the bed and candles in the window.

"Find everything?" she called out.

He shook himself. "Yeah. Listen, Cybil…" He stepped into her studio. "God, how do you work with all that noise?"

She barely glanced up. "What noise? Oh, that." She continued to sketch, using a new pencil, as she'd forgotten the one behind her ear. "Sort of like background music. Half the time I don't hear it."

The room looked efficient and creative with its neat shelves holding both supplies and clever tchotchkes. He recognized the work of the sidewalk artist in one of the paintings on her wall, and the genius of her mother in two others.

There was a complex and fascinating metal sculpture in the corner, a little clutch of violets tucked into a glass inkwell and a cozy divan heaped with more pillows against the wall.

But she didn't look efficient, bent over the big slanted board with her legs folded up under her, the toenails of her bare feet painted pink, a pencil behind one ear and a gold hoop in the other.

She looked scattered, and sexy.

Curious, he walked around to peer over her shoulder. An act that, he admitted, had anyone dared to try on him would have earned the offender a quick and painful death.

"What are all the blue lines for?"

"Scaling, perspective. Takes a little math before you can get down to business. I work in five windows for the dailies," she continued, sketching easily. "I have to set them on paper like this, work out the theme, the gag, the hit, so that the strip can move from start to finish in five connected beats."

Satisfied, she moved to the next section. "I sketch it in first, just need to see how it hangs—you'd say a draft, where you get the story line down, then decide where it needs to be punched up. I'll give it more details, fiddle a bit before I switch to pen and ink."

He frowned, focusing on the first sketch. "Is that supposed to be me?"

"Hmm. Why don't you pull up a stool. You're blocking the light."

"What is she doing there?" Ignoring the suggestion, he tapped a finger on the second window. "Spying on me. You're spying on me?"

"Don't be ridiculous—you don't even have a fire escape outside your bedroom." She looked into her mirror, made several faces that left him staring at her, then started on the third section.

"What about this?" he demanded, rapping the paper on her shoulder.

"What about it? God, you smell fabulous." Pleasing herself, she turned and sniffed him. "What kind of soap is that?"

"Are you going to have this guy take a shower next?" When she pursed her lips in obvious consideration, Preston shook his head. "No. There has to be a line. I was oddly amused when you introduced this parody of me into the script, but—"

He broke off as he heard her front door open and slam shut. "Who's that?"

"That would be Jody and Charlie. So you've gotten a kick out of the new guy?" She stopped sketching and shifted to smile up at him. "I wondered, because you hadn't mentioned it before. You know, some people don't even recognize themselves. They just have no self-awareness, I suppose, but I thought you'd see it if you happened to read the strip. Hi, Jody. There's Charlie."

"Hi." It wasn't an easy matter, even for a happily married woman, to keep her tongue from falling out when she was so suddenly and unexpectedly faced with a well-muscled, naked male chest. "Uh, hi. Are we interrupting?"

"No, Preston just had some questions about the strip."

"I love the new guy. He's really got Emily in a spin. I can't wait to see what happens next." She broke into a wide grin as Charlie exploded out a "Da!" and reached for Preston.

"He calls every man he sees 'Da.' Chuck's a little put out by it, but Charlie's just a guy's guy, you know."

"Right." Absently, Preston ran a hand over Charlie's downy brown hair. "I just want to get something straight about how this thing is going," he began, turning back to Cybil.

"Da!" Charlie said again, arms extended hopefully, smile sleepy.

"Just how close to reality do you work?" Preston asked, automatically taking the baby and settling him on his shoulder.

Cybil's heart simply melted. "You like babies."

"No, I toss them out of third-story windows at every opportunity," he said impatiently, then shook his head when Jody squeaked. "Relax. He's fine. What I want to know is this business here." Shifting the baby, he dropped the comic section on her board.

"Oh, the 'no scale' bit. This is really part one. They'll run the second half of it tomorrow. I think it works."

"Chuck and I fell over laughing when we read it this morning," Jody put in, relaxed again as she watched Preston absently patting the now-sleeping baby.

"You've got these two women here—"

"Emily and Cari."

"I know who they are by now," Preston muttered,

narrowing his eyes at both women. "They're discussing—they're rating, for God's sake—the way Quinn kissed Emily a couple days ago."

"Uh-huh. Chuck laughed?" Cybil wanted to know. "I wondered if men would get it or if it would just hit with women."

"Oh, yeah, he died over it."

"Pardon me." With what he considered admirable restraint, Preston held up a hand. "I'd like to know if the two of you sit around here discussing your various sexual encounters and then rating them on a scale of one to ten before you then give the American public a good chuckle over it with their corn flakes."

"Discussing them?" Eyes wide and innocent, Cybil stared up at Preston. "Honestly, McQuinn, this is a comic strip. You're taking it too seriously."

"So all this about the no scale is just a bit?"

"What else?"

He studied her face. "I wouldn't like to think that when I finally get you into bed, I'm going to read about my performance in five sections in the morning paper."

"Oh, my. Oh, well." Jody patted a hand on her heart. "I think I'll just take Charlie and go put him down for his nap." She eased him out of Preston's arms and hurried out.

"McQuinn." Cybil smiled, tapped her pencil. "I have a feeling that event would be worth the full Sunday spread."

"Is that a threat or a joke?"

When she only laughed, he spun her stool around, then knocked the air out of her lungs with a fierce and demanding kiss. "Tell your friend to go away, and we'll find out."

"No, I'm keeping her. She's all that stopped me from biting your throat when you came in."

"Are you trying to drive me crazy?"

"Not really. It's kind of a side effect." Her pulse had gone from slow shuffle to manic tap dance. "You've got to go. I've finally found a distraction I can't work through. And you're it."

Seeing no reason he should go crazy alone, he leaned down one last time and took her mouth. "When you speak of this—" he caught her bottom lip between his teeth, drawing it erotically through them "—and I expect you will, be accurate."

He walked to the doorway, turning back in time to see her shudder. "No scale?" he said, realizing he suddenly found it not just amusing but gratifying.

When she managed to do nothing more than make one helpless gesture with her hands, he laughed. And was still grinning when he jogged down her steps and out the door.

"Safe?" Jody whispered, poking her head into the doorway.

"Oh, God, God, Jody, what am I going to do here?" Shaken, Cybil stabbed the second pencil behind her ear, knocked the first out of place, and didn't even bother to curse. "I thought I had it all figured out. I mean what's wrong with easing yourself into what promises to be a blistering, roof-raising affair with an incredibly intense, gorgeous, interesting man?"

"Let me think." Holding up a finger, Jody strolled in and picked up the coffee Preston had never touched. "Okay, I've got it. Nothing. The answer to that question is nothing."

"And if you're a little bit in love with him, that only sweetens the deal, right?"

"Absolutely. Otherwise it's fun but sort of like eating too much chocolate at one sitting. You enjoy it when it's going on, then you feel a little queasy and ashamed."

"But what if you went all the way in. What do you do when you've gone over the brink?"

Jody set down the coffee. "You went over the brink?"

"Just now."

"Oh, honey." All sympathy, Jody wrapped her arms around Cybil and rocked. "It's all right. It had to happen sooner or later."

"I know, but I always thought it would be later."

"We all do."

"He won't want me to be in love with him. It'll just annoy him." Turning her face to Jody's shoulder, she let out a shaky breath. "I'm not too happy about it myself, but I'll get used to it."

"Sure you will. Poor Frank." With a sigh, Jody patted Cybil's shoulder, then stepped back. "He never really had a shot, did he?"

"Sorry."

"Oh, well." Jody dismissed her favorite cousin with an absent flick of the wrist. "What are you going to do?"

"I don't know. I guess running and hiding's out."

"That's for wimps."

"Yeah. Wimps. How about pretending it'll go away?"

"That's for morons."

Cybil drew a bracing breath. "How about shopping?"

"Now you're talking." On a quick salute, Jody headed for the door. "I'll see if Mrs. Wolinsky will watch Charlie, then we'll handle this problem like real women."

* * *

She bought a new dress. A slinky length of black sin that made Jody roll her eyes and declare, "The man's a goner," when Cybil tried it on.

She bought new shoes. Mile-high heels as thin as honed scalpels.

She bought new lingerie. The kind women wear when they expect it to be seen by a man who'll then be compelled to rip it off.

And she imagined Preston's wide hands and long fingers peeling the silky-as-cobwebs hose down her legs.

Then there were flowers to choose, candles, wine.

Marketing for a meal she would design to tease the senses and whet the palate for a more primitive kind of appetite.

By the time she got home she was loaded down, and she was calm.

There was a scene to be set, and doing so gave her focus. Because she wanted to take the rest of the day to prepare, because she needed it to be perfect, she wrote a note to Preston and stuck it to her door.

Then she locked herself in, drew a deep breath and took everything up to the bedroom.

She arranged tender lilies and fragrant rosebuds in vases, in bowls, and set them on tables, the dresser, the windowsills. Then she grouped candles, all white, a trio here, a single there, a half-dozen scented tealights on a circle of mirrored glass.

Some she lit so the room would fill with soft light and gentle fragrance while she worked.

She unwrapped two slender-stemmed wineglasses, placed them just so on the low table in front of the curved wicker chaise. Reminded herself to chill the wine.

Facing the bed, she stopped, considered. Would turning down the duvet and sheets be too obvious? Then she laughed at herself. Why stop now?

When it was done, when she could look around the room and see there was nothing that wasn't as she needed it to be, she went down to make the early preparations for the meal she intended to cook.

She listened, hoping he'd begin to play so that some of him would come inside her rooms with her. But his apartment remained silent.

With careful deliberation she chose music for mood, arranging CDs in her changer.

Satisfied, she went back up, laid her new dress on the bed, shivered in anticipation as she set the black lace bra and the blatantly provocative matching garter belt beside it and imagined what it would feel like to wear them.

Powerful, she decided. Secretive and certain.

She shivered again, thrilling to the clutch of lust deep in her center, then went to draw a hot, frothy bath.

She poured wine, lit more candles to promote the mood, before she slipped into the tub. And closing her eyes, she imagined Preston's hands, rather than the frothy water, on her.

Nearly an hour later, she was slathering every inch of her body with cream, sliding her fingers along to make certain her skin was silky and scented, when Preston tugged her note off the front door:

McQuinn, I've got plans. I'll see you later. Cybil

Plans? Plans? She had plans when he'd worked himself into a turmoil over her all day? He read the note again, furious with both of them, as he hadn't been able to get the image of spending yet another foolish evening with her out of his head.

For God's sake, he'd gone out and bought her flowers. He hadn't bought flowers for a woman since...

He crumpled the note in his hand. What else could he expect? Women were, first and foremost, tuned to their own agenda. He'd known it, accepted it, and if he'd let himself forget that single relevant detail with Cybil, he had no one to blame but himself.

She'd see him later?

It appeared she was a game player, after all. But he didn't have to step up to bat.

He turned, marched back into his apartment, where he tossed the lilacs that had inexplicably reminded him of her on the kitchen counter. He flipped her balled note across the room, picked up his sax and stalked out to work off his temper at Delta's.

At exactly seven-thirty, Cybil took the stuffed mushrooms she'd slaved over out of the oven. The table was set for two, with more candles, more flowers precisely arranged. There was a wonderfully colorful avocado-and-tomato salad chilling along with the wine.

Once they'd enjoyed their appetizers and first course, she intended to destroy him with her seafood crepes.

If all went according to plan, they'd polish off the meal with icy champagne and fresh raspberries and cream. In bed.

"Okay, Cybil."

She took off her apron, marched to the mirror to check the fit and line of the dress. She slipped on her heels, added another dash of perfume, then gave her reflection a bracing smile.

"Let's go get him."

She sauntered across the hall, pressed his buzzer, then waited with her heart hammering. Shifting from foot to foot, she buzzed again.

"How could you not be home? How *could* you? Didn't you get the note? You must have. It's not on the door, is it? Didn't I specifically say I'd see you later?"

Groaning, she thumped her fist against the door. Then she jerked upright and blinked.

"I said I had plans. Oh, my God, you didn't get it, did you, you thick-headed jerk? *You're* the plans. Oh, hell." She made a dash back through her open door for her key, realized she didn't have anywhere to put it. With a shrug, she stuck it into her bra rather than waste time running upstairs for a bag.

In thirty seconds flat, she was risking a broken neck by running down the stairs.

"Woman trouble, sugar lips?"

Preston looked over at Delta as he took a break to wet his throat. "No woman. No trouble."

"This is Delta." She tapped a finger to his cheek. "Every night this week you come in here late and you play like a man who's got a woman on his mind. And this man doesn't much mind having her there. Now tonight, you come in early and you're playing like a man who's got trouble with the woman. Did you have a fight with that pretty little girl?"

"No. We've both got other things to do."

"Still holding you off, is she?" She laughed, but not without sympathy. "Some women take more romance than others."

"It has nothing to do with romance."

"Maybe that's your problem." Delta wrapped an arm around his shoulders and squeezed. "Do you ever buy her flowers? Tell her she has beautiful eyes."

"No." Damn it, he had brought her flowers. She hadn't bothered to stick around to take them. "It's sex, not a courtship."

"Oh, sweetheart. You want one, you better do the other with a woman like that."

"That's why I'm better off without a woman like that. I want it simple." He picked up the sax, lifted a brow. "Now, are you going to let me play, or do you want to give me more advice on my love life?"

With a shake of her head, she stepped back. "When you have a love life, *cher,* I'll have advice."

He blew off a riff, listening to the music inside his head. Inside his blood. He let the notes come, but the music didn't take his mind off her. He could use that, as well, he told himself. Here, where sharing was a pleasure. Not with words, where it was often pain.

The notes slipped out, throbbed in the air, sobbed into a wail.

And she walked in the door.

Her eyes, full of secrets, met his through the haze of smoke, held. And the smile she sent him as she slid into a chair made his palms go damp. She moistened her lips, trailed a finger up from the center of the low bodice of the slinky black dress to the base of her throat. And back again.

He watched, his blood swimming, as she crossed long, long legs with a movement so slow, so studied, it had to be deliberate. Surely the way she ran her hand from calf to knee to thigh was designed to make a man's gaze follow the movement.

His did, and his pulse leaped like a wolf on the hunt.

She sat through the song, leaning back in the chair, hooking one arm provocatively over the back. When the notes faded, she traced the tip of her tongue lazily over those hot red lips.

Then she rose, her gaze still locked with his as the music pumped. She ran a hand down her hip, turned on those man-killer heels and started back out. She glanced over her shoulder, sent him a sultry invitation with no more than a lift of eyebrow and left the door swinging behind her.

The oath that came out of his mouth when he lowered the sax was absolutely reverent.

"You going after that, brother?"

Preston crouched to push his sax into its case. "Do I look stupid, André?"

"No." André chuckled and kept on playing. "No, you don't."

Chapter 7

She was waiting on the sidewalk when he came out, standing in the white wash of a streetlight with one hand resting on a cocked hip, her head angled, her lips curved in the barest hint of a smile. It made him think of a photograph, some arty shot perfectly framed and cropped for a classy magazine.

Sex in black and white.

He started toward her, taking more in the closer he came. The short, whiskey-colored hair sleeked to frame her face. The short black dress sleeked to frame her body.

No jewelry to distract the eye.

Mile-high heels designed to showcase mile-long legs.

The only color was on those huge green eyes under sooty lashes and the siren red of her mouth. A mouth, he noted, that was curved in smug, female satisfaction.

He was three steps away when her scent reached

out like a crooked finger and beckoned him the rest of the way.

"Hello, neighbor." She purred it—one more hot bullet to his loins.

He tilted his head, lifted a brow. "Change of plans... neighbor?"

"I hope not." She took the last step, moving into him, deliberately sliding her hands up his sides, over his shoulders, around his neck. Her body fit suggestively to his as she purred again.

Then she laughed, shook her head. "You were the plans, you knothead."

She wondered if it was the announcement or the mild insult that had his eyes narrowing in speculation.

"Is that so?"

"McQuinn." She tilted her head, brought her mouth a whisper from his. Then, with her eyes on his, slowly licked. "Didn't I tell you you'd be the first to know?"

"Yeah." With his free hand he cupped her neck, keeping that wet red mouth tantalizingly close to his. "How fast can you walk in those heels?"

She laughed again, just a little breathlessly now. "Not very. But we've got all night, don't we?"

"It might just take longer than that." He stepped back, and after a moment, held out a hand for hers. "Where did you get the lethal weapon? The dress," he added when she gave him a blank look.

"Oh, this old thing." This time her laugh was warm and rich. "I bought it today, thinking of you. And when I put it on tonight, I was thinking of what it was going to be like when you took it off me."

"You must have been practicing," he said when he

could manage to form words again. "Because you're damn good at this."

"Actually, I'm making it up as I go along."

"Don't stop on my account."

It was amazing, she thought, that a balmy spring evening could suddenly seem as sultry as summer in the Tropics. "Sorry I wasn't more specific in my note. I had a lot on my mind." She turned, delighted that the heels brought her eye level with his mouth. "A lot of you on my mind."

"It pissed me off." It didn't seem so hard to admit it.

"Pardon me if I find that very flattering. When I knocked on your door and you didn't answer, I had essentially the same reaction. I spent a lot of time getting ready for you. You can be flattered."

"It must have taken a while to paint on what there is of that dress."

"Not just that." She'd managed to keep her heartbeat fairly steady, but as she paused at the entrance to their building, it began to plunge and kick. "I made dinner."

"You did?" He wasn't just flattered, he realized. He wasn't just aroused. He was touched.

"A fairly fabulous one, if I do say so myself," she added, backing into the building. "With a sassy little white wine to set it off—and an elegant and icy champagne to go with dessert."

She led the way into the elevator, pushed the button for three, then leaned back against the wall. "Which I thought we could enjoy in bed."

He kept a step away, knowing if he touched her they wouldn't be leaving the elevator for a very long time. "Anything else I should know about these plans of yours?"

"Oh, I don't think you're going to need me to write anything down." She stepped off the elevator, tossed one of those slow smiles over her shoulder and strolled to her door.

He thought if he managed to get inside without exploding, he'd show her he could make plans of his own. "Key?"

"Hmm." Keeping her eyes on his, she slid a finger under the deep scoop of her bodice, touched metal and watched his gaze drop, heat, linger. "Gee." She slid her finger up again, circled it lazily at the base of her throat. "I can't seem to find it. Maybe you can get it for me."

He decided he had news for medical science. It was possible to remain conscious and upright after all the blood had drained out of your head.

He trailed his finger along the inviting swell above the black silk—felt her shiver, heard the catchy intake of her breath. Then dipped down, taking his time, gliding his finger lazily over heated flesh, gently abrading her nipple until her eyes clouded and closed.

"I'd say you're the one who's been practicing," she managed, and made him smile.

"I'm just making it up as I go along."

"Mmm-hmm. Don't stop on my account."

He didn't intend to. Not for hours. "Looks like I found it," he murmured, hooking the key.

"Yeah." She let out a long, long breath. "I just knew you would."

He slid the key home, released locks. "Ask me in, Cybil."

"Come in."

He pushed open the door, backed her inside. Reaching behind, he locked the door. Clamping his hands on her hips, he kept walking.

"Dinner?"

"Can wait." He lifted the phone off the hook as they passed it.

"The wine?"

"Later. Much later." Her heels bumped into the bottom step. This time he smiled. "Keep going."

On legs that had gone weak, she moved up the stairs with her hands braced on his shoulders.

"Ask me to touch you."

"Touch me." She sighed as his hands traveled up.

"Ask me to taste you."

"Taste me." And moaned as his mouth brushed over the rise of her breasts.

When they reached the bedroom door, his teeth scraped along her throat, her jaw, and left her mouth aching for attention.

"Kiss me."

"I will." But he only teased the corners of her lips with the tip of his tongue. "I want the light."

"No, I have candles. They're everywhere." She broke free to grab a matchbook, then fumbled. "I can't. I'm shaking. Isn't that ridiculous?"

He took the matches from her and danced his fingertips along her thigh. "I want you to. Don't move," he ordered, then worked his way around the room setting the candles alight.

The glow shimmered. The scent whispered.

Tossing the matches aside, he moved back to where she stood, her eyes huge and full of nerves, needs and candlelight.

"Now." His hands slid around her waist, down. "Ask me to take you."

She kept her eyes on his. "Take me."

His mouth captured hers, plundered, rocking her with the first punch of the power they'd built between them. She grabbed on, as much to add to the storm as ride it. This was what she wanted, this bold, blistering, battering heat. The crash of senses, the war of needs.

"I want you." She raced wild kisses over his face. "I want you in bed."

Then she gasped as he whirled her around, dragged her back against him. It stunned her to see them reflected in the mirror, to see the gleam of desire in his gaze as it traveled down her body.

"We have all night," he reminded her. "Watch."

He dipped his head to the curve of her neck and shoulder, sharp little bites that had the first helpless sounds catching in her throat.

She watched his hands travel up, saw them, felt them cup her breasts, squeeze, release, slide over silk, his fingers sliding under it, tugging the material. She braced for him to rip.

Then shuddered as he simply let his hands glide over her again, then down. She cried out in aroused shock as he pressed against her center.

His head lifted, his teeth catching the lobe of her ear as their gazes met in the mirror. She'd driven him crazy when she'd walked into the club. He intended to return the favor.

"Tell me you want more."

Her muscles had gone lax, her bones to jelly. "Preston."

He traced his fingers up and down her thighs, felt

the muscles quiver and the flesh heat. "Tell me you want more."

"God." Her head fell back on his shoulder as she fought for air. "I want more."

"So do I."

He moved from silky hose to silky flesh, torturing himself. Her scent was destroying him, the feel of her urging him to take all of her. But he drew it out, even as his own breath became labored; he held back the animal pacing inside him.

Because when he let it go, he knew it would devour them both.

He nipped his way around the back of her neck, her shoulders, while he tugged down the zipper of her dress. He peeled it off her, then bit back a groan.

Sex in black and white, he thought again.

Even through the haze of desire she saw his eyes change. Saw something dangerous flash into them. It shocked her to realize that was what she wanted. The danger, the risk, the glory of breaking whatever choke chain he had on his control.

Power swirled into her as she covered his hands with hers and guided them over her. "I bought this today," she whispered, holding his hands to her breasts. "So you could rip it off me tonight."

She curled her fingers with his, nudged them over the thin silk connecting the lace. And let out one sharp gasp when he yanked the dress apart.

And with that single movement, he broke.

He spun her around, his mouth ravishing hers now, his hands close to brutal as he dragged her to the bed.

He was going to eat her alive, and couldn't stop it. He felt her arch and buck when his hand covered her.

Heard her choked scream as he drove her over the first ragged edge. Then he was tearing at silk and lace, desperate for more.

He feasted on her breasts, the firm fragrant swell of them, while her heart hammered against his mouth. Her hands drove him wild as they pulled at his shirt, as her nails scraped down his back.

Her mouth was as greedy as his, her hands as rough and impatient as they tugged and dragged at his jeans. And when they closed around him, fire burst in his blood.

She rolled with him, tangling in the sheets she'd so carefully smoothed. Panting, shuddering, she wrapped herself around him, bowed up in urgent demand.

When he drove into her, heat into heat, the explosion of pleasure was huge, a fast, hard, turbulent wave that drenched the skin and swamped the soul. With one throaty moan, she matched him for speed and fury.

More was all he could think. He had to have more of her. Clamping her hands on the slim iron poles of the headboard, he plunged deeper. She arched, accepted. Mad on the pleasure of her, he watched her face, absorbing every flicker of shock and delight as he took her higher, and faster, then over so that she sobbed out his name, so that her eyes went dark and blind.

As her body melted under his, he let himself pour into her. Surrendered himself.

His hands continued to hold hers on the rungs, though her fingers had gone limp. His body continued to cover hers while she quaked. He stayed inside her. Mated.

"Are we still breathing?"

He turned his head, felt the pulse in her throat scrambling. "Your heart's still beating."

"Good, that's good. Is yours?"

"Seems to be."

"Okay, then it's probably safe for us to stay here like this for the next five or ten years. I'm pretty sure I'll be able to move by then."

He lifted his head. Though she kept her eyes closed, Cybil was aware she was being studied, imagined that clear blue and focused gaze. And smiled. "I seduced the hell out of you, McQuinn. It was awfully nice of you to return the favor."

"No problem. It was the least I could do."

"Nobody ever made me feel like this before." She opened her eyes. "No one ever touched me this way."

She saw her mistake immediately. The way his eyes shuttered, the way he retreated from the intimacy. If it was light, if it was sexy, if it was dangerous, he was with her. But there was to be no tenderness, no heart, no slippery sentiment, to change the balance.

It made her ache for both of them.

"You've got great hands." She made her smile sassy as she wiggled her fingers under his. "Definitely major-league hands."

"You've got some real contenders yourself." He rolled onto his back, relieved and annoyed with himself for feeling that deep inner jolt when she'd looked at him with so much dazzled emotion in her eyes.

He wasn't going to let things shift into that area between them. Because once it did, it was over. That part of him that was hope and heart had long ago been calcified.

She wanted to curl into him, to curve her body into the warmth of his, but imagined that was another taboo.

Keep it simple, she warned herself, *or he'll walk right out the door.*

So she sat up, instead, flicked her fingers through her disordered hair. "I think that wine would go down well right now, don't you?"

"Oh, yeah." He skimmed his fingers along her calf, because he had to touch, had to keep that connection. "You mentioned something about dinner."

"McQuinn, I have an amazing meal in store for you." She leaned down to give him a careless kiss. "Everything's done but the crepes—seafood crepes, which I will whip up in front of your astonished eyes."

"You're going to cook?"

"Mmm-hmm."

He watched her slide out of bed, walk to the closet on legs that had his blood stirring again. "What's that for?"

"This? It's called a robe," she said with a laugh as she slipped into it. "It's often used to cover nakedness."

He got up, crossed to her and tugged the belt loose again. "Take it off."

A quick thrill shimmied down her spine. "I thought you wanted dinner."

"I do. And I want to watch you cook it."

"Then—oh." She laughed again and pulled the robe together. "I am not cooking crepes naked. That little fantasy of yours is doomed."

He didn't think so. "Actually, I was wondering if you had any more of…" He turned to the bed, found what was left of the lacy black garter belt. "This sort of thing."

Surprised, then intrigued, she lifted her eyebrows. "No intelligent shopper buys only one. I have another little ensemble in red. Break-your-heart, tart red."

His smile spread slowly as he tossed the black lace aside. "Why don't you put it on? I'm really hungry."

Preparing crepes in sexy underwear was not without its risks. Cybil discovered just what it was like to be ravished against the pantry door.

Amazing.

And plundered on the living-room rug.

Incredible.

And being savaged under the hot, beating spray of the shower was an experience she would be more than willing to repeat.

Through the hours of the night he'd reached for her, thrilled her, had never seemed quite able to get enough of her. Or she of him. They'd been so completely in tune, so utterly together, that at times it had seemed his heart had beat inside hers.

The candles had gutted out in their own fragrant pools, and light had been seeping softly through the windows when she'd fallen into an exhausted sleep.

Only to wake alone.

She knew it shouldn't hurt her that he hadn't slept with her, hadn't woken with her. It wasn't to be like that between them. She knew that, accepted that. There would be no soft and foolish words between them, no baring of souls.

The border of intimacy stopped at the physical, with his side of it walled thick. Her heart was her own problem, not his.

How could he know she'd never given herself so absolutely to any other man? Why should he be expected to know that the primitive power of their desire for each other was driven by love on her side?

She rubbed her tired eyes and ordered herself up and out of bed.

She'd walked into the relationship with her eyes open, she thought as she tidied up the bedroom. She'd known its limitations. His limitations. They could be together, enjoy each other, as long as certain lines weren't crossed.

Well, that was fine. She wasn't going to pine and sigh over it. She was in charge of her own emotions; she was responsible for her own actions; and she was hardly going to mope around because she was involved with an exciting, fascinating, interesting man.

"Damn it!" She hurled her shoes into the closet. "Damn it, damn it, damn it!"

Cybil leaped on the bed, grabbed the phone. She had to tell someone, talk to someone. And when it was this vital, there was really only one someone.

"Mama? Mama, I'm in love," she said, then burst into wild tears.

Preston's fingers flew over the keyboard. He'd had less than three hours' sleep, but his system was revved, his mind clear as crystal. His first major play had been wrenched out of him, every word a wound. But this was pouring out, streaming like wine out of a magic bottle that had only been waiting to be decanted.

It was so fully alive. And for the first time in longer than he could remember, so was he.

He could see it all perfectly, the sets, the staging, the characters and everything inside them. The doomed, the damned, the triumphant.

A world in three acts.

There was an energy here, inside these people who

formed on the page and lived on the stage already set inside his head. He knew them, knew how their hearts would leap and how they would break.

The thread of hope that ran through their lives hadn't been planned, but it was there, woven through and tangled so that he found himself riding on it with them.

He wrote until he ran dry; then, disoriented, glanced around the room. It was dark but for the lamp he'd switched on and the steady glow from his computer screen. He hadn't a clue what time it was—what day, for that matter. But his neck and shoulders were stiff, his stomach empty, and the coffee in the cup on his desk looked faintly revolting.

Standing, he worked out the worst of the kinks, then walked to the window, pushed open the curtains. There was a hell of a spring storm going on. He hadn't noticed. Now he watched the flashing of lightning, the scurry of desperate pedestrians rushing to appointments or shelter.

The entrepreneur on the corner was doing a brisk business in the umbrellas, which no one in New York seemed to own for longer than it took the pavement to dry.

He wondered if Cybil was looking out her window, watching the same scene. What she would think of it, how she would turn something so simple and ordinary as a thunderstorm in the city into the bright and ridiculous.

She'd use the Umbrella Man, he decided, work up an entire biography for him, give the figure in black slicker and hood a name, a background, a personality full of quirks. And the anonymous street vendor would become part of her world.

She had such a gift for drawing people into her world.

He was in it now, Preston mused. He hadn't been able to stop himself from opening that colorful door and stepping inside the confusion, the delights, the energy.

She didn't seem to understand he didn't belong there.

When he was inside, when he was surrounded by her, it seemed as though he could stay. That if he let it, life could be just that simple and extraordinary.

Like a storm in the city, he thought. But storms pass.

He'd nearly let himself sink into it that morning. Nearly let himself sink in and stay in that warm bed, with that warm body that had turned to curl around him in sleep.

She'd looked so...soft, he thought now. So welcoming. What had moved through him as he'd watched her in that fragile light had been a different kind of hunger. One that yearned to hold, to sigh out all the troubles and doubts and hold on to dreams.

It had been safer for both of them to leave her sleeping.

He flicked the curtains closed and walked downstairs.

He started fresh coffee, foraged for food, toyed with the idea of a nap.

But he thought of her, and of the night, and knew the restlessness inside him wouldn't allow him to rest.

What was she doing over there?

He had no business knocking on her door, interrupting her work just because his was finished for now. Just because the drum of rain made him feel edgy and alone. Just because he wanted her.

He liked being alone, he reminded himself as he prowled the living area. He needed the edge for his work.

He wanted to sit with her and watch the rain. To

make slow, lazy love with her while it pounded the streets and sidewalks and cocooned them from everything but each other.

Wanted her, he admitted, just a little too much for comfort.

He told himself it was safe enough to want. It was crossing the line from want to need that was dangerous. Just how close, he wondered, was he already skirting that very thin, very shaky line?

When a woman got inside a man this way, it changed him, left him wide-open so that he made mistakes and exposed pieces of himself better left alone.

She wasn't Pamela. He wasn't so blind he believed every woman was a liar and a cheat and cold as stone. If he'd ever known anyone with less potential for cruelty and deceit, it was Cybil Campbell.

But that didn't change the bottom line.

From want to need to love were short, skidding steps. Once a man had taken the fall and ended up broken, he learned to keep his balance at all costs. He didn't want the desperation, the vulnerability, the loss of self that went hand in hand with genuine intimacy. And he'd stopped believing himself capable of those things.

Which meant there was nothing to worry about, he told himself, sipping his coffee and staring at his door as if he could see through it and through the one across the hall. She wasn't asking for anything more than passion, companionship, enjoyment.

Exactly as he was.

She was perfectly aware the arrangement was temporary.

He'd be gone in a few weeks, and their lives would

go comfortably in other directions. She with her crowds of friends, he with his contented solitude.

He'd set his cup down with a violent snap before he realized the idea annoyed him.

They could still see each other from time to time, he told himself as he began to pace again. His house in Connecticut was a reasonable commute from the city. Isn't that why he'd chosen it in the first place?

He came into the city often enough. There was no reason he couldn't make it more often.

Until she got involved with someone else, he thought, jamming his hands in his pockets. Why should a woman like that wait around for him to breeze in and out of her life?

And that was fine, too, he decided as his temper began to rumble like the thunder outside. Who was asking her to wait around? She could damn well hook herself up with any idiot her interfering friends tossed at her.

But not, by God, while he was still across the hall.

He strode to her door, intending to make a few things clear. And opened it just in time to watch Cybil launch herself joyfully into the arms of a tall man with sun-streaked brown hair.

"Still the prettiest girl in New York," he said in a voice that hinted of beignets and chicory. "Give me a kiss."

And as she did, lavishly, Preston wondered which method of murder would be most satisfying.

Chapter 8

"Matthew! Why didn't you tell me you were coming? When did you get in? How long are you staying? Oh, I'm so happy to see you! You're all wet. Come inside, take off your jacket—when are you going to buy a new one? This one looks like it's been through a war."

He only laughed, hefted her off her feet and kissed her again. "You still never shut up."

"I babble when I'm happy. When are you—oh, Preston." She beamed at him out of eyes shining with joy. "I didn't see you there."

"Obviously." Bare hands, he thought, would be the most satisfying. He would simply take the guy with the smug brown eyes and the scarred leather jacket apart piece by piece. And feed each one to Cybil. "Don't let me interrupt the reunion."

"It's great, isn't it? Matthew, this is Preston McQuinn."

"McQuinn?" Matthew ran his tongue around his teeth. He was fairly sure the man braced in the hallway wanted to break them. "The playwright. I caught your work the last time I was in the city. Cyb cried buckets. I practically had to carry her out of the theater."

"I wasn't that bad."

"Yes, you were. Of course, you used to tear up during greeting-card commercials, so you're an easy mark."

"That's ridiculous, and—oh, my phone. Hang on a minute." She darted inside, leaving the men eyeing each other narrowly.

"I'm a sculptor," Matthew said in the same lazy drawl. "And since I really need my hands to work, I'll tell you I'm Cybil's brother before I offer to shake."

"Brother?" The murderous gleam shifted but didn't quite fade. "Not much family resemblance."

"Not especially. Want to see my ID, McQuinn?"

"That was Mrs. Wolinsky," Cybil announced as she dashed back. "She saw you come in but couldn't get to her door in time to waylay you. I'm supposed to tell you she thinks you're more handsome than ever." Chuckling, Cybil grabbed both his cheeks. "Isn't he pretty?"

"Don't start."

"Oh, but you are. Such a pretty face. All the female hearts flutter." She laughed again, then snagged Preston's hand. "Come on, let's have a drink to celebrate."

He started to refuse, then shrugged. It wouldn't do any harm to take a few minutes to size up Cybil's brother.

"What kind of sculptor?"

"I work in metal primarily." Matthew peeled off his jacket, tossed it carelessly over the arm of a chair. It barely had time to land before Cybil snatched it off.

"I'll just hang this in the bathroom to dry. Preston, pour us some wine, will you?"

"Sure."

"She have any beer?" Matthew wanted to know and sauntered over to lean on the counter while Preston moved through the kitchen with a familiarity that had the big brother arching a brow.

"Yeah." He plucked out two, popped the tops, then took out the wine for Cybil. "You work in the South?"

"That's right. New Orleans suits me better than New England. Weather-wise, it gives me more room to work outside if I want. Cyb hasn't mentioned you. When did you move in?"

Preston lifted his beer, noted Matthew's eyes were nearly the exact color of Cybil's hair. Like good aged whiskey. "Not long ago."

"Work fast, do you?"

"Depends."

"Preston." Cybil heaved a sigh as she came back. "Couldn't you have used glasses?"

"We don't need glasses." Matthew grinned, keeping a challenging eye on Preston. "We'll just drink our beer like real men, then chew up the bottle."

"Then you probably don't want any dainty cheese and crackers, or girlie pâté to go with it."

"Says who?" Matthew demanded, and slid onto a stool. "You used to have four of these, didn't you?"

"Oh, Preston borrowed one. What are you doing in New York, Matthew?" She stuck her head in the fridge.

"Just some quick preliminary business for my show this fall. I'm only here for a couple days."

"And you checked into a hotel, didn't you?"

"Your revolving-door policy drives me crazy." Matthew gestured toward Preston with his beer. "You've lived across the hall for a bit, right? So you know what goes on in here. It's terrifying. She lets…" He shuddered dramatically. "People in here."

"Matthew is a professional recluse," Cybil said dryly as she began preparing a small feast. "You two should get along famously. Preston doesn't like people, either."

"Ah, finally. A man of sense." Matthew aimed one of his quick, crooked smiles at Preston and decided he might like him, after all. "I let her talk me into staying here once," Matthew continued, stealing a cracker. "Oh, the horror. Three days, people dropping in, talking, eating, drinking, standing around, bringing their relatives and pets."

"It was only one little dog."

"Who insisted on sitting in my lap, without invitation, then ate my socks."

"If you hadn't left them lying on the floor, he wouldn't have eaten them. Besides, he only chewed them a bit."

"It's all a matter of perspective," Matthew concluded. "And you see, in a civilized hotel, the only people who drop in are housekeeping and room service—and they knock first and very rarely bring along small, toothy dogs." He reached over, pinched her chin. "But I'll let you cook me dinner, darling."

"You're so good to me."

"You ever had Cyb's homemade chicken potpie, McQuinn?"

"Can't say I have."

"Well, watch me sweet-talk us into some."

It was an interesting way to spend the evening, Preston thought later, watching Cybil relate to her brother.

The ease of affection, humor, occasional exasperation. He remembered it had been like that between him and his sister. Before Pamela.

After that, there had still been affection, but the ease of it had vanished. All too often he had felt an awkwardness that had never been there before.

But awkwardness wasn't a problem with the Campbells. They cheerfully told embarrassing stories about each other, and when that paled ganged up to tell him about their absent and therefore defenseless sister and any number of cousins.

By the time he left, he was wondering if he could work bits of them into act 2, for a little comic relief.

Work, Preston decided, since Cybil was likely to be occupied with family for quite some time yet, was his best hope for the rest of the night.

"I like your friend." Matthew stretched out his legs and swirled the brandy Cybil had opened in his honor.

"That's handy—so do I."

"A little on the sober side for you."

"Ah, well." She settled in beside him on the sofa. "A little change of pace now and again can't hurt."

"Is that what he is?" Matthew gave her earlobe a tug. "I noticed you two didn't waste any time getting locked together when I so accommodatingly strolled upstairs to make a phone call."

"If you were making a phone call, how do you know what we were doing down here? Unless you were spying." She smiled sweetly, fluttered her lashes and got another jerk on the ear.

"I wasn't spying. I just happened to glance down the stairs at one very strategic moment. And since he looked at you any number of times during the evening like he knew you'd be a lot more tasty than your chicken pot-pie—which was great, by the way—I cleverly put two and two together."

"You were always bright, Matthew. I suppose it's reasonable to say, since you're being nosy, that Preston and I are together."

"You're sleeping with him."

Deliberately, Cybil widened her eyes. "Why, no—we've decided to be canasta partners. We realize it's a big commitment, but we think we can handle it."

"You always were a smart-ass," he muttered.

"That's how I make my fame and fortune."

"Now you're making it turning McQuinn across the hall into Emily's elusive and irritable Quinn."

"How could I resist?"

Matthew drummed his fingers, shifted. "Emily thinks she's in love with him."

Cybil said nothing for a moment, then shook her head. "Emily is a cartoon character who pretty much does what I tell her to do. She's not me."

"She has pieces of you—some of your most endearing and annoying pieces."

"True. That's why I like her."

Matthew blew out a breath, frowned into his brandy. "Look, Cyb, I don't want to horn into your personal life, but I'm still your big brother."

"And you're so good at it, Matthew." She leaned over to kiss his cheek. "You don't have to worry about this. Preston didn't and isn't taking advantage of your baby sister." She took Matthew's brandy, sipped, handed it back. "I took advantage of him. I baked him cookies, and ever since he's been my love slave."

"There's that mouth again." Uncomfortable, he pushed off the sofa, paced a bit. "Okay, I don't want the details, but—"

"Oh, and I was so looking forward to sharing all of them with you, especially the home videos."

"Shut up, Cybil." Working his way from uncomfortable to embarrassed, Matthew dragged a hand through his hair. "I know you're grown-up, and you're seriously cute in spite of that nose."

"My nose is very attractive." She sniffed with it.

"We all worked hard to make you believe that, and you've overcome that little deformity so well."

She had to laugh. "Shut up, Matthew."

"All I want to say is…be careful. You know? Careful."

Her eyes went soft as she rose. "I love you, Matthew. In spite of that annoying facial tic."

"I don't have a facial tic."

"We worked hard to make you believe that." Laughing again, she slipped her arms around him for a fierce hug. "It's so nice to have you here. Can't you stay longer?"

"Can't." He rested his cheek on the top of her head. "I'm going up to Hyannis for a couple days. I'll hang out, do some sketching. Grandpa wheedled."

"He's the champ. Is Grandma pining for you?" Cybil asked, leaning back to grin.

"Fretting herself down to skin and bones. Why don't you come up? Give him a bonus. And that way we can spot each other when he starts on why we're not settled down and raising a pack of little people."

"Hmm. Well, he has called here a couple times in the last few weeks—hasn't given me a chance to call first." She considered, juggling time and duties in her head. "I'm enough strips ahead to take a couple of days. I do have a meeting day after tomorrow, though, that I shouldn't break."

"Come up afterward." He angled his head when he saw her mull it over, hesitate. "You can ask your canasta partner to drive up with you. We'll have a tournament."

"He might enjoy that," she murmured. "I'll check with him. Either way, I'll come."

"Good." And, Matthew thought, he hoped Preston accepted the invitation. He would love to see Daniel MacGregor work him over.

Since it was after midnight when Matthew went off to his hotel, Cybil told herself to go upstairs to bed. She hadn't gotten much sleep the night before—and neither had Preston. The reasonable, the practical, thing to do was climb into bed, shut off the light and get some much-needed rest.

So she walked across the hall and pushed his buzzer.

She was beginning to think he'd gone to bed, or down to the club, when she heard the rattle of locks.

"Hi. I never offered you a nightcap."

He glanced over her shoulder, back at her face. "Where's your brother?"

"On his way to his hotel. I opened some brandy, and—"

She didn't manage the rest, or even much of a squeak of surprise as he yanked her inside, kicked the door closed and shoved her against it. Her mouth was much too busy being assaulted by his.

When he switched to her neck, she managed to suck in a breath. "I guess you don't want any brandy." Since he was already dragging off her shirt, she returned the favor. "Or after-dinner mints."

The force of need that had slammed into him the moment he'd seen her was outrageous. He couldn't stem it, even with his hands rushing over her to take. Greedy, his mouth crushed back on hers while he pulled her head back to dive yet deeper.

And she strained against him, just as urgently, just as desperately, groaning in pleasure as he tugged her trousers down her hips.

Whatever she had was his.

He filled his hands with her breasts, then his mouth descended, sucking, nipping while her nails bit, arousing points of pain, into his back. Her skin, like warmed silk, drove him to possess. Desire, a freshly whetted blade, twisted as he moved down her until her hands vised on his shoulder and her breath was only gasping sobs.

Not possible, not possible to feel so much and survive, was her last coherent thought. Then he used his mouth on her, his fingernails raking lightly down her body as with lips and teeth and tongue he drove her beyond reason.

She heard her own cry of shocked release dimly, struggling for air as her system rocked from the hot explosion of pleasure. Destroyed, she sagged against the door, utterly open to him.

Surrender only fanned the flames.

His hands slipped, slid, over her damp skin. His mouth continued its relentless assault, demanding more, still more, until her body began to quiver again. Until he felt her begin to heat and move and stretch toward the next peak.

He left her groaning, traveling back up her body, slicking his tongue over flesh that tasted erotically of salt and woman. His hands were rougher than he intended as he dragged her to the chair, pulled her down on him, lifted her hips.

His eyes met hers, watching, watching as that soft, clouded green darkened and blurred, watching as those long lids flickered, watching still as he lowered her.

Now, as she closed around him, surrounded him in hot, slippery heat, their groans mixed. Her head fell back, exposing that lovely white arch of throat where a pulse beat in wild hammer blows.

And she began to ride.

The pace was hers now, and it was fast and fierce. Each thrust of hips slapped them both toward the dark swirl of delirium. He craved it, that moment when sanity ripped away.

Bright arrows of sensation, each separate and sharp, stabbed through him. The sumptuous taste of her flesh in his mouth, the wet silk texture of it as his hands sought more of her, those low, animal sounds in her throat and the sheer wonder of her face flushed with pleasure and purpose.

He teetered on the edge, struggling to hold on another instant, just one more instant where he could no longer tell where she began and he left off. But she closed around him, a glorious fist of triumph, and, breathing his name, dragged him over with her.

Then, as she had before, she melted onto him. The sensation of having her head lie on his shoulder, her lips against his throat, spread a hazy glow through him. Closing his eyes, he held on to it, and to her.

He remembered what she had said to him before. No one had ever touched her as he had.

No one, he thought, had ever reached him as she had. But, however clever he was with words on paper, he didn't know how to begin to tell her.

"I wanted to get my hands on you all evening." That, at least, he could say without risking either of them.

"Mmm. And to think I nearly went up to bed." With a long, contented sigh, she nuzzled his hair. "I knew this chair was perfect for you."

A chuckle rumbled in his chest. "I was thinking of having it recovered. But now I'm having it bronzed."

She leaned back, cupping her hands on his face. "I love those little unexpected pockets of humor in you."

"It's not funny," he said in serious tones. "It's going to cost me a fortune."

He expected her to laugh, a sound he'd grown to depend on. But her smile was wistful, her eyes soft. "Preston." She murmured it, then lowered her mouth to his.

The slow, deep, gentle kiss stirred the soul rather than the blood. It reached into him, brushed hesitant fingers over his heart and made him yearn for something he refused to believe in.

Something struggled to shift inside him, made his hands tremble with the effort to hold it still and steady. But the sweetness of it seeped in, left him reeling.

He crossed over that thin line between want and need, and felt himself stumble terrifyingly close to the edge of love.

She sighed, pressed her cheek to his. And wished.

"You're cold," he murmured, feeling her skin chill.

"A little." She kept her eyes squeezed tight another

moment, reminding herself you couldn't always have everything you wished for. "Thirsty. Want some water?"

"Yeah, I'll get it."

"No, that's all right." She slid off him, leaving him slightly baffled by the sense of loss. "Do you have a robe?"

He worked up a smile again. "What is this obsession you have with robes?"

"Never mind." She snatched up his shirt and pulled it on. "Matthew likes you," she commented as she walked into the kitchen.

"I like him." He could take a deep breath now. Could, he told himself, regain his balance now. "The piece up in your studio. That's his work?"

"Yeah. Terrific, isn't it? He's got such a unique vision of things. And watching him work—if he doesn't murder you—is an amazing experience."

She opened a bottle of water, poured a tall glass to the rim, then drank down nearly a third before moving back to Preston. She didn't notice his blink of surprise when she settled, cozy as a cat, into his lap.

"So anyway," she began, offering him the glass, "how do you feel about taking a little trip?"

"A trip?"

"A couple of days in Hyannis Port. Matthew's going up to see our grandparents—the MacGregors—and I thought I might do the same. Grandpa loves to complain that we don't visit enough. It's a great place. The house is…well, I can't describe it. But you'd like it. You'd like them. Want to get out of Dodge for a bit, McQuinn?"

"It sounds like a family thing." It struck him as odd, and totally out of character, that he should feel so unhappy with the idea of her being away for a couple of days.

"With The MacGregor, everything is a family thing. Grandpa loves people. He's over ninety, and has the most amazing energy."

"I know. He's fascinating. They both are." He glanced back as she frowned at him. "I know them. Slightly. They're acquaintances of my parents."

"Oh? I didn't realize. I told you the rather convoluted family connection, didn't I? MacGregor to Blade. Blade to Grandeau. Grandeau to Campbell. Campbell to MacGregor, not necessarily in that order."

"Don't start. It makes my ears ring."

She laughed, dutifully kissed them. "Well, since you know them and you've met Matthew, it wouldn't be like dropping yourself in on a group of strangers. Come with me." She ran her lips from his ear to his neck. "It'll be fun."

"We could stay right here in this chair and have even more fun."

She chuckled warmly. "There are dozens and dozens of rooms in Castle MacGregor," she murmured. "And in many of them, there are big...soft...beds."

"When do we leave?"

"Really?" Thrilled at the idea, she leaned back. "Day after tomorrow? I have a meeting midmorning. We can leave right after. I can rent a car."

"I have a car."

"Oh." She cocked her head. "Hmm. Is it a sexy car?"

"How do you feel about four-door sedans?"

"It's probably very sturdy, very reliable. I appreciate a sensible car."

"Then you're not going to like my Porsche."

"A Porsche?" She giggled in delight. "Oh, tell me it's a convertible."

"What else?"

"Oh, yeah. Tell me it's a five-speed."

"Sorry, it's a six-speed."

Her eyes widened. "Really? *Really?* Can I drive?"

"Of course. If by the day after tomorrow the icicles have finished forming in Hell, you're at the wheel."

Pouting only a little, she began to play with his hair. "I'm an excellent driver."

"I'm sure you are." He decided it would be much more productive to distract her than to listen to her try to change his mind. He rolled the cold glass over her naked back, making her gasp and arch so that her breasts flattened delightfully against his chest.

"Now...what do you think we could accomplish if we laid this recliner back?"

"All manner of amazing things," she murmured, turning her neck to give his teeth better access. "Did you know my grandfather owns this building?"

"Sure. He told me about the apartment when I was looking for a place. Turn like...yeah, that's the way."

"He told you about the apartment?" Somehow he'd managed to shift so that his body covered hers, distracting her from a niggling thought just beginning to form in her mind. "When did he... Oh, God, you're so awfully good at that."

"Thank you. But I'm about to get much better."

Chapter 9

The house The MacGregor built stood arrogantly on the cliffs above a surging sea. Nothing about the old gray stone was sober. Everything about it, from its spearing towers and jutting turrets, to the snapping flag that carried the crest of the clan, shouted pride.

He had built as he'd intended to, on a sturdy foundation, with grandiose vision. And he had built to last.

The wild and rambling roses that would bloom brilliantly come summer did nothing to soften the effect but only added to that sense of magic.

"Stop," Preston murmured, and laid a hand on Cybil's arm. "Stop the car."

Because she understood, and was pleased to see the sight of that fanciful structure affect him as it always did her, she braked gently.

"It's like a fairy tale, isn't it?" She leaned on the

steering wheel to study the house through a driving curtain of rain. "Not one of the wimpy G-rated versions, but one with blood and guts."

"I've seen photographs. They don't come close."

"It's not just a house. It's the most generous of homes. Whenever we visited we'd always find something new. Something marvelous."

As she would this time, she thought. With Preston. "It shows well in the rain, doesn't it?" she commented.

"I imagine it always shows well."

"You're right. You should see it in the winter. We always come up during Christmas. The snow and the wind turn it into something frozen out of time. And last year, just at the end of summer when the roses were tumbling and the sky was so hard and blue you waited for it to crack like an egg, my cousin Duncan got married here. But in the rain…" She smiled dreamily, leaning on the wheel. "It feels like Scotland."

"Have you ever been?"

"Mmm. Twice. Have you?"

"No."

"You should. It's your roots. You'll be surprised how much they tug at you when you breathe the air in the highlands or look out at a lowland loch."

"Maybe I will. I might want a couple of weeks to decompress when the play's finished." He turned his head, lifted his eyebrows. "How's the car handling for you?"

"Since you've only let me drive it for approximately forty-five seconds, it's difficult to be sure. Now, if you let me take it out for a spin tomorrow…"

"Even your powers of persuasion aren't going to get you behind the wheel longer than it takes to go up the drive."

Cybil shrugged carelessly, thought, *We'll see about that,* and drove decorously up the hill, parked. "Thank you very much." She gave him a light kiss, and the keys.

"You're welcome."

"Let's not worry about the bags now. We'll make a dash for it and see how long it takes to have whiskey and scones by the fire."

She pushed open the car door, ran like a bullet through the rain, then stopped on the covered porch to shake her head like a wet dog and laugh.

For ten full seconds, he couldn't move. He could only stare at her, through the shimmering curtain of rain, her cap of hair sleek and soaked, her face alive with the delight of it. He wanted to think it was desire, straight and uncomplicated. But desire rarely struck so deeply or had fingers of fear clawing at the gut.

If he couldn't ignore it, he'd deny it. He stepped into the rain, let the wind slap at his cheeks like a teasing woman as he walked to her. And while she laughed, he yanked her hard against him and took her mouth with a kind of violent possession.

For once her hands only fluttered helplessly as the sudden, almost brutal, kiss staggered her. But she tasted the desperation on his mouth, felt the barely restrained fury in the body that pressed to hers. And her hands reached for him, stroked once, then held.

"Preston."

He heard her murmur through the roaring in his brain that was like the rain and the sea battering against him. The soft sound of her voice had him gentling his hold, then the kiss, before he forced himself to draw back.

"With all your family around," he managed, and skimmed her dripping hair behind her ear in an absent gesture that made her heart flutter foolishly, "I might not be able to do that for a while."

"Well." She breathed deep, hoping to settle herself. "That ought to hold me." And smiling, she took his hand and pulled him inside.

There was warmth, immediate and welcoming.

Bright swords and shields glowed on the walls. It was, after all, the home of a warrior and one who had never forgotten it. There was the scent of flowers and wood, and of age that speaks of dignity rather than dust.

"Cybil!" Anna MacGregor came down the wide stairs, her soft face aglow with pleasure. Her sable hair was swept back, her deep-brown eyes clear and smiling as she held out her arms to take Cybil into them.

"Grandma." She breathed deep, exhaled lavishly. "How can you always be so beautiful?"

With a laugh, Anna squeezed tighter. "At my age the best you can hope for is presentable."

"Not you. You're always beautiful. Isn't she, Preston?"

"Very."

"You're never too old to appreciate a considerate lie from a handsome young man." Anna shifted, keeping one arm around Cybil's waist as she held out a hand. "Hello, Preston. I doubt you'll remember me. You couldn't have been more than sixteen the last I saw you."

"About," he agreed, taking her hand. "But I remember you very well, Mrs. MacGregor. It was at the Spring Ball in Newport, and you were very kind to a young boy who wanted to be anywhere else."

"You remember. Now I am flattered. Come, let's get you warmed up. Rain's cold this time of year."

"Where are Grandpa and Matthew?"

"Oh." Anna laughed lightly as she led them down

the hall into what the family called the Throne Room. "Daniel's got poor Matthew hammering on the pump for the pool. He says it's acting up, and you know how your grandfather is about his daily swim. Claims it keeps him young."

"Everything keeps him young."

The term for the room was apt, with Daniel's regal high-back chair dominating a great space carpeted in scarlet. The furnishings were old and massive, the carvings deep. Lamps were already lit against the gloom, and a fire blazed boldly in the big hearth.

"We'll have tea. I imagine Daniel will insist we add whiskey to that and use company as an excuse for it. Sit, be comfortable," she invited. "If I don't let him know you're here, I'll never hear the end of it."

"You sit," Cybil insisted. "I'll go. I'll have the tea sent along on the way."

"You're a good girl." Anna patted Cybil's hand as she sat by the fire. "You always were." Anna gestured to the chair beside hers. "Preston, Daniel and I saw your play in Boston some months ago. It was powerful, and wrenching. Your family must be so proud of what you've accomplished."

"Actually, I think they were more surprised."

"Sometimes that amounts to the same thing. We never really expect our children or our siblings, no matter how we admire them, to exhibit real genius. It brings us a jolt, and we think—how could I have missed that all those years?"

"You know my family," he said quietly. "So you'd know the play cut very close to home."

"Yes, I know. Sometimes a wound needs to be lanced or it festers. Is your sister well?"

"Yes, she has the children. They center her."

"And you, Preston? Is it your work that centers you?"

"Apparently."

"I'm sorry." Annoyed with herself, Anna lifted her hands. "I'm prying—and I usually leave that to my husband. I'm interested because I remember that young boy at the Spring Ball and the way he looked after his sister. It reminded me of the way Alan and Caine always looked after Serena—and how it irritated her as it appeared to irritate…it's Jenna, isn't it?"

"Yes." He smiled now. "It used to drive her crazy." But the smile soon faded. "If I'd done a better job of it years later, she'd never have been hurt."

"Preston, you didn't hurt her," Anna reminded him. "And, truly, I didn't mean to take you back there. Will you tell me about what you're working on now, or do you keep such matters secret?"

"It's a love story, set in New York. At least, that's the way it's turning out."

His gaze flicked past her shoulder when he heard laughter rolling down the hall. Yes, Anna thought, that seemed to be the way it was turning out.

"Haven't you given the man a whiskey yet, Anna?"

Daniel stepped into the room and simply dominated it. Size, presence and that great booming voice that refused to thin with age. His eyes glittered blue as the lochs of his homeland; his hair and rich full beard were stunningly white.

"Is that any way to welcome a man after he's come in out of the rain and brought up my favorite grandchild from the city?"

"Oh, fine," Matthew muttered, trailing in behind

him. "When you wanted your pool fixed *I* was your favorite grandchild."

"Well, it's fixed now, isn't it?" Daniel said, and with a bark of laughter slapped Matthew on the back with the affection a father grizzly might show to his cub.

"It's good to see you, Mr. MacGregor." Preston crossed the room, hand extended to shake. But for Daniel this was rarely sufficient when he'd taken an interest in a man. He clapped Preston into a hug with the force of a steel trap biting closed.

"You're looking fit, McQuinn, and a good drink of whiskey always makes a Scotsman fitter."

"You'll have a drop in your tea, Daniel," Anna warned him as she rose to fetch the decanter.

"A drop." For a big man, he could still manage to sulk like a child. "Anna."

"Two drops," she conceded with a smile tugging at her mouth. "Tell me, Preston, do you smoke cigars?"

"Not as a rule, no."

Anna turned, angled her head in warning at Daniel. "Then if I come across you with one in your hand, I'll know who stuck it there before he dashed out of the room."

"The woman'll nag you to death," Daniel muttered. "Well, sit down, boy, and tell me how you and Cybil are getting on."

Little alarm bells sounded in Preston's head. "Getting on?"

"Neighbors, aren't you?"

"Yeah." Relieved, Preston sat. "Across-the-hall neighbors."

"Pretty as a primrose, isn't she?"

"Grandpa." Cybil sighed as she wheeled in a loaded

tea tray. "Don't start on McQuinn. He hasn't even been here ten minutes."

"Start what?" Daniel narrowed his eyes at her. "Are you pretty or not?"

"I'm adorable." She laughed and kissed his nose. While she was close, she whispered in his ear. "Behave and I might tip a bit of my whiskey into your tea while she's not looking."

Daniel's teeth flashed in a grin; his eyebrows wiggled. "There's a lass."

"You won't believe these scones, McQuinn." Satisfied she'd bribed The MacGregor, Cybil loaded a small plate. "I can't quite pull them off. Mine are close, but not quite there."

"Cybil's a fine cook," Daniel agreed, scowling when he watched his wife measure a measly two drops of whiskey into a cup for him. "You've been feeding the man a bit from time to time, haven't you, lass? Like a proper neighbor."

"She made us all a potpie last night." Matthew loaded a scone with strawberry jam. He'd promised to be a buffer, he remembered. "Preston, you want whiskey or are you making do with tea?"

"I'll take the whiskey, thanks. Neat."

"And how else would a man drink it?" Daniel muttered, pouting into his teacup. "So you've had a taste of our Cybil," he added, and watched with a barely suppressed grin as Preston nearly bobbled a scone.

"Excuse me?"

"Her cooking." Daniel's eyes radiated innocence. *Oh, aye,* he thought, *I've got you on the reel, laddie.* "Woman who can cook like my darling here ought to have a family to feed."

"Grandpa." Cybil tapped her finger on her whiskey glass.

When a man was torn between his drink of choice and his granddaughter's future, what choice did he have? Sacrifices, Daniel mused, had to be made. "What man doesn't appreciate a hot meal well made, I'd like to know? You can't disagree with that, can you, lad?"

Somehow, somewhere, there was dangerous ground, was all Preston could think. "No."

"There!" Daniel pounded a fist, made plates rattle. "Hah! McQuinn's a good and honorable name. You've done proud by it."

"Thanks," Preston said cautiously.

"But a man your age should be thinking of what comes after him. You must be thirty by now."

"That's right." *And how the hell do you know that?* Preston wondered.

"A man gets to be thirty, it's time to take stock, to consider his duties to name and family."

"I've got a few years left," Matthew whispered to Cybil.

She merely elbowed him. "Do something," she hissed.

"If he turns it on me, it's gonna cost you."

"Name your price."

"Oh, I will." And cheerfully throwing himself on the sword, Matthew dropped into a chair. "Grandpa, I haven't told you about this woman I've been seeing lately."

"Woman?" Distracted, Daniel blinked, then zeroed in on his grandson. "What woman would that be? I thought you were too busy building your big metal toys to pay any mind to women."

"I pay them plenty of mind." Matthew grinned, lifted his whiskey in salute. "This one's something special."

"Is she, now?" Shifting gears, Daniel settled back. "Well, it would take a special lass to catch your eye for more than a blink."

"Oh, I've been looking at this one for a while. Name's Lulu," Matthew decided on the spot. "Lulu LaRue, though I think that's her stage name. She's a table dancer."

"Dances on tables!" Daniel roared as his wife choked back a laugh, then continued to drink her tea. "Naked on tables?"

"Of course naked. What's the point otherwise? She's got the most amazing tattoo on her—"

"Naked, tattooed dancing girls! I'll be damned, Matthew Campbell. You want to break your dear mother's heart? Anna, are you listening to this?"

"Yes, of course I am, Daniel. Matthew, stop teasing your grandfather."

"Yes, ma'am." Matthew shrugged, grinned and watched Daniel's eyes narrow into blue slits. "But I don't see why I can't have a naked, tattooed dancing girl if I want."

Much later, after the rain had passed and night had fallen and Preston had slipped into her room to take advantage of her and the big four-poster bed, Cybil hummed in contentment.

It had been a near perfect day.

Perfect enough that she let herself curl up against the man she loved and pretend, in this fairy tale world, that he had scaled the walls of the castle to find her. And love her. And stay with her for always.

"Tell me something," he murmured, too relaxed to worry about how soothing it was to lie there with her arm draped over him, her head in the curve of his shoulder and their bodies sharing a lazy, intimate warmth.

"Okay. Despite exhaustive research, the exact number of angels who can dance on the head of a pin has never been fully documented."

"I thought it was 634."

"That's mere speculation. Nor in related studies has it ever been fully discovered precisely how many frogs one must kiss before finding the prince."

"That goes without saying. But…" He loved the way she chuckled as she shifted closer. "What I really wanted to know—and you would be the handiest authority on the subject—is what the hell was all that with your grandfather at tea?"

"Which all?" She lifted her head, skimmed her hair back from her brow, then rolled her eyes. "Oh, that all. I didn't warn you because I had the pathetic hope that it wouldn't be necessary. The fault is entirely mine."

She shifted, rolling over so that her body lounged cozily over his. "Do you know you have wonderful eyes, McQuinn? They're almost translucent, like I could dive right into that moonlight blue and just disappear."

"Is that a genuine comment or an evasion of the subject at hand?"

"Both." But since it had to be dealt with, she sat up, kissed him, then reached for the robe she'd tossed at the foot of the bed earlier.

"Why do you have to cover up whenever you talk to me?"

She glanced over, and to his surprise, flushed a little. "A latent puritanical streak?"

"Incredibly latent," he noted, but only smiled as she belted the robe. "Now, about your grandfather and his sudden interest in my family name—or as he put it during dinner—the good blood, strong stock in my ancestry."

"Well, McQuinn, you're a Scotsman."

"Third-generation Rhode Islander."

"Hardly matters in the vast and historic scheme of things."

She rose and poured them a glass to share from the pitcher of ice water that had been placed on the bedside table. "I'll apologize first," she said, without looking at him. "But hope you'll understand Grandpa means well. It's all out of love, and he wouldn't have done it if he didn't like you."

Something much too akin to nerves moved into Preston's stomach. "Done what, exactly?"

"I didn't realize it—or it didn't sink in fully until we got here. It should have," she murmured, sitting on the bed and handing him the glass before she'd sipped herself. "The other night when you mentioned how you knew each other and he'd put you onto the apartment across from mine, I should have latched on to it. Well." She jerked her shoulders. "It wouldn't have mattered anyway."

"What, Cybil?"

She blew out a breath, lifted her lashes and looked directly into his eyes. "He's picked you out for me. It's just that he loves me," she said quickly. "And he wants what he thinks is best for me—that's marriage, a family, a home. And that appears to be you."

It wasn't nerves, Preston discovered. It was outright terror. "How the hell did he come to that conclusion?" he demanded, and set his water back on the table with a hard click of glass on wood.

"It's not an insult, McQuinn." Her voice chilled several frigid degrees. "It's a compliment. As I said, he loves me very much, so he obviously thinks a great deal of you if he believes you'd make me a proper husband and be a good father for the many great-grandchildren he hopes I'll give him."

"I thought you didn't want marriage."

"I didn't say I did. I said he wanted it for me." Her chin jerked up before she got out of bed again, stalking to the bureau to snatch up her brush and drag it over her hair. "And the fact that you're so obviously appalled is incredibly insulting."

"I suppose you think it's amusing."

"I think it's sweet."

"You think it's sweet for your ninety-something grandfather to pick out men for you?"

"He isn't grabbing them off the street corner for me to audition." Ridiculously hurt, she slammed down the brush. "You needn't panic, McQuinn. I'm not buying my trousseau or booking chapels. I'm perfectly capable of finding my own husband when and if I want one. Which I've already said I don't."

She tossed her head and, for lack of something better to do with her hands, wrenched open a jar of cream and began to slather it on her hands.

"Now, I'm tired, and I'd like to go to bed. And since you don't care to sleep with me after sex, you should go."

Was it just temper, he wondered, or was there something more in the reflection of her eyes in the mirror? "Why are you angry?"

"Why am I angry?" she said quietly, unsure if she wanted to weep or scream. "How can someone who writes about what's inside people with such insight, such sensitivity, ask a question like that? Why am I angry, Preston?"

She turned then because it was best to face the issue head-on. "Because you're sitting there in the bed we just shared, still warm from me and utterly baffled, completely shocked that someone who loves me thinks there could or should be something more between us than sex."

"Of course there's more between us than sex." His own temper started to twitch as he grabbed his jeans and tugged them on.

"Is there? Is there really?"

The cool, flat tone had him looking over, had the sneaky worm of guilt sliding into him. "I care about you, Cybil. You know I do."

"You find me amusing. That's not the same thing."

Yes, there was more than temper, he realized before she turned away. There was hurt. Somehow he'd hurt her again without plan or purpose. He took her arm, firmly turned her back. "I care about you."

Her heart, already too much his, softened. "All right." She touched a hand to his, squeezed, released. "Let's forget about it."

He wanted to agree, to keep it simple. But the smile she'd tossed him before she'd walked to the window hadn't reached her eyes. And those eyes had been wounded. "Cybil, I don't have more than that."

"I didn't ask for more than that. The moon's come out. All the clouds have been blown away. We can walk the cliffs tomorrow. It's a little chilly, though." Absently, her heart weeping in her breast, she rubbed her arms. "I think we need another log on the fire."

"I'll do it."

The fire in the fieldstone hearth still burned bright and cheerful. But he took a log from the carved box, sat it on the flames, then watched them rise up, lick, curve greedily around it.

For a time the only sound in the room was the crack and the hiss of wood being consumed.

Maybe it was because she didn't ask, so deliberately didn't ask, that he was compelled to tell her. "Would you sit down?"

"I like standing here looking at the stars. You can't see the stars in New York. It's all the lights. You forget to look up, much less wonder where the stars are. In Maine, where I grew up, they filled the sky. I never realize I miss them until I see them again. You can get along, very well, for long periods, without a lot of things. Hardly even noticing you're missing them."

When his hands came to her shoulders, she tensed, an instinctive movement it took concentrated effort to undo. But she smiled when she turned. "Why don't we go out and get a better look at them while they're there."

"I want you to sit down and listen to me."

"All right." Struggling to be casual, she walked to one of the deep chairs in front of the fire. "I'm listening."

He sat beside her, leaned forward in his chair and kept his eyes on her face. "I always wanted to write. I can't remember otherwise. Not the novels my father had hoped for. It was always plays. Everything was very clear in my head. The stage, each set, the movement of the actors, the precise angle and quality of the lights. Often, maybe too often, that was the world I lived in. You come from a prominent family, one with a lot of social obligations and demands."

"I suppose that's true."

"So do I. I tolerated that end of it, enjoyed it occasionally, but for the most part just tolerated or eluded it."

"You value your privacy," she said. "I understand that. My father's the same, and Matthew."

"I valued it. I needed it." Too restless to sit, he rose to wander the room. "I love my parents, my sister, no matter how little we sometimes understand one another. I'm sure I hurt them countless times with small acts of carelessness, but I do love them, Cybil."

"Of course you do," she began, but said nothing more when he shook his head.

"My sister, Jenna, she was always so outgoing, so easy with people. She's a lovely woman. She wasn't quite twenty-one when she married. Married my best friend from college. I introduced them."

It still scraped him raw to think of that. The first step in the whole miserable journey had been his. Glancing at the water, he wished it were whiskey.

"They were great together," he murmured. "Shining with love, full to bursting with hope and plans. Jacob came along just over a year later. And less than a year after that she was pregnant again and glowing with it."

He stuck his hands in his pockets, moved to the window. But he didn't see the stars. "About that time, my first play was being produced. Locally, just a small theater group, but a place with cachet. My father's an important writer, so that made his son's work of some interest."

"It's of interest on its own," Cybil declared, and he glanced back, grateful to her for understanding his need for that separate legitimacy. But she would, he thought, because of who she was and from what she'd come.

"Now I certainly hope so. But not then, not right at the start. And it was vital to me that my work stand on its own and not lean on his. Part of that was pride," he continued thoughtfully. "But part of it was respect. Whatever the reason, this play, this first of mine to be produced, was incredibly important to me."

Because he turned away, seemed to need a moment to gather himself, she spoke again. "I didn't sleep at all the night before my first strip came out. However much I loved the work, I couldn't have stood it if people thought I was using my father's accomplishments as a stepping stone."

"Some always will," Preston murmured. "You can't let it matter. The work has to matter most, and this play did to me. There wasn't any aspect of it I wasn't involved in—the set designs, the staging, the casting, the rehearsals, lighting cues. All of it."

She smiled a little. "I imagine you drove everyone, including yourself, insane."

"I'm sure I did. The company had a lot of talent. The actress who played the lead was stunning, certainly the most beautiful woman I'd ever seen. She dazzled me."

He faced her. "I'd just turned twenty-five, and I was hopelessly in love with her. Every minute I spent with her was a gift. Just to watch her onstage, saying lines I'd written, that had come from me. Having her look at me and smile and ask me if that was how I meant it to be. The more I became involved with her, the less the play meant to me."

Even now it burned inside him, what he'd tossed aside. And what he'd had stolen. "She was gentle. Oh, and sweet. Even a little shy when she wasn't onstage. I made excuses to be with her, then began to realize she was making them to be with me. We became lovers on a Sunday afternoon, in her bed, and afterward, she cried on my shoulder and told me she loved me. I think I would have cut off my arm for her at that moment."

Cybil folded her hands in her lap and wondered what it would be like to be loved like that by a man like him. She didn't speak because she could see there was more. And what was left still caused him pain.

"For weeks," he continued, "my world revolved around her. The play opened, garnered very decent reviews. All I could think was that the play had been the vehicle that had given her to me. That was all that mattered."

"Love should matter most."

"Should it?" He laughed shortly and the cynical light was back in his eyes. "But words last, Cybil. That's why a writer should take care with them."

Love lasts. She wanted to say it, nearly did, but she could already see his hadn't.

"I bought her gifts," he continued, "because they made her happy, took her dancing or to the club because she loved to be with people. She was so beautiful I thought she deserved to be showcased. She needed the right clothes, the right jewelry, to be showcased in, didn't she? So why not buy them for her? And if she needed a little to tide her over, why not write her a check? It was only money, and I had more than enough."

Cybil could see where it was going, or thought she could. She wanted, so badly, to go to him, to slip her arms around him in comfort. But it wasn't unhappiness in his voice, in his eyes; it was bitterness.

"She had talent, and I wanted to help her become an important actress. Why not use my influence—or my father's, my family's—to boost her career?"

"You loved her," Cybil said quietly, already hurting for him. "What you wouldn't have used for yourself, you would use for someone you loved."

"And that makes it right?" He shook his head. "No, it's never right to use someone else. But I did. She talked about marriage, shyly again, almost wistfully. I hesitated there. Her career needed her attention. We could wait to settle down. After the play, I told her, after she began to move up, we'd go to New York and we'd both *own* theater. We'd own it together."

Together, he thought, was all too often a word that didn't hold true. "Then one day she came to me, weeping, shaking, so pale you could almost see through that beautiful skin. She told me she was pregnant, and lovely, terrified tears slipped out of her eyes and down her cheeks. She blamed herself, begged me not to abandon her. Where would she go, what would she do? She had little money. She was afraid. She thought I would hate her."

"No," Cybil whispered. "You wouldn't hate her."

"Of course I didn't. I didn't hate her, I didn't blame her. I was afraid, I was shaken, but part of me was thrilled. The decision had been taken out of my hands. I didn't need to be practical now but could marry her, start a life with her."

He prowled now, restless in the cage of his own past. "Money was no problem. I'd come into a large part of my inheritance at twenty-five, would come into more at thirty. Money wasn't a problem," he said again, then lifted the poker and jabbed viciously at the logs blazing.

"I dried her tears, and I held her, told her everything would be fine. It would be wonderful. We'd be married right away. We'd stay in Newport until the baby was born, then we'd go to New York just as we'd planned. It would be three of us instead of two, but we'd be happy. We had a touching parting scene as she left to go back to her little apartment—to rest and call her family and tell them the wonderful news. We agreed to go to my parents after the show that evening and tell them.

"I started making plans almost immediately. Imagined myself as her husband, as the father of the child we'd made together."

"You wanted the baby," Cybil said, remembering the ease with which he'd held little Charlie.

"Yes, I did."

He turned to her then, his back to the fire. But the heat that pumped from the flames couldn't reach the cold memories left inside him. "I wanted her, and the child, and the life I imagined we could make together. And while I was floating on that particular cloud my sister came to my door."

He could still see it, still bring it back. Every movement, every gesture. Another play on another stage. "Like Pamela, she was weeping, she was trembling, she was pale. And like Pamela, she was pregnant. Further along, just showing, so I was worried at the state she was in. She clung to me, sobbing and sobbing, and finally managed to tell me her husband was having an affair."

His voice changed now, darkened, flattened, as did his eyes. "She told me that she'd dashed back home, leaving Jacob with my mother, because she'd forgotten something. They were to be out all day, so she wasn't expected back only an hour after she'd left. Wasn't expected to walk in and find her husband scrambling back into his trousers and a woman in her bed. Her own bed."

"Oh, Preston, how horrible for her." She rose then, wanting to comfort. "How awful for your family. She must have…" She trailed off as it clicked. The scenes he'd been painting for her, the scenes he'd painted in his play. "Oh, no. Oh, God."

He stepped back from the sympathy she offered. "Her name was Leanna in *A Tangle of Souls,* but she was pure Pamela. Beautiful and clever and cold. A woman who could act without rehearsing the lines. Who could play a man brilliantly, all for money, for power, for the possibilities. She would have married me for those things, and to give a socially prominent name to the baby my closest friend, my sister's husband, had planted in her. But I was no longer in the mood."

"You loved her, and she hurt you. Hurt all of you. I'm so sorry."

"Yes, I loved her, but she taught me. You can't trust the heart. My sister trusted hers, and it almost destroyed her. If she hadn't had Jacob and the baby on the way, I think it would have. They needed her, and that's what got her through."

"But you didn't have that."

"I had my work, and the satisfaction of facing the woman who'd cut through our lives. She wept and she swore it was all a lie. Some terrible mistake. She begged me to believe her, and I very nearly did. She was that good."

"No," Cybil murmured. "You were in love. You'd have wanted to believe her."

"Either way. We argued, and some of the layers on that perfectly presented mask of hers fell away. I saw her for what she was. A schemer, a liar, a cheat. A woman who thought nothing of seducing and sleeping with another's husband for pleasure and going from him to another man for gain. But she finished the run of the play." He smiled thinly. "The show must go on."

"How did you stand it?"

"She was good, and it was only a matter of reminding myself the work was more important than she was, more important than anything else." He arched a brow. "You think that was a cold decision on my part?"

"No." She laid her hands on his shoulders, then on his cheeks, wondering that he couldn't see the hurt was still there. "No, I think it was brave." Then she leaned into him, held him, sighing when his arms finally came around her. "She didn't deserve even the smallest piece of your heart, Preston. Then or now."

"Now she's only an interesting character in a play. I won't give anyone that much ever again. I don't have it to give."

"If you believe that, you've let her take more." She lifted her head, and her eyes were drenched. "You've let her win."

"Nobody won, my sister, my friend, me. Three lives damaged, and all she got from it was a few auditions. Nobody won," he murmured, and brushed a tear from her cheek with his thumb. "Don't cry. I didn't tell you to make you cry, just to help you understand who I am."

"I know who you are, and I can't help hurting for you."

"Cybil." He brought her close again. "If you keep wearing your heart that close to the surface, someone's going to come along and break it."

She closed her eyes but didn't tell him someone already had.

Chapter 10

It was time, Daniel decided, to have a private little chat with young Preston McQuinn. It was simple enough to lure the man up into his tower office while Cybil was busy with Anna in another part of the house. And Matthew—well, the boy was likely off somewhere or other looking for inspiration for one of his metal toys.

Matthew's sculptures invariably brought Daniel both puzzlement and pride.

"Have a seat, lad. Stretch out your legs." Daniel walked to the bookshelf, took out a copy of *War and Peace* and chose a cigar out of the hollow. "Will you have one?"

Preston only lifted a brow. "No, thanks. Interesting literature, Mr. MacGregor."

"Well, a man does what he can to keep his woman off his back." Daniel ran the length of the cigar under his nose, sniffing in appreciation, sighed in anticipation as he sat, then took his time lighting it. Part of the pleasure was in the small and delightful steps.

He unlocked the bottom drawer in his huge oak desk, took out a large carved shell and set it in the center of his blotter as an ashtray. Following that came a tiny battery-operated fan. It was the newest of Daniel's attempts to keep Anna from sniffing him out.

"Wife doesn't want me smoking." The pity of it had Daniel shaking his head. "And the older she gets, the sharper her nose. Got one like a bloodhound," he muttered, then settled back, sighed. "Now, then."

"What if she comes up?" Preston wanted to know.

"We worry about that if and when, boy, if and when." But his healthy fear of his wife's wrath had him nudging the little fan closer. "So tell me, your play's going well for you?"

"Yes, it is."

"I'm not only asking as an investor, I want you to know. I'm interested in you."

"Mmm-hmm."

"Admire your father's work. Got some of his books around here." Daniel leaned back in the enormous leather chair, puffed out smoke. "A bird tells me that Hollywood's taken quite an interest in your work, McQuinn."

"You've got a good ear for birds."

"I do indeed. How does it sit with you, this movie business?"

"Well enough."

"You play poker, don't you, McQuinn?"

"I've been known to ante up occasionally."

"I'll wager you play a fine game of it. You're not one to give your hand away. I like that." Contemplatively,

Daniel tapped his cigar on the shell. "You'll be in New York a few more weeks?"

"Another month, anyway. Most of the work on the house should be done by then."

"A fine big house, too, by the sea." Daniel smiled as Preston narrowed his eyes. "The birds tell me all manner of things. It's good for a man to have a house of his own. Some of us aren't meant to live in a hive, with people buzzing through the next wall. We need our own space, for ourselves, for our family. Room to spread out," he continued, gesturing. "A place where a man can go to have a damn cigar in his own house without being nagged half to death."

As Daniel scowled, took another puff, Preston's lips twitched.

"True enough," Preston agreed. "Though I wouldn't say my house is anywhere near the scale of yours."

"Young yet, aren't you? You build as you go. And you'd need the sea, as I did, having grown up with it outside your door."

"I prefer it to the city." Since he wasn't quite sure where the conversation was headed, Preston didn't relax quite yet. "And if I had to live in a suburban development I'd likely slit my throat in a week."

Daniel laughed, puffed and eyed Preston through the cloud of smoke. "You're a man who needs his privacy, and that's a reasonable thing. But when solitude and privacy become isolation, it's not always healthy, is it?"

Preston angled his head. "I don't see any neighbors mowing their yards and trimming their hedges when I look out the windows of Castle MacGregor."

Daniel's grin flashed in his beard. "That you don't, McQuinn. But while private we are, isolated we aren't.

You know Cybil grew up by the sea, as well." He clamped the cigar between his teeth. "Along the coast of Maine, where her father guarded his privacy like a pit bull."

"So I've heard," Preston said mildly.

"Her father's a good man for all he's a Campbell." Idly, Daniel drummed his fingers on the edge of his desk. "Time was a highlander'd sooner bed down with rats and weasels than let a Campbell through the front door. You don't hold the '45 against him and his, do you, McQuinn?"

It took him a minute, possibly longer, to realize Daniel referred to the Jacobite Rebellion over two hundred years before. Thinking a laugh would be out of place, he disguised it with a cough. "No," he said, very seriously. "Times change. We have to move on."

"Right enough." Pleased, Daniel thumped a fist on the desk. "And as I said, he's a good man, and his wife's a fine woman. Comes from good stock herself. Their children do them proud."

At sea, Preston merely nodded. "I'm sure you're right."

"Of course I'm right. You've seen for yourself, haven't you? She's a bright and lovely woman, my Cybil. A heart big as the moon, warm as the sun. She draws people to her just by being. There's a light about her, don't you think?"

"I think she's unique."

"That she is. There's no deceit in her, or guile," Daniel continued, his blue eyes sharp and focused. "Too often she puts her own feelings aside to spare another's. Not that she's a doormat, not with that good Scots' blood in her. She'll spit when she's cornered, but she's more likely to hurt herself before she'd hurt another. Causes me some worry."

Though he was hearing no more than he'd seen for himself, Daniel's words had Preston shifting uncomfortably in the chair. "I don't think you have to worry about Cybil."

"It's a grandparent's right, duty, and pleasure if it comes down to it, to worry about his chicks. She wants a place to put all the love she holds inside her. The man who engages that heart of hers will live his life lucky."

"Yes, he will."

"You've had your eye on her, McQuinn." Daniel leaned forward now. "I don't need birds to tell me that."

More than my eye, Preston thought with an inward wince. "As you said, she's a lovely woman."

"And you're a single man of thirty. What are your intentions?"

Well, Preston thought, that was cutting straight to the core. "I don't have any."

"Then it's time you got some." To punctuate, Daniel banged his fist on the desk. "You're not blind or stupid, are you?"

"No."

"Well then, what's stopping you? The girl's exactly what you need to lighten up that serious nature of yours, to keep you from burrowing into a cave like a bear with indigestion." Eyes narrowed, he jabbed out with the cigar. "And if I didn't know you were just what's best for her, you wouldn't be within arm's reach, I can tell you that."

"You put me in arm's reach, Mr. MacGregor." Feeling trapped, and furious because of it, Preston pushed out of his chair. "You dumped me on her doorstep, under the guise of doing me a favor."

"I did you the finest favor of your life, lad, and you

should be thanking me for it, instead of looking murderous."

"I don't know how the rest of the family and acquaintances handle your button pushing, but I can tell you I don't appreciate or need it."

"If you didn't need it," Daniel disagreed in a roar, "why are you still moping about something that's gone—and never really was—instead of taking hold of what is?"

The temper that had been heating Preston's eyes turned to ice. "That's my business."

"It's your flaw," Daniel disagreed, more pleased than not to watch the anger, and the control. "And a man's entitled to one or two. I've had over ninety years in this world to watch people, to measure them, to see them as they are. I'll tell you something, McQuinn, that you're either too young or too stubborn to see for yourself— you match, the pair of you. One balancing the other."

"You're wrong."

"Hah! Damned if I am. The lass wouldn't have asked you to this house if she wasn't already in love with you. And you'd not have come unless you were already in love with her."

So he goes pale at that, Daniel thought, sitting back again with satisfaction. Love, for some, was a scary business.

"You've miscalculated." Preston spoke softly as his stomach clenched into a dozen tight fists. "Love has nothing to do with what's between Cybil and me. And if I hurt her. When I hurt her," Preston corrected, "you'll own part of the blame for it."

He stalked out, leaving Daniel puffing on his cigar. Hurt was part of love, he acknowledged. Though he'd suffer for knowing his precious girl would ache a bit along the way. And yes, he'd own part of the blame for it. But when the man stopped wriggling like a stubborn trout on the line and made her happy... Well then, who would own the credit, he'd like to know, if it wasn't Daniel MacGregor?

And laughing, he finished his cigar in secret delight.

Cybil was sorry the trip to Hyannis had put Preston in a prickly mood. One, she thought, that hadn't completely reversed itself after a week back in New York.

He was a difficult man. She accepted that. Now that she knew the full story of what he'd been through, what had been done to him, she didn't see how he could be otherwise.

It would take him, a man with that much sensitivity, that much heart, a long time to trust again. A long time to allow himself to feel again.

She could wait.

But it hurt. She couldn't stop it from hurting when he turned away from her just a little too quickly, or barricaded himself against her with his work, his music or the long, solitary walks he'd begun to take at odd hours.

Walks where he made it clear he wanted to be alone, that he didn't want to share with her.

She told herself his work was giving him trouble—though he never talked about his play with her any longer. She imagined he didn't think she could understand the pain, the joy, the frustration of his work or what parts of himself it could swallow. That stung, but she told herself she accepted it.

She'd always been able to lie to herself more easily than she had to others.

Her own work had taken a new turn and was involving more of her time and energy. The meeting she'd had just before leaving for Hyannis had been a vital one. But she'd told no one. Not family, not friends, not her lover.

Superstitious, she supposed, as she climbed out of a cab in front of her building. She'd been afraid to say it out loud and jinx it before it was real.

Now it was.

She pressed a hand to her heart, felt it thud in hard, excited beats. Heard herself giggle. Now it was very real, and she couldn't wait to tell everyone.

Maybe she'd have a party to celebrate. A loud, silly, joyful bash of a party.

Champagne and balloons. Pizza and caviar.

As if preparing for it, she danced up the steps. She had to call her parents, her family, to grab Jody so they could squeal at each other.

But first, she had to tell Preston.

She used the knuckles of both fists, rapping a cheerful tattoo on his door. He'd be working, she thought, but this couldn't wait. He'd understand.

They had to celebrate. Glug champagne in the middle of the afternoon, get a little drunk and stupid and make crazy love.

When he opened the door she was shining like a sunbeam.

"Hi! I just got back. You won't believe it."

He was rumpled, unshaven, and resented the fact that one look at her could yank his mind right out of his play. Just one look. "I'm working, Cybil."

"I know. I'm sorry. But I'm going to burst if I don't tell somebody." She lifted her hands to his face, rubbed them over the stubble. "You look like you could use a quick break anyway."

"I'm in the middle of things," he began, but she was already breezing in.

"I bet you haven't eaten lunch. I just had the most incredible lunch at this new hot spot uptown. Why don't I fix you a sandwich and we'll—"

"I don't want a sandwich." He heard the edgy snap to his voice, didn't bother to soften it as he stalked to the stove to pour coffee that had been ripening for hours. "And I don't have time for one. I want to work."

"You have to eat." She had her head inside his fridge, then brought it out again when she heard him go upstairs. "Oh, for heaven's sake." She blew out a breath, rolled her eyes and started up after him.

"Okay, forget the sandwich. I just have to tell you how I spent my day. God, McQuinn, it's dark as a tomb in here." Instinctively, she marched to the window, started to throw open the drapes.

"Leave them alone. Damn it, Cybil."

Her hand froze, then dropped away, as slowly, as completely, as her mood. He was already at the keyboard, she noted, already closed off from her, just as he closed himself off from the life that surged and pulsed outside his curtained window.

He worked with lamplight and stale coffee. And with his back to her.

Nothing that was inside her, that had been bubbling like a geyser, mattered to him.

"It's so easy for you to ignore me," she murmured. "To dismiss me."

There was no mistaking the hurt in her voice. He

braced himself against it, refused to feel guilty. "It's not easy, but right now it's necessary."

"Yes, you're working, and I've got some nerve, don't I, interrupting genius, interfering with such a grand enterprise. One I couldn't possibly understand."

Irritated, he flicked a glance at her. "You can work with people hovering. I can't."

"Then again," she continued, "it's easy for you to ignore and dismiss me at other times, too, when work has nothing to do with it."

He pushed away from the keyboard, shifted toward her. "I'm not in the mood to argue with you."

"And, of course, it always comes down to your moods. If you're in the mood to be with me or be alone. To talk to me or be quiet. To touch me or turn away."

There was a hint of finality in her tone that had panic skating up his spine. "If that didn't suit you, you should have said so."

"You're right. Absolutely. Exactly right. And just now it doesn't suit me, Preston, to be treated like a mild annoyance easily swatted aside, then picked up again when you have a moment. It doesn't suit me to have what matters to me shrugged off as unimportant."

"You want me to stop work and listen to how you spent the day shopping and having lunch?"

She opened her mouth, closed it again, but not before one small sound of hurt had escaped.

"I'm sorry." Furious with himself, he got to his feet. She looked as if he'd slapped her. "I'm streaming toward the end of this, and I'm distracted, nasty." He dragged his hands through his hair because she hadn't moved, hadn't stopped staring at him with those wide, wounded eyes. "Let's go downstairs."

"No, I have to go." Because she could feel ridiculous tears stirring in her throat, burning there. "I have some calls to make, and I have a headache," she said, lifting a hand to rub at her throbbing temple. "It makes me irritable. I think I need some aspirin and a nap."

She started out, stopping when he laid a hand on her arm. He felt her tremble and absorbed a hard wash of shame. "Cybil—"

"I don't feel well, Preston. I'm going home to lie down."

She broke free, rushed out. He winced as he heard the slam of the door. "You stupid son of a bitch," he muttered, rubbing his fingers against his eyes. "Why didn't you just kick her a couple of times while you were at it?"

Disgusted with himself, he paced the room, shoving his hands in his pocket, then pulling them out again to yank at the drapes.

The sun was brilliant, streaming through the glass, making him narrow his eyes in defense. Maybe he did close himself off from what was on the other side, he thought. He worked better that way. And he didn't have to justify or explain his work habits to anyone.

He didn't have to hurt her that way.

But damn it, she'd burst in on him at the worst possible time. He was entitled to his privacy, to his space when the work and the words were racing through him.

He didn't dismiss her. He didn't ignore her. How the hell did you ignore someone who wouldn't get out of your mind no matter what else was sharing the space with her?

But he'd been trying to, hadn't he? Very deliberately trying to do both, ever since the little session with Daniel MacGregor in his tower office in Hyannis Port.

Because the clever, canny, meddling old man was right.

He was already in love with her.

If he ignored it, dismissed it, kept pushing it just a little further out of reach, it might go away before it got a good, firm grip on him.

He wasn't risking love again, not when he knew exactly what it could do to twist heart and soul, to wring every drop of blood out of them. He wasn't going to allow himself to become that vulnerable to her.

He'd get over it, he told himself, and pulled the curtains shut again. He'd put things back on balance and they'd both be happier.

And as far as his insufferable behavior of the last few days, he'd make it up to her. She hadn't done anything to deserve it, except exist. She'd done nothing but give, he thought. He'd done nothing but take.

Knowing work was out of the question, he went downstairs. He considered going across the hall, knocking, leading in with the apology he owed her. But she was entitled to her privacy, as well, he decided. He'd give it to her and take a walk.

He didn't think about buying her flowers until he saw them, bright and sunny in an outdoor cart. Not roses, he mused. Too formal. Not the daisies—they were cheerful but ordinary. He settled on tulips in butter yellow and creamy white.

The minute they were in his hand, he felt lighter.

He kept walking, realizing he'd gone on too long without taking the time to really let his mind clear. As it did, he thought more about what she'd said in that brief, dark scene in his room.

Just how often had she nudged aside her own moods,

her own needs, to accommodate his? The MacGregor had hit that one, as well. It was her nature to think about the needs of those she cared about before her own.

He'd never known anyone as selfless, generous or unfailingly happy in her own skin. He'd stopped being all those things, except when he was with her. When he let himself really *be* with her.

She'd been so excited when she'd burst into his apartment. He'd become so used to seeing her that way he hadn't considered it might have been something special that had put that shine in her eyes.

He'd taken care of that quickly enough, he thought viciously.

And he'd taken her for granted, he realized, almost from the first moment.

He could change that. And would. He'd give her back as much as he took, put them on equal ground. So when the time came to step back from each other—and it would—they might have a chance to do so as friends.

He simply couldn't imagine his life without her as part of it any longer.

He stayed out the rest of the afternoon, into early evening. When he went to her door with flowers, he didn't feel foolish. He felt settled. And when she opened it, he felt right.

"Did you get some rest?"

"Yes." She'd dived into sleep the way a rabbit dives into a thicket. To hide. "Thanks."

"Feel like company?" He brought the tulips up into her line of sight. And when she stared at them, he recognized simple shock. "And tulips?"

"Ah…sure. They're wonderful. I'll get a vase."

Just how much had he left out, he wondered, if his

bringing her a handful of flowers stunned her? "I'm sorry about this afternoon."

"Oh." So the flowers were an apology, she thought, as she took a blue glass vase from a cupboard. She shook off the vague disappointment that they hadn't been for no reason at all and turned to smile. "It doesn't matter. It's what you get when you disturb a bear in his den."

"It matters." He laid a hand on hers over the tulips. "And I'm sorry."

"All right."

"That's it? A lot of women would make a man grovel a little."

"I don't care for groveling much. Aren't you lucky?"

He lifted her hand, turning it over to press his lips to the palm. "Yes. I am." And for the second time he saw blank shock on her face.

He'd never given her tenderness, he realized, amazed at his own stupidity. Never given her the simple glow of romance. "I thought, if you're feeling better, you might like to go out to dinner."

She blinked. "Out?"

"If you like. Or if you're not feeling up to it," he continued, coming around the counter, "we can have a quiet dinner in. Whatever you want," he murmured, cupping her face to brush his lips over her forehead.

"Who are you? And what are you doing in Preston's body?"

He chuckled, then kissed her cheeks, one, the other. "Tell me what you want, Cybil."

To be touched like this. Looked at like this. "I… I can just fix something here."

"If you want to stay in, I'll take care of dinner."

"You? *You?* All right, that's it. I'm calling the cops."

He drew her into his arms, held her. "I'm not threatening to cook. We'd never survive the night that way." He nuzzled her hair, stroked it. "I'll order in."

"Oh, well, all right." He was holding her, she thought dizzily. Just holding her, as if that was enough, as if that was everything.

"You're tight." He murmured it, sliding his hands up to rub at the tension in her shoulders. "I don't think I've ever known you to be knotted up. The headache still bothering you?"

"No, not much."

"Why don't you go up. Soak in the tub until you're relaxed. Then you can put on one of those robes you're so fond of and we'll have a quiet dinner."

"I'm fine. I can…" She trailed off as his mouth skimmed hers, retreated, then returned, softly, gently, sweetly enough to dissolve her knees.

"Go on up." He drew her away, smiling as she stared up at him with slumberous, confused eyes. "I'll take care of everything."

"All right. I guess I'm a little unsteady yet." Which might explain why she wasn't entirely sure how to get upstairs in her own apartment. "The, ah, number for the pizza place is on the phone."

"I'll take care of it." He gave her a nudge toward the steps. "Go relax."

"Okay." She started to the steps, up, then stopped and turned back to study him. "Preston?"

"Yeah?"

"Are you…" With a half laugh she shook her head. "Nothing. Never mind. I won't be long."

"Take your time," he told her. It was going to require

a bit of his to make certain everything was ready for her when she came back down.

If the hint of romance nearly shocked her speechless, he thought she'd have a hard time forming a single word by the time the evening he was planning was over.

He picked up the phone, punched the button on memory next to Jody's name. "Jody? Preston McQuinn. Yeah. Listen, does Cybil have a favorite restaurant around here? No, not the diner," he said with a laugh. "We're moving upscale. Let's try French and fancy."

He had to grin at Jody's long, three-toned "Oh," then scribbled down the name she gave him. "I don't suppose you'd have the number handy. You do, huh? You're a genius. Now, let's see if you can hit three for three. Which dessert on their menu sends her into a coma? Got it, thanks. Special?" He glanced upstairs, grinned. "No, nothing special. Just a quiet dinner in. Thanks for the tip."

He laughed again as Jody continued to shoot out questions. "Hey, we both know she'll tell you all about it tomorrow."

He hung up, dialed the restaurant and outlined his needs. Then, metaphorically pushing up his sleeves, got down to work.

Chapter 11

She did as he'd suggested and took her time. She needed it to adjust to this strange new mood of his. Or was it a side of him, she wondered, he just hadn't shown her before?

How could she have known he had such sweetness in him? And how could she have predicted that his showing her, giving her that sweetness, would make it so much more difficult for her to stay in control of her own feelings?

She loved him when he was careless and cross, when he was amused and amusing, when he was hot and hungry. How much more could she love him when he was kind and caring?

He was making an effort, she thought, to apologize to her for hurting her. And he didn't even know, not really, just what he'd done. But it mattered enough—she mattered enough—for him to want to make it right again.

How could she say no?

A quiet, casual evening at home would be good for both of them. He didn't like crowds, and at the moment, she didn't have the energy for them herself. So they'd eat pizza in front of the TV, be easy with each other again. They'd laugh, talk about something unimportant and make love on the sofa while an old movie flickered on the screen.

They'd make things simple again. Because simple was really what was best for both of them.

Steadier, she belted a long, silky blue robe, flicked her fingers through her nearly dry hair, and started downstairs.

She heard the music first. Low, dreamy. The kind that set the pulse for seduction. It didn't puzzle her for long. After all, the man liked his music. But when she was halfway down the steps, she saw the candles burning. Dozens of them, with pinpoint flames that flickered and swayed.

He was standing in that shimmering light, waiting for her.

He'd changed into trousers and a black shirt and had shaved off the two days' growth of beard. His hand was already held out for hers, and she stepped down to take it, more than a little dazzled at the way the light glinted on his hair and deepened the blue of his eyes.

"Feeling better?"

"I'm fine. What's going on here?"

"We're having dinner."

"The set's a little elaborate for..." He raised her hand to his lips, nibbled lightly at her knuckles, and had the breath strangling in her throat. "Pizza," she managed, and he only smiled.

"I like looking at you in candlelight. Seeing what it does to your eyes. Those exotic, enormous eyes," he murmured, and drew her close to kiss them gently closed. "And your skin." He trailed his lips over her cheek. "That impossibly soft skin. I'm afraid I've put bruises on it forgetting just how soft it is."

"What?" Her head seemed to be circling slowly.

"I've been careless with you, Cybil. I won't be tonight." He lifted her hands again, kissed them again, and had her heart stumbling.

"I have something for you," he told her, and picked up a small square box with an elaborate pink bow from the counter.

Instantly, she whipped her hands behind her back. "I don't need gifts. I don't want them."

He frowned, puzzled at the shaky edge in her voice. Then realized she was thinking of Pamela. "It's not because you need them, or ask for them, or anything else for that matter. It's because they made me think of you." He held the box out. "Open it before you decide. Please."

Feeling foolish, she took the box, gently removed the bow. "Well, who doesn't like presents?" she said lightly. "And you missed my birthday."

"I did?"

He said it with such guilty surprise she laughed. "Yes, it was in January, and just because you didn't know me is really no excuse for not giving me a present. So this will…" She stopped, stared into the box at the earrings, two long dangles of hematite in the shape of a dozen tiny, foolish fish. Like minnows on the line.

She laughed, rolled with it as she took them out, held them up and shook so they would clack together. "They're ridiculous."

"I know."

"I love them."

"I figured you would."

Eyes sparkling, she slipped the thin wire backs through her ears. "Well, what do you think?"

"They're you. Definitely."

"It's such a sweet thing to do."

She tossed her arms around him, kissed him lavishly enough to have his blood heating. Then he heard the sniffle.

"Oh, God, don't. Don't do that."

"Sorry." She pressed her face to his throat. "It's just—flowers and candles and silly fish all in one night. It's so thoughtful." But she drew a long breath, blew it out, stepped back. "There, all clear."

"Thank God." He brushed his thumb over her lashes where a tiny tear clung. "Ready for champagne?"

"Champagne?" Baffled, she lifted her hands. "Well, it's tough not to be ready for champagne."

She watched as he stepped into the kitchen, took a bottle from her own crystal ice bucket and began to open it. What in the world had gotten into him? she wondered. Suddenly, he was relaxed, happy, romantic...

"You finished your play! Oh, Preston, you finished it."

"No, I didn't. Not quite." He popped the cork, poured the wine.

"Oh." Trying to puzzle it out, she angled her head as he turned, handed her a glass full of straw-colored, bubbling wine. "Then what are we celebrating?"

"You." He touched his glass to hers. "Just you." He laid a hand on her cheek, then lifted his own glass to her lips.

She tasted the wine, a froth on the tongue, silk in the throat. But it was the way he looked at her that made her head spin. "I don't know what to say to you."

"Well, there's an unprecedented event." Smiling, he brought the wine to his own lips, tasted it. Tasted her.

"Ah, so this is all a ploy to shut me up." Chuckling, relaxed again, she enjoyed the champagne. "Very clever, aren't you?"

"I haven't even started." He took the glass from her, set it aside, then drew her into his arms. Even as she lifted her mouth, expecting the kiss—expecting, he was sure, demand and heat—he skimmed his cheek over hers and began to move to the rhythm of the music. "I've never asked you to dance."

"No." Her eyes drifted closed. "You haven't."

"Dance with me, Cybil."

She ran her hands up his back, laid her head on his shoulder and fell into the music and him. They danced, swaying together in the kitchen washed with candle glow.

When his lips grazed her jaw, she turned her head so that his mouth cruised over hers. Her pulse was slow, slow and thick, her limbs weak as water.

"Preston." She murmured it, rising on her toes to give him more.

"That must be dinner," he said against her lips.

"What?"

"Dinner. The buzzer."

"Oh." She'd thought the buzzing was in her head, and had to brace a hand on the counter for balance when he left her to release the outer door.

"I hope you're not disappointed," he commented, unlocking her door. "It isn't pizza."

"Oh, that's all right. Anything's fine." How was a woman supposed to eat when her stomach was full of tiny, energetic butterflies?

But her eyes widened when, rather than a delivery boy, two tuxedoed waiters appeared at the door.

She watched, astonished, as with discretion and efficiency they arranged food on the table Preston had already set with her best dishes. In less than ten minutes, they were gone, and she'd yet to find her voice.

"Hungry?"

"I… It looks wonderful."

"Come, sit down." He took her hand again, led her to the table in front of the window, then bent to brush a kiss at her nape.

She must have eaten. She would never be able to remember what, or how it had tasted. Her innate powers of observation had deserted her. All she could see was Preston. All she would remember was the way his fingers had brushed hers, how his mouth had skimmed over her knuckles. How he had smiled and poured more wine, until her head was swimming with it.

How he had looked at her when he'd risen and held out a hand for hers to bring her to her feet. The way her heart had tripped when he'd lifted her right off them and into his arms.

She suddenly seemed so delicate. So vulnerable when she trembled. Even if he'd wished it otherwise, he couldn't have been anything but gentle.

He carried her up the steps, into the bedroom, and laid her on the pillows. He lit the candles as he had once before, but this time when he turned to her, when he came to her, his touch was feather soft.

And he took her, dreaming, into the kiss.

He gave more than he'd thought he had left in him. Found more in her open response than he'd believed possible. If she trembled, it wasn't triumph he felt but tenderness.

And he gave it back to her.

Slow, silky, sumptuous kisses. Long, liquid, lingering caresses. He had her floating on some high, lace-edged cloud where the air was full of perfume and the world beyond it insignificant.

Gently, he slipped the robe from her, the glide of his hands sending silvery shivers along her skin and shimmering warmth beneath it. Through dazed eyes she watched as he drew back, as his gaze followed the lazy trail of a single fingertip over her body.

"You're so lovely, Cybil." Those suddenly intense blue eyes met hers. "How many times have I forgotten to tell you? To show you?"

"Preston—"

"No. Let me do both. Let me watch you enjoy being touched as I should have touched you before. Like this," he murmured, skimming his fingertips over her.

Her breath caught, and the cloud beneath her began to rock. Then he lowered his head and let his mouth follow the path his fingertips had blazed.

Now she was drowning, slowly floating beneath the surface of a warm dark sea. Helpless there, drifting with only his hands and lips to anchor her. And that first wave came in a long, liquid crest that washed through her system to leave it weak and heavy with pleasure.

He wanted to have her steep in it, sate her with it. No sharp flash this time but a slow burn. He explored and exploited every inch of her, lingering when her breath quickened, savoring when her body arched on each steadily building delight.

And his blood swam with it; his heart jolted until he was as lost and open as she.

He murmured her name as he slipped into her, moaned it as she wrapped around him in welcome.

With long, deep thrusts, he moved in her while their mouths met in a soft and stirring kiss. In a slow, sleek rhythm, she moved under him while their hands met to complete yet another link.

They swallowed each other's sighs, gripped each other's hands as they let themselves shatter.

And he was there when she awoke, holding her, as he'd held her while they slept.

"It's definitely number one of the modern-day Top Ten Most Romantic Evenings." Jody expertly changed Charlie's diaper, cooing at him between commentary. "It knocks that Valentine's Day carriage ride around the park and dozen white roses with diamond-chip earrings attached that my cousin Sharon experienced down to a poor second place. She's going to be peeved."

"No one's ever paid that much attention," Cybil murmured, hugging one of the teddy bears in Charlie's vast collection. "Not just the you-know."

"But the you-know." Jody cocked her eyebrows as she fastened Charlie's fresh diaper. "That was excellent, right?"

"It was spectacular. You know that scene in *Through the Mist,* where Dorian and Alessa find each other after being cruelly separated by her evil, ambitious uncle?"

"Oh." Jody rolled her eyes, lifting Charlie up to bounce him. "Do I ever. I was up till two reading that book, then I woke up Chuck." She smiled reminiscently. "We were both a little tired the next day but very, very loose. Anyway—" she shook herself, before carrying Charlie into the living room so he could practice his crawling "—it was that good?"

"It was better."

"No way."

"It was like having him take my heart out and hold it, then give it back to me."

"Oh, man." Weak-kneed, Jody slipped into a chair. "That's beautiful, Cyb. Just beautiful. You ought to write a romance novel yourself."

"But it wasn't just that. It was all of it. Everything." Still giddy, she threw her arms out and twirled in a circle, making Charlie rock back on his butt and clap in delight.

"I'm so in love with him, Jody. I didn't think you could be this much in love and not have it all just come steaming out of you. There shouldn't be room inside for it all."

"Oh." Jody's sigh was long and loud. "When are you going to tell him?"

"I can't." With a sigh of her own, Cybil picked up Charlie's red plastic hammer and tapped the oversize head on her palm. "I'm not brave enough to tell him something he doesn't want to hear."

"Cyb, the guy's crazy about you."

"He's got feelings for me, and maybe, maybe if I can wait, if he realizes I'm not going to let him down, he'll let himself feel more."

"Let him down?" The very idea ruffled Jody's feathers. "You never let anyone down. But maybe this time you're letting Cybil down."

"He's got reasons to be careful," she said, then shook her head before Jody could speak. "I can't tell you about it. They're his own."

"Okay."

"Thanks. I've got to go. I have a million errands to run. Need anything?"

"Actually, I do. If you're going out anyway."

"I'll just add it to the list. I've got a few things to pick up for Mrs. Wolinsky, and I told Mr. Peebles I'd see if the green grapes looked good at the market. Just let me find my shopping list."

"I'm only asking because you're going out anyway and because it's you." Jody bit her lip, then grinned. "Don't tell anybody what you're getting for me, okay?"

"I won't." Absently, Cybil dug through her purse. "I know that list is in here somewhere."

It took longer than she'd expected—but Cybil found shopping usually did. Then, by the time she'd delivered the goods to Mrs. Wolinsky, the grapes—which had looked appetizing enough for her to buy a pound of her own—to Mr. Peebles and knocked on Jody's door, it was after five o'clock.

She hissed in frustration when Jody didn't answer. It appeared her friend could stand the suspense, though Cybil herself wanted instant gratification. But either Jody had taken Charlie out for a little walk or she was visiting one of the other neighbors and they'd both just have to wait.

Arms loaded, Cybil took the elevator up.

And grinned like a fool when she saw Preston waiting for her in the hall. "Hi."

"Hi, neighbor." He scooped the bags out of her arms,

then bent down and kissed her. "Hold it," he said when she dropped back from her toes to the balls of her feet. "Let's do that again."

"Okay." Laughing, she wound her arms around his neck, shifted back to her toes and put a great deal more energy into the greeting. "How's that?"

"That was fine. What have you got in here? Bricks?"

Searching for her ever-elusive key, she laughed again. "Food mostly, and some cleaning supplies. Some this and some that. I picked up a few things for you. The apples looked very good, and they're better for you to snack on while you're working than candy bars or stale bagels."

She found her key with a little *aha!* and unlocked the door. "Oh, and I got you some ammonia—it'll take care of that grime you're letting build up on your windows."

"Apples and ammonia." He set the bags on the counter. "What else could a man ask for?"

"Cheesecake, straight from the deli. It was irresistible."

"It'll have to wait." He spun her around, off her feet, and began to twirl with her.

"Well, you're in a mood, aren't you?" Grinning, she bent down to kiss him. "If your smile got any bigger, I might fall in."

"You'd be better than cheesecake. I finished the play."

"You did?" The hands that were braced on his shoulders slid around to hug his neck. "That's wonderful. That's great."

"I've never had anything move so fast. It still needs work, but it's there. All there. You had a lot to do with it."

"Me?"

"So much of you kept jumping into it. Once I stopped trying to push you back out, it just raced."

"I'm speechless. What did you write about me? What was I like? What did I do in it? Can I read it?"

"So much for speechless," he noted, and set her back on her feet. "After I fiddle with it a bit more you can read it. Let's go to the diner and celebrate."

"The diner? You want to go celebrate something like this with spaghetti and meatballs?"

"Exactly." And he didn't give a damn if it was sentimental. "With you, where you once took a struggling musician out for a hot meal."

"Did you put that in there? About me paying you? God."

"You'll like it, don't worry."

"What's my name—in the play, what's my name?"

"Zoe."

"Zoe." She pursed her lips, considered, then the dimple fluttered at the corner of her mouth. "I like it."

"Nothing ordinary quite fit. She kept tossing them back at me." He laughed a little, shook it off.

"You look so happy." She reached up, brushing at his hair. "It's nice to see you look so happy."

"I've been doing a lot of that lately. Come on. Let's go."

"I have to put the groceries away, fix my face. Then we'll go."

"Go fix whatever you think's wrong with your face. I'll put them away."

"All right. They actually have places," she called out as she ran up the stairs. "They don't just get tossed into cupboards."

"Just make it fast," he told her, and started pulling things out of the first bag.

He'd been going crazy for the past hour, just waiting for her to get back so he could tell her. Tell her first. And to tell her, to find a way to tell her, that somehow, somewhere, over the last few weeks, everything had changed for him.

And though he'd fought it, ignored it, denied it, it had changed nonetheless. He realized that for the first time in much, much too long, the sensation he continued to feel was simple happiness.

She was right. He looked happy. He was happy. But it wasn't just the play. It was Cybil, and it had been all along.

She made him happy.

It had come out in his work. There was an underlying glow of hope in this play he hadn't intended to put there when he'd begun. But it was just there—shimmering and impossible to resist. The way she was.

It had come out in his life when she had come into his life. With cookies and chatter and compassion. With generosity and laughter and verve.

What he felt for her—what she, being who she was, had given him no choice but to feel—filled him, completed him and, he thought, in a very real sense saved him.

The last line of his play said it, he mused.

Love heals.

With a little time, a little effort, he thought, he had a chance of making the kind of life with her he'd stopped believing really existed.

He reached in the second bag, pulled out a box. And

felt the world that had so recently gone rock steady, waver, shake and fall away under his feet.

"I was going to change, but I decided not to waste the time when we could be celebrating." She clattered down the steps at a dead run, the foolish earrings he'd given her swinging. "I just have to call Jody, see if she's back yet. Then we're out of here."

"What the hell is this, Cybil?" Pale, coldly furious, he tossed the home pregnancy test kit on the counter. "Are you pregnant?"

"I—"

"You think you're pregnant, but you don't tell me. What? Were you going to pick your time, your place, your *mood,* then let me in on it?"

The color of excitement and pleasure that had been glowing in her cheeks drained so that she was as pale as he now. "Is that what you think, Preston?"

"What the hell am I supposed to think? You waltz in, all smiles, not a care in the world, and there's this." He rapped a finger on the box. "And you're the one who claims she doesn't play games, doesn't tell lies. What else is keeping this from me but both of those?"

"And that makes me like Pamela, doesn't it?" All the joy that had shimmered in her heart throughout the day turned to ashes, cold and gray. "Calculating, deceitful. Just one more user."

He had to steady himself, to calm, but the slash of betrayal where he had finally, finally, decided to trust was ripping through him. "This is you and me, no one else. I want an explanation."

"I wonder if there's ever really been a you and me and no one else," she murmured. "I'll give you an explanation, Preston. I picked up apples for you, grapes for 1B and several small items for Mrs. Wolinsky. And I picked up that handy little will-it-be-pink-or-blue kit for Jody. She and Chuck are hoping they're expecting a baby brother or sister for Charlie."

"Jody?"

"That's right." Every word she spoke hurt her throat. "I'm not pregnant, so you can relax on that score."

"I'm sorry."

"Oh, so am I. I'm terribly sorry." Her eyes ached as she picked up the box, examined it. "Jody was so excited when she asked me to buy this. So hopeful. For some people the idea of making a child is a joyful one. But for you," she went on, putting the box down, making herself look at him, "it's a threat, just a bad memory of a bad time."

"It was a poor reaction, Cybil. Knee-jerk."

"You could say instinctive, I suppose. What would you have done, Preston, if it had been mine? If I'd been pregnant? Would you have thought I'd tricked you, trapped you, done it on purpose to ruin your life? Or maybe you'd have wondered if I'd been with another man and was laughing at you behind your back."

"No, I wouldn't have thought that." The very idea shocked him. "Don't be ridiculous. Of course I wouldn't have thought that."

"What's ridiculous about it? She did it—why not me? Why the hell not me? You let her jump right back in here. You're the one who left the door open for her."

"You're right. Cybil—"

She stepped back sharply when he reached for her. "Oh, don't. I can't quite figure out if you think I'm just another calculating bitch or pathetically malleable. But I'm neither. I'm just me, and I've been nothing but honest with you. You had no right to hurt me like this, and I had no right to let you. But that stops now. I want you to go."

"I'm not going until we settle this."

"It's settled. I don't blame you for it. I'm just as much at fault. I gave too much and expected too little. You were honest with me. 'This is all I have. Don't ask for more,' you said. 'This is what I am. Take it or leave it.' It's my own fault that's what I did. But I won't be doing it anymore. I need someone in my life who respects me, who trusts me. I'm not settling for less. So I want you out."

She strode to the door, flung it open. "Get the hell out."

Because in spite of the fire in her eyes, they were swimming with tears; despite the fists her hands were clenched in, they were shaking. He went to the door, but he stopped, looked at her.

"I was wrong. Completely wrong. Cybil, I'm sorry."

"So am I." She started to slam the door, then drew a deep breath. "I lied. I haven't always been honest with you, but now I will be. I'm in love with you, Preston. And that's the pity of it."

He said her name, started toward her, but she shut the door. He heard the locks snap into place.

He pounded on the door, cursed through it. He paced the hallway, then stalked into his own apartment to call her. But she wouldn't answer.

He tried pounding again, and finally feeling that everything he'd begun to treasure in his life was slipping away, he tried begging. But she was upstairs, with that door closed, as well, and couldn't hear him as she wept in the dark.

Chapter 12

"I ought to go find the son of a bitch and break his legs, his arms. Then his neck." Grant Campbell paced the kitchen of the home he'd built with his wife, his mood as dark and rough as the sea that thrashed outside.

"That wouldn't stop her from hurting." Gennie turned from the window where she'd been watching for her daughter and studied her husband.

Long and lean, she mused, and still just a bit dangerous. So much the man she'd fallen in love with all those years ago. And so much more.

"It'd make me feel a hell of a lot better," Grant muttered. "I'm going out to get her."

"No, don't." Gennie laid a hand on his arm before he could storm out the door. "Let her be awhile."

"It's dark," he said, and felt helpless.

"She'll come in when she's ready."

"I can't stand it. I can't stand the look he put in her eyes."

"She has to hurt before she can heal. We both know that." Because they both needed it, Gennie slipped into his arms, rested her head on his shoulder. "She knows we're here."

"It was easier when one of them would fall down. Scrape or break something."

"You didn't think so then." Her laugh was as warm as it had been when he'd first met her; her voice was rich and recalled the scent of magnolias in full bloom. She tipped back her head, cupped his face. "You always hurt more than they did."

"I just want to put her on my lap, make it go away." He lowered his brow to Gennie's. "Then I want to rip the bastard's lungs out."

"Me, too," she said, pleased when he chuckled.

That was how Cybil saw them when she came in the room. The two of them standing in the kitchen, standing close, their eyes on each other's.

And that, she decided, that bond, that intimacy, was what she wanted. What she'd been willing to give.

She walked to them, slipped an arm around each to make a circle. "Do you know how many times in my life I've come in here and seen the two of you just like this? And how lovely it is?"

"Your hair's wet." Grant rubbed his cheek over it.

"I was watching the waves crash." She tilted her head to kiss him. "Stop worrying so, Daddy."

"I will. When you're fifty. Maybe." He patted her cheek. "Want some coffee?"

"Mmm, no. Nothing really. I think I'll take a hot bath,

then snuggle into bed with a book. It always worked for me when I was a teenager working off a crush."

"During those crises, I ran your bath," her mother reminded her. "Why break tradition?"

"You don't have to do that, Mama."

"Let me fuss." Gennie slipped an arm around her shoulders.

With a sigh, Cybil let herself be guided out. "I was sort of hoping you would."

"Your father needs to be alone to pace and curse your young man."

"He's not my 'young man,'" Cybil muttered as they started up the wide, circular stairs Grant had designed to echo the narrow, metal ones in the lighthouse just beyond the house. "He never was."

"But you're not a teenager now." Gently, Gennie turned Cybil as they moved into the bedroom where Cybil had dreamed her young-girl dreams. "And this isn't a crush."

The tears came again, spurting out of her center, flooding her heart, throat, eyes, as she shook her head. "Oh, Mama."

"There, baby." She led Cybil to the bed, still covered with its colorful quilt, and, sitting beside her, opened her arms.

"I want to hate him." Burrowing into the comfort, Cybil wept and clung. "I want to hate him. If I could, for just a little while, I'd stop loving him."

"I wish I could tell you that you would. I wish I knew. Some men are so hard, so baffling." Gennie rocked her daughter as she spoke. "I know you, sweet baby. I know if you love him there's something in him that makes him worthy of it."

"He's wonderful. He's horrible. Oh, Mama." Cybil leaned back, weeping still. "He's just like Daddy."

"Oh, God help you." With a half laugh, Gennie gathered her close again.

"I always loved the story." Her breath hitched, and she gratefully took the tissue Gennie snagged from the box near the bed. "The story about how you met—when your car broke down in the storm and you were lost, and you stumbled on the lighthouse where he was living like a hermit. And he was so cranky and rude."

She paused to blow her nose, while Gennie stroked her hair and added, "He couldn't wait to get rid of me."

"The way he tells it, you burst in on him. And he was annoyed because you were wet and beautiful." Cybil sighed and studied her mother's face with its honey-toned skin, its strong bones, the lovely fall of dark hair that framed it. "You're so beautiful, Mama."

"You have my eyes," Gennie said softly. "That makes me feel beautiful."

Tired after the storm of tears, Cybil wiped them dry. "We're just wrong for each other," she said at length. "Preston and I. He's so fiercely private, so absorbed in his work. But it's not that he doesn't have humor."

She sighed, rose, walked to the window so that she could see the moon on the water. "Sometimes he can be incredibly charming, unexpected, delightful. He's so moody you never know what's going to pop up. And there's this amazing sensitivity, and you realize he's almost afraid to trust, to feel. Then he touches you, and you're lost. All the things that he is, all of those complicated things he is, are there when he touches you. But he still doesn't quite let you in."

"Good Lord. He *is* like your father. Cybil, you have

to do what's right for you. But if you love him this much, you may never be happy unless you at least try to work things out with him."

"He thinks I'm frivolous." The fighting edge came back in her voice, pleasing Gennie enormously. "And that my work is less important than his just because it's different. He doesn't trust me. He thinks he can flick me off like a gnat one minute, and he can't keep his hands off me the next."

She whirled around, ready to spew out more complaints, and saw her mother smiling. "What?"

"How did you find another? I thought I had the only one."

"Grandpa found him."

Gennie's smile sharpened, her aristocratic eyebrows arched. "Oh," she said in the regal tone Cybil recognized as dangerous. "Oh, really."

For the first time in more than twenty-four hours, Cybil smiled.

Preston scowled and shoved his sax back in his case. Damn the woman. He couldn't even play out his frustration. He certainly couldn't work, which he'd proven after spending most of a miserable day between staring at his screen and going across the hall to bang on Cybil's door.

That was before he'd finally realized she wasn't inside anymore.

She'd left him. Which he decided was the smartest thing she'd done since she'd met him. And after brooding over it, he'd figured out the best thing he could do for both of them was to be gone when she got back. From wherever the hell she'd gone.

He was going back to Connecticut in the morning. He could tolerate construction workers, plumbers, electricians and whoever else would descend on him on a daily basis for the next few weeks. But he couldn't tolerate living across the hall from a woman he loved and couldn't have due to his own stupidity.

Everything she'd said to him had been completely true. He had no defense.

"I won't be around for a while, André."

The piano player looked up through the haze of smoke from the cigarette between his lips. "That so?"

"I'm heading back to Connecticut tomorrow."

"Uh-huh. Woman chase you away?" Brow cocked, André stretched back. "That your tail I see between your legs, brother?"

With a short, humorless laugh, Preston picked up his case. "See you around."

"I'll be right here." When Preston's back was turned, André jerked up his chin, signaling his wife, then stabbed a thumb in Preston's direction.

With a nod, she glided over to block Preston's exit. "Leaving early tonight, sugar lips."

"I haven't got anything in me. And I want an early start in the morning. I'm going back to Connecticut."

"Back to the boonies?" She smiled, hooked her arm around his shoulders. "Well, let's have us a goodbye drink, 'cause I'm gonna miss your pretty face."

"I'll miss yours, too."

"Not just mine," she said, then held up two fingers to the bartender. "That little girl put the blues into you, and you can't put them all in your sax. Not this time. Not with her."

"No, not with her." He lifted his glass. "That's over."

"Why's that?"

"Because she said it is." He drank, let the fire course through him, but found it didn't quite warm his insides.

Delta let out a short laugh. "When did a man take that for an answer?"

"When the woman means it, this man takes it."

"McQuinn." Delta patted his cheek. "You sure are a fool."

"No argument. That's why it's over. I ruined it—I have to live with it."

"You ruin it—you have to fix it."

"When you hurt someone that much, they've got the right to lock you out."

"Honey, when you love someone that much, you've got the right to pick that lock, then do a lot of crawling on your hands and knees." She turned, studied him eye to eye. "You love her that much?"

He turned his glass, watched the whiskey through the smoke. "I didn't know there was this much. That there could be."

"Sugar lips." She kissed him. "Go pick yourself a lock."

He shook his head, tossed back the rest of his drink, then started the walk home.

Delta was wrong, he told himself. Sometimes you couldn't fix it. You couldn't pick the lock, and you were better off not trying. Why should she let him back in? He carried the image of how her face had paled, how her eyes had gone huge and hollow—and how the tears had swirled in them over the heat of anger.

He didn't have any right to ask her to listen. To let him crawl or beg or play on her sympathies.

And he didn't realize he'd started to run until he'd

reached Jody's door, out of breath, and was pounding on it.

"For God's sake." After checking the peep, Jody wrenched open the door and hitched her robe closed. If Chuck didn't sleep like a rock, she wouldn't have had to race out of bed before the noise woke the baby. "It's after midnight. Are you crazy?"

"Where is she, Jody? Where did she go?"

She wrinkled her nose, lifting her chin with a dignity that was difficult to maintain in a robe covered with pink kittens. "Are you drunk?"

"I had one drink. No, I'm not drunk." He'd never felt more sober, or more desperate. "Where's Cybil?"

"Like I'd tell you after you broke her heart. Go back up to your hole," she ordered, pointing dramatically. "Before I wake up Chuck and some of the other people around here. They might just lynch you on the spot." Her bottom lip trembled. "Everyone loves Cybil."

"So do I."

"Right. That's why you made her cry her eyes out." As her own threatened to fill, Jody dug a ratty tissue out of the pocket of her robe.

All Preston could do was close his eyes against the vicious guilt. "Please tell me where she is."

"Why should I?"

"So I can crawl, and give her a chance to kick me while I'm down. So I can beg. For God's sake, Jody, tell me where she is. I have to see her."

Jody sniffled into the tissue, but the eyes over it had cleared. And now they narrowed as they studied Preston's face and saw pale desperation. "You really love her?"

"Enough to let her send me away if that's what she wants. But I have to see her first."

What could a romantic heart do but sigh? "She's at her parents' in Maine. I'll write it down for you."

Rocked with relief, stunned with gratitude, he had to close his eyes again. "Thanks."

"If you hurt her again," she muttered as she scribbled on the back of an envelope, "I'll hunt you down and kill you with my bare hands."

"I won't even put up a fight." He blew out a breath. "Are you, ah…"

She glanced over, then smiled and laid a hand on her belly. "Yeah, I'm 'ah.' I'm due on Valentine's Day. Isn't that perfect?"

"It's great. Congratulations." He took the envelope she handed him. Then stuffed it into his pocket, framed her face in his hands and kissed her. "Thank you."

She waited until he'd dashed out, then exhaled, long and sharp. "Oh, yeah," she murmured as she closed and locked the door. "I can see how that could work into a no scale. Definitely no-scale potential." Then she closed her eyes, crossed the fingers of both hands. "Good luck, Cybil."

"The MacGregor." Grant said the words through clenched teeth, his dark-brown eyes snapping as visions of murder and mayhem danced through his mind. "Interfering old goat."

Because it was a sentiment Grant had expressed in various terms any number of times since she'd told him the night before of Daniel's matchmaking plot, Gennie didn't bother to suppress the grin. Her husband adored Daniel MacGregor.

"I thought it was 'meddling old blockhead.'"

"That, too. If he wasn't six hundred years old, I'd kick his butt."

"Grant." Gennie set down her sketch pad, deciding the lovely old maple she'd been sketching would be in full leaf rather than tender bud before her husband stopped pacing. "You know he did it out of love."

"Didn't work, did it?"

Gennie started to speak; then, hearing the sound of a car, turned, shielding her eyes against the slant of the midmorning sun. She felt a little ripple go through her heart. "I'm not so sure of that," she murmured.

"Who the hell is that?" It was Grant's usual sentiment when someone dared to trespass on his staunchly guarded privacy. "If that's another tourist, I'm getting the gun."

"You don't have a gun."

"I'm buying one."

She couldn't help it. Gennie sprang to her feet, tossed the sketchbook down on the glider and threw her arms around him. "Oh, Grant, I love you."

The feel of her broke through his darkening mood like sun through storm clouds. "Genviève." He lowered his head, took her mouth. His blood stirred and his heart warmed. "Tell whoever that is to go away and never come back."

Gennie kept her arms around him, laid her head on his shoulder and watched the gorgeous little car fight its way down the narrow, rutted road Grant refused to have repaired. "I think that's going to be up to Cybil."

"What?" Grant's eyes narrowed as he shifted his gaze to watch the car's progress. "You figure that's him? Well, well," he said, and would have pushed his way clear if his wife's arms hadn't tightened around him. "I'm going to be able to kick some butt, after all."

"Behave."

"The hell I will."

Preston spotted them as a particularly nasty bump snapped his teeth together. He'd been too busy cursing whoever considered this ditch in the middle of nowhere a road to notice much more than the next rut, but as his gaze was drawn up, he saw the couple standing in the yard of a rambling white farmhouse.

Not really standing, he thought. Embracing. There on the grass just greening with spring, beside an old-fashioned glider positioned to nestle between graceful shrubs, were the parents of the woman he loved.

He wondered which one of them would kill him first.

Resigned, he muscled the car down the lane and scanned the place where he would likely be buried in a shallow grave.

He'd seen it before, he realized, in the work of Genviève Campbell. She'd painted here, he thought, with love and with brilliance. The romantic old whitewashed lighthouse that loomed over the cliff, the tumbling rocks that showed color and age in the morning light, the bent and twisted trees—all had been pulled together to form a place and a painting of wild beauty.

The house, with its gleaming white paint, its many windows and cozily covered porch, the tidy flower beds waiting for the spring that would come late to this part of the world, offered simple comfort.

Cybil had grown up here, he thought, in this wild and wonderful place.

He stopped the car, but the sense of relief that his bones could now stop rattling couldn't compete against nerves. The couple on the lawn had turned to watch him. Even at a distance, Preston could see the sentiment on the rugged face of Cybil's father.

And the sentiment wasn't *welcome*.

He stepped out of the car, determined to live long enough to see Cybil and say his piece. After that, he supposed, all bets were off.

No wonder, Gennie thought, as she watched Preston cross the yard. No wonder she'd fallen so hard. Feeling Grant tense, she dug her fingers into his waist in warning. He vibrated like a pit bull on a choke chain.

"Mrs. Campbell. Mr. Campbell." Preston nodded but knew better than to offer his hand. It would be very hard to type with a stub. "I'm Preston McQuinn. I need Cybil—need to see Cybil," he corrected, flustered.

"How old are you, McQuinn?"

Preston's brows knit at the unexpected question delivered in slow, measured tones that didn't dilute the threat. "Thirty."

Grant inclined his head. "You want to live to see thirty-one you get back in that car, put it in reverse and just keep going."

Preston kept his eyes level, unconsciously rolling his shoulders like a boxer preparing for a bout. "Not until I've seen Cybil. After that, you can take me apart. Or try to."

"You're not getting within ten feet of her." Grant set Gennie aside as if she weighed little more than a child's doll.

As he took a menacing step forward, Preston kept his hands at his sides. Cybil's father could have first blood, he decided. He'd earned it.

"Stop it!" Gennie dashed between them, slapped a

hand on each of their chests. She sent her husband one withering look, then offered Preston the same.

He had a moment to think he'd just been chastised by a queen, then his heart stumbled. "She has your eyes." He had to swallow. "Cybil. She has your eyes."

And the soft green of them warmed. "Yes, she does. She's on the cliff, behind the lighthouse."

"Damn it, Gennie."

Before he could stop himself, Preston lifted a hand to the one she pressed to his heart. He could feel his own thundering beat. "Thank you."

He lifted his gaze to Grant's, held it. "I won't hurt her. Not ever again."

"Damn it," Grant muttered again when Preston started for the cliffs in long, determined strides. "Why did you do that?"

With a sigh, Gennie turned back, took her husband's face in her hands. "Because he reminded me of someone."

"Like hell."

She laughed. "And I think our daughter's going to be a very happy woman very shortly."

He let out one exasperated sigh. "I should've gotten just one punch in, on principle. Damn, if he wasn't going to let me."

Then Grant glanced over, watched Preston disappear behind the wide white base of the tower. "I might've been able to do it if one look at your eyes hadn't cut him off at the knees. He's stupid in love with her."

"I know. Remember how scary that is?"

"It's still scary." With a laugh, he pulled her against him again. "The boy's got guts," Grant mused. "And being your daughter, Cybil will twist them into knots for a while before she forgives him."

"Of course she will. He deserves it. Daniel was right about them," she added.

"I know." Grant grinned down at his wife. "But let's not tell him for a while and make him suffer."

She was sketching, sitting on a rock with the wind ruffling through her dark hair, her head bent over the pad, her pencil flying.

The sight of her stole his breath. He'd driven through the night, through the morning, all the while trying to imagine how he would feel when he saw her again. For once his imagination had fallen far short.

He said her name, then realized his shaky whisper wouldn't carry over the sounds of wind and water. He started down the narrow beaten path toward the sea.

Maybe she heard him, or perhaps his shadow changed her light. Or maybe she simply sensed him. But her head came up, and her eyes whipped to him. Emotions stormed through them before they turned the chilly green of a winter sea.

Then, as if his presence didn't matter in the least, she began to sketch again. "You're a long way from home, McQuinn."

"Cybil." His throat felt rusty.

"We're not much on visitors around here. My father often talks about mining the road. Too bad he hasn't gotten around to it."

"Cybil," he said again, while his fingers itched to touch her.

"If I'd had any more to say to you, I'd have said it

in New York." *Go away!* her mind screamed. *Go away before the tears come back.*

"I have something to say to you."

She flicked him a disinterested glance. "If I'd wanted to hear it…same goes." She closed her sketchbook, rose. "Now—"

"Please." He lifted a hand, but when her eyes flared in warning dropped it again. "Hear me out. Then if you want me to go, I'll go. You're too…fair," he said for a lack of a better word, "not to listen."

"All right." She sat back on the rock, opened her sketchbook again. "I'll just keep working, if you don't mind."

"I—" He didn't know where to begin. All the speeches he'd rehearsed, all the pleas and promises, deserted him. "My agent ran into yours yesterday."

"Really? What a small, insular world we live in."

He might have winced at that biting tone, but he was too busy looking at her. "He told her about the series— the television series they're going to do based on your strip. She said it was a major deal."

"For some."

"You didn't tell me."

She spared him another glance. "You're not interested in my work."

"That's not true, but I can't blame you for thinking it. I worked it out, time-wise. The day you came to see me, almost bursting with excitement. You'd come to tell me, and I ruined it for you. I—" He broke off, had to turn away and stare out over the green and restless sea. "I was distracted by the play, and more, what I was feeling for you. What I didn't want to feel for you."

Her fingers tightened and she broke the tip of her

pencil. Furious with herself, she stuck it behind her ear and dug in her small tool bag for another. "If that's what you came to say, you've said it. Now you can go."

"No, that's not what I came to say, but I'll apologize for it, and tell you I'm happy for you."

"Whoopee."

He shut his eyes, fisted his hands. So, she could be cruel, he thought, when it was deserved. "Everything you said to me the night you threw me out of your life was right. I let something that had happened a long time ago stand in front of now. I used it to cut myself off from the best thing that's ever happened to me. I watched my sister's world shatter, saw her struggle to function over the betrayal and the pain, to raise her son alone and give birth to another before the ink was dry on her divorce papers."

How could she hold herself aloof from that, Cybil thought, as she closed her book again? How could she be unmoved? "I know it was hell for her, for both of you. No one should have gone through what your sister did, Preston."

"No, they shouldn't. But people do."

He turned back, met her eyes. Already, he thought in wonder, already there was sympathy in them. "It would work, wouldn't it, if I used my sister to play on your compassion? That's not what I want to do. Not what I'm going to do."

He walked to where the land fell off, where it seemed to have been hacked by an ax to form a wall that faced the churning sea. Gulls screamed overhead, swooping down with flashes of white wings, then rising up again to soar.

She came here, he thought, here to this place whenever she visited her childhood home. Came here on those rare times when she needed to be alone with her thoughts.

It was only right, he supposed, that he finally gave her his thoughts, and the feelings behind them, in a place that was hers.

"I loved Pamela. What happened between us changed me."

"I know." She would have to forgive him, Cybil realized as she could feel her heart softening. Before she let him go.

"I loved her," he repeated, turning toward her again, stepping forward. "But what I felt for her isn't a shadow, isn't even a pale substitute, for what I feel for you. What I feel when I think of you, when I look at you. It overwhelms me, Cybil. It makes me ache. It makes me hope."

Her lips trembled open. Her heart began to beat in a quick, almost painful rhythm she recognized as joy. She saw on his face what she'd never really believed she would see. Struggling to absorb it, she looked away, down the long, rocky coast that seemed to stretch into forever.

"For what?" she managed. "What does it make you hope for?"

"Miracles. I hurt you. I've no excuse for it." He spoke quickly, terrified she would tell him it no longer mattered, that it was too late. "I attacked when I thought you might be pregnant because I was angry at myself. Angry that part of me was thinking that having a baby with you would be a way I could keep you."

When her head whipped around, her eyes wide with shock, he dragged his hands through his hair. "I knew you didn't want marriage, but if you'd been… I could have pushed you into it. And my only defense against that kind of thinking, against using something like that, was to turn on you."

"Pushed me into marriage?" was all she could say. Staggered, she rose, walked a few feet away to stare blindly down into the thrashing waves. How was she supposed to keep up with this? she wondered. How had it all changed so fast?

"It's no excuse, but you have a right to know I never thought you'd planned it or tricked me. I've never known anyone less calculating than you. Cybil, you're a warm, generous woman, with a capacity for joy unlike anyone else I've ever known. Having you in my life…you made me happy, and I think I'd forgotten how to be."

"Preston." She turned back, her vision blurry with tears.

"Please, let me finish. Just hear me out." He grabbed her hands now, gripping hard. "I love you. Everything about you staggers me. You said you loved me. You don't lie."

"No." She saw him clearly now. The exhaustion in his eyes, the tension in his face. If he hadn't been holding her hands so tightly she would have tried to smooth it all away. "I don't lie."

"I need you, so much more than you need me. I know you can get over me and move on. You're too resilient, too open to life, not to. Nothing would stop you from being what you are. You can tell me to go. You'll forget me. Whatever part I played in your life won't keep you from being happy."

He kept his eyes on her face, surrendering everything to the desperate whirl of emotion inside him. "And I'll never in my life get over you. I'll never stop loving you or stop regretting everything I did to push you away from me. You can tell me to go," he said in a voice strained taut with emotion. "And I will. Please God." Helpless, he lowered his brow to hers. "Please don't tell me to go."

"Do you believe that?" she said quietly. "Do you really believe I could forget you?" Amazed at how steady her voice, and her heart was, she waited until he lifted his head and looked down at her. "Maybe I could get over you and be happy. But why should I risk it? Why should I tell you to go when I want you to stay?"

He let out the air clogging his lungs. Even as her lips began to curve, he pulled her against him, kept her there, swaying with relief. She felt him shudder once as he pressed his face to her shoulder.

"You didn't let me ruin it." His voice was raw, and his heart seemed to batter against hers until it moved inside her.

"No, I didn't." She held on, rocked with the knowledge that he had so much feeling for her in him. This strong, stubborn, serious man was weak for love of her. "I couldn't. I need you, too."

He held her away from him, his heart in his eyes as he skimmed his thumbs over her cheeks. "I love this face. I thought I lost it." He brushed his lips over her brow, her eyelids. "I thought I lost you, Cybil. I can't..."

His mouth covered hers. He meant to be gentle, to show her she would be cherished, but emotion raged through him, wild and strong as the sea below them. All of it poured into the kiss.

When he drew back, her eyes were wet. "Don't cry."

"You're going to have to get used to it. We Campbells are an emotional lot."

"I figured that out. Your father wants to break me into very small pieces."

"When he sees you make me happy, he'll let you live." She grinned, and laughter bubbled out. "He'll love you, Preston, and so will my mother. First because I do, then because of who you are."

"Moody, rude, short-tempered?"

"Yes." She laughed again when he winced. "I could deny it, but I'm such a lousy liar." She took his hand in hers and began to walk. "I love it here. This is where my parents met and fell in love. He lived in the lighthouse then, like a hermit, guarding his work, irritated that a woman had come along to distract him."

She shot him a sidelong look. "He's moody, rude, short-tempered."

The similarity had him grinning. "Sounds like a very sensible man." He brought their joined hands to his lips. "Cybil, will you go to Newport with me and meet my family?"

"I'd like that." She glanced up, her head angling when she saw that familiar intense expression in his eyes. "What?"

He stopped, turned to her in the shadow of the great light with the water warring against the rocks below. "I know you don't want marriage or a house in the country. You like living in New York in the center of things, and I don't expect—you'd like the house," he said, interrupting his own thoughts. "It's a great old place, near the coast like this. Anyway," he continued, shaking his head as she remained silent, just looking at him, "I don't expect you to change your lifestyle. But if you decide, later on, that you want to marry me, make a home and a family with me, will you tell me?"

Her heart did three wonderful and stylish handsprings, but she only nodded. "You'll be the first to know."

Telling himself to be content with that, he gave her hand a quick squeeze. "Okay."

He started to walk again, surprised when she stopped, pulling back so that both their arms were extended, linked only by warm fingers. "Preston?"

"Yeah?"

"I want to marry you, make a home and a family with you." The smile lit up her face as he gaped at her. "See, you're the first to know."

Hope spun cheerfully into bliss. "Sure." He brought her stumbling into him with one quick jerk. "But did you have to keep me dangling for so long?"

Then she was laughing as he swung her off her feet, spinning her in dizzy circles.

* * * * *